P9-BZS-079

Praise for Valerie Hansen
and her novels

"*Second Chances* by Valerie Hansen
will put a smile on your face."
—*Romantic Times BOOKreviews*

"*Love One Another* by Valerie Hansen is a
serious story with some great moments."
—*Romantic Times BOOKreviews*

VALERIE HANSEN

Second Chances

Love One Another

Steeple
Hill®

Published by Steeple Hill Books™

If you purchased this book without a cover you should be aware that this book is stolen property. It was reported as "unsold and destroyed" to the publisher, and neither the author nor the publisher has received any payment for this "stripped book."

STEEPLE HILL BOOKS

Steeple
Hill®

ISBN-13: 978-0-373-65275-4
ISBN-10:   0-373-65275-5

SECOND CHANCES AND LOVE ONE ANOTHER

SECOND CHANCES
Copyright © 2001 by Valerie Whisenand

LOVE ONE ANOTHER
Copyright © 2001 by Valerie Whisenand

All rights reserved. Except for use in any review, the reproduction or utilization of this work in whole or in part in any form by any electronic, mechanical or other means, now known or hereafter invented, including xerography, photocopying and recording, or in any information storage or retrieval system, is forbidden without the written permission of the editorial office, Steeple Hill Books, 233 Broadway, New York, NY 10279 U.S.A.

All characters in this book have no existence outside the imagination of the author and have no relation whatsoever to anyone bearing the same name or names. They are not even distantly inspired by any individual known or unknown to the author, and all incidents are pure invention.

This edition published by arrangement with Steeple Hill Books.

® and TM are trademarks of Steeple Hill Books, used under license. Trademarks indicated with ® are registered in the United States Patent and Trademark Office, the Canadian Trade Marks Office and in other countries.

www.SteepleHill.com

Printed in U.S.A.

CONTENTS

SECOND CHANCES   11

LOVE ONE ANOTHER   261

Books by Valerie Hansen

Love Inspired

The Wedding Arbor #84
The Troublesome Angel #103
The Perfect Couple #119
Second Chances #139
Love One Another #154
Blessings of the Heart #206
Samantha's Gift #217
Everlasting Love #270
The Hamilton Heir #368

Love Inspired Suspense

The Danger Within #15
Out of the Depths #35

VALERIE HANSEN

was thirty when she awoke to the presence of the Lord in her life and turned to Jesus. In the years that followed she worked with young children, both in church and in secular environments. She also raised a family of her own and played foster mother to a wide assortment of furred and feathered critters.

Married to her high school sweetheart since age seventeen, she now lives in an old farmhouse she and her husband renovated with their own hands. She loves to hike the wooded hills behind the house and reflect on the marvelous turn her life has taken. Not only is she privileged to reside among the loving, accepting folks in the breathtakingly beautiful Ozark mountains of Arkansas, but she also gets to share her personal faith by telling the stories of her heart for Steeple Hill's Love Inspired line.

Life doesn't get much better than that!

SECOND CHANCES

Blessed are the peacemakers;
for they shall be called the children of God.
—*Matthew* 5:9

This book is dedicated to all the special people whose calming influence and wise counsel bring daily peace to all our lives.

Prologue

An orange glow danced across the night sky. Flames curled around the three-storey frame structure, licking the thick layers of old paint and bubbling them to ashes, then consuming the dry wood beneath. Firelight radiating through the window of eighteen-year-old Belinda Carnes's bedroom turned the pale pink interior walls a sickly yellow.

Shocked awake, she bolted out of bed, ran to the window and stared at the fire next door. In the street below, her father was shouting, pleading, "Somebody do something. Dear God, do something!" The sound of his anguish tore at her heart, making her temporarily forget the terrible quarrel they'd had only hours before.

"Daddy!" Grabbing her robe, Belinda made a dash for the stairs. Their house was full of smoke, making it difficult to see or breathe. Maybe it was on fire, too!

She rocketed into the street, auburn hair flying, her robe clutched around her slim body, her feet bare. "Daddy! Where are you?"

The first fire truck was already shooting water on the flames as others arrived. "Get back!" someone shouted. Belinda ignored the order. She had to find her father. He was all she had left.

A team of volunteer firefighters ran by, dragging a bulging hose. Several of the men were part of her father's congregation. Gasping to catch her breath, Belinda looked at the church that had been her second home since before her mother had died. She didn't have to know much about firefighting to know the historic building, her father's pride and joy, was beyond saving.

Blossoming spray from the hoses drifted over the appalled onlookers like icy mist over a river. Wending her way through the crowd, Belinda overheard more than one angry person place the blame for the terrible inferno on Paul Randall, the misfit teenage son of a convicted arsonist.

They were wrong. They had to be. She was sure Paul had left town right after her father had ordered him out of their house and out of her life for good. The bitterness of that altercation echoed in her throbbing head.

"Leave my daughter alone," her father had shouted just hours ago.

Paul had stood his ground, feet planted firmly apart on the front walkway, fists clenched in defiance. "We're in love. We're going to get married, with or without your blessing. There's nothing you can do about it."

"We'll see about that."

"I'm leaving town tonight and Belinda's coming with me," Paul had said flatly.

"No, she isn't." Her father had held out his hand to her, his commanding voice as forceful as if he were warning his congregation about the wages of sin. "Belinda is going to go away to college in the fall, just like she promised her mother. By the time she gets her degree she'll be wise enough to make the kind of choices that will affect her whole life. Right now, she's far too young."

Caught between her vow to her late mother and the angry young man who insisted they marry immediately and run away together no matter what the consequences, Belinda had felt trapped. Weeping, she'd stepped to her father's side. No words were necessary. Her actions had spoken for her.

"Fine. I'll go," Paul had yelled, cursing to accentuate his mood. "But I'll show you. You'll be sorry. You'll *both* be sorry. You just watch."

Even now, Belinda imagined she could still hear the echo of Paul's vehement threats. When he'd lost his temper and threatened her father she'd glimpsed a side of him she'd never seen before. A part of his character that had truly frightened her. And now the church was on fire. Thank goodness Paul was long gone! If he were still in town, he'd be the first one *she* suspected, too.

Belinda was so distraught she could hardly breathe, hardly think. Blinking back tears, she worked her way through the twisted maze of hoses lying in the street. Behind her, the upper windows of the old church began to shatter from the intense heat and the pressure of the water being hurled against them.

As she drew closer to her father she saw two men restraining him to keep him from trying to enter the burning building. "Thank you, God. He's safe," she whispered, grateful beyond belief.

All she could think about was getting to her father so she could tell him how sorry she was about the church and how much she loved him, in spite of their recent argument.

Suddenly, strong, masculine hands grasped her from behind. Held her fast. Told her, "It's not safe to be out here barefoot."

Panicking, Belinda twisted to stare at him. Her eyes widened. It *couldn't* be Paul...but it was. She immediately tried to jerk free. "Let go of me!"

Scowling, Paul released her, held his hands in the air and took a step back. When he said, "Sorry," it sounded a lot more like sarcasm than penitence.

"What are *you* doing here?"

"I heard the sirens so I came by to make sure you were all right."

Fire reflected in the depths of his almost-black eyes, making him appear sinister, dangerous. Belinda's already broken heart hardened at the sight of him, at the realization that all her wonderful excuses for his innocence were useless now that she knew he was still hanging around the area. "Stop lying, Paul," she countered. "You came here to gloat and you know it."

He combed his fingers through his long, thick, dark hair, pushing it back as he shook his head. "You have a really low opinion of me, don't you?"

"I only know what I see. You said you were leaving town hours ago. Why didn't you *go?*"

Paul's jaw clenched, but he kept his outward cool. "I was packing. I knew your father banished me from this town but I didn't know he was timing me or I'd have hurried."

"Leave my daddy out of this. Haven't you done enough to hurt him already?"

"Me? Hurt *him?* All I did was fall in love with his daughter!"

Paul saw Belinda's tear-filled glance dart briefly in the direction of the burning church before returning to him. Suddenly understanding, he nodded. "I should have known. I thought you were different but you're just like the rest of them, aren't you?" His arm swept in an arc that took in the whole chaotic scene. "You blame me for this. All of you do." He shoved his hands into the pockets of his worn leather jacket. "It figures. My father made a mistake and went to prison for arson, so I'm guilty by association. Right?''

The unfair accusation stung, made her even more defensive. ''You said it. I didn't.'' Standing firm, she refused to let him off the hook. ''You were supposed to be long gone by now. Admit it. You only hung around so you could watch my father suffer.'' Pent-up emotion made her tremble. ''Get away from me! I never want to see you again. Ever.''

''Fine with me. I'm glad your old man decided that I'm not good enough for you. He did us *both* a favor. Goodbye, Belinda. Have a nice life.''

With tears running down her cheeks, Belinda pressed her fingertips to her lips to stifle her sobs as she watched Paul elbow his way through the throng of hostile onlookers, mount his motorcycle and roar away. She realized she was saying goodbye to more than Paul Randall. She was also giving up the naive belief that her love was enough to change him, to save him from the negative effects of his dysfunctional upbringing.

Admitting she'd been wrong about him was breaking her heart.

Chapter One

Belinda Carnes was busy sorting local business files in the tall cabinet at the rear of her office when she heard the familiar ding of the electric eye that monitored the front door. She smoothed her skirt and breezed around the corner into the reception area with an expectant smile, recognizing her visitor immediately. "Sheila! Hi."

"Aren't you going to say, 'Welcome to Serenity. How can the Chamber of Commerce help you'?"

"Nope. I save that speech for the tourists." Belinda's smile widened. "And I leave out the part about the ticks and chiggers eating us alive all summer. What's up?"

"You mean you haven't heard?"

"Heard what? What are you talking about?"

"He's back."

"Who's back?" The fine, auburn hair at the nape of Belinda's neck began to prickle.

"Don't play dumb with me," Sheila said. "You know very well who I mean. Verleen saw that lawyer, Paul Randall, coming out of the market downtown. He'd been buying groceries. Bags of them. I'd say that means he plans to stay with those ancient aunts of his for quite a while."

Belinda blinked rapidly and paused to digest her friend's comments. The whole idea of Paul being anywhere nearby tied her stomach in knots, made her pulse speed. "I'd heard he was going to help the Whitaker sisters with the legalities of their real estate deal but I didn't think he'd actually come here to do it. What gall."

"What do you mean?"

"It's a long, complicated story." She sighed. "Let's just say Paul didn't turn out to be the wonderful guy I thought he was."

"Oh? What makes you say that?"

"You mean you haven't heard the gossip yet? Amazing. The way rumors fly in this town, I'd have thought you'd already know the whole story."

"I'd rather hear it straight from you," Sheila said with undisguised interest.

Belinda filled her in concisely, trying to leave out any supposition. She concluded with, "No one has ever proved who was—or wasn't—responsible for setting fire to the church…but nobody had any real motive except Paul."

"Wow. No wonder you don't want to come face-to-face with him."

"I'm glad you understand."

"Yeah, well…" A sly smile lifted Sheila's lips. "That's really too bad. I hear Randall is the best-looking guy around. And rich. I was kind of hoping you might want to introduce me to him. There aren't that many eligible men in this area, you know."

Belinda was flabbergasted. "You'd be interested in him, even after what I just told you?"

"Why not? Lots of us do crazy things when we're teenagers. It looks to me like he's reformed."

Shaking her head, Belinda made a face at her friend. "Not reformed. Just turned his talents to getting back at Serenity by legal means. Don't forget the lawsuit against the town fathers a few years back. When he proved land-use discrimination and the councilmen had to back down, they all lost face. Half of them weren't reelected."

"So? That's just business."

"Not in a close-knit town like this one. Around here, it's considered a vendetta. That's another reason I don't want anything to do with him."

"Guilt by association, you mean? I'm surprised you don't already have a problem with that. I hear that you used to tell everybody you were going to marry Paul."

Belinda blushed. "I was just a high school kid with a stupid crush on the only boy in town my father refused to let me date. In other words, a typical teen-

ager. Besides, that was ten years ago. Believe me,
I'm cured and everybody knows it...especially me.''

"Being young doesn't mean you can't fall in love
for keeps," Sheila countered. "My mom got married
when she was seventeen. She and Dad are still doing
okay."

"My parents had a wonderful relationship, too.
Everything changed when my mother died, though.
The only thing that saved Daddy's sanity was focus-
ing all his energy on his church."

"The one that burned down?"

"Yes." The memories of her late father's subsequent slide into depression brought Belinda's
thoughts full circle. "The doctors said he died from
a heart attack but I think he just gave up caring about
anything, even his own life, after he lost the church."
She hardened her heart. "Getting back to Paul Randall. I don't care where he stays or what he does
while he's here as long as I don't have to deal with
him. I'll be delighted if I never lay eyes on him again."

"You sound like you really mean that."

"I've never meant anything more in my whole
life."

Paul managed to keep himself occupied all afternoon by strolling around town and stopping to make
casual conversation whenever he got the opportunity.
He was amazed at how few of the old-timers recognized him at first. And at how shocked they looked
when he identified himself. Clearly, they remem-

bered the punk kid with the perpetual chip on his shoulder and were having trouble believing the changes he'd made in his image. *Good,* he thought, satisfied. That was exactly what he'd intended.

Beginning at the Mom and Pop café and gas station located next to the only traffic light in town, he worked his way through the pharmacy and the farm bureau office, then strolled the last block to the town square. A green, close-cropped lawn surrounded the courthouse. Most of the benches in the shade of the maple trees were occupied by old men, heads nodding sleepily. As usual, Serenity was so serene it gave him the willies.

Paul snorted in self-derision as he entered the hardware store on the north side of the square. All the businesses on that block faced the old brick courthouse, which meant he could stand on the opposite side of the square and position himself to look directly at the door to the Chamber of Commerce without attracting undue attention.

Ever since he'd learned Belinda worked there, he'd been trying to ignore that particular office. And he'd failed miserably. It looked like he was either going to have to pay his old flame a visit and try to clear the air, or resign himself to his grinding gut and buy a giant supply of antacids to calm the ulcer that usually flared up when he was under a lot of stress.

Paul opted for the visit. He'd written dozens of letters to Belinda over the years but had never mailed any of them. Initially, he'd focused on defending himself until he'd realized how futile that was. Later, he'd simply apologized for his anger. The last attempt had been a letter of condolence when he'd heard that her father had died. Worried that it might seem inappropriate because of his volatile past association with the man, he'd torn it up instead of sending it.

Remembering, he paused near the front of the hardware store, just inside the door.

"Something I can help you with, mister?" the skinny, slightly stooped proprietor asked. "You'd best hurry. We're about to close."

Paul snapped out of his reverie and smiled pleasantly. "Sorry. I was just looking, anyway. Do you happen to know how late the Chamber of Commerce stays open?"

"Till five, like the rest of us," the man said. "Why?"

"Just wondered."

"You're not from around here, are you?"

Chuckling, Paul shook his head. That was at least the tenth time that day he'd been asked the same question in exactly the same words. "Nope. I'm an outsider. Definitely an outsider." He offered his hand. "The name's Randall. The Whitaker sisters are my great-aunts."

Accepting Paul's hand, the proprietor shook it heartily. "Well, well. I didn't know Miss Prudence and Miss Patience had kin in these parts. Where'd you say you was from?"

"I settled in Harrison after I got out of law school," Paul told him. "I'm just visiting here."

"Well, if you're fixin' to repair that old house of theirs, we got the best selection of plumbing and electrical parts in the county."

"I'll keep that in mind. Thanks for your time." When the man opened his mouth and began to add to his sales pitch, Paul headed for the door. "I can't stay and talk right now, but I'll be sure to check back with you later. I need to run over to the Chamber office before it closes."

"Tell Miss Belinda I said howdy."

"Right." Waving a congenial goodbye, Paul crossed the wide, shady street at an angle and started to jog across the courthouse lawn. The digital clock in front of the bank on the north-west corner read four fifty-five.

All afternoon Belinda had fidgeted at her desk, eagerly awaiting quitting time so she could close the office. She'd already straightened the racks of brochures and maps several times and dusted everything in sight. All that was left to do was turn off the lights, lock up and make a dash for home. The sooner the better.

At five minutes to five, she started for the door, the click of her heels echoing in the empty office. Surely all the evenings she'd stayed open late would make up for leaving a few minutes early this time. One hand was poised over the Open sign, the other reaching for the lock, when a dark-haired, sophisticated-looking man in navy blue slacks and a sky-blue sport shirt appeared at the door.

He was tall, broad-shouldered and moved with an athletic grace. His hair was cut in the smooth, full style of a successful executive, except that it was long enough in the back to brush against his shirt collar.

Belinda's heart recognized him a few seconds before her brain agreed. She froze in mid-motion, sorely tempted to slam the door and bolt it. She didn't care if she did represent Serenity. That didn't mean she had to be nice to the likes of Paul Randall.

He glanced at his gleaming gold wristwatch. "I thought I still had a few minutes."

"Sorry. The office is closed."

"Too bad," he said with a wry smile. "I need some information about this interesting little town."

Belinda was not about to let him get the upper hand. "Fine." She grabbed a random handful of colorful brochures pertaining to the area and thrust them at him. "Here."

"I'm afraid that won't do," Paul said, stepping through the half-open door.

She gave ground. "I told you. The office is closed." The spicy aroma of his aftershave affected her strongly and made her want to put even more distance between them.

Paul's smile grew into a self-satisfied grin as he looked her up and down. "Humor me. I have as much right as anybody to be treated with respect. All I want from you is a few facts.''

Whether she liked it or not, he'd made a good point. Fair was fair. Besides, it wouldn't do to let on that she was still mad enough at him to make her blood boil. A contrary man like Paul Randall would probably enjoy seeing that she was upset, and she wasn't going to give him that satisfaction.

Circling him widely, hurriedly, Belinda said, ''All right. What can the Serenity Chamber of Commerce do for you? I'll give you two minutes.''

Paul's gaze met hers, challenged it, held it. ''I'm good, but I'm not *that* good. Perhaps I'd better come back tomorrow when you have more free time.''

And make me go through this emotional turmoil all over again? No way! The smartest thing she could do was give him the information he wanted, right now, and be rid of him.

''That won't be necessary,'' she said, pleased at how calm and businesslike she sounded in spite of her quaking insides and righteous indignation. She rounded the end of the counter to put a solid physical barrier between them. ''What is it you need?''

''Well… A list of the commercial property within four blocks in any direction from my aunts' estate, for starters.''

''You need to go to the county office for that and you know it,'' Belinda said, scowling. ''What do you *really* want?''

Inwardly tense, Paul kept his posture relaxed, his

smile as enigmatic as he could make it. He'd known that facing Belinda again would be difficult but he'd had no idea what a strong, gut-level reaction he'd have to her. That had been such a surprise he found he could hardly think straight, let alone come up with reasonable-sounding excuses for tracking her down while he was in town.

The most sensible option was probably to tell her the plain truth. The minute he'd set foot in Serenity again he'd felt he had to see her, to talk to her, to make her understand that he hadn't been responsible for the loss of her father's church. He was good at arguing court cases. It should have been easy to present a logical defense of his innocence.

Unfortunately, Paul had to admit he was currently standing on a foundation of emotional quicksand and sinking fast. Any notion he'd had about being permanently immune to Belinda's charms had vanished the moment he'd faced her again. If anything, the attraction he felt now was stronger than ever. That conclusion didn't astonish him nearly as much as the fact that the memory of her rejection still hurt.

If it hadn't been for her cautious expression and stiff, standoffish posture he might have foolishly relaxed his guard and told her how he felt, then and there. Which would have been the dumbest thing he'd done for ten years. Sharing some information about his professional concerns, however, didn't seem like such a bad idea. At least it would give him something intelligent to say.

"I was hoping you'd have time to bring me up to speed on the way Serenity is developing. You know. New business trends, population demographics, that kind of thing. Sort of an overview of what you see as the future of the town."

"Why me?"

"Because you've not only lived here for a long time, your job has put you right into the center of commerce." He quickly pressed on, hoping to sway her decision before she had a chance to think it through. "So, since you're about to close the office, how about I make reservations at Romano's for tonight? We can relax and talk over dinner."

"You've got to be kidding. No way!" Belinda's heart was racing and her mouth was as dry as the bottom of Lick Creek in mid-July! Didn't he remember anything about their last day together? About their quarrel? About the things she'd said to him? The passage of time had not changed her mind. Too many unanswered questions remained. Important questions. Questions she wasn't sure she wanted to ask because hearing the answers might prove too painful.

"Why not? Got a date with your doctor friend? I hear you two are quite a couple."

Obviously, Paul had been prying. "That's none of *your* business," she said stiffly.

"I see."

Belinda was surprised when he didn't immediately argue or try to manipulate her. As a practicing attorney he was obviously used to getting the results he wanted. Waiting for his counterattack, she pressed her lips into a thin line.

"Well, maybe some other time," Paul said, straightening and smiling woodenly. "I'll call you."

She noticed that his smile no longer brought a mischievous sparkle to his dark, compelling eyes. His gaze had grown shadowy, brooding, the way it used to be. The way it had been the night of the awful fire.

That memory was enough to keep her from holding back any longer. "No. I don't want you to call." Belinda shook her head firmly for emphasis. "We have nothing more to talk about."

Smile fading, he turned to leave. His voice sounded emotionless when he said, "For once, you may be right."

Belinda stopped by her grandmother Eloise's that evening. Eloise had sprained her ankle and was supposed to stay off her feet as much as possible. She wasn't behaving, of course. Belinda hadn't expected her to listen to medical advice, not even Sam's, which was why she'd decided to drop in and volunteer to cook the evening meal.

Standing at her grandmother's stove, Belinda got more and more distracted as she began to contrast the differences between Sam and Paul. Sam was steady, comfortable, and he fit effortlessly into her daily life. She'd never had a moment's worry about what he might be doing or who he might be with. On the other hand, being around Paul had always made her feel disquieted, as if she were standing at the edge of a precipice in a stiff wind and was about to be blown over the edge. Even now, though he'd looked as refined as any other professional man, his presence had sent a chill up her spine and made the hair on the back of her neck prickle.

Daydreaming, she nearly burned the black-eyed peas she was fixing as a side dish.

Eloise hobbled up to rescue the smoking pot and stirred rapidly. "Goodness me. That was close."

"Sorry. I guess I wasn't paying enough attention."

"No problem. I got to 'em in time." She paused, then asked, "So, tell me, how was Paul Randall?"

Whirling, Belinda stared. "How did you know I'd seen him?"

"Lucky guess." Eloise set the pot off to the side and plopped her slightly overweight body into a kitchen chair. "Well? Was he polite? Did he show his raisin', or did he manage to behave himself?"

"If you mean, did he grab me and kiss me senseless the way he used to, the answer is no. He's more out-of-place in Serenity than ever, but he didn't say or do anything embarrassing."

"That's a relief. You never know what might get back to Sam if somebody was to see you and Paul acting too friendly."

"Don't be silly. I'm not even friends with Paul. Not anymore. Besides, Sam's not the jealous type.

He may be practical to a fault but he's also predictable. He'd never jump to conclusions." Belinda turned off the stove and scooped thin strips of sautéed steak and onions from her frying pan into a serving bowl. "He's completely logical. That's why I believe him when he says Serenity's going to boom. He's even bought the building where his office is. Says he's planning to add another wing to it."

"Well, well. I suppose that explains why he was so keen on being voted president of the Chamber. I'm not real happy to hear he wants to start changin' things, though." She lowered her voice to add, "'Course, he's not from around here, so you never know."

Pensive, Belinda recalled what Paul had always said about not being accepted by the established core of Serenity's population. In his case, he was right. It wasn't that folks were cruel. Some newcomers just fit in better than others, especially if they made an effort to become a useful part of the community. Sam was making that effort. Paul and his father never had.

She remembered the first time she'd set eyes on Paul. His father had come to Serenity because of his late wife's shirttail relation to the Whitaker family and landed a job as a mechanic at the local gas station.

Paul had shown up for his first day as a senior at Serenity High sporting threadbare clothes, a worn leather jacket and a sullen, uncooperative attitude. Belinda had viewed him more as a lost soul than a rebel and had offered friendship. In no time, she'd fallen head-over-heels in love. She sighed. Too bad Paul's feelings for her hadn't been strong enough to overcome their differences.

"I'd like some of that before it gets cold," Eloise gibed, gesturing toward the bowl Belinda was holding. "Unless you plan on keepin' it all for yourself."

The comment brought her back to the present with a jolt. "Of course not. I…I was just afraid it was too hot for you to handle, that's all."

"Oh? With that faraway look in your eyes I figured you might be thinking about how you felt when you ran into your old boyfriend today." She grinned. "Was *he* too hot to handle, too?"

"Gram! Shame on you. Wash your mouth out!" Cheeks flaming, Belinda took her place at the table and refused to acknowledge her grandmother's triumphant expression. It was impossible to ignore her jubilant comments, however.

"Aha! I thought so. Good! Maybe now we'll see some action around here. A little honest competition should shake up Sam Barryman and get things moving. He may not be perfect but he's the best catch around…and a doctor, to boot. You two have been courtin' for a whole year. It's time he got serious and asked you to marry him. Fish or cut bait, I always say."

Belinda stared at her plate without seeing it. Sam had already asked her to be his wife—more than once—and she'd put him off. At the time, she hadn't realized what was stopping her. Sam was personable and reliable, he went to her church, and she was truly fond of him. So why not make a commitment? Why, indeed. Now that she'd been around Paul again, she was beginning to understand that the problem lay with her, not with Sam.

And she didn't like that conclusion one bit.

The Whitaker estate was a run-down relic from a bygone era. It was also a prime piece of real estate, which was why Paul had decided to spend a few extra days poking around in Serenity. He knew his elderly twin aunts had no spare funds with which to have the place independently appraised. He also knew that the sale of the property was their last chance to provide for the fulfillment of any dreams beyond day-to-day subsistence. At eighty-three, they didn't have the option of going back to work teaching if they wanted anything more than the basic necessities.

He wheeled his black Lexus into the circular driveway of the old frame house and parked. The narrow track branched so that visitors who had arrived by carriage in the old days could enter by the front door, then send their driver to the back to stable the horses without having to turn the team around. The carriage house in the rear had eventually been converted into a garage.

Pausing in the quiet of the late evening, Paul gripped the steering wheel and took a deep, settling breath. Maybe he'd made a mistake by coming here. Even Aunt Patience, usually the sprightly, happy twin, had been acting reserved. Prudence, on the other hand, had always moped around as if she'd just lost her best friend, so he couldn't tell if she was glad he'd responded to her request for legal help or not.

But that wasn't his real reason for questioning the wisdom of his decision to visit Serenity, was it? He immediately pictured Belinda. They'd had some really good times together. On her eighteenth birthday she'd snuck away to spend the afternoon at the river with him. Her auburn hair was longer back then, with golden highlights glistening in the sun, and she'd pinned it up because the weather was so hot and sticky.

They'd walked beside the slow-flowing water, pausing in the shade to share a tender kiss. Paul remembered her wide, innocent, blue eyes looking at him as if he were the perfect man. Faint freckles had dotted her pale skin.

She'd wrinkled her nose and made a silly face, pleading with him. "Come on. It's just a picnic. Please? Promise you'll go with me?"

"A *church* picnic," Paul had said.

"So? Daddy won't bite."

"I'm not so sure. He didn't look real pleased when I sat down next to you last Sunday."

She giggled. "I know. Wasn't he funny? It was like he preached his whole sermon right to you."

"Yeah. I noticed." Paul grimaced. "I felt like a bug under a microscope."

Belinda slipped her arms around his waist and stepped into his embrace. "I'm so sorry. That was partly my fault. When Daddy asked me why I was spending so much time with you, I told him I was trying to get you converted."

"I don't need saving," Paul recalled telling her. Back then, he'd seriously considered walking the aisle some Sunday just to please her and make points with her father. Fortunately, he'd decided there was no way he could fake salvation, any more than he could convince the sanctimonious residents of Serenity that he was just as good as they were.

Pensive, he sighed. Funny how things had worked out. His father had ruined his own life by making lousy choices, had left the stigma of a convicted arsonist on his only son and had seen to it that they stayed ostracized by living a transient, antisocial life.

Yet it was that same miserable existence that had made Paul so determined to succeed, to earn enough money to change his lifestyle and make himself into someone entirely different. A professional man people could look up to. Respect.

And that strategy had worked until he'd faced Belinda Carnes again and sensed her continuing distrust. He'd hoped she'd give him some sign that she might be willing to forgive and forget. Maybe even take up where they'd left off. After her clear rebuff today, however, he knew better.

Innocent until proven guilty didn't apply to him. Not in Serenity. Belinda obviously still blamed him for setting fire to her father's church. Chances were, so did almost everybody else in town, even if they didn't have the guts to say so to his face.

Paul's jaw muscles tightened, and his forehead furrowed. He didn't care what the others thought of him, but Belinda's opinion mattered. A lot. Whether they ever got back together or not, it was imperative that he prove to her he'd been innocent of any wrongdoing.

He sure wished he knew how he was going to do that.

Chapter Two

Belinda smiled and waved when she saw Sam Barryman's sporty red Camaro pulling into her driveway at precisely nine-thirty on Sunday morning. It was hard to remember exactly when Sam had started taking her to church. He hadn't asked. He'd simply begun showing up. For the past six or eight months she'd accepted his presence without question. This morning, however, she found it strangely annoying.

Tall, blond and athletic, the doctor bounded up the front steps to her house and held the door open for her. "Good. You're on time. I'm glad to see my suggestions worked."

"I beg your pardon?" Belinda wrinkled her brow.

"My suggestions. About getting you organized," he said, ignoring her negative expression. "Can't have my future wife running around being late all the time."

Belinda couldn't decide which assumption she wanted to object to first. Having spent the past few days soul-searching, she decided on the farthest-reaching one. "I told you, Sam. We're good friends. There's no reason to spoil a great relationship by getting married."

"So you say." He slipped his arm around her waist and escorted her down the porch steps, not letting go until they reached his car. As he opened the passenger door for her he said, "If you weren't such a prude we could be having a lot more fun right now, though."

Belinda rolled her eyes. "We've been over and over this subject, Sam. It's not open to discussion."

Chuckling, he circled the car and slid behind the wheel. "Okay. But I'm not going to wait for you forever."

"I've never asked you to wait for me at all. That was your idea."

"Because you're worth it." He flashed her a toothpaste smile and reached over to pat her hand as he drove. "All I have to do is figure out how to make you wake up and realize I'd be the perfect husband for you."

Belinda wanted to refute his claim but something held her back. Was it possible Sam was right? Could she be making a terrible mistake? It was conceivable. Sam was a nice enough person, and according to her late father she'd never shown good judgment where men were concerned.

Lost in thought she smoothed the skirt of her silky teal blue dress, admiring the beautiful fabric. The dress was one of her favorites, even though Sam had admitted he didn't care for it. He preferred she wear tailored outfits in more subdued colors, especially when she accompanied him to Chamber dinners or other business functions. She didn't really mind.

When it came to attending church, however, she wanted to feel uplifted, joyful. Bright colors helped her do that. So did singing. When the organ, piano and choir voices filled the sanctuary with heavenly music, she was transported to a time of carefree childhood, when her family had been intact and she hadn't imagined she'd one day feel so alone. So abandoned. So…

Oh, stop! Belinda ordered in disgust. *You're being ridiculous. You have much more to be thankful for than a lot of people do. You should be ashamed of yourself.*

She truly was ashamed. After all, she still had Eloise and a whole church-full of dear friends, not to mention the other people in Serenity who cared about her. It was a wonderful place. Even with its small town politics and petty rivalries it beat living in a big city, where most neighbors didn't even know each other's names. Or care to learn them.

Sam's voice jarred her reverie as he wheeled the Camaro into the church parking lot. "Well, we're here. What are you thinking about? You looked awfully serious just now."

"Serenity," Belinda said, smiling. "The town, not the frame of mind. Sometimes I can hardly believe how perfect this place is."

"Hold that thought," he teased. "It's excellent PR for the Chamber of Commerce."

"I know." She looped her purse strap over one arm, cradled her Bible and got out. "Remember that the next time I ask for a raise."

"I will." As they started for the large, redbrick church he offered her his arm, waited until she took it, then leaned closer to add, "Of course, if you were my wife, you wouldn't have to worry about working."

Belinda decided it was wisest to treat his comment lightly. She batted her lashes, gazed at him melodramatically and said, "Oh, sugar pie, you mean I'd get to stay home with all twelve of our kids?"

Sam's resulting chuckle sounded more like choking than laughing. "How about we start with one or two?" He raised an eyebrow. "Or were you kidding?"

Stifling a giggle she told him, "I was kidding. I can't believe you thought I was serious."

"I never know with you. Your moods can be really hard to read sometimes."

"Oh?" Belinda was about to ask for clarification when she felt a tingle at the nape of her neck. She shivered. Looked back. A dignified man wearing dark glasses and driving a shiny black Lexus was pulling into the parking lot. She didn't have to stare to know it was Paul Randall.

Her ire rose. How *dare* he follow her to church!

Inside the sanctuary, Belinda tried to forget who she'd seen arriving. She and Sam were seated in the third row, as usual. Since she couldn't see Paul in front of her, she assumed he had to be somewhere behind. Was he far away? Close by? If she peeked over her shoulder, would she spot him? Catch him watching her so she could give him an appropriately disapproving look in return? The thought of meeting his intense gaze sent a frisson of electricity zinging up her spine.

The congregation stood for the first hymn. Sam offered to share his hymnbook, but Belinda didn't need it. She'd memorized the words to most of the songs as a child because if her father's church door had been open, she and her mother were expected to be there. Truth to tell, she hadn't concentrated on her father's sermons nearly as well as she should have. The beautiful, inspiring music, however, had always captured and held her attention.

"Blessed assurance…" Voice clear and sweet, she sang the first few words, then suddenly quieted. Directly behind her an accomplished baritone was harmonizing with so much feeling and skill it took her breath away. He sounded familiar. Acting on impulse, she glanced over her shoulder, certain she had to be mistaken. She wasn't. Paul Randall was standing in the next row back, singing his heart out!

"...of glory divine..." Sam elbowed her and thrust the open hymnal at her again. Hands trembling, Belinda grasped one side of it and stared at the printed page. Looking at the words didn't help a bit. Her mind was whirling so fast she couldn't focus. All she could do was listen in awe.

It was like a miracle! Paul sounded as if he really meant what the song was saying. Whenever she'd managed to drag him into church as a teen he'd acted so sullen he hadn't even opened his mouth, let alone shown any musical talent. What a magnificent voice he had! She could listen to singing like that all day and never tire of it.

The hymn ended. Belinda followed Sam's lead and quietly sat down, but her spirit was still soaring. Paul's voice had touched every nerve in her body, echoed from the corners of her heart and lifted her soul to a higher plane.

What a shame he isn't in the choir, she thought absently. Logic immediately contradicted the notion. *Bad idea.* It would strain her already tenuous emotions if she had to see Paul sitting with the other members of the choir every Sunday. Good thing he didn't actually live around here! Imagining him as an active member of her church was probably nothing more than emotional regression, she reasoned, wishful thinking left over from her youth.

Taking a shaky breath, Belinda decided that was

exactly what was happening. At eighteen, she'd hoped and prayed that Paul would join her father's church, settle down and become a productive member of the community, someone she could introduce to everyone, including her dad, without feeling she had to make excuses.

Now, all that had changed. She had matured. Her father had died. Whether or not Paul Randall had truly bettered himself was no longer her concern. If he hadn't returned to Serenity she might never even have thought of him again.

Her conscience immediately disagreed, forming a stern but silent, *Ha!* Focusing on the stained-glass window behind the preacher, she escaped into silent prayer.

Oh, Father, forgive me. You've blessed me so much. Why can't I be satisfied and thankful and not want things that are bad for me? Sighing, she added, *Things like Paul Randall.*

As if the timing were preordained, the congregation began to sing a second hymn. There was no way Belinda could fight the emotional impact that Paul's impressive voice had on her, so she gave up trying. Closing her eyes, she drank in the deep vibrations the way the thirsty Ozark hills soaked up the first spring rains.

When she finally opened her eyes, Sam was staring at her as if she'd just committed an unpardonable sin.

In a way, she agreed with him.

* * *

Paul decided to linger in the parking lot outside the church and lay in wait for Belinda and Sam after the service concluded. When he'd chosen a seat behind them he'd convinced himself he was only doing it to force Belinda to introduce him to Sam. That was partially true. He did want to meet the doctor for the first time on a social level so he could size him up better.

What Paul hadn't anticipated, however, was how being so close to Belinda for a whole hour would affect him. Or how his thoughts would wander and his perception intensify whenever he looked her way.

He noticed she was wearing her hair shorter these days. It lay smoother and curved under gently, just touching her shoulders, with the sides tucked behind her ears. Delicate pearl earrings reflected the shimmering blue of her dress. The color was like sunlight reflecting on rippling water. It reminded him of the summer days they'd walked along the banks of the Strawberry River, holding hands and stealing kisses. At that time, he'd assumed they were simply seeking privacy, which was just fine with him. The more chances he could get to kiss her, to hold her, the better. In retrospect, he supposed Belinda had wanted to go to private places like that because she'd been ashamed to be seen in public with him.

And speaking of public, Paul mused, she and her boyfriend had just come out of the church and were headed his way. He purposely stepped forward to block their path. When Belinda looked at him their eyes met. Held. Paul called upon his battle-seasoned courtroom smile. "Good morning, Ms. Carnes."

Cheeks reddening, she mumbled, "Good morning."

He continued to smile amiably. "Aren't you going to introduce me to your friend?"

Why not? Maybe then Paul would believe she and Sam were a steady couple and leave her alone, like she'd asked. Belinda managed to tear her gaze from Paul's long enough to look over her shoulder at Sam. "Dr. Sam Barryman, Paul Randall."

Paul was the first to reach out. "Pleased to meet you." He wondered for a long moment if the doctor was going to refuse to shake his hand.

"Same here," Sam finally said, grasping his hand firmly, briefly. "You're that lawyer, aren't you? I'd heard you were in town."

Paul chuckled. "I imagine everybody has. Word travels pretty fast around here. Actually, I came to advise my aunts on the sale of their property." Striking a deliberately casual pose, he shrugged. "But I guess you know that, too." When Sam didn't comment, he went on. "Folks tell me you've managed to make a place for yourself in Serenity. That's not an easy thing to do. Congratulations."

"Thanks." Sam slid his arm around Belinda's waist and urged her away. "Well, nice to have met you, Randall."

"Same here." A cynical smile lifted one corner of Paul's mouth. Now that he'd met the doctor, he had the advantage, which was how he liked it. Sam Barryman was a smooth operator. Everything about him looked good—his professional demeanor, his expensive suit, his perfectly styled hair…the hometown girl he was courting. But something about him wasn't quite right. When Paul had looked into his eyes he'd seen a brief flash of wariness that didn't belong there, assuming the man was as honest as his reputation implied.

Thoughtful, Paul watched him hurry Belinda away. For a guy who had nothing to hide, good old Sam sure was in a rush to leave. Maybe it was time to press him a little harder and see how he reacted. He started after the retreating couple.

Belinda disengaged herself from Sam's possessive grasp as they approached his car. "What's the matter with you?"

"I don't know what you're talking about."

She saw him glance toward the church, so she did the same. Her heart skipped a beat. Paul was rapidly following them! Could Sam be getting jealous, just like Gramma Eloise had predicted? It sure seemed like it. And by the way, where *was* Eloise? She rarely missed a Sunday service.

Paul slowed as he approached. "Whew. I didn't realize how muggy it was out here." He shed his suit jacket and loosened his tie as he smiled at Belinda. "I meant to tell you, that dress looks great on you. It reminds me of summer days like today."

Since Sam was standing so close, it was easier to relax and casually accept the compliment. ''Thanks. It's a favorite of mine.''

''I can see why.''

Behind her, Sam opened the car door. ''Belinda?''

''Sorry,'' Paul said quickly. ''Don't let me keep you. We can always arrange a time to get together later and talk.''

Belinda couldn't believe his arrogance! She'd innocently acknowledged one comment about her dress and he immediately assumed that was all it took to win her over. What conceit! She stiffened defensively. ''I told you before, Paul. I don't think you and I should have anything more to do with each other.''

He nodded. ''I'm afraid you misunderstood me. I meant that Dr. Barryman and I needed to have a private talk. I suppose it is inevitable that I'll bump into you again, though. This is a pretty small town.'' The corners of his mouth lifted in a smug-looking smile. ''Tell you what. I promise to do everything I can to avoid you. How's that sound?''

''Wonderful.'' Feeling like an idiot, Belinda shaded her eyes and focused her attention on Sam. ''Okay. What's going on here? Why does Paul want to talk to you in private? I'm starting to feel like I've come in halfway through a complicated movie and can't make sense out of the plot.''

She saw the doctor set his jaw stubbornly, so she

turned back to Paul. "Well? I'm waiting. Which one of you is going to fill me in?"

"I have no objection," Paul said, maintaining his casual air. "It has to do with the sale of the Whitaker estate."

"Why do you need to talk to Sam about that?"

"Because your boyfriend, here, is up to his eyeballs in the deal. I'm surprised he didn't tell you."

Frowning, Belinda said, "So am I." It was bad enough that Sam was keeping an important secret from her. To learn about it from smug, gloating Paul Randall was much worse.

At that moment, if someone had asked her to choose which of the two men was more irritating, she'd have been hard-pressed to decide.

By the time Sam dropped her off at home, Belinda had managed to find out very little about his plans. All he'd say was that he had some wealthy silent partners whose interests he needed to protect, and that what he was trying to accomplish would be good for Serenity. She'd been around him long enough to know he couldn't be badgered into revealing more details until he was ready.

Since he hadn't offered to take her out for Sunday dinner the way he usually did, she assumed he was miffed. Well, too bad. If he expected her to ever consider him husband material, he was going to have to accept the fact that she expected to be treated as an equal partner in any serious relationship.

She opened the passenger door and stepped out as soon as Sam stopped his car in her driveway. "Thanks for the ride."

He leaned across the seat. "Belinda?"

Pausing, she bent down to see what he wanted.

"Is it true?" he asked.

"Is what true?"

"You and Randall. I'd heard a few rumors but I didn't pay much attention to them. I figured you'd never go for a guy like that. I mean, his father was a bum with a prison record, wasn't he?"

Belinda's stomach tightened, though not from hunger. "Paul's father was an auto mechanic when we met. What the man may have done before he and Paul moved to Serenity is none of my business." *Or yours.*

"And they lived in a shack out behind Butch's gas station where the old man worked?"

"It was a trailer, not a shack," she answered. "It was the best poor Mr. Randall could do, under the circumstances. Paul worked odd jobs to help out...." She paused, then added, "Until he went away to college."

"I've heard all about the night he left," Sam said, "but I won't go into that because I don't want to bring up memories that are painful for you."

Oh, right, Belinda thought. *As if you haven't already.* "Why are you asking me so much about Paul?"

"I've found it pays to know my enemies."

"Paul's not your enemy. Besides, there's absolutely nothing between us. Not anymore."

Sam began to smile at her. "I know that, honey. I just wanted to see if you were in a good position to help me out. I think you are."

"Help you? How?"

"I need to find out what Randall's plans are for the Whitaker place and how close we are to coming to terms during negotiations." His grin grew. "If you and I work together, we'll have a definite advantage."

Belinda refused to believe he was asking her to become some kind of amateur spy. Sam would never do that. He might be overly practical but he wasn't nefarious.

"What I have in mind is for the good of Serenity," Sam added. "I promise. You'll see. The whole town will benefit."

"From *what*?"

Chuckling, Sam straightened, making her bend lower to look him in the eye. "Oh, no, you don't. I'll let you in on my plan when the time comes. Until then, it's my little secret. All you have to do is be your charming self and report whatever Randall tells you about my project."

"Didn't you hear what I said to Paul this morning? I never intend to see him again, let alone talk to him."

Sam looked triumphant. "On the contrary. You're going to see Randall this coming Wednesday night."

"I am? How? Where?" Her heart began to pound at the thought. The sticky afternoon air no longer seemed to contain enough oxygen, no matter how rapidly she breathed.

"At the business dinner I told you about last week. We'll be representing the Chamber, remember?"

"Yes, but…"

"I guess I forgot to mention that it's at the Whitaker house. That location wouldn't have been my choice, but we'll make the best of it. Now that I've seen what kind of man Randall is, I'm certain he'll be there." He paused and slipped the car into gear. "I know he said he liked that dress, but wear that simple black dress of yours instead, so he keeps his mind on the deal, will you? I'll pick you up Wednesday at six-thirty sharp."

As Belinda watched him drive away, she was surprised how aggravated she was. Sam's attitude made her feel like blurting out a few colorful phrases that had never before passed her lips. She wouldn't do it, of course. It was wrong to curse, even if what she said didn't actually take the Lord's name in vain.

But after the morning she'd just had, she certainly understood what drove people to say such things!

Boy, did she.

Chapter Three

Restless, Belinda immediately changed from the teal dress to shorts and a loose shirt, then walked over to her grandmother's house rather than phoning to see why she hadn't been in church that morning. Eloise had ventured into the garden in spite of her sore ankle and was carefully watering a bed of new seedlings. She smiled a greeting.

Belinda pushed her bangs off her forehead. "Whew. I can see why you're out here watering. It's sure hot today."

"No kidding."

"So, what's new? How come you missed church?"

"I didn't miss it." Eloise shot her a brief glance, then squeezed the trigger of the sprayer again and went back to watching the spritzing water.

"You were there this morning? I didn't see you."

"I sat way in the back with Verleen and Miss Mercy. We get a much better view of all the goings-on from there. And now that the church has those hearing assistance doodads, we don't have to be so close to the front to keep from missing the important stuff."

Eyes twinkling, Belinda gibed, "You three never miss a thing, and you know it. I'm surprised you don't sit up in the sound booth and train binoculars on the rest of the congregation through that little window."

"Ooh, good idea!"

"I thought you'd like it."

Eloise waited a moment, then said, "So, tell me all about your morning."

"It was interesting, to say the least." Belinda blew a noisy breath. "Paul Randall showed up in church, but I'm sure you know that already. I don't understand why he didn't just go to services with his aunts."

"And have to choose whether to go to Patience's big, fancy church over in East Serenity, or Pru's little one? That's a no-win situation. The boy's not crazy."

"He's also not a boy anymore." She pulled a face. "You were right about Sam getting jealous of him."

"Aha! I knew it. Wonderful!"

"Not exactly," Belinda said cynically. "I don't think I like Sam as well when he's acting so possessive."

"Nonsense. That's a man's way of showing you he cares. They're not very good at putting it into words, you know."

Belinda shook her head. "No, I *don't* know. Dad was always hugging Mom and telling her he loved her. He used to hug people in his congregation, too. I don't remember him doing it much after Mom died, though." She hesitated, then decided to go on. "At home, he acted like he was mad at me all the time. I would have given anything to get one of his big bear hugs in those days."

"Oh, honey..." Eloise laid aside the sprayer and enfolded her in a motherly embrace. "Your daddy didn't mean anything by it. He was just hurting and afraid."

"Afraid?" She stepped back to study her grand-mother's expression. "Of what? He was always preaching about the strength we should draw from our Christian faith. How could he have been afraid?"

"Because he was human. Preachers are, you know. I think he pulled away from everybody be-cause he couldn't bear to be hurt again." She ca-ressed Belinda's cheek. "He loved you very, very much. That was why he acted so strict about every-thing. He was just trying to protect you."

Sniffling, Belinda made a wry face. "Well, it worked. I'm probably the only twenty-seven-year-old virgin in Serenity...or in the world, for that matter." The rosy color rising on Eloise's cheeks made her laugh.

The older woman giggled, too. "I don't know how you've managed to avoid getting carried away." The pink in her cheeks darkened, and her eyes were bright. "I was a very respectable girl, but I'm not sure I could have resisted your grandpa much longer than I did. We were too much in love to want to wait."

Belinda sighed, shrugged. "I suppose that's the key. Love, I mean. Sam says I'm a prude. He's right."

"You haven't been tempted?"

"Some," Belinda admitted. "But we always managed to stop before it was too late."

"Was Sam upset? Men have very fragile egos, you know."

With a smirk and a quick shake of her head, Belinda looked bravely into Eloise's eyes. "Sam didn't have a thing to do with it," she said. "He wasn't the man I was with when it happened."

Belinda would never forget the night she and Paul had almost stepped across the line. The balmy spring evening was so lovely it was as if it had been made especially for lovers. For them. She'd ridden close behind him on his motorcycle, reveling in the perfect opportunity to wrap her arms around his waist and lay her cheek against his back.

Paul had pulled over just outside Sylamore, on a bluff overlooking the river. Reluctantly, she'd released her hold on him and they'd strolled hand in hand toward an immense, flat-topped boulder at the edge of the scenic-view parking area.

Sighing, she'd said, "Look how clear the sky is. You can even see the Milky Way tonight."

He'd drawn her into his embrace then, and kissed her soundly, passionately. "All I want to look at is you."

Weak in the knees, she'd slipped her arms around his neck and held tight. "Oh, Paul. I love you so much."

"I love you, too, Belinda. I just wish..."

"What?" she whispered against his lips.

"Let's go sit down." Paul led her to the boulder, climbed it and reached to pull her up beside him. He took off his leather jacket and spread it out. "Here. Sit on this so you don't get your clothes all dirty."

So filled with happiness she thought she'd burst, Belinda did as he asked and snuggled as close to him as she could get. She'd just begun to imagine what it would be like to spend the rest of her life in Paul's arms when he said, "I may be going away soon."

That was unthinkable! "No!" Throwing herself at him, Belinda held on as if he were bidding her a final goodbye that very night. "You can't leave. You can't. Please don't go!" Frantic, she threaded her fingers through his long, thick hair and began raining kisses over his face, his neck, his chest.

Paul had managed to keep his youthful urges pretty much under control until that moment. She heard him moan and felt his hands start to rove over her back, then come up under her arms to touch her where no one else ever had.

"Run away with me," Paul begged, an emotional catch in his voice. "Marry me, Belinda. Marry me."

She'd almost said yes to more than marriage that night. Breathing hard, her heart pounding, she'd fought her own desires until the immense effort had brought tears to her eyes. One kiss, one forbidden touch, had led to another and another and another.

That was when she'd opened her eyes, looked at the canopy of stars, recognized God's magnificent handiwork and been reminded of her vow to her Heavenly Father. Somehow, she'd mustered the strength of will to push Paul away in spite of his protests.

To this day, she didn't know how she'd talked herself into it.

Paul spent the next two days shuttling between Serenity and his office in Harrison, checking tax records and trying to find out if Sam Barryman had the financial backing he claimed. By late Tuesday afternoon he was back in Serenity, waiting for his secretary to call with more information. He poured himself a tall glass of the lemonade his aunts had made and took it out to their front porch.

Prattling, Patience trailed him. "Can you believe it? She went shopping and was so late for her hair appointment she had to go straight to Angela's!"

"Who? Aunt Prudence?" He tipped the frosted glass and drank half its tangy contents.

"Of course. Who else is the bane of my existence? I made her the appointment because I wanted us both to look decent for tomorrow night. Oh, the lovely parties our family used to host in this very house. And now we'll get to do it again, right here, one last time."

"It's not exactly a party," Paul reminded her. "It's a business dinner."

Patience flipped a hand in the air, bracelets jingling. "Oh, who cares. We're entertaining. That's all that matters to me. You're such a sweetheart to offer to pay for it all." She patted his arm and smiled wistfully. "I can't wait to get my money out of this old place and take off on a world cruise."

"It might be best to invest the profits and use the interest instead of dipping into the principle."

"Oh, pooh," Patience said. "My sister can stick around here and sulk away her life if she wants to. I'm going to get out and have some fun." She smoothed her cap of silver hair. "Which reminds me. Since Prudence has our station wagon, can you give me a lift to the beauty salon?"

Paul checked his watch. "In another half hour or so. I'm waiting for an important call. I told my secretary I could be reached at your number."

"Oh! Oh, dear. I'm afraid that won't do. I have to be there in fifteen minutes," she said, casting him a bright grin. "I have an idea. I can borrow *your* car."

Paul nearly strangled on his lemonade. "My new Lexus?"

"Yes! I've always wanted to drive a beautiful car like that. It'll be the thrill of my life." Displaying a pitiful expression she said, "I don't have a lot of time left to collect great experiences like that, you know."

What could he say when she put it that way? Patience's reflexes still seemed keen enough to cope with a short trip across town. She was quick-witted and sprightly, which made her seem more youthful than her twin, even though Prudence always stressed that she was eleven minutes younger.

Sighing in resignation, he reached into his pocket and held out his keys. "Promise you'll be careful?"

She drew an imaginary X across her chest with a long, lacquered fingernail. "I promise. Now be a dear and back it out for me, will you? I have trouble judging distances in those fancy mirrors."

"How do you know you do?"

Patience giggled behind her hand. "I'm afraid I've been naughty. I've been sitting in your lovely black car and pretending to drive it." She clapped her hands. "This time, I won't have to pretend!"

Paul rolled his eyes and sighed. Great-Aunt Patience certainly knew how to get whatever she wanted. In her prime, she must have been a real femme fatale. He couldn't help wondering why she and her twin had turned out so differently.

"Prudence tells me Patience is having the whole affair catered," Eloise informed Belinda when she stopped by after work the following Tuesday. "All except for my special carrot cake. Pru wanted me to make one as a surprise."

"Great. If dinner's no good, I'll just wait for dessert and fill up on your delicious cake."

Grinning broadly, Eloise got up and started for the kitchen. She was limping noticeably. Belinda frowned. "How's your ankle?"

"Fine. It hardly bothers me at all if I stay off it. Just makes me mad is all. I'd like it better if I didn't have to act my age."

"Sixty-five isn't old," Belinda argued. "What if you were in your eighties like the Whitaker twins? Besides, since when did you act your age?"

Eloise laughed. "Probably never. I suppose that's what keeps me feeling so young. At least most of the time." Wincing, she plopped down in a kitchen chair and pointed to the refrigerator. "I've got to sit a spell. The cake's in there. Take a peek."

Opening the refrigerator door, Belinda immediately spotted the lavish dessert and lifted it out with great care. "Oh, it's beautiful! You really outdid yourself this time."

"I wanted it to be extra nice so I used slivered almonds and made a sweet cream cheese icing. Putting it on that footed glass plate dresses it up a lot, too." She carefully propped her ankle on the chair next to her. "So, can you deliver it for me?"

"Me?" Belinda's heart did a back flip and landed in a lump in her throat. "When?"

"Well, I suppose you could take it with you when you and Sam go to dinner at the Whitakers', but it would be much better if it was already there when the caterers arrive. That way, we can be sure Pru won't be disappointed."

Reflecting upon the time of day and the fact that the spinster sisters would undoubtedly be home, Belinda got control of her vivid imagination and forced herself to calm down. Paul had kept his promise to avoid her. She hadn't seen him since Sunday morning. There was no reason to assume he'd be at his aunts'. And even if he was, so what? The problem wasn't Paul, it was *her.*

"Okay," Belinda said with a nod. "I can drop it by on my way to the city council meeting."

"Uh-oh. I forgot this was Tuesday. No wonder you didn't change your clothes after work. Never mind, dear. I'll take it myself."

"No, you won't. You'll stay right where you are and rest that ankle. Is there anything else you need before I leave?"

"No. I'm fine. I'll have a pizza delivered for supper. Stop by after the meeting if you like and we can share the leftovers."

Belinda chuckled. "Are you sure? The way those meetings drag on it could be midnight before I'm free."

"I don't mind a late visit as long as it's you," Eloise said fondly.

Carefully balancing the cake, Belinda leaned sideways to kiss her grandmother on the cheek. "Wow. Love and pizza. An unbeatable combination. I have the perfect life."

"I think you'll find there's a little more to a perfect life than that."

"Oh, I hope not." Belinda made the exchange into a silly joke to keep from taking herself too seriously. "I was just getting the pepperoni part figured out."

Belinda parked her white Tercel on the tree-lined street in front of the Whitaker house, immensely relieved to see that there was no black Lexus in the narrow driveway. She closed her eyes and whispered, "Thank you, God."

Not that she was scared of running into Paul. She just saw no reason to face him again unless she was forced to. Clearly, the Lord agreed, because the man was gone.

Balancing the heavy glass cake plate, Belinda detoured around an overgrown cedar and made her way along the side of the dilapidated old house. A fat yellow cat sat in the middle of the back porch, licking its paw to wash its face and regally ignoring her presence.

Belinda didn't want to put the cake down or balance it in one hand to knock on the kitchen door so she called through the screen. "Miss Prudence? I brought your cake."

No one answered. By nudging the bottom of the warped wooden frame with the toe of her shoe, she was able to pry the screen door open and duck through safely before it banged shut behind her. Except for the tabby cat roosting on top of the refrigerator and the black-and-white kittens playing with a catnip mouse under the table, the house seemed deserted.

"Oh, well. No problem," Belinda told herself, easily deciding what to do. She'd just tuck the cake into the refrigerator where it belonged and be on her way. That would preserve the freshness of the cream cheese icing and also keep the house cats from helping themselves to a taste after she left.

She yanked open the refrigerator door. Her jaw dropped. So did a package of wilted lettuce and a roll of premade biscuits. The cardboard cylinder around the biscuits popped open as it hit the floor. Startled, Belinda almost made the terrible mistake of jeopardizing the cake in her efforts to stem the avalanche.

At her feet, biscuit dough was slowly expanding through the break in the package. One of the black-and-white kittens was sneaking up on it as if it were dangerous prey. Looking from the crammed refrigerator shelves to the large, footed glass plate, Belinda muttered, "What in the world am I going to do with *this?*"

Her gaze centered on the odd bowls and half-empty packages of food she could see near the front of the shelves. Could she ever clear a big enough place? Maybe. In an hour or so. Give or take a day.

One thing was certain. She was going to be late for the council meeting.

Paul was upstairs, on the phone to his secretary, when he thought he heard the back door slam. Relieved, he assumed Patience had finally brought his car home.

As soon as he finished his conversation he started downstairs to give her a chance to tell him about the fun she'd had with his poor Lexus. It was insured, of course, but that didn't mean he'd welcome a dented fender. Or a dented great-aunt!

His running shoes made little sound on the carpet. It wasn't until he was almost to the kitchen that he heard the soft singing of a woman. That wasn't Patience. Or Prudence. It sounded like… Belinda?

Slowing his pace, Paul approached with caution. After her insistence that she didn't want to see or talk to him, Belinda couldn't possibly be there. It had to be a trick of his imagination. Or a singing burglar with a high, sweet voice, he countered, purposely mocking himself.

He reached the doorway. There was no need to look. Now that he was close enough to hear every word of her gospel song, he was certain his visitor was Belinda Carnes. But why? What was she up to?

And why give herself away by making unnecessary noise?

Frowning, Paul leaned against the doorjamb, silently watching her. She was poking around in the refrigerator, a no-man's-land if he'd ever encountered one. Open bowls, cups and plates were stacked on the closest end of the counter. Wrapped packages of food were piled high on a chair she'd pulled over beside her and she was cautiously sniffing the contents of a large Mason jar, apparently checking them for freshness.

He waited until he thought she was about to step back, then calmly said, "Hello."

Belinda screeched, jumped and whirled around, all at the same time. The quart jar she'd been holding slipped out of her grasp. It hit the floor flat on its bottom, broke and spurted spaghetti sauce straight up in the air like a garlic-flavored geyser. What didn't get on her splattered all over the chair, cabinets and floor.

Heart pounding, she confronted Paul. "What did you do that for!"

"Me?" It was all he could do to keep from bursting into laughter. "I'm not the one who got caught raiding somebody else's refrigerator."

"I wasn't raiding it!"

"Oh? It looks to me like you were." He gestured toward the food she'd spread out. "What's all that?"

"It's…" Her anger increased when she saw the

runny red splotches dotting everything, from the floor to the top of the counter and beyond. "A mess."

"That's true."

"This is not funny, Paul."

"Oh, I don't know." A broad grin was spread across his face. "It looks pretty funny from over here."

"Oh, yeah? Well, it doesn't from where I'm standing, and I'll thank you to butt out."

He shrugged nonchalantly. "Okay. If that's what you want. I suppose it won't hurt the floor much more if you walk over to the sink to get the paper towels yourself." With a chuckle he added, "You might want to slip your shoes off first, though. I hope they were red to start with."

"No. They were white," Belinda snapped, disgusted. "White linen. And new. I'll probably have to throw them away now."

"Not to mention chucking a lot of the stuff on the chair," he said, pointing.

"I can't do that. It's not mine." Worried, she surveyed the chaos, unsure where to begin.

"Well, I can," Paul said firmly. "I've been looking for a good excuse to dump a lot of those scraps before my aunts make the mistake of eating them and wind up with food poisoning. Wait there. I'll go get a big trash can from outside."

He returned almost immediately and set a black rubber trash can at the perimeter of the exploding sauce circle. "Here you go."

"Thanks." Belinda's conscience was really starting to bother her. She'd snapped at Paul and told him she didn't want to even talk to him, yet here he was, volunteering to help. "It's really nice of you to pitch in like this."

"I beg your pardon?" Arms folded across his chest, he stood back and stared at her.

She didn't like the shrewd look in his eyes or his posture of authority. "You were going to help me."

"I don't think I said that, exactly." The corners of his mouth lifted in a sly smile. "I believe I said I'd bring you a can. I did. I trust you to decide what's worth keeping and what should be tossed out." He raised one hand as if administering an oath. "I hereby promote you from refrigerator raider to garbage sorter. Go for it. Get busy. I'll just watch."

"Why you…you…" Belinda barely managed to squelch the desire to tell him off. There she stood, in her ruined shoes and dripping skirt, while he made stupid jokes at her expense. Him and his spotless shirt and perfectly creased jeans and detestable attitude of superiority. What Mr. Paul Randall needed was to be taken down a peg. And she was just the one to do it.

Struggling to keep her rising temper a secret, she said, "I don't want to track this mess all the way to the sink. Would you mind handing me the roll of paper towels?" It nearly choked her to add, "Please."

For a few long seconds it looked as if Paul wasn't

going to comply. Finally, he turned and strolled to the sink and back. Sidestepping a splash next to the chair, he held the roll of towels out to her at arms' length.

Belinda couldn't quite reach it without moving her feet beyond the main sauce puddle. "You think you're standing far enough away?" she asked sarcastically. "I won't bite."

"Maybe not, but you sure are a mess." Paul chuckled heartily. "The stuffy Serenity Chamber of Commerce should see you now!"

If her conscience had ever possessed the slightest chance of stopping her, Paul's mocking, overbearing attitude had erased it. He was going to get what he deserved and more. Right now.

She bent, and filled her hands with cold, spilled spaghetti sauce and flung it at him as she straightened. "Oh, yeah? Well, let's see how *you* like it."

Paul saw determination light her expression, but his subconscious refused to believe what was happening until it was too late. Gooey globs of sauce caught him in the side of the head and trickled down his neck. He yelled like he'd been scalded. "You little brat!"

Belinda was elated. It was high time somebody in Serenity stood up to Paul Randall. How funny he'd looked before he'd realized what she was doing! Laughing till her sides hurt, she saw his expression sobering. He cast around, finally reaching for the sugar bowl on the kitchen table, then lifting it above her head.

Belinda ducked and backed away, her arms raised to ward him off. "I'm warning you. Don't you dare, or…"

"Or what?" Paul's large hand closed around her wrist, held her fast in spite of her struggle to escape. "What will you do? Tell dear old Sam? Ooh, I'm scared."

Sam was the *last* person Belinda wanted to tell about her willing participation in such a childish tussle. "I don't need anybody to help me get the best of you, mister," she shouted. "I can do it alone."

"Oh, yeah?"

"Yeah." With her free hand she reached up to spread the sauce across his cheek, adding to the mess because her fingers were still coated with red, too.

Paul immediately upended the sugar bowl over her head, then let her go with a sarcastic remark, "There, darlin'. That should help you be a little sweeter."

"Why, you…" Belinda felt as if he'd dumped a whole pail of grit in her hair. Sugar granules were trickling over her scalp and down her neck like sand in an hourglass. Without thinking, she squeezed her eyes shut and leaned forward to bat at her loose hair. Unfortunately, she'd forgotten that her fingers were still smeared with sauce. When she realized what she was doing, she began to shake her hands like a kitten who'd just stepped in a dish of milk and didn't know what to do with its wet paws.

"Hey," Paul taunted, "it looks like you're making marinara sauce in your hair. I love that stuff. I usually mix mine in a bowl, though."

Belinda was so furious she was speechless. At that moment it didn't matter to her if they were in someone else's house or not. They'd already made such an awful mess it couldn't get much worse. Paul Randall, however, could get considerably dirtier. She'd see to it. It would serve him right.

Still bent over, her hair hanging down to hide her face, she peered at the assortment of food she'd stacked on the chair. Most of it looked too old and too dry to stick to anything…except maybe whatever treasure lurked in a margarine tub that was within easy reach.

She grabbed the plastic container and popped off the lid, thrilled to see it still held half its original contents. She scooped up a handful of the greasy yellow margarine, straightened with a screech and lunged straight at Paul.

He didn't catch her hands in time to stop the attack. A gob of margarine plopped onto his shoulder. Without hesitation, Belinda smeared what was left of it on his cheek. "There. You've always been too slippery for your own good, anyway. Now you can *slide* your way out of town instead of riding off on that stupid motorcycle of yours."

Jaw clenched, Paul grabbed a red and white whipped cream can from the counter, aimed it at her face and pushed the trigger. The can spit and fizzled ineffectively.

Belinda stood her ground, laughing at his futile efforts to even the score. "You lose."

"Oh, yeah?" He began to shake the can frantically, then turned it upside down. Glaring at her through narrowed eyes, he started to advance, whipped cream nozzle at the ready. "I *never* lose, lady. Not anymore."

Putting up her hands to ward him off, she started to back away. Maybe it was time to call off the hostilities. Judging by the angry, determined look on Paul's face, maybe it was *past* time. Belinda decided to quit while she was ahead. "Truce, truce!"

"Truce, my eye," Paul said menacingly. He wiped his slippery cheek on the sleeve of his shirt and took a slow step toward her. Then another.

She squealed. Ducked. Turned to run. Scrambling, she slipped on the wet floor and lost her balance.

"Crazy woman..." Paul dropped the whipped cream can and lunged to catch her. If his hip hadn't wound up accidentally braced against the counter, their mutual momentum might have carried them both to the floor. Just in time, his arms closed safely around Belinda's waist.

"Let me go," she screeched, twisting and fighting back.

"Hold still and calm down," he countered. "I'm trying to help you."

"Oh, sure, you are." She pounded her fists hard

against his chest. "Just like you helped my father's church, right?"

"You never give up, do you?"

Suddenly, the back door slammed. They both froze. Paul wheeled to face the noise, swinging his wriggling burden around with him.

Already short of breath, Belinda gasped. The Whitaker sisters were standing just inside the door, their mouths open, looking totally stunned.

Prudence recovered first. She gave a little squeak, snatched up the nearest cat and clasped it to her breast, holding the poor Siamese so tightly it began yowling and struggling to escape.

Arching one thin, plucked eyebrow and starting to smile, Patience said, "Well, well. Look at the naughty children."

Paul tried to explain. "Aunt Patience, I..."

She ignored him and began to reminisce. "I remember a few food fights Pru and I had when we were girls. But I can see we were rank amateurs compared to you two. We didn't have *nearly* this much fun!"

Chapter Four

Struggling to free herself from Paul's grasp and regain some semblance of dignity, Belinda whispered, "Let me go."

"If you insist." He didn't right her, at first. He also didn't fully release her. Off balance, she started to fall, shrieked and instinctively threw her arms around his neck. Paul steadied her once again. "I thought you wanted me to let you go?"

"I do. I..." Flustered, Belinda made the mistake of looking directly into his eyes. The awareness she saw there took her breath away, made her realize she wasn't the only one feeling momentarily unstable. Unless her imagination was running away with her, Paul was as surprised as she was to be so deeply affected by their physical closeness.

In the background, Patience giggled behind her hand. "I hope you plan on cleaning up this place before the party tomorrow night. My poor sister washed and waxed the floor just this morning.''

''I certainly did,'' Prudence said, almost in tears. ''Whatever possessed you to ruin my beautiful kitchen?''

Paul recovered his emotional and physical balance. Sobering, he carefully set Belinda aside. ''It was an accident. We'll take care of it.''

''We?'' Scowling, Belinda studied him. ''I thought you said I was on my own.''

''That was before you covered me with sauce,'' he countered. ''Since I'm now as big a mess as you are, I might as well help you.''

Belinda decided he had a valid point. Partial imprints of her hands decorated the shoulders and back of his shirt. His collar and chest were dotted with the same dull red, his cheek and right arm were greasy, and he'd had to step into the puddle on the floor to save her from falling. They were in the sauce together.

Paul pulled a handful of paper towels off the roll and spoke to his aunts. ''This could take a while. Why don't you both go watch television or something?''

Prudence was more than willing. Muttering to her cat she hurriedly carried it from the kitchen. Patience, however, simply shook her head, pulled a chair as far away from them as she could get without leaving the room and sat down to watch. ''Not on your life, Paul, dear,'' she drawled. ''You two go right ahead.

I wouldn't miss the rest of your little spat for the world.''

He was scowling when he turned to Belinda and said gruffly, "This is all your fault."

"I beg your pardon. I wasn't the one who started it."

"You were, too."

"Was not," she insisted. "*You* made me drop the tomato sauce. Remember?"

"I didn't rub my own face in it," Paul muttered. "And speaking of rubbing my face in something, what did you mean by that crack you made about your father's church?"

"You know very well what I meant."

"Maybe I'm dense. Spell it out for me."

Belinda glanced at Patience and turned aside. "Not now," she told him, keeping her voice low. "This is not the time to discuss it."

"You're absolutely right," he said soberly. "The time we should have discussed it was ten years ago." He abruptly thrust the paper towels at her. "Here. I suggest you start by cleaning yourself off so you don't make things worse."

She jerked the roll out of his hand. "I don't know how it could get much worse. My clothes and shoes are ruined."

"And my shirt isn't?"

"Yeah, well, sorry about that. Guess I lost my temper."

"Tsk tsk. What would your stuffy friends say?"

"That I'm human, just like everybody else."

"And what about good old Sam? What would he say?"

Belinda's breath caught. She'd forgotten all about her promise to meet Sam. "Oh, dear! What time is it?"

Paul glanced at the clock on the far wall. "After seven. Why?"

"I'm missing the council meeting. I promised Sam I'd be there tonight. He'll be really upset when I don't show up."

"So, call the town hall and explain."

Making a wry face, Belinda said, "Oh, sure. That's a great idea. And what do you suggest I tell him?"

One corner of Paul's mouth began to lift as his glance traveled over her. "You have a point there. I suppose it wouldn't do to say you had a slight accident, because then he'd assume you were hurt and want to doctor you. And you certainly can't tell him the whole truth. Or can you?"

"Of course I can," she countered, trying to sound more convinced than she actually was. "Sam's a reasonable person. He'll understand that I had to come here first to deliver Gram's cake. Everything else was accidental."

"Everything?" One dark eyebrow rose.

"Well, almost everything." She eyed the door to the hall. "I don't dare walk on the carpet to get to the phone in the hall, though."

Paul was quick to offer a solution. "You won't have to go anywhere if you use my cell phone." He looked to his aunt. "I left it out in the car. Would you mind?"

Patience smiled sweetly and got to her feet. "Not at all, dear. As long as you promise you two won't do anything else exciting while I'm gone."

Blushing, Belinda bent to pick up the whipped cream can and said the first thing that came to mind. "Don't worry. I'm sure Paul will behave himself from now on."

The moment the words were out of her mouth she realized she might have inadvertently rekindled his antagonistic attitude. Uneasy, she glanced at him. Instead of taking offense, however, he'd resumed his unemotional, professional demeanor. That was too bad. Even as a youth he'd always taken life too seriously. The times she'd managed to get him to relax enough to smile and be candid were some of her fondest memories. Even the food fight they'd just had was better than seeing him sulk.

Moving mechanically, Belinda wiped off her hands, slipped out of her shoes and padded to the sink to wash. She was drying her hands and forearms when Patience returned with the portable phone and gingerly handed it to her.

"Thank you." Hoping that Sam would have his telephone in his pocket, as usual, Belinda dialed the number from memory. He answered almost immediately.

"Belinda? Where are you? The meeting's started."

"At the Whitakers'. I was de—"

"What are you doing there?" he interrupted.

"As I was trying to tell you, I stopped here to deliver a cake for Gram and I got delayed."

Sam's voice became a whisper. "All right. No harm done. Are you on your way now?"

"No. I—I don't think I'll be able to make it."

"What are you talking about? Just tell the old ladies you have to go and walk out the door."

"It's not as simple as that," she said softly, cupping the small phone in her hands and mimicking Sam's hushed tone.

Before she could explain, Paul called loudly to her. "Hey, Belinda, do you want me to throw your shoes away or are you going to try to salvage them?"

She covered the mouthpiece with her hand. "Hush."

"Why?" Paul asked, raising his voice even more. "You said you were going to tell him everything."

"Not now!" she countered. "He's in a meeting."

"What difference does that make?" Paul was beside her in three rapid strides. He held out his hand. "Here. Give me the phone. I'll take care of it."

Belinda resisted. "I'll bet you will."

"Look. Do you trust him or not?" Paul challenged.

"Of course I do."

"Then there shouldn't be a problem."

The only way to prove her faith in Sam was to hand over the phone. By the time Sam asked, "What's going on there?" he was talking to Paul.

"Nothing important," Paul answered calmly. "Your girlfriend just had a little accident with some spaghetti sauce." He paused. "That's right." He listened for a moment. "No, we weren't eating it. We were flinging it at each other. Believe me, you don't want her showing up at that meeting looking like she does now." He chuckled wryly. "Too much garlic. The sugar I added didn't seem to sweeten her up much, either."

Belinda couldn't hear Sam's reply, but judging by the smug look on Paul's face she imagined it was pretty colorful.

"No, no," Paul said. "You stay right there. She'll be fine. We'll take good care of her. If she decides she can't drive home the way she is, I'll get one of my aunts to loan her something else to wear. That should be an interesting sight, don't you think?"

Wide-eyed, Belinda watched Paul begin to grin as he listened. Then he said, "Same to you," and pressed the button to break the connection.

Hands on her hips, she waited impatiently. "Well? What did Sam say?"

Paul shook his head. "Word for word? Believe me, you don't want me to repeat it." He looked at the clock. "I figure we have about ten minutes, tops, before he charges in here to rescue you, so let's get to work on this mess. Half the blame is yours. I don't intend to get stuck cleaning up all by myself.''

''You really think Sam will come to my rescue?'' The notion made her feel surprisingly special.

''I don't know about him,'' Paul said flatly. ''But if you were my girl and I'd gotten a call that you were in trouble, *I* would.''

When Paul finally went outside to get a second trash can, Belinda took advantage of his absence to slip off her panty hose and throw them away. Disappointed, she sighed deeply. Paul had been wrong about Sam showing up. Almost two hours had passed with no sign of the doctor, and they were done with the basic cleaning. Thankfully, they'd been able to keep the peace while they worked.

Patience had been upset when Paul had insisted that they dispose of so many leftovers. Eventually, she'd stopped arguing and gone to join her sister in the den.

Terribly weary all of a sudden, Belinda leaned against the edge of the counter, closed her eyes and talked to God while she waited for Paul to return. ''Oh, Father. It's been ten years since I prayed for that impossible man to come back to me. I've changed my mind. You know I have. Please, please tell me You're not answering that old prayer *now*.''

The screen banged noisily. Her eyes popped open. Paul had shed his stained dress shirt, leaving only his plain white T-shirt and denim jeans. His hair was mussed, his dark eyes bright. It ought to be against the law to look that appealing, Belinda mused, annoyed that she'd noticed in the first place. When he began to smile a little she was glad she had the kitchen counter to lean on.

"You look beat," he said with a resigned sigh. "Why don't you go on home. I'll finish up here."

"I can't. I still have to mop the floor."

"I'll do that, too."

"Oh, sure."

Paul chuckled softly. "Trust me. Thanks to a hitch in the Navy, I'm a real expert with a mop."

That was a surprise. "You were in the service?"

"Uh-huh. I joined because it seemed like the best way to further my education." *And to get far away from my past,* he thought.

"I'm impressed."

"Well, don't be. I hated every minute of it. I never was real good at taking orders."

Belinda's weariness helped lower her guard so that she spoke more from her heart than from her head. "No kidding. You used to be a terrible rebel. I think that was one of the things I liked best about you."

"What?" His brow knit. "Why?"

"I don't know. Maybe because I'd led such a sheltered life. My father had a lot of strict rules about how his only daughter should behave. I was always afraid of accidentally breaking one of those rules. When I met you, I saw what it was like to have freedom, to enjoy life."

Paul's loud, abrupt response made her jump. "Ha! I'd have given anything to have a father who cared where I was and what I was doing. Just a normal, everyday dad. A guy who fit in and acted like everybody else's father."

Stunned, Belinda paused to sort out her thoughts. "I'm sorry. I guess I never understood. I knew your dad had problems. We all knew. I just assumed you *wanted* to be different."

"Why? Because I acted like I didn't care?" Snorting with self-derision, he crossed the kitchen to bring her the empty trash can. As he set it down, a plaintive mewing diverted his attention. One of the black-and-white kittens seemed to be wedged in the narrow space between the refrigerator and the end of the cabinet.

When he reached down to rescue it, it hissed at him. "Hey, this little guy's got guts." Paul held the shivering kitten to his warm chest and petted it to soothe it. "He's so scared he's about to shake apart, but he knew he couldn't run away so he stood up to me."

In awe, Belinda softly asked, "Is that how *you* felt? About having to live in Serenity, I mean."

Paul saw pity in her eyes. Pity and welling tears. He wanted neither. Especially not from her. Disgusted with himself for accidentally letting down his defenses, he sought to remedy the situation. "Of course not. I was talking about this cat. What did you think I meant?"

"Nothing. I didn't realize you'd changed the subject, that's all." She reached out. "Better give him
to me. He's leaving little footprints all over your
shirt. He must have stepped in a spot of sauce that
we missed."

Paul reluctantly did as she asked. "Okay. As long
as you don't intend to try to give him a bath."

"Of course not. I'll just wipe his paws with a
damp cloth so he doesn't track up the floor. He and
his mama can do the rest." Moving slowly and mur-
muring endearments to the frightened kitty she made
her way to the sink, squeezed out one of the kitchen
towels they'd used to wipe down the cabinets and
gently washed its feet.

"There you go. See?" she crooned. "That didn't
hurt a bit, did it?" Cradling the kitten against her
with one hand she turned her attention to Paul and
began to dab at the faint, tiny paw prints on his
T-shirt with a corner of the damp towel.

"Leave it alone. It's okay," he insisted.

"It'll just take a second...."

Paul's hand closed around hers, stilling her efforts.

Confused, Belinda raised her eyes to meet his. He
didn't speak. He didn't have to. The look in his eyes
was warning enough. It sent prickles shivering over
her skin and raised the fine hairs on her arms into
goose bumps.

Time sputtered to a standstill, pausing until the
kitten mewed a plaintive distraction. As soon as Be-

linda broke eye contact with Paul to glance down, the intimate mood was broken.

"I'll take him," Paul said, releasing his hold and pushing her hand away while relieving her of the tiny ball of fur. "You'd better get going. It's late."

Yes, she thought sadly. *It's way too late…for a lot of things.*

Especially for her and Paul Randall.

That was the heartbreaking part.

Belinda didn't remember any details of her trip home. She didn't even realize she'd arrived until she automatically turned left into her own driveway.

Her car's headlights swept across a parked red Camaro. Evidently, Sam had decided to avoid confronting Paul and had gone to her place to wait instead. *Terrific.* She knew she should feel delighted to see him, but in truth, he was the last person she wanted to talk to right now. She also knew she had no choice.

Heaving a sigh of resignation, Belinda climbed out of her car and started for the front porch. In the yellow glare of the porch light she could see Sam on the top step. The night was warm, clear and humid. He'd shed his suit coat and tie and rolled up the sleeves of his shirt.

"Hi," Belinda said. "The back door's unlocked. You could have gone inside where you'd be more comfortable. I have to leave the air conditioner on or the house gets so hot I'd never get it cooled down enough to sleep comfortably.''

"No way. Out here is fine.''

She assumed he was being solicitous of her spotless reputation. "How sweet.''

"What is?'' Sam frowned at her as she climbed the steps toward him, then stood aside so she could unlock the door.

"Worrying about what other people will think of me if they see you acting too at home here. Once a rumor like that gets started it's almost impossible to stop, especially in a close-knit town like Serenity.''

"I suppose you're right. I hadn't thought of that. I stopped by to make sure you were all right and decided to stay out here because I heard Snuffy barking. You left her loose in the house. You know how I feel about that dog.''

"Oh.'' What a disappointment. Belinda paused at the door, blocking his entry and making sure her overly friendly beagle didn't charge out and jump all over him. "I'm sorry, Sam. It's late, and I'm beat. I'm not going to ask you in.''

Sam sounded disgusted. "Why not? You just spent hours at the Whitakers' with Randall. *That* certainly won't help your reputation.''

"We weren't alone. Besides, it couldn't be helped.'' Watching the doctor's glance take in her soiled, disheveled appearance, she ordered, "Stop staring at me like that. You look like you just bit into a wild persimmon before the first hard winter freeze.''

''What's that supposed to mean?''

''Sorry. I forgot you aren't from around here. Wild persimmons are real sour, like the look on your face. The frost makes them sweet.''

Shoving his hands into his pockets, Sam apologized. ''Okay. I'm sorry, too. I suppose this is partly my fault. I did tell you to talk to Randall whenever you got the chance.'' He raised an eyebrow and stopped scowling. ''So, what did you find out?''

That he knows how to mop a floor and likes kittens, Belinda thought. She said, ''We didn't talk about the sale of the house at all, I'm afraid. We spent the entire time cleaning up the food I spilled trying to get Gram's cake to fit into Miss Prudence's refrigerator.'' She gestured at her skirt. ''As you can see, it was a terrible mess.''

''That's an understatement.''

The disappointment in Sam's expression told her far more about his true disposition than she wanted to know. When he gently laid his hands on her shoulders and bent to kiss her, she presented her cheek. ''Good night, Sam.''

''Good night, honey.'' He hesitated as if he might say more, then wheeled and started for his car. ''Remember, I'll pick you up at six-thirty tomorrow evening.''

The balmy night air wasn't warm enough to keep Belinda from shivering as she watched him drive away. She folded her arms across her chest and hugged herself. In all the confusion she'd forgotten their dinner date.

Normally, she enjoyed Sam's company. Ever since Paul had returned, however, she was beginning to feel like a tasty bone being fought over by two hungry, possessive dogs, each tugging her in opposite directions. There were already imaginary teeth marks on her poor, confused psyche.

And speaking of dogs… Now that Sam had gone, it was safe to let Snuffy out. "Come on, baby. The coast is clear," she said, opening the door all the way and bending to greet her loving pet. Panting and leaping at Belinda, the brown, white and black beagle dashed onto the porch.

"I'm glad to see you, too." Belinda chuckled. Nose to the ground, Snuffy was instinctively following tracks. She circled the place where Sam had stood, then trailed him to the driveway, stopping where he'd gotten into his car. Apparently satisfied, she gave a sharp, resonant bark and bounded back to Belinda.

"Yes, girl, he's gone." Belinda ruffled the dog's pendulous ears while it eagerly sniffed the hem of her skirt. "That's spaghetti sauce. And you can probably tell I was around a few cats, too."

Snuffy wagged her tail and cocked her head, looking at her mistress expectantly. "No, baby. I didn't bring you a kitty to play with, although that may not be such a bad idea. At least you'd have somebody to keep you company while I'm at work." Belinda's voice softened, sounded more like she was speaking to a child. "Are you lonesome when I'm gone, sweetheart? Huh? Are you?"

The exuberant dog began licking her bare toes. "Hey! Stop that. It tickles," she said with a soft laugh. "If you're trying to tell me I need a bath, you're right. Come on. I'm putting you in the back yard where you can't get into trouble. Then I'm going to treat myself to a long, long shower. I've certainly earned it."

With a series of short, happy barks, the little beagle dashed around the house ahead of Belinda and darted through the open gate, skidding to a stop next to its red plastic food dish.

Amused, Belinda grinned and nodded as she latched the gate behind her and headed for the back door. "Okay. You win. First, I'll feed the dog."

And then I'll crash, she added, noting once again how tired she was. Must be from all the hard scrubbing and cleaning she'd had to do.

Her conscience immediately contradicted her. Who was she kidding? She was beat because she'd spent so much time dealing with Paul…with her reactions to him.

Belinda started to mentally argue, then stopped. There was no use denying that a spark of affection remained between them. But that was all it was. All it could ever be. When their lives had briefly converged ten years ago, they might have had a chance to find a happy middle ground. But no more. Paul had his successful law practice and the perfect new life he'd worked so hard to make for himself in Harrison. And she had Serenity, the only place where she'd ever felt truly at home.

The last thing Paul wanted to do was go back.

The last thing she wanted to do was go forward.

Chapter Five

Sam didn't say anything about her choice of clothing when he picked her up for their dinner engagement, but Belinda was certain he noticed she wasn't wearing the simple black sheath he'd suggested.

To be fair, she had gotten it out of the closet and considered it, but she just didn't feel like being so somber. This was summer in the Ozarks. Bright color was everywhere. Most people had a myriad of beautiful flowers in their yards, or filling planter boxes, or cascading over the sides of baskets hung in the shade of old-fashioned covered porches like hers. Some gardeners, Eloise included, had all three. And a lush vegetable garden, to boot.

Besides, the black sheath was a terrible choice for hot, muggy weather, and today's temperature had been particularly high. Belinda figured it was bad enough that she had to wear panty hose. She wasn't about to purposely make herself even more uncomfortable.

That line of reasoning had led her to pick out a pale pink sleeveless dress with a short, open-knit jacket in a darker rose. The outfit was far from businesslike. It was, however, pretty. And cool. It also set off the reddish glint in her hair, and she felt good wearing it. That was the most important thing.

When they arrived at the Whitaker mansion, she was doubly glad she'd dressed lightly. Sam parked beneath an enormous walnut tree that grew next to the driveway, but the temperature was still uncomfortably high, even in the shade.

"Whew!" Belinda fanned herself with her hand as she climbed out of the car. "I'm afraid working in an air-conditioned office has spoiled me."

"Yeah. Me, too." Sam used his folded handkerchief to blot beads of perspiration from his forehead. He took her elbow, urging her toward the elaborate, once regal porch. "Come on. Let's get inside before we melt."

"I don't think I've ever gone in the front door here," she said candidly. "When I was little, Gram used to bring me by to visit Miss Prudence all the time. I'd usually sit on the back porch and eat her homemade sugar cookies while she and Gram talked."

Sam was already banging the brass knocker. "That's nice. But you need to remember this is not a social call. Keep your mind on the reason we're here.''

"To get the Whitaker sisters to sell the place to you and your partners. I know.'' She made a face at him. "Don't you think it's about time you told me what your plans are?''

"When I'm ready.'' Sam raised his arm to rap again just as the door swung open.

Belinda watched his countenance rapidly darken. Her gaze instinctively followed his. The humid air became cloying. Nearly unbreathable. When Paul smiled at her, she felt suddenly faint.

"Come in, come in,'' Paul said, stepping out of the way. "Glad you could make it.''

Sam shook his hand. Belinda refrained. By using Sam as a buffer, she was able to enter the house gracefully while still managing to avoid Paul's touch. Thankfully, he didn't seem to notice the slight.

Acting the affable host, Paul led the way into the formal parlor. High ceilings helped cool the room by giving the rising warmer air a place to go. Portable electric fans were strategically placed to stir the cooler air below.

The Whitaker sisters were seated together on the brocade settee. An older man Belinda didn't recognize was the sixth person in the room. Paul introduced him as Milton Boggs, a friend from Harrison, but Belinda suspected there was an ulterior motive for his presence. Evidently, Sam felt that way, too, because he eyed the thin, balding man with suspicion.

"So, what brings you to Serenity?" Sam asked him as they politely shook hands.

Boggs shrugged casually. "Not much. It is nice to get away once in awhile. See the sights. Serenity is a lovely town. You must be thankful you chose to bring your medical practice here."

"I am. I intend to spend the rest of my life here." He drew Belinda closer to his side. "You know. Settle down. Get married. Raise a family."

She stiffened. Glanced at Paul. Nothing in his expression indicated that Sam's declaration had upset him. Either he truly didn't care or he was very good at masking his feelings. Maybe both.

Sam escorted her to a chair across the room and stood beside it like a sentry on guard duty. Looking for some way to relieve the tension, Belinda noticed the items on the tea cart and smiled at Prudence. "I was just telling Sam about your wonderful sugar cookies. I see you've made some."

"Yes. Mayor Smith phoned and said he was going to be late so I decided to serve these while we wait. Sister made the lemonade. Would you like a glass?"

"Yes, please."

Patience put ice cubes into a tumbler and filled it with lemonade. Before Sam had a chance to offer to fetch it for her, Paul had taken on the task. He also put two cookies on a napkin, then delivered everything with a polite smile. "Here you go. How about you, Doc? Lemonade?"

"No, thanks."

Belinda had to concentrate hard to keep her hand from trembling as she took the glass and cookies from Paul. It helped that he was looking at Sam instead of at her. She perched on the edge of the chair, napkin in her lap, and smiled woodenly.

"You look a bit peaked," Patience observed. "Are you feeling all right?"

"I'm fine." Belinda wasn't about to admit she hadn't felt light-headed until she'd encountered Paul again. She took a sip of lemonade and peered at him over the rim of the frosty glass. He looked so cool, so unruffled. His slacks were pressed, his shirt was crisp and white and his smile was enigmatic.

She pulled a face, disgusted with herself for paying so much attention to him. Being attracted to Paul Randall in the first place, in spite of herself, then being thrust into such close proximity to him, was liable to make this one of the most difficult evenings she'd ever spent.

"Oh, dear," Prudence said, noting the change in Belinda's expression. "Sister didn't forget to add sugar again, did she?"

Paul answered for her. "No, Aunt Pru. I tasted the lemonade. It's perfect, as usual." A knowing grin spread across his face. "I think Ms. Carnes may be reliving the little problem she had in your kitchen yesterday."

"*I* had? And what do you mean, *little* problem?" Belinda bristled. "That was a full-blown disaster, and you know it."

"I have to agree with you there," he gibed. "I wish I'd thought to grab my camera and snap a picture of you."

The image that immediately flashed into Belinda's mind was one of Paul, staring at her photo and dreaming, just as she'd often done with an old high school picture of him.

Paul saw a softening of her expression, a glassy shimmer in her lovely blue eyes, and he wondered what she was thinking. Whatever it was, he didn't think it was wise to ask. Especially not in front of Sam. Instead, he said, "Sure. I might need that kind of solid evidence for blackmail some day."

Belinda made another disgusted face. "What would you charge me with? Breaking and entering?"

"Nope. Just breaking…jar breaking." He started to chuckle. "And maybe butter smearing, if I could find a legal precedent for it."

Belinda was relieved when the mayor finally arrived and everyone gathered in the formal dining room. Its flowered wallpaper was faded, and the drapes were a bit frayed at the hem, but it was still easy to envision how elegant the room had once looked. Unless she missed her guess, the mahogany table and chairs were Chippendale.

The caterers had set up their silver serving dishes

on a massive matching sideboard and were standing beside it, waiting to begin.

"This is beautiful," Belinda told the elderly sisters as she admired the lavishly set table. "I didn't know you had such fancy china and crystal."

"The silverware was Mother's," Patience said proudly. "And she helped me collect the china for my hope chest. The stemware was our aunt Nettie's."

"Yes," Prudence agreed. "She willed it to both of us and we hated to split up the set, so I gave my half to Sister."

"Not that it made one whit of difference," Patience observed, beginning to pout. "Since neither one of us ever left home, it's stayed right here, anyway."

"Oh, and I suppose that's *my* fault? Nobody told you you couldn't leave."

Belinda had never known the sisters to act so openly antagonistic. Of course she usually saw them separately, especially since Grandma Eloise was closer friends with Prudence. Unsure of what to say next, she looked to Paul. It was obvious that he, too, was surprised by their mutual outburst.

"Well," Paul offered, his voice calm and even, "neither of you will have the problem for much longer, once you sell the house."

"That's another thing," Prudence said stiffly. "I don't care what my sister decides to do or where she wants to go. I've given the matter a lot of thought and I'm perfectly content right here. I'm not leaving.''

"It's those stupid cats of hers," Patience explained. "She's afraid they won't be happy anywhere else." She huffed and plunked down into the chair Paul had pulled out for her. "Sister never did have the sense God gave a goat when it came to dumb animals."

"Oh? Well, at least my animals can be trusted to never turn on me. Not like some people I might mention."

"You wouldn't know a friend if she came up and bit you," Patience argued.

"*My* friends don't bite."

"You know very well what I meant," her sister countered. "If you'd get out once in a while you might actually enjoy yourself the way I do."

"I wouldn't want to be like you if that was the only choice in the world," Prudence said, her voice shrill. "All you ever think about is yourself."

"That's not true, and you know it!"

Paul tried to call a peaceful halt to the argument by holding up his hands. When that didn't work, he put two fingers in his mouth and whistled. Everyone froze.

"That's better," he said with a tolerant smile. He signaled the caterers to begin serving. "I think we'd better eat. The soup is probably getting cold."

"We didn't order soup." Patience sounded miffed.

Paul laughed softly and shook his head, looking

from one of his testy aunts to the other. "I know we didn't. But if I thought it would quiet you two down, I'd go open a can of the stuff and fix it myself. Now, can we eat in peace? Please?"

"If that's what you want, dear," Patience said amiably. Her sister merely nodded in sullen agreement.

How different the two women were, Belinda mused. She'd always thought it would be loads of fun to have a twin. Watching the Whitaker sisters interact was starting to make her thankful she was an only child.

But it would be nice to have somebody else she could feel close to besides Gram, she thought. A contemporary who truly cared and understood her. Someone who belonged to her and she to them. A sense of belonging was one of the things that had blessed her so when she'd given her life to Jesus. No matter where she was or how bad the circumstances seemed to be, He was always there. Always ready to help.

All she had to do was get her pride out of the way, stop being stubborn, and surrender to His will. It sounded like a simple enough act. It wasn't.

Sometimes, like now, when she was so confused by her rampant feelings that she hardly knew her own name, it was practically inconceivable.

During dinner, Belinda was relieved that Mayor Smith chose to distract everyone by telling tales of

Serenity in its early days. She'd heard various versions of his stories often, which was just as well, since she couldn't have paid close attention if her life had depended upon it. Eating her dinner with Paul seated directly across the table was hard enough. Taking part in a discussion that required the assimilation and processing of unfamiliar information would have been impossible.

"'Course, I was just a boy back then," the mayor said, "but I do recall the way this place here looked. It was the finest estate in the whole county, maybe even the whole state of Arkansas. Had everything, a big house, fine stables, grand gardens..." He paused to blot perspiration from his balding pate with a folded handkerchief. "It had the best kitchen garden, too. Me and a couple of other boys used to dare each other to swipe watermelons out of it. We used to sneak in from the back side, off of Old Sturkey Road. Nowadays, I'd be lucky to be able to *walk* that far—" he patted his paunch "—let alone run, totin' a humongous melon!"

Patience covered her mouth delicately with her napkin and tittered. "You should have seen those boys! I used to hide with Papa and watch from up in the carriage house loft. He got the biggest kick out of it. Especially watching you, Ira."

The mayor gasped. "He knew?"

"Of course, he did. It was a game to him. That was why Sister and I were always needling you to do it again."

Belinda had held her tongue as long as she could. "That doesn't seem like a very good way to raise children. It sounds to me like he was condoning stealing."

"I suppose it does, these days," Patience answered, thoughtful. "But back then Papa gave away lots more than our family ate. Everybody knew all they had to do was ask and they could have whatever they needed."

Looking relieved, the mayor wiped his brow again. "That's true. Come to think of it, I suppose that's why my pa never whipped me for doing it. Anyway, I turned out all right, so I guess no harm was done."

Belinda noticed a mischievous twinkle lighting Patience's grayish-blue eyes. "Well, I don't know about that, Ira," the older woman drawled, "you *did* become a politician."

Laughter filled the room. Forgetting herself, Belinda made the mistake of relaxing her guard and looking at Paul.

His eyebrows arched in acknowledgment and challenge. "Just goes to prove you never can tell, doesn't it?"

Before Belinda could decide how best to respond, Prudence jumped to her feet and grasped the edge of the table. "Stop talking about hiding and spying on people! All of you. It's not funny, it's a mean, nasty habit, especially when a person's own family is involved." The color drained from her face.

"Aunt Prudence..." Paul was beside her in seconds. "Are you all right?"

"No. I'm not all right," she wailed. "I just wish... Oh, dear..." When Paul put his arm around her shoulders she hid her face against his chest.

He stroked her thin back. "This whole business about selling the house has been hard on everybody. You're probably overtired. If you've finished eating, why don't we let Aunt Patience take you up to your room so you can get some rest?"

"No! Not her," Prudence cried. "She's the worst of them all."

Paul was at a loss. He looked at Sam. "In that case, would you mind checking her out, Doctor? I've never seen my aunt act like this, before."

"Humpf," Patience said, making a sour face. "I have. Plenty of times. Don't worry. There's not a thing wrong with her that gettin' her own way won't cure. She just wants to distract us, keep us from talking about the sale of this monstrosity of a house."

Sam got to his feet. "Well, as far as I'm concerned, she's been successful. I can't see any reason to continue negotiations when one of the primary parties to the deal is so unwilling to sell that she's making herself sick over it." He rounded the end of the table and reached for Prudence's wrist, timed her heartbeats, then looked at Paul. "She's a little overwrought, but her pulse is strong and steady. I can prescribe a mild sedative if you want."

"I don't need any pills," Prudence insisted, sniffling. "I'll just go lie down for a bit and I'll be fine."

Paul hesitated to release her. Instead, he started to guide her from the room. She shook off his touch. "I can manage." Lifting her misty gaze, she blinked back tears. "I want you to stay right here and be my lawyer, like you promised. Make sure Sister doesn't pull another one of her dirty tricks and sell my house out from under me."

"You know she wouldn't do that, Aunt Pru."

"Ha!" Prudence glowered at her twin through reddened eyes. "Don't kid yourself, boy. There are lots of things she'd do, given half a chance. I should know. I've spent the last eighty-some years watching her do them."

Sam took Paul's place beside Prudence. "I'll handle this," he said. "You come, too, Belinda. Miss Whitaker and I are going to go have a little chat, and I want you there. I think you'll find it interesting."

"Of course." Belinda didn't care for Sam's overbearing attitude. However, she did want to help calm Prudence down, so she gently cupped the woman's elbow and followed his orders. He was *not* at his most likable when he was acting so superior or hinting that there was some cloak-and-dagger plot afoot. She'd much rather he'd have simply said whatever he intended to say and gotten it over with, instead of drawing her away from the others.

Others? Belinda countered silently. *You mean Paul Randall, don't you?* Of course she did. He was the reason she didn't want to leave the party, didn't want to go up to Prudence's room with Sam.

Sighing, she sobered. Sam might not realize it, but he'd been wise to take her away from the man she had once loved. The more time she spent with Paul the more she rued the mistakes of the past. The more she wished she could somehow make amends.

Was *that* why the Lord had brought him back to Serenity? she wondered abruptly. Was she supposed to show him how to forgive all the people, including herself, who had accused him and driven him out of town?

Disgusted, Belinda huffed. Fat chance. You can't very well teach it if you can't *do* it, and she was still furious with Paul. As much as she hated to admit it, she was also holding a grudge against her late father for having stood between them. Which meant she was far from the ideal example of Christian love.

Some peacemaker! God wasn't going to use her to lead *anybody* down the path to forgiveness and harmony until she'd mastered the concept herself.

Maybe by the time she was as old as the Whitaker sisters she'd have figured it all out. Then again, maybe it was going to take her even longer.

Lost in thought, Belinda escorted Prudence up the winding staircase to her second-floor bedroom. Sam followed.

"I'm glad you agreed to come up here with us, Miss Whitaker," Sam said, closing the door behind all three of them. "I've been wanting to speak with you in private."

Prudence snorted in obvious disgust. "Ha! Don't start tryin' to sweet-talk me, Sam Barryman. I'm wise to men's tricks. I may look older than dirt but I'm far from senile. This house is not for sale. Period."

Back ramrod straight, chin jutting out, she plopped down on the edge of the bed and crossed her arms defensively, looking for all the world like a naughty child who'd been sent to her room for misbehaving.

Sam ambled over to join her. Leaning against the carved post that held up the bed's canopy, he said, "I don't want your house, Miss Whitaker."

That was a surprise to Belinda. Curiosity got the better of her. "You don't? But I thought…"

"You thought what I wanted everybody to think," Sam said smugly. "Actually, it's only the vacant property I'm interested in. I couldn't care less about this old wreck of a house. It's more of a liability than an asset."

Belinda stared at Sam, then looked at Prudence. Compared to her present ashen complexion, she hadn't been a bit pale before. "You…you don't want my house?"

"No. I don't. I intend to build a clinic and a small hospital on this site. We all know Serenity desperately needs adequate medical facilities. Think of it. We might even name the place after your family."

Prudence grew pensive. "I suppose Father would

have liked that.'' A faraway look filled her eyes. Her voice grew thready. ''I always listened to Father. My sister didn't, but I did. When Father said Eldon wasn't good enough for me, I sent him away.''

Sam shot a questioning look at Belinda. Confused, she shrugged and said, ''This is the first I've heard about anything like that, Miss Prudence. Did it happen a long time ago?''

''Long time?'' The elderly woman sighed deeply. ''Yes. A very long time ago.'' Another heart-wrenching sigh. ''Eldon loved me. I know he did. If *she* hadn't interfered I'm sure I could have convinced Father to give us his blessing.''

Prudence snapped to the present. ''Sister can't be trusted. Never could. That's why I don't believe she only wants to sell this place so she can run off and travel. She's got something else up her sleeve. Well, whatever it is, she's not going to get away with it.'' Her frigid gaze lit on the doctor. ''And neither are you, mister.''

None of the guests could help overhearing the loudest of the conversation coming from the floor above. The party broke up when the mayor excused himself and Patience talked Milton Boggs into taking a stroll in the garden with her.

Paul politely walked everyone to the door, then returned to the foot of the staircase and quietly bowed his head to listen. All was quiet. Apparently, Prudence had calmed down. What a shame she was so upset with her sister. He wished he could think of some way to reconcile them.

Belinda started down the stairs. She paused at the landing when she spotted Paul at the bottom. If she hadn't been on a mercy mission she would have waited until he'd walked away so she wouldn't have to pass right by him. Unfortunately, any delay was likely to cause Sam to come looking for her, which would only complicate matters.

Steeling herself for the encounter with Paul, she stood tall and announced her presence as she continued to descend. "Miss Prudence is having trouble resting. I'm going out to the car for Sam's medical bag."

The sound of Belinda's voice gave Paul a jolt. His head snapped up. He watched her approach with his heart in his throat. She'd never looked lovelier. Every time he saw her he had the same kind of gut-level reaction, the same kind of thoughts. She was floating down the stairs like a vision from his dreams, coming to him quickly, surely, the way he'd so often fantasized she would.

Her steps slowed as she reached the ground floor. The hand she'd placed on the smooth banister slid to a stop, bumping against his. The contact sent a tingle up her arm that tickled the fine hairs at the back of her neck and made her shiver.

Paul jerked his hand away. "I'll get the bag for you. Just tell me what it looks like."

"I'm not sure." Jiggling the set of car keys in her

hand, she smiled. "Sam said it was in the trunk. With luck, there's only one bag to choose from."

When Paul reached to take the keys from her, she held them away. "Uh-uh. Sam's very particular about his car. I'm the only other person allowed to touch it."

"How special," Paul taunted. "Does he let you polish it, too?"

"As a matter of fact, we did give it a fresh coat of wax recently. It was one of those balmy evenings a week or so before this heat wave started."

"That figures." He couldn't help smirking. "Want to polish *my* car? You're obviously a pro."

"In your dreams, Randall," she countered, breezing past him and heading for the front door.

By the time Belinda returned with Sam's medical bag, Paul was nowhere to be seen. To her dismay, she was terribly disappointed he hadn't waited for her.

Nevertheless, she whispered, "Thank you, Father. You know better than I do what's best for me. I just wish..." She broke off. "Never mind, Lord. You rescued me from that man once. I'm not going to put myself in the position where You have to do it again."

Pausing at the foot of the stairs, her hand on the banister, she waited for the sense of peace she'd grown to expect when she relinquished control of her life to the Lord.

This time, it didn't come.

Chapter Six

By the following morning, Belinda had managed to rationalize away her uneasy feelings about being thrust into the latest situation involving Paul Randall. One of her biggest failings had always been trying to figure out what God had in mind for her long before He was ready to reveal it. This time, she was determined to avoid making that mistake.

She wasn't, however, ready to sit by and watch the Whitaker sisters lose out on a chance for a rosy future simply because one of them was suffering from emotional problems. Before she could implement her plan to telephone her grandmother and ask for background information, the older woman showed up at the Chamber office on her own. Belinda took it as a good sign.

"I'm glad you stopped by," she told Eloise, giving her a hug. "I was going to phone you."

"Phone me about what, dear?"

"The party at the Whitakers' last night."

Eloise brightened. "Oh, goodie. I'm dying to hear all the juicy details. How did it go? Was my cake a success?"

"The cake was wonderful, as usual. I hardly got a chance to taste it before Sam and I had to take Miss Prudence up to her room, though."

"Oh, dear! Was she sick?"

"Not exactly. Unless acting weird counts. One minute she seemed fine and the next she was nearly hysterical. She kept rambling on about how awful Patience was. Sam finally had to give her an injection so she could rest."

"Poor Pru. I knew she was getting worse, but I had no idea she'd regressed that far."

Folding her arms across her chest, Belinda said, "I think it's time you told me exactly what's going on."

"I don't know if I should."

"Well, I do. Sam says the poor woman's liable to have a nervous breakdown if we don't figure out what's really bothering her and help her deal with it. As her best friend, I figure you must know."

"Well... Okay." Eloise followed Belinda to her windowless office and sank into the nearest chair. "I suppose it's too late for the story to do any more damage than it already has."

Belinda pulled up another chair. "Is it something

really bad? The way Prudence was carrying on last night, you'd think Patience had committed murder.''

"I suppose it does seem like a terrible crime to Pru. She was never the same after Eldon Lafferty jilted her.''

"She did mention someone named Eldon.''

Eloise nodded. "He was the Whitakers' gardener. He and Prudence had a lot in common, a love for plants, an uncanny understanding of animals—they even went to the same little church. The problem was, Mr. Whitaker didn't consider a gardener to be a suitable match for his daughter and he told her so.'' She paused, smiling wistfully. "Things were different back in those days. Folks set a lot of store by the unwritten rules of society. And young women obeyed their fathers.''

"Surely, when Prudence got older…''

"By that time, it was too late,'' Eloise said. "Eldon was long gone.''

"But why is she so mad at Patience?''

"Because Patience stole Eldon away from her right before everything came to a head. I think that was what made old man Whitaker so mad. He couldn't stand seeing *both* of his daughters smitten.''

"How awful. For everybody.''

"No kidding. I don't suppose poor Eldon even knew what hit him when Patience started to flirt with him. You know how she is. She's never done anything halfway. And Pru's always been shy, so she didn't know how to fight back. When she lost the man she loved, first to her sister and then to fate, she became sort of a recluse. If it hadn't been for her teaching job, I don't think she'd have set foot out of that house again.''

Touched, Belinda shook her head. ''What finally happened to the gardener?''

''Nobody knows. Word was that the girls' father paid him off and sent him away. Pru never heard a word from him. To save face, she started telling everybody she was the one who'd told him to go.''

The sad story was painfully reminiscent of Belinda's loss of Paul. Thoughtful, she sighed. ''I suppose it's way too late to try to find Mr. Lafferty and bring him back.''

Eloise gasped. ''Don't you dare! That wouldn't accomplish a thing except to start the feud all over again. Pru is sure Eldon would have come to his senses and admitted he still loved her if he'd stayed in Serenity. When Patience got herself involved with him she ruined everything. There's no way to change that.''

''I guess you're right. I just wish I knew how we're going to help Miss Prudence let go of the past and begin to enjoy her life.''

Eloise snorted. ''How do you know she isn't enjoying it? Just because she chooses to be a loner doesn't mean she isn't happy. She loves her cats, she gardens some when her health permits and she goes to church on Sundays. That doesn't sound like such a bad life to me." She laughed. "Matter of fact, it sounds a lot like *mine*."

"And mine," Belinda agreed, feigning a sulk. "No offense, but I'd rather have a little more excitement than that."

"Oh? You mean like you had the other day? I heard about the food fight you had with Paul Randall."

"No! Of course not! I don't know what came over me." She felt her cheeks growing uncommonly warm.

"I do," her grandmother offered. "You stopped trying to be the perfect preacher's daughter for once. You let yourself go and had some good, clean fun. Right?"

Belinda's face burned with embarrassment. "I wouldn't exactly call it clean. It was more like messy temporary insanity." She started to grin shyly. "It was fun, though."

"Good. I'd rather see that than have you wind up a bitter old woman like Pru. She has hundreds of things to be thankful for every day, yet she doesn't recognize them because she's so busy concentrating on all the real or imagined wrongs she's suffered. Drives me crazy. I declare, if she wasn't so dear to me, I'd disown her."

Belinda's smile grew cautious. "You aren't going to disown me, are you, Gram?"

"Not in a million years." Eloise chuckled and patted her granddaughter on the arm. "You're a smart cookie. You know a blessing when you see one. I intend to stick around and watch you and your Sam walk down the aisle. You'll make a beautiful bride.''

Try as she might, Belinda couldn't visualize the doctor standing at the altar in his tuxedo, waiting for her. Oh, she could see herself as a bride and as someone's wife, someday. Just not as Sam's.

What about Paul? That wayward thought was enough to make her heart skip a beat. Then reason intervened. She and Paul had nothing in common. Not goals, not lifestyle, not even love. Especially not love. Romantic stirrings were exciting but they were no substitute for all the other elements missing from their relationship. Like trust, for instance. If she ever found out for sure that he actually had been responsible for the church fire, as she'd once so strongly suspected, there would be no way she could ever forgive him.

Unwilling to accept the logic of her conclusions, Belinda tried to imagine herself as Paul's bride, to make herself believe such an unlikely wedding could take place.

To her utter chagrin, she found she couldn't picture that scenario, either.

Belinda walked Eloise all the way out to the sidewalk and gave her a parting hug. ''I'm glad you stopped by.''

''Me, too. Sure you won't change your mind about coming to lunch with us? Verleen, Mercy and I would love to have you. We're going to that new pizza place to splurge.''

"Thanks, no. I'm way behind in my work. I'll just run across the street and grab a quick sandwich at the café.''

"Okay. But you'll be missing a real treat. Not only is the pizza very good, I made Verleen promise to keep her upper plate in while we were out in public.''

Belinda giggled. ''*That* should be a real plus.''

"I thought so.'' She squeezed her granddaughter's hand and turned to leave without watching where she was going. If Belinda hadn't pulled her back in time she would have crashed right into Paul Randall's chest.

Startled, Eloise gave a high-pitched gasp. "Aagh! Where did you come from?''

"Originally or recently?'' he quipped, hands outstretched to catch her if need be. "Are you all right?''

Leaning on Belinda for support and fanning herself with her open hand, she said, "Goodness, no. You scared the life out of me. I think I'm about to have the vapors!''

You're not the only one, Belinda thought. Disgusted with herself for reacting that way, she was looking forward to the day when the unexpected sight of Paul Randall didn't make her woozy.

Eloise continued to emote. "Oh, me. Oh, my.''

Amused by the older woman's theatrics, Belinda picked up on the mood and spoke more candidly than she would have otherwise. "He's had that effect on me before, too, Gram. But don't tell him. He's liable to get a swelled head."

Paul laughed. "Hey, I don't mind…as long as my new hat still fits."

"What hat? I've never seen you wear a hat."

"Actually, I seldom do," he drawled, "but a friend talked me into buying a good Stetson a couple of weeks ago and I'd hate to see that much money go to waste."

"You? Pretending to be a cowboy?" Belinda's eyebrow arched. "That I'd like to see."

"I suppose it could be arranged."

She waved her hands in front of her as if to erase the idea. "Forget it. I was only kidding."

"You could be missing out on a good thing," Paul countered. "I already had the boots."

"Isn't that a little out of character for you? What happened to your old leather-jacketed motorcycle image?"

"Ah, well… My friend assured me women like the clean-cut, Western look much better," he told her with a slight reddening of his tanned complexion. "Says it works like a charm for him."

"So, you decided to become a counterfeit cowboy, too?" Jealousy tweaked Belinda's conscience. "Pretending to be something you're not just to impress people seems terribly unfair to me." She took a breath, intending to go on with the impromptu lecture, when Eloise elbowed her in the ribs.

"Be nice, dear. You and I would rather be wearing sandals and shorts in this miserable, humid weather. Yet here we are, all decked out in heels and these wretched panty hose. Does that make us fakes?"

"Of course not." Belinda pulled a face of disgust, stressing it even more when she noticed that Paul looked highly entertained. "But I *have* to dress this way for work. Grown men don't have to play cowboy."

Laughing softly, affably, Paul said, "You've lived here so long you don't notice what's right under your nose. Do you think every man who's wearing camouflage-colored clothing and an orange cap is on his way to the woods to go hunting?" He swept his arm in a wide arc that took in the whole town square, including the courthouse in the center. "Look. You won't see more camo than this on the first day of deer season. There's no difference between that and the Western look."

He had a valid point. Sort of. People did seem to recreate themselves at will these days. Belinda was thinking about conceding when Eloise piped up. "Right. Well, I'd best be going. Verleen gets testy if she takes her antacid and then doesn't get to eat on time. Bye-bye."

Paul watched her breeze off. "I like your grandmother. She's quite a character. Is she your father's mother?"

"No. My mother's."

"I don't remember you being so close to her before."

"I wasn't." Belinda sighed, thinking. "Gram came to stay with my dad and me for a little while after Mom died. That was a mistake. She and Daddy fed off each other's grief so much that neither of them was healing. When she realized what was happening, she left us alone."

"That must have been hard on you, too."

Amazed, Belinda stared at him. "How did you know?"

He stuck his hands into the pockets of his slacks and shrugged. "Been there, done that, as they say."

"You used to tell me your mother had been gone so long you didn't even recall what she looked like."

"Well, maybe I exaggerated a little."

"You did? Why?"

"You'd lost your mother a lot more recently than I'd lost mine." His eyes were bleak for only an instant. "I didn't want to have to lie about how long it took me to get over it. I figured, if you knew the truth, you'd ask me about it and I didn't think I could explain without making things worse. Especially for you."

"That's kind of sweet…in a dumb way."

"I'm a prince among men." Paul half smiled. "So, how about lunch? You free?"

The lie almost stuck in her throat when she said, "No."

"Okay. It was just a thought."

"Sorry." Belinda wished he'd give up and go away before her galloping guilty conscience got the better of her.

"Actually, I was hoping we could set aside our differences long enough to talk about my aunts' problems over lunch. I need a woman's perspective on their crazy behavior. But if you're too busy…"

There was something about his sincere concern for others that softened her heart. She shook her head pensively. "I must be crazy to even *consider* going out to eat with you."

"At last we agree on something," Paul quipped. "So, does this mean you've changed your mind? You'll come?"

"Well… Okay. But we have to keep it short. I'm only doing this because Gram told me a very interesting story about your family this morning and I'd like to hear your version. Wait right there. I'll go get my keys so I can lock up."

Paul watched her walk away and disappear into her private office. He blew air out of his lungs with a noisy whoosh. It was getting harder and harder to maintain a casual bearing when Belinda was nearby. He'd thought his courtroom experience had made him a pretty good actor until he'd come back to Serenity and tried to act unaffected in her presence. Choosing the right words to face a stubborn jury was nothing compared to the stress of trading lighthearted quips with her!

Disgusted with himself, he reviewed their most recent conversation. Why in the world had he told her about giving in when his friend had dared him to buy the Stetson? And if that weren't bad enough, he'd announced that the hat was supposed to help him attract women! What nonsense. He hadn't even taken it out of the box since he'd been fool enough to buy it. He exhaled another sigh. Judging by the last few minutes, his normally logical thought processes must be seriously out of whack.

Good thing he wasn't going to have to spend a lot more time around Belinda. He was already a basket case. If his illogical desire to please and impress her got much worse, there was no telling what he might say or do.

Paul shook his head, snickering at himself. He was getting too emotionally involved for his own good. His main reason for being in Serenity was to aid his aunts. Second, he wanted to prove he was innocent of any wrongdoing in the fire that had burned down the old church. Those were reasonable goals. Maybe even attainable ones.

Stepping back in time and taking up where he and Belinda had left off, however, was neither. They'd never had a chance in the first place. As a rational adult he knew that their youthful dreams of happiness had been nothing more than the innocent longings of two lonely kids who'd believed they were madly in love.

Love? Paul felt his gut knot as he remembered holding her tight and promising he'd always care.

Maybe they had once loved each other, as well as either of them knew how. And maybe he was still harboring some of those same tender feelings. But that didn't mean he and Belinda were compatible enough to build a successful future together.

Wishing wasn't enough. It never had been.

Chapter Seven

They settled on a short walk across the town square to a locally run café that advertised their daily lunch special would be served in less than fifteen minutes, or the order was free. In twenty years, the management had never failed to deliver.

Belinda's problem was forcing herself to eat once she got her food. Paul had removed his tie and rolled up his shirt sleeves, making him appear more at home in the casual surroundings. Seated across the narrow table, he was stirring a glass of iced tea and watching her intently.

She'd ordered the special, a hot roast beef sandwich, hoping that the gravy would help her swallow past the lump in her throat. If she was ever going to develop a fatal case of indigestion, this was probably the meal that would do it.

"I hate to see you have to rush so," Paul said

amiably. Resting his elbows on the table, he concentrated on her. "So, you eat and I'll talk first. What was it you wanted to know about my family?"

"Ummpf." Mentally comparing Paul to the waitresses who always waited until your mouth was full before asking if the meal was satisfactory, Belinda finally managed to choke down the bite in her mouth. "Gram said both your aunts were once in love with the same man. What do you know about that?"

Paul rocked back, his brow furrowed. "Nothing. Are you sure that's what happened?"

"Pretty sure. Supposedly, Prudence fell in love with the family gardener. When Patience started flirting and won him away from her, their father blew his stack and sent the guy packing."

"Sounds about right for this town," Paul said cynically.

"It wasn't the town's fault. That was the way things were done in those days. Girls—good girls—didn't go against their fathers' wishes." Her words hung in the air between them like a heavy curtain.

Finally, Paul said, "Seems to me that practice hasn't changed much. At least not in your case. You always did what your father wanted, too."

Belinda laid aside her fork and blotted her lips with her napkin to give herself time to carefully choose a reply. Then she looked straight at Paul. "I tried to. After Mom died, I was all Daddy had left. You didn't know him like I did. If I'd gone away with you, the way you wanted, I don't know what would have become of him. Especially after…'' Her voice trailed away.

''After the fire, you mean. Go ahead. Say it. Someday, I'm going to convince you I wasn't involved. I just haven't figured out how to come up with the proof.''

''It's way too late for that, and you know it,'' Belinda declared, which was why she couldn't quite believe he was being sincere, even though she wanted to.

Nodding, Paul soberly agreed. ''Let's drop the subject. That was a bad time for everybody.''

''Some good did come out of it,'' she said, seeking to focus their discussion on more positive aspects. ''Have you ever considered what our lives might have been like if I *had* run off with you?''

''Meaning?''

''We were kids, Paul. I hadn't graduated from high school and you had no marketable skills. I doubt you'd be where you are now if you'd had me tagging along while you struggled to get an education. And I'd have been miserable, feeling guilty and worrying about abandoning my dad. You'd probably have wound up so frustrated you'd have chucked all your big plans just to try to make me happy. It was a no-win situation. For both of us.''

His attitude softened. ''When did you get so smart?''

''When I finally grew up and realized that our parting was all for the best. We're old enough now to look back and see that the Lord is always faithful, just like He promised, even though it's hard to understand what's going on at the time.'' She heaved a deep, sorrowful sigh. ''I wish I could take all the kids I know, shake some sense into them and prove that *no* situation is ever hopeless.''

''Sounds to me like you've tried,'' Paul said.

''I have.'' Leaning back in her chair and remembering, Belinda slowly shook her head. ''One of the young people in our youth group at church recently tried to end her life because of a fleeting disappointment she would probably have laughed at a few years from now.''

''Is she all right?''

''Yes, thank God—literally. But it could just as easily have ended the other way. The whole concept of kids considering suicide makes me frantic.''

''And frustrated. I know what you mean.''

She pushed her plate aside. ''I suppose you do. You've had your share of serious setbacks to overcome, too. I really am glad to see how far you've come.''

When he answered there was an underlying hostility to his tone in spite of his efforts to subdue it. ''Ah, yes. My triumph over my unrefined upbringing. The kid with the jailbird father actually made it through college and law school. Imagine that. What a surprise.''

Belinda's cheeks flushed. ''I didn't mean it like that.''

"Oh? Then how did you mean it?"

"I was trying to give you a compliment." When he seemed unmoved, she added, "You have to believe me, or…"

"Or what?" One dark eyebrow arched. "You'll start throwing food at me again? In public? You'd better not or you'll ruin your first-class reputation. I may not have to live in this town, but you do."

She could see the righteous anger draining out of Paul's expression. His dark eyes were beginning to sparkle. *Oh, thank You, God, he believes me,* Belinda prayed, rejoicing inside. Now, if she could just keep from putting her other foot in her mouth, maybe their relationship wouldn't get any more strained than it already was.

"I could always fall back on the excuse I used when Gram asked me about the food fight," Belinda said.

"Which was? Let me guess. You blamed the whole ruckus on me?"

"No! And wipe that smirk off your face. I didn't blame any of it on you. I claimed temporary insanity."

"Not a very original defense."

"Well, it's the truth." Vivid memories of the silly altercation made her grin so broadly her cheeks hurt. "But now that I think about it, you were so self-righteous and smug after you scared me into dropping that jar of sauce, it's no wonder I splashed you. You were practically asking for it."

"Oh, really?"

"Yes, really." Belinda leaned forward to stare at him and reinforce her point. He didn't even blink. She, on the other hand, felt an immediate jolt of awareness as their gazes met. Her skin tingled. Her stomach churned. Her mouth went dry while her palms began to perspire. She laced her fingers together on the table to still their barely perceptible trembling and watched in awe as Paul placed his large, warm hands over them.

"I suppose it's best if we agree that I drove you to act up," he told her in a hushed voice. "Otherwise, word could get around that we were actually having fun, and Sam might start to think he was getting a fruitcake instead of a normal bride."

Belinda tried to pull her hands free, but Paul held them fast, so she quit struggling rather than attract unnecessary attention. "What made you bring *that* up?"

"I just thought I should remind you of who you are. And who I am." *Not to mention get my own dangerous thoughts back on track,* he added to himself. "And while we're at it, how about telling me what secret project Sam has up his sleeve."

"You're as bad as he is!"

"There's no need to insult me," Paul said, only half kidding.

Feeling the relaxing of his grip, Belinda slowly withdrew her hands and placed them in her lap so she could clasp them together out of sight. "I will ask Sam to fill you in, though. His idea is really wonderful. I don't see any reason he wouldn't want to share it.''

''I can,'' Paul said flatly. He leaned back in his chair and nodded thoughtfully. ''Okay. Ask him. A few more days one way or the other won't matter. I have to go to Harrison to catch up at the office. Tell him I expect to be back at Aunt Prudence's by next Saturday at the latest.''

He pulled out his wallet and handed Belinda a business card, then picked up the bill for their lunch and stood beside the table. ''My secretary can take a message if I'm not in the office.''

Belinda held Paul's card by its edges and stared at it for long seconds. *Look, Daddy,* she thought sadly, *you were wrong. Paul did amount to something after all. I knew it. I told you he would.*

When she looked up again, Paul had finished paying their bill and was on his way to the door. Dozens of other customers in the café were watching him leave, too. As soon as he was out of sight, everyone's attention turned to the table where Belinda sat. A few folks smiled. The rest peered at her sideways or peeked from under lowered lashes while they tried to appear uninterested.

The scenario struck her so funny she felt like climbing up onto the seat of her chair, waving her arms and announcing in a loud voice that she was *not* on a date, was *not* seeing Paul behind Sam's back and was *not* a bit interested in the handsome attorney.

Talk about more fodder for the gossip mill! A forthright denial like that would only serve to focus on her actions and increase unwarranted suspicion. Everybody was probably going to think she and Paul were an item, anyway, especially since he'd held her hands in public. If she went out of her way to deny there was anything romantic in their relationship, they'd be *positive* she was lying.

Belinda was taking a last sip of her iced tea when her breath caught in her throat and the tea slid down the wrong way. She sputtered. Gagged. Coughed into her napkin so loudly she sounded like a beached seal. And no wonder! She'd choked on a lot more than a swallow of tea. She'd choked on the truth.

In the middle of the sip, it had suddenly occurred to her that it *would* be a lie if she insisted she wasn't having any romantic thoughts in regard to Paul Randall. And not just a little lie—a real doozie!

Blushing, she jumped to her feet, hurried out the door and headed back to work.

The Chamber of Commerce office fronted on the town square and faced the brick-and-stone Fulton County courthouse. According to the engraved cornerstone, that building dated back to the eighteen hundreds. Sometimes, Belinda wished she were part of that simpler era, when time moved more slowly and life was less complicated. She was leaning on the counter, gazing out the window, when Sheila popped in with a bright, "Hi!"

"Oh, hello." Belinda straightened, stretched.

"I brought you a soda," Sheila said, handing over one of the white plastic cups she carried. "With ice. I know you don't like to drink them out of a can."

"Thanks. I can use the caffeine lift."

Sheila giggled. "No kidding. You looked like you were asleep on your feet when I got here."

"I was just daydreaming."

"About what? Hey! Were you planning how to set me up with that lawyer friend of yours, like I wanted?"

Belinda pulled a face. "Actually, no. I was imagining how peaceful things used to be, back when Serenity was first being settled."

"Peaceful? Oh, brother. You do have on rose-colored glasses, don't you? Life was *hard* back then."

Belinda mused, while she sipped her cold soda. "I suppose you're right. People did have to work more to accomplish things, unless they were wealthy and could afford lots of servants, of course."

"You mean like the Whitakers? I understand they used to be the richest folks in town. Which reminds me. You never told me how the dinner at their place went. I'll bet it was really elegant. With the right designer and enough money, that old mansion could be turned into a real showplace."

"It was a showplace, once," Belinda said. "But I'm afraid it'll never be one again."

"Why not? Whoever buys it can fix it up."

Sighing, she shook her head. "I suspect the old house is going to be demolished, instead."

"Oh, what a shame!"

"No kidding." Sipping, thinking, Belinda finished her soda and disposed of the cup. "I shouldn't say any more. Not yet. I haven't gotten Sam's permission to talk about his plans yet."

"His *permission?*" Sheila nearly choked on the notion. "Oh, pul-eeze."

"That's just common courtesy. It doesn't mean I'm not thinking for myself. Sam took me into his confidence because he trusted me, and I intend to live up to that trust."

Sheila chuckled wryly. "You know, sometimes you act like you *do* belong in another century."

"I think I'll take that as a compliment," Belinda said with an amiable smile. "Besides, the rules haven't changed in thousands of years. The Ten Commandments are still as valid as they always were."

"I suppose you're right. I don't have trouble keeping most of them, but I sure do wish the one about not coveting had been left out." She peered at Belinda. "Which brings me back to my original question…how's it going between you and Paul Randall?"

"Fine."

"Mmm, that's what I heard. Seems you and he had a hot and heavy lunch in the restaurant across the square. They say he grabbed your hands and practically held you prisoner. Is that true?''

"Of course not!''

"He never touched you?''

"I didn't say that.'' Belinda felt a blush warming her cheeks. ''But he didn't force me to go or make me stay there. I could have left anytime I wanted.''

"Uh-oh. That's what I was afraid of. You didn't want him to let go of you.''

"I didn't say that, either!''

"You didn't have to. I can see it in your face. Guess I'd better find a new prospective husband for myself. It looks like you aren't going to want to share Paul.''

"There's nothing to share,'' Belinda insisted. ''We're just old friends—I mean acquaintances—who happened to eat lunch together so we could discuss his aunts.'' Contemplating Sheila's last observation, Belinda wrinkled her brow and pressed her lips into a thin line. ''What do you mean you can see something in my face? There's nothing there to see.''

"Wanna bet? Every time I mention Paul's name your eyes glass over and you look like your mind is taking a vacation.''

"I do not. I can't. I mean… Oh, dear. Tell me you're kidding.''

Sheila shrugged. ''Sorry. No can do. I know you too well to miss the signs. If you didn't want to hear the truth, you shouldn't have reminded me of the Ten Commandments.''

"Okay," Belinda said, squaring her shoulders and dealing with the problem in a no-nonsense fashion. "I'll accept the fact that you can see a change in me. We're both women and we're close friends, so that figures. Now, tell me, do you think it's as obvious to other people?''

"Like who? Paul?"

"No! I don't have to worry about Paul. He's never understood me. I'm talking about Sam."

"Not a chance. Sam Barryman is too busy thinking about all the ways he can make more money to notice if you get a little spacey once in awhile." She giggled. "I do think it's dumb to be seen in too many places with Paul if you're still interested in Sam, though. Some busybody is liable to carry tales.''

"I'm not trying to hide anything," Belinda insisted. "There's nothing to hide.''

"Then why are you worried about what Sam might think?''

That question floored Belinda. If she never intended to marry Sam, why be concerned? Simply wanting to avoid hurting his feelings was an insufficient answer. Was she still being influenced by her grandmother's advice regarding a possible future with the doctor? Perhaps. Yet there was more to her current uneasiness than that. She and Sam had been dating for nearly a year. Their relationship *was* in a comfortable and untroubled rut. Was it wrong to want to remain within the safety of that rut, even if she never intended to commit to him for keeps?

Sheila waved a hand in front of Belinda's eyes. "Yoo-hoo. Wake up. I asked you a question."

"About Sam," Belinda murmured. "I know. That's what I was thinking about."

"And?"

"And Sam knows how I feel. He respects my decision. As long as he doesn't start insisting that I agree to marry him, the way he used to, nothing between us needs to change."

"You mean, he's proposed and you've turned him down?"

"Don't look so shocked. Marriage is serious business. I'm not ready to make that kind of lifelong commitment."

"You were ready ten years ago, when Paul Randall was in line to be the groom."

"No," Belinda said cynically, "I only thought I was ready. Talk about naive. I figured, since I'd asked God to make my wedding happen and I was doing my best to follow all the rules in the Bible, I couldn't fail. What a shock it was when I learned *I* wasn't the one running the universe."

"Do you think you'll ever settle down with Sam?" Sheila asked softly.

Sighing and shaking her head, Belinda said, "I sure wish I knew."

"Yeah," Sheila said with a brief nervous chuckle. "I'll bet poor old Sam does, too."

* * *

Belinda waited until she figured Sam would be through seeing patients for the day, then phoned his office. His receptionist put her call through without delay.

"Hi. It's me," Belinda began. "How are you?"

"Beat. This has been one of those days. I had three emergencies before nine."

"Is everybody okay now?"

"Yes," he said with a weary sigh, "but it shows how badly we need our own hospital. I don't want anybody to suffer because I don't have access to the equipment I need to help them."

"Neither do I." Belinda had never heard Sam express such purely altruistic sentiments. Moved by his clear concern for others she asked, "Would you like to come for dinner tonight?"

"Maybe tomorrow. I didn't sleep much last night and I have a surgery scheduled for seven in the morning so I'm going to bed early." He yawned, then added, "Want to go to bed with me and keep me company?"

The man seemed to have a special knack for ridding her of any tender feelings toward him almost as soon as she acknowledged them, didn't he? "Please, Sam. Don't start."

"I know, I know, you're not that kind of girl. If I had a nickel for every time…"

Rather than let him continue in that vein, Belinda purposely interrupted. "Getting back to your plans for building a hospital. I saw Paul today. He—"

"I know you did. I even know where you had lunch."

"Good. Do you also know what we talked about?"

"Not everything."

She could sense Sam was smiling on the other end of the line. That was a good sign. "Basically, Paul wanted me to tell him what your plans were for the Whitaker property," Belinda explained.

"Did you?"

"Of course not. I wouldn't break your trust."

"At this point, I can't see that it matters much. All he'd have to do is ask Prudence, providing she remembers what we talked about. She was pretty out of it the other night."

"Only because she's so scared of change," Belinda said wisely. "The Whitaker house has become her refuge. According to Gram, the only time Miss Prudence was away from home for more than a few hours, after she turned twenty-one, was when her father was in the hospital in Little Rock. She wanted to stay close so she spent the night in the city."

"All the more reason she should support my project," Sam said. "I'll remember to mention that the next time I talk to her. In the meantime, tell Randall as much as you want. Say whatever it takes to convince him he belongs on our side. He'll be a valuable ally if the old lady refuses to listen to reason."

"I suppose you're right."

"As always," Sam quipped.

Belinda didn't feel much like trading witty remarks. Instead, she bid the doctor a simple goodnight. As she hung up the phone she closed her eyes and sighed. Sheila was right. The most important elements in Sam's world were prestige and profit. People finished a distant third.

Was Paul any different? she asked herself. His concern seemed to be for his aunts, yet his focus was on how much money they could get for their property and how best to invest it.

Which made him sensible, not nefarious. It was as big a sin to waste what the Lord had given them as it was to try to unfairly squeeze more money out of the deal. Nobody purposely went out and announced to the world, "Here I am. Cheat me."

Picturing the naïveté of the Whitaker sisters made Belinda uneasy. In the area of high finance they seemed little more than lambs being led to the slaughter. Given free rein, Sam would try to convince them to accept his offer because of all the good they'd be doing for the town, just as he'd already told Prudence.

On the other hand, what was Paul's motive for offering his professional advice? He'd never been particularly close to either of his great-aunts until recently. Before he and his father had arrived in town ten years ago, the sisters hadn't even mentioned having a grandnephew. Her eyes widened in alarm. Maybe he wasn't related at all!

I'm getting paranoid, Belinda thought in disgust.

Why would Paul's father lie about being Whitaker kin?

Her imagination was quick to answer, *Why not? He lied about his arson conviction until Daddy found out the truth and made a big scene.*

Remembering, she sighed and shook her head. Paul had always refused to tell her much about his early upbringing but he'd never lied about what he did disclose. She knew his mother had died while his father was in prison and he'd spent over a year in various foster homes. When his father was paroled, he'd reclaimed Paul and they'd come straight to Serenity.

The first minute Belinda had seen young Paul, she'd cared about him. He'd looked so determined, so angry, so stand-offish, so tough…and so lost. The truth had been hidden in his veiled glance but Belinda had recognized it immediately. She'd seen that same look in her own eyes plenty of times since her mother had gone home to be with the Lord.

She and Paul Randall were soul mates. It was as simple, and as complicated, as that. Belinda blinked back tears. Befriending him had been the right thing, the Christian thing, to do. Her only mistake had been in assuming that the emotional bond they'd shared was the same as the love between a husband and wife. It wasn't, of course. She knew that now.

But if her teenage tears and heartfelt prayers had been enough, the closeness she and Paul had experienced might someday have blossomed into the kind of perfect love between a man and a woman that lasted forever. The kind of love she'd seen and felt in her own home when she was growing up.

That kind of love was a special, precious gift from God.

One she'd been searching for all her adult life.

One she had yet to find.

Chapter Eight

For Belinda, the days seemed to crawl by until the weekend. On Saturday morning, she was so keyed up she decided to put on her shorts and work off her nervous energy in her garden. Snuffy was with her, running in circles and darting into the bushes to track invisible rabbits while Belinda dug out stubborn weeds from among the snapdragons by her front porch.

Paul will be back soon, she told herself over and over, immediately countering with, *it doesn't matter to me.*

Which, of course, was a fib. "I sure hope, since I'm only lying to myself, it doesn't count," she muttered, incorrectly assuming she was alone.

Eloise was close enough to overhear. "Why should you do that?"

"Oh!" Belinda jumped. "You startled me, Gram. Where did you come from?"

"I walked over. I hadn't seen you in a few days so I baked you some cookies." She held up a clear plastic baggie. "See? Your favorite."

"When it comes to your cookies, they're *all* my favorites." Smiling, Belinda got to her feet and dusted off her hands. "Cookies for breakfast sounds perfect. I haven't had anything to eat since last night. Come on in. I'll make us some coffee."

Following her to the door, Eloise asked, "Did you and Sam have a nice time at the movies last night?"

Belinda stopped in her tracks, nearly causing a collision. "How did you...? Never mind. I know. So, which branch of the Serenity grapevine tattled?"

Eloise giggled. "I heard the news from Patience. It seems she and Paul's friend Milton were sitting in the very last row of the theater. That's probably why you and Sam didn't notice them."

"Patience *Whitaker?*"

"Don't look so shocked," the older woman remarked, unconsciously primping with her free hand. "Gray hair does not mean a person's life is over."

"But...Patience?" Belinda couldn't get over the idea.

"She's a lot more likely candidate than Prudence."

"Well, *that's* true, I suppose."

"So," Eloise said with a grin and a nod toward the door, "are we going to have coffee, or not? If not, I'm going on over to Verleen's. She's always got a fresh pot brewing. Even in the summertime.''

Paul got directions from his aunts and drove past Belinda's house twice before he decided to stop. It was that or take the chance of being reported to the police by her snoopy neighbors. The ones across the street had already gathered on their porches and were staring at him as if he were a dangerous criminal.

He pulled slowly into the drive and parked. Before he could get his car door open all the way, a black, brown and white dog raced up, scrambled across his lap and landed beside him on the car seat.

Temporarily startled, Paul put out his hand so the friendly little beagle could take a sniff before he began petting it on the head. It responded by wagging its tail so hard it nearly fell off the seat. Paul steadied it. ''Whoa! Where did you come from? Huh?''

The dog spun in tight circles beside him, clearly excited and eager to have discovered a new friend.

Paul laughed. ''We're not going for a ride, if that's what you want. But I guess we'd better ask the lady who lives here where you belong so you don't run out into the street and get hurt.''

Reacting to his kindly tone of voice, the dog leaped up to try to lick his face.

Paul caught it to keep it from dancing in his lap. It scrambled and wiggled against his chest, still trying to wash his face, as he got out of the car and started toward Belinda's front door. *What a lucky break.* If he'd engineered the diversion himself, he couldn't have chosen a more useful or cooperative accomplice.

Luck has nothing to do with it, he corrected, realizing he'd fallen back into his old way of thinking. He'd been praying for an easy way to approach Belinda Carnes, and the Lord had provided it. He just hadn't expected his answer to arrive in the form of a friendly little dog.

He climbed the stairs, knocked on the metal frame of the screen door and called, "Excuse me. Anybody home?"

"Just a minute."

At the sound of Belinda's voice, the little dog's feet paddled the air so hard Paul almost dropped it. He clamped his hands around its rib cage and held it out so it wouldn't scratch a hole in his shirt. Or in him.

Belinda began to grin and shake her head when she got close enough to see Paul's dilemma. "You'd better put her down or give her to me before she runs herself to death getting nowhere," she said, laughing as she pushed the screen door open. "How did you manage to catch Snuffy in the first place? She's usually pretty shy around strangers."

"Oh?" He handed the dog over, watching the mutual joy of the reunion. "Then I suppose you won't believe she jumped into my car with me as soon as I opened the door, huh?"

"Not hardly." Lowering the energetic dog to the

ground, Belinda spoke to it as if it were a child. "Gramma's here, Snuffy. Go find Gramma and tell her you want a cookie."

Paul shoved his hands in his pockets and struck a purposely casual pose as the dog dashed off. "How about me? I like cookies, too."

"Yes, but you don't live here."

"True. I did return your dog, though. Of course, I didn't know she was yours at the time, but I should still get credit for doing a good deed."

"I suppose you're right," Belinda conceded. She gave the screen door a push. "Come on in. My grandmother's visiting so the neighbors probably won't be too scandalized."

"Want me to stand out here and announce it before I come in?" Paul teased. "That lady across the street looks real worried."

"No more than usual," she said, waving to the woman past Paul's shoulder and calling, "Hi, Liz," as she ushered him in.

Snuffy returned in a whirl, sniffed Paul's shoes, then headed for the kitchen. "Just follow the dog," Belinda told him. "She's on the right track."

"What energy! If those cookies will do that for her, I'd like to order a couple of dozen for myself."

Belinda laughed gaily. "I think it's more a matter of heredity than what she eats. She's been like that ever since she was a puppy. Once she outgrew the tendency to trip over her own ears when she put her nose to the ground, she's been on the run. If I ever saw her walk anywhere, I'd figure she was sick.''

"I think she's cute," he said. "Real lovable."

Like her mistress.

"Thanks. She seems taken with you, too. Are you sure you don't have liver treats in your pockets? Snuffy's a sucker for those.''

"Not the last time I looked." Paul chuckled. "But I'll try to pick some up before I visit the next time, just in case she doesn't remember she likes me.''

"Good idea." She swallowed hard as what he'd said registered fully. "Visit the *next* time?''

"Just making conversation," Paul replied. He sauntered into the small kitchen and greeted Eloise warmly. "Good morning. Nice to see you again. I was going to say it's nice to run into you—again, but I didn't want you to think I was making fun of our near collision at Belinda's office last week.''

"That was funny, wasn't it?" Eloise held out a plate. "Would you like a cookie? I made them myself.''

"I'd love one. Snuffy tells me they're excellent.''

Belinda broke in as she handed Paul a cup of steaming coffee. "You're not going to believe this, Gram. Snuffy actually made up to Paul.''

"Well, of course she did," Eloise said, reaching down to ruffle the little dog's silky ears. "She's a sweet little thing. Aren't you, baby?''

"But she doesn't like—" Belinda broke off in

mid-sentence, leaving an unmistakable hole in their conversation.

"Who doesn't she like?" Paul asked quietly. "Sam?"

When Belinda didn't reply, her grandmother answered for her with great enthusiasm. "Of *course* she likes Sam. Everybody likes Sam."

"Maybe not everybody," Paul muttered into his cup.

Belinda felt trapped between defending Sam out of loyalty and insisting on the absolute truth. Not that her grandmother would listen to anything negative about the man she'd already decided would make a perfect grandson-in-law. At this point in the conversation, Belinda figured she'd be lucky if she could merely get away with changing the subject.

"Oh, Paul!" she blurted, louder than she'd intended. "I forgot to ask. Do you take sugar or cream in your coffee?"

"No. Black is fine."

"Okay. Um, if you change your mind..." Her heart sank when Eloise interrupted to continue with her praise of Sam.

"I've told Belinda over and over she should count her blessings that a wonderful man like Dr. Barryman is so serious about her."

Paul's eyebrows raised. "Is he." It wasn't a question.

"Oh, yes," the older woman went on. "I'm sure

it's just a matter of time before they announce their engagement.''

''Are you planning on baking the wedding cake?'' he asked. ''You really should. You're a wonder in the kitchen. That cake you made for Aunt Pru was delicious.'' He saluted her with the remains of a cookie. ''So are these.''

Eloise blushed at the compliment, then raised the cookie plate. ''Thank you. Have another?''

''I don't want to eat Snuffy's share.''

Giggling, Eloise said, ''Don't worry. I can always bake more. I was thinking of making oatmeal-raisin this afternoon. If you like that kind, I'd be glad to do up some extras for you.''

Belinda stood back and watched their conversation with amazement. In the space of a few minutes, Paul had managed not only to stop Gram's gushing over Sam, he'd also persuaded her to bake him cookies! No wonder he was so successful in court. The man was a marvel at subtle manipulation. In Belinda's view, that didn't make him sociable, the way Gram was seeing him, however. It made him risky to trust.

''So, Paul, you never said why you stopped by,'' Belinda interjected. ''Is everything okay?''

He paused long enough to take another sip from his cup and smile casually. ''As okay as it gets when both my aunts are under the same roof. I did ask Aunt Patience about the problem you and I discussed. She denies everything.''

When his glance darted toward Eloise, Belinda

quickly relieved him of his nearly empty cup and took him by the arm. "Let's go out into the garden and talk about it, shall we? Gram needs to get home to make those cookies she promised us, and I wouldn't want my neighbors to think you and I were up to anything in here by ourselves."

"I do?" Eloise sounded confused.

Belinda smiled sweetly and nodded. "Yes, dear, you do. Paul may not be in town much longer, and you wouldn't want to disappoint him, would you?"

"Of course not. I'll get right to it." She breezed happily off on her mission, calling, "See you later."

As soon as Eloise shut the door behind her, Belinda dropped Paul's arm. Her shoulders drooped. "Sorry about all that Sam business. She has a one-track mind."

"And your happiness seems to be the track it's on. That speaks well of her devotion to you."

"I suppose so."

Paul had felt a jolt of pure pleasure when Belinda had taken his arm. Now that she'd let go, the loss of contact was bothering him a lot more than he liked to admit, even to himself. The confines of the small kitchen seemed to be closing in on him, urging him to step close to her again. To reach out and renew their physical connection. To take her in his arms and kiss her, in spite of everything her grandmother had just said about her feelings for another man.

Walk away, his conscience insisted. *Forget about*

Belinda and walk away. Now. Before you do something you'll be sorry for.

Would he be sorry? He doubted it. He might feel guilty but he couldn't picture himself wishing he hadn't kissed her. The notion whirled around in his mind, sounding more and more plausible as he contemplated it.

He stepped closer, almost without realizing he'd moved. Belinda was looking at him, her lips slightly parted, her eyes wide and misty. *She knows what I'm thinking. What I want.* The wishes of their hearts were in tune again, the way they used to be so long ago!

If she backed away or showed any sign of resistance he'd stop, Paul told himself. He gently laid his hands on her shoulders, felt her tremble beneath his touch. Everything was perfect, the faint, floral fragrance of her hair, the openness of her expression, the smoky blue yearning in her eyes. Paul felt as if he were nineteen again and so much in love with this woman he'd die if he couldn't hold her in his arms one more time.

The idea that he should ask her permission to kiss her flitted in and out of his mind and was quickly dismissed as idiotic. Suppose she turned him down simply because she thought she should? He didn't want to put any more obstacles between them. They already had enough of those for a dozen relationships!

Belinda saw the glow of desire light Paul's gaze,

sensed the runaway rush of his shallow breathing as it sped to match hers. In awe, she lifted her hands and placed them on his warm, broad chest. His heart thundered beneath her palms. Barely able to stand, she closed her eyes, lifted her chin and waited for the inevitable.

All along, Paul had assured himself he could call a halt to his irrational action any time he wished. Then Belinda had touched him, and his willpower had vanished like a wisp of smoke in a gale. His arms closed around her.

Forcing himself to move slowly, to be gentle, he pulled her to him and bent his head to prepare for the kiss, aware that she knew exactly what he was going to do and was meeting him boldly, on equal terms.

So close he could feel her warm breath on his face and see her lashes flutter, he paused for an instant to savor the experience. First he'd taste the sweetness he remembered, then deepen the kiss if Belinda seemed at all responsive. He'd make it both a last kiss and a first kiss, hello and goodbye, chaste yet innocently romantic.

It was a fine plan—in theory. The instant Paul's lips joined with hers, however, all rational thought disappeared in a mighty surge of emotion. The sweetly pliant mouth he remembered so well was responsive, all right! It was kindling a need within him that was so bright, so fiery, he had to fight to maintain any semblance of self-control. This was not the timid, repressed girl who had ridden behind him on his motorcycle and kissed him on the banks of the Strawberry River. This was a woman. A fearless woman. One who wouldn't run away from love the way she used to.

He'd known early on that his heart was in deep trouble. That was understandable, given their mutual history. This was the first inkling he'd had, however, that the *rest* of him wasn't far behind.

Belinda felt as if she were floating in a half-asleep, half-awake state. She knew her arms were wrapped around Paul's neck, and she felt his hands moving over the back of her T-shirt in a slow, sensual caress, but she couldn't be absolutely sure she wasn't dreaming. Truth to tell, she sincerely hoped she *was* dreaming. The alternative was unthinkable!

Tensing, she chanced a peek. Reality was waiting on the other side of her lowered lashes. Handsome, enticing reality. This couldn't—shouldn't—be happening. Not to her. Not now. Not here. Oh, but it felt so good, so right.

In another second I'll push him away, she assured herself, only half believing it. *Just a second or two. Maybe a minute. Maybe…* Reminded of the night Paul had first asked her to marry him, she sighed. Maybe she shouldn't have sent their chaperone off to bake cookies. *Yeah, no kidding!*

This situation is my fault, Belinda reasoned, trying hard to focus her scattered thinking. The sensations of Paul's closeness were so overwhelming she could scarcely breath, let alone form coherent ideas. Only one thing was clear. They weren't kids anymore. If they stayed in each other's arms and kept kissing the way they were, their shared temptation was liable to sweep away the moral principles that she, at least, held dear.

That mustn't happen! She hadn't saved herself for all those years to waste her virginity on a man she'd probably never see again once his business here was concluded.

Marshaling her defenses, Belinda managed a slight resistance, hoping that would be enough to convince Paul they were making a big mistake. To her astonishment, his hold slackened. He was letting her go! Without a fight!

Filled with intense relief and remorse, she whispered the first prayer she'd thought of since Paul had swept her into his embrace, a simple, heartfelt, "Thank God."

"You should thank Him," Paul said hoarsely, his lips moving lightly against her cheek. "If I didn't know this was wrong and care what the Lord thought of me, you'd be in serious trouble, lady."

"I know." Belinda leaned away from him to look into his eyes. Latent passion still showed in his expression. No doubt Paul could see the same telltale emotion in hers. "I had no idea...." Embarrassed, she lowered her glance and stepped back.

Paul's hands slid gently down her bare arms till

he could grasp her hands. "I've wanted to do that since I first walked into your office."

"You have?" Misty-eyed, she searched his face for sincerity and found it.

"Yes," he said softly, "but that's no excuse. I'm sorry. Really sorry."

What could she say? That she wasn't sorry? Perish the thought, even though it was true. No man had ever kissed her like Paul just had—not even Paul himself. It was amazing. And scary. All sorts of inappropriate notions had arisen out of that one kiss and were racing madly around the fringes of her consciousness. She'd been wrong when she assumed her prior temptation was as bad as it could get. What had happened between Paul and her ten years ago was *nothing* compared to this! Maturity definitely had its drawbacks.

Penitent, he watched her, waiting for a response. Any response. Finally he asked, "Speak to me? Please?"

And say what? she wondered. Dealing with her flood of confusing feelings was hard enough without being required to chat coherently, too.

Belinda pulled her hands from his and backed away, hoping the added distance would help her focus. It did. A little. It also let her see how truly apologetic Paul was. His broad shoulders slumped, his hair was mussed, his brow was wrinkled, his mouth was pressed into a thin line, and the muscles were twitching at the joint of his jaw.

Poor guy. He looked awful. He also looked as endearing as a lost puppy, which made Belinda glad she'd put the length of the kitchen between them. She refused to lie and say she hadn't wanted him to kiss her. Besides, that wasn't what he'd asked or what he obviously wanted to hear.

Sympathetic, she said simply, "I forgive you."

Paul's resulting smile lit up the whole room, bathing Belinda in its sweetness and making her heart skip.

"Hey, that's good news," he told her, followed by a deep, relieved sigh. "You had me worried for a minute."

When he started to take a step toward her she held up her hand like a traffic cop. "Hold it right there, mister. I said I forgave you. I didn't say I wanted to repeat the mistake we both made when we... You know."

Paul nodded and raked his fingers through his thick, dark hair. "Oh, yeah. I know, all right."

"Then you do understand my problem."

"If it's anything like mine, I sure do," he said, eyeing the back door. "Tell you what. Snuffy and I will meet you in the yard. Join us when you're ready, and we can finish our discussion outside, the way you wanted."

Temporarily at a loss, Belinda began to chuckle at her befuddlement. "I'd love to. You wouldn't happen to remember what we were talking about, would you? I don't have a clue."

Paul paused, his hand on the doorknob, and looked at her with a mischievous little-boy expression. "I think it had something to do with my family. Or maybe it was your grandma's cookies." He shrugged. "Oh, well. I'm sure we can find something to discuss once we get out in the sunshine where it's safe." *And stop thinking about what just happened between us.*

With a quiet snort of self-derision, he turned and left the room. He didn't know about Belinda, but he was *never* going to forget that kiss.

Or the woman who had shared it.

Chapter Nine

Belinda talked to herself, and to the Lord, for a few minutes before she gathered her courage, poured more coffee and went to join Paul in the back yard. He was seated on the grass under a maple tree, leaning against the stout trunk. Snuffy had crowded in next to him and was poking his hand with her nose, trying to coax him to pet her. Obviously, the dog considered Paul a part of her extended family. Belinda wished she could say the same.

"I brought you a fresh cup of coffee." She held his mug higher. "Sorry, we're out of cookies."

Paul got to his feet and brushed himself off, chancing a cautious smile as he accepted the coffee. "My loss. I guess if Snuffy can stand to be deprived, I can, too."

"I could offer you one of her dog biscuits," Belinda teased, quickly backing away. "I'm sure she wouldn't mind sharing. For some reason, she seems to be madly in love with you.''

"Animals can be pretty discerning." He glanced at her over the rim of his mug as he took a sip. "You should pay attention. When Snuffy doesn't warm up to a person there's probably a good reason."

"If you're referring to Sam, forget it. The problem is, he doesn't happen to like dogs. That's all."

"Sounds like a bad sign to me," Paul said. "You were always nuts about animals."

"I can adjust." Belinda knew he was purposely needling her, trying to get her to say something negative about Sam, and she refused to take the bait.

Paul chuckled low, obviously amused.

"What are you laughing about?"

"You." He moved two lawn chairs into the shade under the maple and waited for Belinda to join him. When she didn't, he sat in one of them and continued, "In case you don't know it, you're the most stubborn, inflexible woman I've ever met. When you said you'd be able to adjust, the idea struck me funny."

"I am not stubborn!"

He gestured at the spare chair. "Oh? Then why are you standing way over there in the hot sun instead of sitting here in the shade by me? I promise I won't lay a hand on you again. Cross my heart."

What could she do? If she stood her ground, Paul could claim he was right about her being standoffish. But he looked so good, so appealing, casually sitting there drinking coffee and petting her dog with his free hand, that she wondered if she could manage to approach without letting her mind wander to places it had no business going.

She compromised by moving the empty chair farther from his before sitting in it. "There. Happy now?"

"That's a little better," Paul said with a wry smile. "You don't have to be afraid of me, you know."

It's myself I'm afraid of, she thought cynically. "I'm not afraid of you."

"Maybe that was a bad choice of words. Nervous might be closer."

"You're getting warm," she said, blushing when she realized belatedly that that particular phrase could also have a physical meaning. "I...I mean, you do make me kind of uncomfortable."

"I can tell." Saddened, Paul thought back to the long-ago church fire and Belinda's outspoken negative reaction to him in its aftermath. Given that history, he supposed he couldn't blame her for continuing to feel uneasy, even if she couldn't pinpoint exactly why.

What he wanted to do at that moment was jump to his feet, grab her by the shoulders, look her in the eye and shout to the housetops that he was innocent. If he were still as big a fool as he'd been when it had all happened, he might have made the mistake of trying—and maybe frightened her worse, he realized with a start.

Fortunately, he was able to conceal his momentary lapse. His nonchalant facade remained firmly in place while he pondered his dilemma. Life was like a court of law. Overt emotion was no defense against false accusations. If anything, it harmed the situation. Facts were what he needed. Later, he'd drop in at the local newspaper office and see what their archives had to say about the aftermath of the fire. At this point, any clue would be a blessing.

Belinda took a deep breath and slowly sipped her coffee, finally managing to focus on something other than her current proximity to Paul. "I did speak to Sam about his project," she offered. "He said I can tell you. He's planning to build a hospital."

"Wow." Paul's eyes widened. "He doesn't think small, does he?"

"You mean you really didn't know?"

"No. Not the details. All I'd been able to find out was that some property, including my aunts' twenty-plus acres, was being considered for rezoning to commercial. I assumed Sam wanted to build apartments or a small shopping mall like the one his office is in now." Paul paused, speculating, as he shook his head slowly in disbelief. "A hospital will cost a fortune."

"I'm sure he's thought of that. He has partners, of course. And ties to a larger health system. It's a feasible plan. We've needed a facility like that in Serenity for a long time."

"That's true. I hope he can put the deal together."

"You do?"

Paul chuckled low. "Yes, Belinda, I do. I'm not a monster. All I want is a fair deal for my aunts. Don't you think they deserve to be properly compensated for a prime piece of real estate?"

"Of course, but…"

"Do you think I should be willing to lower the asking price, no matter how a reduction affects Patience and Prudence, simply because your boyfriend intends to use the property for a good cause?"

She made a face. "When you put it that way, it sounds really unfair."

"Good. It's supposed to." Paul got to his feet and handed her his half-empty cup. "I'd better be going. Tell Sam I'm still working on Aunt Prudence. I expect to have her consent to sell within the next week or so. The rest will be up to him. If he truly wants the Whitaker estate, he's going to have to pay fair market value."

"I'll tell him."

"*Only* about the property," Paul warned. "I don't think it's a good idea to mention what took place in your kitchen this morning, do you?"

Her cheeks turned crimson. "Of course not! That was just…"

"For old times' sake," he suggested with a wry smile. "Goodbye, Belinda. Have a great life."

She sat very still, watching him turn and walk away. His farewell words had been so much like the ones he'd used when he'd left town all those years before, they were causing her actual physical pain. *Have a great life,* Paul had said. Funny, she'd assumed she already was until he'd shown up in Serenity and proved otherwise.

Eloise was in the midst of baking, just as she'd promised, when Belinda dropped in. "Whew! It's a good thing you have air-conditioning, Gram." She made herself at home at the kitchen table and began to nibble warm cookie crumbs. "You'd better not do too much. Your ankle is liable to swell again if you don't rest it."

"I know." Eloise sighed. "I was only going to make those cookies for Paul. Then Verleen called. There's going to be a pie supper down at the community center tonight."

"Really? I hadn't heard a thing about it."

"It's a benefit for that poor family over on Highway Nine. The ones that got burned out a few days back. I think their name was Nichols."

"I remember now." Belinda grinned. "Their name is Penny. But you were close. Only four cents off."

"Hush," Eloise ordered good-naturedly. "You know I have a terrible memory for names. I still don't know half the folks in our church, except by their faces, and I've been a member for fifteen years."

"True. But we've added a lot of new members lately, too. Besides, at your age you can get away with it. Between my job at the chamber and Sam's political position, I'm expected to remember everything about everybody.''

Eloise stopped mixing the sliced peaches, sugar and dry tapioca in her bowl and made a grumpy face. ''What do you mean, at my age?''

''Okay, so you're a *young* grandmother. You're still a grandmother. Mine. And I'm proud of you.'' She gave the older woman a hug and a quick kiss on the cheek. ''Tell you what. Why don't you take a break? I'll finish the pies you've started.''

''I wish you would finish what *you've* started,'' Eloise said, rolling her eyes toward the ceiling in a show of maternal frustration. ''When are you and Sam going to stop dragging your feet and get married?''

''Who says you don't remember things?'' Belinda quipped. ''It seems to me your memory's been working overtime on that particular subject.''

''I just want you to be happy.'' Handing over the bowl and spoon, Eloise sank wearily into the nearest chair. ''I've been married and I've been single. Believe me, married is much, much better.''

''Only if you're married to the right man.''

''That's what I've been trying to *tell* you. If you play too hard to get, Sam may find somebody else. Then where will you be?''

Where, indeed? The thought of being dumped by Sam Barryman made Belinda feel oddly content. The sensation was similar to the peace she usually sensed when she knew she was doing God's will. *How strange.* Not that she could rely on her emotions to behave in a rational manner, given what had happened that morning. Still, maybe the Lord was trying to use Paul's kiss to open her eyes.

She began to flour the board so she could roll out the first bottom crust. "As you always say, Gram, if the good Lord wants something to happen, it will."

"Providing we don't come along and mess up His plans."

"Or try to help Him too much instead of trusting in His leading?" Belinda added astutely. "Of course, you wouldn't know anything about doing that, would you?"

"At least I recognize a good thing when I see it."

"So do I. Believe me, so do I." Inwardly, Belinda mocked herself for immediately picturing Paul. What was good for one kind of woman, however, wasn't necessarily good for any other kind. She and Paul had grown apart. Far apart. No amount of wishing or praying could change that. They couldn't spend the rest of their lives standing in her kitchen and kissing passionately, no matter how wonderful it had been. There was a lot more to life, to happiness, than that, like it or not. It was easy to admit she definitely did *not* like it.

"Hey!" Eloise shouted. "Not so thin. What do you think you're making? A pizza?"

"Oops." Belinda looked at the enormous circle of dough. Even the best cook could never successfully lift that flimsy a crust into a pie plate. She started to gather it up and squeeze it into a ball. "Sorry. Guess I was daydreaming. I'll roll it out again."

"If you do, you'll take it to the benefit with *your* name on it. That crust'll be as tough as shoe leather."

"Fine. I'd like to have a pie to donate. If nobody bids on it I'll buy it back myself."

Eloise bumped her aside with her hip and commandeered the rolling pin. "You may have to. Wrap that ruined dough in waxed paper and refrigerate it until I'm through with my pies. I'll save you enough for a bottom crust. You can use your overworked pastry to make a lattice top."

"Yes, ma'am." Belinda watched her grandmother's capable hands fly into action.

The older woman threw a handful of dry flour onto the table, spread it around with her hand and kept working while she talked. "You were daydreaming about Sam, I hope."

"I have been thinking of Sam and me," Belinda conceded, "but I doubt you're going to like what I've decided."

Eloise stopped rolling and turned to stare. "You aren't thinking of breaking up with him?!"

"Actually, I was. It's not fair to keep seeing Sam when I don't love him."

"Of course you do. You just refuse to admit it." She grimaced. "It's that Paul Randall, isn't it? You've got some crazy idea you still love him, even after what he did to your poor father. Shame on you, Belinda Carnes."

"Paul said he's planning to prove to me that he didn't start the fire. He sounded very convincing."

"If he's so blasted innocent, why did he run away?"

"Well, because…" Belinda had no ready excuse.

"See? You don't know. That's because you aren't sure what the real truth is, either." Raising her eyebrows, she peered at Belinda and added, "The apple never falls very far from the tree, as they say."

"Fine. I blamed him without any proof, so why shouldn't you. But tell me this, Gram, if you really believe Paul is so evil, why are you baking him cookies?"

Eloise went back to her pie crust, rolling with a vengeance. "Christian charity."

"Phooey." Belinda paced across the room and back. "I know you. If you honestly believed Paul was guilty, you wouldn't even speak to him, let alone give him cookies."

"I would so."

"Good," Belinda drawled knowingly, "then I can count on you to take a peace offering out to the flat-lander who bought the Beasley place, then sued the pants off the city when they ordered him to clean it up. Right?"

The look of dismay and astonishment on her grandmother's face was so comical Belinda almost laughed out loud. Nodding with perception she said, "Uh-huh. That's what I thought."

* * *

The pie supper at the community center was scheduled to begin at seven that night. Belinda decided to go early so she could help set up the folding chairs. One whole wall was taken up by long tables of donated baked goods for the pie auction. Household goods and clothing intended for the family's personal use were stacked on the floor beneath the tables. Some of the things were new. Others were whatever the giver could spare.

The room filled up quickly. Mr. and Mrs. Penny sat in the front row with their three children, accepting hugs of condolence and sniffling with gratitude for the bounty they were about to receive. Belinda had added her own offering, as well as Eloise's, to the table of baked goods and was choosing a chair for herself when Sam breezed in.

"Sorry I'm late," he said. "The Barlow kid cut his toe. They called me at home and I had to meet them at my office so I could stitch him up and give him a tetanus booster."

"You're not late," Belinda assured him. "We haven't started yet."

"I know. I'm the auctioneer."

Surprised, she glanced around the room. Many of the usual volunteer auctioneers were present. "Why you?"

"Probably because this benefit was my idea," he said, boasting. "It was the perfect opportunity to announce my plans for a hospital, especially if I was the one in charge. So I made sure I was." He cocked his head toward the crowd and spoke quietly. "Look. Half the town is here, and they're all in a charitable mood. The atmosphere couldn't be better."

"You didn't do this for the burned-out family?"

Sam shrugged it off. "Of course I did. If I hadn't thought of it, somebody else would have. They always do. I just didn't see any reason to waste a good stroke of luck so I made a few calls and got the ball rolling."

"I see." And she did see. Sam Barryman might be a great doctor and a successful businessman, but his priorities and his sense of divine guidance were seriously flawed. Where she saw the hand of God, Sam gave all the credit to luck, instead. She sighed. His present attitude was just one more confirmation that her decision was the right one. She and Sam would never be happy together. Their motivations were simply too different.

He patted her arm. "Have a seat and watch the master at work, honey. I'll bet we raise more money tonight than we ever have before."

"I hope so." She managed a smile as she watched him make his way down the center aisle, stopping along the way to shake hands and greet people as if he were running for political office. Truth to tell, he had already done a lot of good for Serenity. Business was booming. And if he was successful in getting a hospital built, the benefits to the town would be enormous.

But at what cost? She'd seen Miss Patience arrive

with store-bought baked goods, as usual. There was no sign of her twin sister, however, which wasn't surprising, since Prudence usually avoided crowds. What would that poor old woman do if she no longer had her house as her sanctuary? And what would become of all those cats she doted on as if they were her children? No wonder she'd been so adamant about not selling.

"Oh, Father," she whispered. "I think I see what You've been trying to tell me."

The pieces of the puzzle began to slide into place in her mind. People's happiness was more important than monetary gain. One look at the crowd gathered together to comfort and support a family in need proved that. Some of the folks who were giving most freely had little to offer, yet they'd come because they cared about each other.

Belinda cared, too. Poor Miss Prudence deserved to stay in her house for as long as she wanted to and was able to care for herself. Like it or not, Sam was going to have to find another suitable piece of property for his hospital, and Belinda intended to tell him so. Soon.

She smiled in spite of the seriousness of her decision. When she'd decided to break up with Sam the path was being prepared for her, just like the Bible promised. It was a good thing. The minute she openly sided with Prudence, Sam was going to be absolutely furious.

At that point, breaking up was probably going to sound like a real good idea to him, too.

Since it was customary to bid way too much for the pies and other baked goods, then serve them to everyone in attendance as soon as the sale concluded, Sam opened the auction with a short spiel about his plans for the new hospital. Then he got down to the business at hand.

An hour later he was almost finished auctioning everything on the baked goods table. He raised the last pie in the air, balancing it on the flat of his palm to display it. "Here we go, folks. Don't give up on me yet. We've got one more to sell before we eat."

Eyeing the slightly lopsided pie with undisguised skepticism, he drawled, "Looks like peach. Don't know who made this poor little thing, but that doesn't really matter, does it? This is all for a good cause. What am I bid?"

Silence reigned. Belinda had no trouble recognizing her amateur effort. In a community where many women still prided themselves on their expertise in the kitchen, her lack of culinary skill was something of an embarrassment.

"How about two dollars? Do I hear two?" Sam asked, chuckling.

Belinda raised her hand and called out, "Five."

A few curious people turned to look at her. From the back of the room a burly farmer hollered, "She ought to know what it's worth. That's one she brought.'' An undercurrent of laughter began to ripple through the crowd.

If Belinda had thought she could successfully crawl under her folding chair and hide from everybody, she would have tried to do it. Masking her hurt feelings, she managed to smile at Sam and catch his eye long enough to say, ''It is peach.''

Jockeying the pie plate, he grinned at her. ''In that case, I bid ten dollars myself. Going once, going twice...''

''Fifty dollars!''

Every head swiveled, especially Belinda's, even though she'd recognized the new bidder's deep voice the moment she'd heard it. Paul Randall was standing in the back of the room, feet braced apart, arms folded across his chest, visibly defying his rival to up the bid.

''I have fifty.'' Sam's voice lacked its former enthusiasm. ''I'll make it fifty-five. Do I hear sixty?''

Without hesitation Paul shouted, ''Seventy-five.''

Belinda wasn't the only one who gasped. All eyes snapped to Sam, waiting to see what he'd do. If that hadn't been her pie on the auction block, Belinda would have found the whole scenario pretty funny.

Gritting his teeth, Sam countered, ''Eighty.''

''One hundred dollars,'' Paul shouted. Before Sam could respond, he doubled his own offer. ''On second thought, make that *two* hundred.''

The wooden gavel cracked down on the speaker's

stand. Belinda didn't hear Sam say, "Sold," because the meeting hall was echoing with so much cheering and loud applause.

Belinda had volunteered to help Verleen and some of the other women dish up the food, so she reported for duty right after Paul won the bidding war for her pie.

"That was some sale," Verleen said. "I never seen a peach pie that looked quite like that last one. Guess you should of made a bunch of 'em."

Belinda stifled a giggle. "No kidding. Gram gave me her leftover fixings after she finished making four pies of her own."

The older woman squinted at the crowd. "Is Eloise here? I didn't see her."

"No. The poor thing was dead on her feet by the time the last pie came out of the oven. Her ankle was bothering her a lot, too, so I talked her into staying home. It's hard to get her to take it easy, though. Lying around is not in her nature."

"Nor mine. I s'pose Dr. Sam would've slapped Eloise in that hospital of his if it'd been built already."

Her attitude gave Belinda pause. "You don't sound as thrilled about it as I thought you'd be. We do need a place like that, you know."

"That don't make it fun to visit." Verleen continued to section the spice cake in front of her. "Glad you brought Eloise's pies for her, though. Every dollar helps. We did pretty good tonight."

"I'll say."

"Did you see May Penny cryin'? She was real touched. Must a blowed her nose a hundred times."

Nodding, Belinda busied herself putting slices of cake and pie onto small paper plates while people crowded around, hoping to get a taste of their favorite.

She was so preoccupied with trying to satisfy the demand, she didn't look at who she was serving until a familiar voice asked, "Do you suppose I can get a piece of the one I bought? I've never eaten two-hundred-dollar pie before. I'd kind of like to see what it tastes like."

His genial smile took her breath away. "Paul. Hi."

"Hi, yourself. How come you didn't tell me about this benefit when I saw you this morning? I almost missed the bidding."

Belinda shot a sidelong glance at Verleen, happy to note she was chattering away with her cronies instead of paying attention to Paul. "I didn't know about it then. These benefits are usually planned in advance, but this one's for a family that was recently burned out. They needed a lot of help right away."

"So, it came up on the spur of the moment?"

"Yes." She tried to hand him some dessert. "Here. Try this one. Gram made it."

"Like I said, I'm waiting for a piece of the one you made."

"You may be sorry."

"I'll take my chances," Paul said, noting that Sam

was wending his way through the crowd, heading straight for Belinda. "Just give me my pie and I'll stop bothering you."

"You're not…" When she felt an arm slip around her waist she tensed and jerked so badly she nearly dropped the thin paper plate and its contents. "Sam! You scared me."

"Did I? I guess you must have been thinking about something else, huh?"

Belinda didn't like the way Sam was glaring at Paul—or the way Paul was returning a similar look— so she thrust the plate into Sam's free hand to occupy it, then snatched up an identical piece and handed it to Paul. He thanked her politely and turned away.

Sam stayed, so Belinda found something for him to do besides glare at Paul's retreating figure. "We're about to run out of plastic forks, Sam. Would you mind getting another case out of the storage cupboard?"

She saw him continuing to concentrate on what was going on across the room and followed his line of sight. It looked as if Paul was preparing to leave!

Apparently Sam thought so, too, because he stopped acting like he was guarding her and went to do as she'd asked. Saving her deep sigh until he was out of hearing range, Belinda finally let it go with a whoosh. "Oh, boy."

Beside her again, Verleen cackled. "If them two was boys instead of grown men, they'd be mixin' it up out behind the barn, honey, instead of throwin'

their money around to impress you. You'd best pick
one and stick to him before they both run off.''

"I can't,'' Belinda said with a disgusted pout.
"Neither one of them is right for me.''

"According to Eloise…''

Belinda interrupted. "I know what Gram thinks.
She's told me often enough.''

"So?''

"So, she's wrong. I'm sure of that now. There's
no way I'd ever be able to convince myself to marry
Sam.''

"What about the other one?'' Her already wrinkled brow creased in thought. "Hey. Wait a minute.
Was he the kid who burned down your daddy's
church? He was, wasn't he? Lots of folks said he'd
been seen hangin' around, kind of like he was casing
the place, just before the fire.''

"Paul was there to see *me*,'' Belinda said with
conviction. "That's why he came back that night. He
was worried about me.''

"That so? Then why'd he take off afterward and
hightail it out of town like he did?''

Sobering, Belinda shook her head. "Gram asked
me the same question. I suppose that's partly my
fault. There was so much confusion, and I was so
worried about what might happen to Daddy, I'm
afraid I accused Paul of being responsible, too.''

"Makes sense. He probably did it.''

"No. No, I don't think so anymore.''

"Eloise tells me he had plenty of good reason to

be mad at your daddy, that's a fact.'' She snorted. ''Yes, sir.''

Belinda opened her mouth to contradict, then shut it again without speaking.

Nodding solemnly, Verleen said, ''Sometimes it's best to let sleeping dogs lie, you know. 'Specially if you've been bit by that particular one before.''

Chapter Ten

The following Sunday morning was going to be the day Belinda came right out and told Sam she could never marry him. She'd thought it all through. It would be easy to steer their conversation in that direction while he drove her home after church.

By ten-thirty, however, she was still standing on her front porch, waiting and wondering if she was going to get the chance. She allowed him fifteen more minutes, then hopped into her car and raced toward church.

"Please, Lord, just get me there on time and I promise I'll never speed again," she muttered. "You know how I hate to be late."

Which is a personal problem, she countered. *God is not responsible for my quirks.* Penitent, she retracted her earlier prayer and lightened up on the gas. "Sorry, Father. I know better. I should be thankful

I'm able to go at all. If I'm late, it'll be Sam's fault, not mine. Or Yours. I'll just sneak in the back door and grab the first seat I see so I don't disturb the service."

Unless Paul Randall is nearby, she added to herself. In that case, she might have to walk the aisle, even if that did call undue attention to her tardiness. It was better to be a little embarrassed in front of her friends than to wind up forced to sit too close to Paul again.

Then why go at all? a voice within her asked.

Because I belong in church, Belinda answered. Nothing said she couldn't visit a different church once in awhile, though. She brightened. What a wonderful idea! Miss Prudence's little church was right on her way. Instead of passing it, she could stop there with time to spare. The plan was perfect. She'd been wanting to talk to Prudence, anyway, and apparently the Lord had used Sam's tardiness to send her in the right direction. What a blessing!

Rejoicing, Belinda wheeled into the unpaved parking area surrounding the one-room church. Cars and trucks all faced the sanctuary, radiating out like spokes of a wheel, with the white-painted church as the hub. Spiritually, it *was* the hub, she thought, happy she'd decided to stop.

Grinning at the prospect of worshiping here, she hurried to the open door and was greeted warmly by an elderly gentleman she suspected was the pastor. His grip was firm and sure, his eyes brimming with love. "Good morning! We're so glad to have you with us."

"Thank you," Belinda said. She peered past his shoulder. "Is Miss Prudence Whitaker here? I understand this is her church."

"It most certainly is." Stepping aside, he gestured. "She always sits right up front. First row. We can't afford a sound system like the bigger churches have, and she can hear better from up there. Please. Go on in. I'm sure she'll be proud to see you."

"I hope so." Considering her prior support of Sam's plans to develop the Whitaker estate, she wasn't quite sure what Prudence's reaction would be when she showed up.

Starting down the aisle, Belinda began to picture herself as one of the kids in Miss Whitaker's old fourth-grade class, being called up to the teacher's desk for correction. She lowered her gaze and watched the toes of her shoes moving along the hardwood floor, just as she had when she'd been Prudence's student years ago. *How funny!* Although she hadn't reminisced about those days in a long time, her subconscious apparently still hid a gut-level desire to please her former teacher.

Smiling at the absurdity of her reaction, Belinda reached the front of the church. Prudence was there, as promised. The fold-down wooden seats looked like they had once belonged in an ancient movie theater. There were two empty spaces between Prudence and the center aisle.

"Miss Prudence?" Belinda asked quietly. "Are these seats taken?"

"Why…no." She brightened immediately and turned slightly to better face Belinda. "What a lovely surprise! Is your grandmother with you?"

"No. Sorry." Belinda took the seat closest to her former teacher. "I was running late this morning, and it seemed like the Lord was telling me to stop here as I drove by, so I did."

"How sweet." Prudence patted her hand. "And how interesting."

"Isn't it! I love it when stuff like this happens. Which reminds me. We need to talk after church. I've been thinking, if you want to stay in your house, you have a perfect right to. All we have to do is figure out how to make it feasible." She saw tears begin to glisten in the old woman's blue eyes.

"What a lovely thought," Prudence said softly.

One more empty chair remained between Belinda and the aisle. She was sitting sideways with her back to it when someone reached past her to hand Prudence a well-worn Bible.

Crowded, Belinda straightened in the narrow seat. "I'm sorry, I…" Her mouth dropped open, then slammed shut. "You! What are you doing here?"

"Bringing my aunt the Bible she left in the car," Paul said gruffly, "and going to church." One eyebrow arched. "What are *you* doing here?"

"I was passing by and…"

Prudence leaned forward to speak quietly to her

nephew. "Belinda couldn't have ulterior motives, dear. We came in my station wagon, not your car. Remember? So she couldn't have known you were here." She sat back, cupped her hand around her mouth and whispered to Belinda, "Don't worry about him. He's been a grump ever since Sister talked him into letting her borrow his new car again this morning." She giggled. "And besides, I suspect you scare him a bit."

"Me?" Belinda started to glance at Paul, then changed her mind. "I do?"

The older woman nodded, offering no further explanation. Sitting primly in her seat, she opened her hymnal as a pianist began to play an introduction.

In the confines of the narrow seats, Paul's shoulder butted against Belinda's, and she couldn't help feeling the warmth of his arm radiating through the sleeve of his suit coat. If there had been any extra room she would have scooted farther away, for her sake as well as for his. Unfortunately, the seats were all fastened together, so distancing herself wasn't an option.

Droplets of perspiration distracted her as they started to trickle down the back of her neck. She blotted her forehead. A sound system wasn't the only thing this sanctuary lacked. It also had no air-conditioning. If it hadn't been for the ceiling fans, the place would have felt like an oven by the time the service was over. It already reminded her of a rain forest, humid and close.

She wished she could slip off her short jacket without bumping into Paul's arm. She wished she'd worn something cooler. She wished she could sneak away and remove her sticking panty hose before she cooked in them.

And that wasn't the half of it. Belinda grimaced. She sure wished she'd known Paul was going to be here. And she wished Sam had picked her up on time, the way he always did. She also wished she'd had sense enough to keep on driving instead of stopping at the tiny church when she felt the urge! Any of those things would have helped her avoid this predicament.

What a mess! There she was, a captive of good manners and her strict upbringing, sandwiched in next to the one man who only had to look at her to hopelessly muddle her thoughts. If she got up and left now, Miss Prudence would be embarrassed in front of her whole church family, not to mention what an impolite action like that would do to Belinda's already overworked conscience.

You're supposed to find peace in church, she told herself, confident that God would provide for her needs as soon as she surrendered and let Him take over. *Oh, please, Lord?* she prayed silently. Things couldn't possibly get worse than they already were, so it stood to reason they had to get better.

Slowly accepting that logical conclusion, Belinda was starting to relax when the congregation got up to sing. She looked right and left. Hymnbooks were apparently as scarce here as everything else. Prudence was already sharing hers with two women on her opposite side.

Singing the first verse of the old hymn from memory, Belinda faltered on the second and felt a gentle nudge to her right. Paul held out his hymnal, wordlessly offering to share. She grasped her half of it out of habit, realizing too late what a revealing mistake she'd made. Her hands were shaking so badly the pages wiggled!

Paul cradled her hands beneath the book and steadied them. His touch was sure and gentle. It should have had a calming effect. It didn't.

Before the third verse ended Belinda was feeling so light-headed she began to wonder if she'd get away with blaming her weakness on the high air temperature if she fainted dead away!

By the end of the service most of the women were fanning themselves vigorously. The men sat there and sweated, stoic as usual. When the final amen came, Belinda was relieved to note that everybody else seemed as eager to get out of the sweltering church as she was.

Prudence took her arm and started up the aisle. "Maybe it's my age, but every summer seems hotter to me."

"It was very warm this morning," Belinda agreed. "I'm spoiled. My church has air-conditioning."

"I know. So does Sister's. But a little place like this can't afford that kind of thing."

Paul was walking directly behind them. "They could if someone gave them an endowment," he said. "You could do that, you know, if you agreed to sell the estate."

"But I don't want to leave the house Father built." She tightened her hold on Belinda's arm. "You don't know how sick it makes me to even think of selling. Belinda understands. Don't you, dear?"

"Of course I do." She shot a quick, warning glance over her shoulder at Paul, then focused on her elderly companion, speaking sympathetically. "There has to be some way you can keep your place." Behind her, she heard Paul's derisive snort, so she added, "Well, there does. All we have to do is put our heads together and think of it."

Prudence was blinking rapidly, her eyes moist. "Will you join us for Sunday dinner? Please?"

"I don't know, I…" She would have begged off if Paul hadn't butted in.

"I'm sure Ms. Carnes has other plans, Aunt Prudence."

Belinda managed a calm, self-possessed smile and said, "Actually, I don't. Sam stood me up this morning. I suppose he had some kind of medical emergency that he had to take care of."

"Then you'll come with us!" Prudence almost jumped up and down with joy. "You and I haven't had a chance for a nice chat in years. I want to hear all about your ideas for my house.''

''I haven't worked anything out yet.''

''That's all right. You will. You always were a bright child. So eager and well-behaved.''

Belinda was basking in the praise when Paul spoiled it. ''This isn't elementary school, Aunt Pru. And you don't have your father's money to keep that house going anymore.''

That was a surprise to Belinda. ''You don't?'' She looked at Paul. ''They don't?''

''No, they don't,'' he said flatly. ''Between Patience's extravagances and Prudence's philanthropy, they're broke. If it weren't for their pensions and social security, they'd starve to death.''

''It's not that bad,'' the older woman insisted. ''The good Lord provides for our needs. He always has and He always will.''

Belinda saw Paul roll his eyes and sigh. She, too, believed that God was faithful, but she also knew that He expected His children to take good care of whatever He'd given them. If the sisters had wasted their inheritance, it was doubtful they could count on God to bail them out.

Sensitive to Prudence's mood, she kept that opinion to herself and pointed to her white car. ''I'll follow you. Where are we going to eat?'' If looks could have killed, she'd have been pushing up daisies, thanks to the icy glower Paul sent her way. Apparently, when he'd bid her that final-sounding goodbye and told her to have a great life, he'd meant it to be *very* final.

"The Linden's buffet over in East Serenity is about the only place open on Sunday," Prudence explained. "We thought we'd try it out. I hear it's very good."

"Fine. I'll meet you there." She began to back away. "If I'm late, go ahead and start without me."

"I wonder why she thinks she might be late?" Prudence mused. "We're all leaving here at the same time."

Paul held the passenger door for his aunt, watching Belinda make her way to her car. "I suspect she wants to go check on the doctor first."

"Of course she does. Why didn't I think of that?"

Paul slammed the door and circled the station wagon, muttering to himself, "I wish *I* hadn't."

Belinda dashed home to change clothes, make sure Snuffy had plenty of cool drinking water and check her answering machine for recent messages. There were a few seconds of semi-incoherent babbling from Sheila, but Sam hadn't called, which meant that he must still be involved with a patient. While she was changing, she sent up a quick prayer for his success and the health of whomever he was working on. In less than ten minutes she was on her way to the restaurant.

From the outside, Linden's looked like the normal coffee shop it once had been, but the interior now contained an enormous buffet. Belinda hadn't eaten there very often in the past year or so because Sam didn't like the noise of all the diners or the task of dishing up his own meal. She paid the cashier at the door, glad she'd decided to arrive alone rather than make Paul feel obligated to buy her dinner. At this point, the less she owed him, the better.

The after-church crowd had filled nearly every seat. If Paul hadn't been taller than average she might have had trouble spotting the secluded booth he and his aunt occupied.

Arriving a bit breathless, Belinda tossed her purse onto the bench beside Prudence. "Whew! I've never seen the place this full."

When Paul started to stand, she waved him down. "Sit. Eat. I'll go fill a plate and be right back."

"I wish I'd gone home and changed, too," Prudence observed. "She looks so refreshed."

"Yeah, I see that," Paul grumbled. He'd shed his suit coat and tie and rolled up his shirt sleeves, but he still didn't feel nearly as cool and collected as Belinda looked. She'd put on a yellow sundress with tiny shoulder straps and pulled her dark auburn hair back with a matching ribbon. Her cheeks were flushed, the way they'd looked right after he'd kissed her, and her eyes sparkled like sunlight on rippling water. The result was so awesome he had trouble forcing himself to stop staring.

By the time she returned, he'd managed to regain a semblance of self-control and go back to his meal.

"So, did you find Sam?" Paul asked as she scooted into the booth next to Prudence.

"Sam? No, why?"

"I thought that might be why you were delayed."

Belinda laughed softly. "Nope. All I wanted to do was go home and get out of my hot outfit. Sam's a big boy. He can take care of himself. He doesn't need me."

"Does *he* know that?" Paul asked with an enigmatic grin.

"I doubt it. Sam is a nice guy, but he has a little trouble listening to any ideas other than his own." She smiled at Prudence. "As you already know."

The elderly woman made a sour face. "I certainly do. If I'd been younger, or stronger, I'd have grabbed that confounded needle of his and given him a taste of his own medicine right in the—!"

"Aunt Pru!" Paul leaned across the table toward her and placed a finger to his lips. "Hush. If you get upset again you'll have everybody thinking Sam was right to give you that sedative."

"That's okay," Belinda countered, seeking to lighten the mood, "if they haul you off and lock you up, I'll bake you a cake with a file in it so you can escape."

Glad for a diversion, Paul took up the challenge of wits. "I don't know that I'd count on that plan, Aunt Pru. I know what her cooking is like. If I were a jailer, I'd immediately suspect that anything that crudely made had to be a ruse." To his delight, Belinda's eyes widened in disbelief, then narrowed with indignation.

"Oh, yeah? What makes *you* such an expert?"

Pleased, Paul smirked. "I've been eating all my life."

"No kidding? Well, if you're referring to the pie I made for the benefit last night, I'll have you know that it earned the most money on record."

"No doubt. I remember that part vividly." Watching her cheeks reddening, he decided he'd better stop teasing. "Sorry. I couldn't resist. Your pie actually tasted very good, judging by the sliver I managed to get of it."

"Shame on you," Prudence scolded. "Belinda was just trying to cheer me up."

"So was I." He concentrated on carving the slice of ham on his plate. "What we really need to do is focus all this wasted brainpower on a solution to your problems."

"I think Sam should find a different piece of land," Belinda offered. "Then Miss Prudence could keep her house."

"For awhile," Paul agreed. "Trouble is, the place is falling apart and there's no money to properly repair it. Before long, it won't be worth saving."

"Sam doesn't intend to save it." Laying down her fork, Belinda blotted her mouth on a paper napkin.

"Are you sure about that?" Paul saw her nod.

A quiet sniffle from Prudence drew their attention. "That house is special to me because Father built it.

I wouldn't mind so much if I thought the place would survive even if I moved away. I'm afraid my old house is too much of a dinosaur, though, just like Sister and me.''

Belinda disagreed. "It should be a national treasure." She sat very still as the idea formed. "Like a historical monument! It was the first estate in this county, maybe this whole end of the state. Paul? What do you think?''

Mulling over her suggestion, he finally shook his head. "That won't help. Even if we do convince some organization to step in and preserve the house, that still doesn't give Aunt Pru any place else to live. If she doesn't sell, she won't have the money to re-settle.''

Disappointed, Belinda conceded he was right. However, something else, something tenuous, kept trying to gel in the back of her mind. How could the sisters sell the house and preserve it at the same time? Who would be nuts enough or philanthropic enough to pay for it, then turn around and give it back? Certainly not Sam. Unless...

A clever plan was beginning to take shape in Belinda's mind. If she could present her idea with enough emphasis on personal gain and community prestige, there just might be a chance Sam would go for it.

Paul stood. "I'm going to go get some dessert. Can I bring you ladies something?''

"I'll have cheesecake, please,'' Prudence said.

Belinda said, "Me, too. Thanks." Waiting until Paul had left the table, she told her elderly companion, "I don't want to get your hopes up but I have an idea how you can keep your house from being destroyed and still get enough money to buy yourself another nice place to live."

"How?"

"I'm going to suggest that Sam buy the entire estate, just like he'd planned, then deed the residence back to the state as a historical site. There's plenty of room on the rest of the property for his hospital, and I'll bet he can claim the gift of the old house as a whopping tax deduction."

Misty-eyed, Prudence grasped her hand, squeezing hard. "Oh, dear. Do you really think that will work?"

"I hope so," Belinda said. "I'm just glad I thought of it before I broke up with Sam and made him too mad to listen to me."

"Broke up? You're not going to marry him like Eloise thought?" The old woman's gaze drifted across the room to the crowded buffet table where her grandnephew waited in line for their dessert. "Does that mean you've decided to marry Paul?"

"No!" Belinda blurted, attracting the attention of a few nearby diners. She lowered her voice. "No. I could never let myself get serious about him."

"Why not?" Drawing a shaky breath, Prudence answered her own question. "Oh, my. It's because of that awful fire, isn't it? You still blame Paul."

"Not exactly," Belinda said, hedging. "I don't want to suspect him. The trouble is, I'll never know for sure what happened that night, and as long as there's any doubt I'll have to keep dealing with it. I can't forget. I've tried."

Prudence pressed her fingertips to her lips and began to weep silently. Finally she lowered her hands and said, "Paul didn't do it. I *know* he didn't."

"It's sweet of you to believe in him," Belinda told her, "but I'm afraid you're prejudiced."

"No! You don't understand. I know Paul didn't set that fire because I was there!" she whispered hoarsely. "The whole thing was my fault!"

Belinda tensed. "What are you talking about?"

"It was an accident," the old woman said between sniffles and halting breaths. "I didn't mean to do it." Prudence's bony fingers were tearing her napkin to shreds in her lap. "Promise you won't tell? Promise?"

So shocked she could hardly think, Belinda nodded woodenly. "What happened?" Flabbergasted, she stared at her elderly companion. Did she dare believe what she'd just heard? Or was the surprising confession merely a fib designed to clear the way for Paul? Speaking of which...

Belinda's head snapped around. Paul was turning from the dessert table with three small plates in his hands. There was no way she could sit here and waste time making polite conversation when what she wanted to do was take her former teacher by the shoulders and shake her until she spilled the whole story.

Grabbing Prudence's hand, she slid out of the booth and ordered her to do the same. "Come on."

"Where are we going?"

"To the ladies' room. Where we can talk privately."

"What about Paul?"

"He's the reason we can't stay at the table." Belinda was clearly growing angry. "And I'm not about to wait for a better time. Ten years of blaming the wrong man for a crime he didn't commit is quite long enough, thank you."

She had to force herself to slow her pace so Prudence could keep up. Fortunately, they had the rest room to themselves when they entered. Belinda whirled. "Okay. Let's have it. How did you start the fire? And this had better be good."

"It…it was a candle," Prudence managed to say between shuddering sobs. "I lit it when I went to the church that night to meet Eldon."

"Eldon Lafferty? I thought he was long gone."

"Everybody did. But he wrote to Sister all the time. I recognized his handwriting on the envelopes."

This scenario was so bizarre it was beginning to sound almost plausible. "If Miss Patience knew where he was, why didn't she say something to somebody? Why let everybody think he'd disappeared?"

"Because Sister never got her letters," Prudence said with a shaky intake of breath. "I kept them for myself."

Belinda was losing patience at the convoluted telling of the tale. "Okay. Get to the point. What does that have to do with the fire in Daddy's church?"

"I told you. I was meeting Eldon there." She reached for a paper towel to blot her tears. "I took a candle with me to put in the window because that was the secret signal we'd arranged."

"This is unbelievable," Belinda said. "Why didn't you just turn on the lights?"

"Because I didn't want to make anybody suspicious. Besides, I thought if I kept the light real dim, Eldon wouldn't know it was me instead of Sister until I'd had a chance to explain, to tell him how much I still loved him. But he recognized me right away. We had a terrible row. I forgot all about my candle until much later, when I heard the sirens." She burst into renewed weeping. "I should have known it was a sin to sneak around that way. But I was so lonely. And I'd missed him so much."

Overcome by the portent of everything she'd learned, Belinda sagged against the rest room sink. "I understand that part. I just don't know why you never spoke up."

"I couldn't! What would people think? And what was the use? Paul was long gone, and nobody was ever arrested."

"You have to tell him," Belinda insisted.

"I can't! He's like the son I never had."

"All the more reason you owe it to him." She straightened, her chin high, her mind made up. "I'll give you until tomorrow morning. If you don't tell him the truth by then, *I* will."

Leaving Prudence behind to wash off her tears and pull herself together, Belinda started to return to the table where Paul waited. She'd thought she could bluff her way through the rest of the meal, but the moment she saw him, her stomach did a flip-flop and her resolve vanished.

Totally confused, she couldn't decide whether she loved him the way she used to, or hated him for running away from trouble when she'd needed his moral support so badly. Only one thing was certain, there was no way she could sit across a table from that man and make polite conversation without him being aware that something important had changed between them. The best thing to do was make a hasty exit.

Paul started to rise as she approached. "Where's Aunt Prudence?"

"In the ladies' room. She'll be back in a jiffy." Belinda retrieved her purse. "I have to be going."

His abrupt "no" took her by surprise.

She quickly recovered, waving gaily as she turned to make her escape. "Sorry. Can't be helped. Bye."

"No. Wait! Eat your dessert," he called after her.

Belinda ignored him. Almost to the door, she heard another familiar voice that brought her up short. It sounded like Sam's! Puzzled, she paused long enough to glance at the nearby tables. It *was* Sam. And he was with another woman!

Belinda faltered, her eyes widening in disbelief as the woman looked up. Sheila? Her so-called best friend?

Irate, Belinda stomped over to their table and concentrated all her pent-up irritation on Sam. "What are *you* doing here?"

Sam leaned to look past her with a scowl. "I could ask you the same question. I saw you sitting over there with Randall."

"Leave him out of this. Where were you this morning? I had to leave for church without you."

"Had to? Or *wanted* to?" Sam asked. "I was only a couple of minutes late. You could have waited."

"You're *never* late. You told me so when you were giving me tips on punctuality. Remember?" She turned to her friend. "And as for you..."

"I tried to phone you first," Sheila insisted. "I left a message on your answering machine. Honest. Play it. You'll see."

In the back of her muddled mind Belinda did recall fast-forwarding through a confusing message from Sheila. Any other time she'd have been quick to acknowledge it. Right now, however, it was all she could do to keep from shouting.

Paul chose that instant to step behind her and explain. "I noticed the doctor was here. That was why I wanted you to stay at our table and eat your dessert." He made a token effort to take her arm. "Are you okay?"

"No. I am *not* okay," Belinda said angrily, jerking out of his grasp and stomping toward the exit. "Everything is a mess, especially me."

Paul followed. "Oh, I don't know. You look pretty good from here."

"Ha!" She straight-armed the door and plunged through. She wanted so badly to break her promise and tell him all about the candle that she had to grit her teeth to keep from doing it. In self-defense, she concentrated on her seething anger, instead. She was mad at everybody—Prudence, Sam, Sheila and Paul, not to mention being furious at herself for assuming the church fire had to have been caused by arson simply because that was what everyone else had believed.

"Can I take you home?" Paul asked quietly. "I don't think you should drive when you're so upset."

"I'm fine. I'm not upset," Belinda insisted.

"Then let me go get Aunt Prudence and we'll at least follow you."

Belinda had no intention of waiting for Paul to coax his weeping aunt out of the rest room. When he turned and entered the restaurant, she made a dash for her car and sped away.

Chapter Eleven

By the time Belinda got home, Sheila had left another message on her answering machine. This time, it was easier to tell what she was saying. Penitent, Belinda immediately returned the call.

"Oh, thank goodness, it's you!" Sheila burst out. "When you walked up to that table and got so mad I thought for sure you'd hate me forever."

"It's..."

"I know. It's inexcusable to go out with Sam and not tell you, only I didn't have the chance. He just showed up. I mean, we didn't have a date or anything. And by that time you weren't home. I know. I tried to phone you before I said I'd go anywhere with him. You'd told me you weren't serious about him, so..." She began to cry. "I'm so sorry."

"Whoa. I'm sorry, too. You caught me at a bad time, and I overreacted. I shouldn't have taken my frustrations out on you. I'd already made up my mind to stop seeing Sam, anyway.''

Sheila sniffled. ''You had? You're not just saying that to make me feel better?''

''I *do* want it to make you feel better,'' Belinda said, feeling lower than something that had just crawled out from under a wet, slimy rock, ''because it's the absolute truth.''

''Did you decide that on account of Paul? I about fell out of my chair when he walked up and grabbed you.''

''There you go, assuming things again. He did *not* grab me.'' Cradling the receiver, Belinda slipped off her shoes and plopped into a chair. Snuffy rolled over at her feet for her customary tummy rub, and Belinda rested her feet against the dog's ribs, wiggling her toes for Snuffy's pleasure.

''Well, he tried to,'' Sheila said. ''What was going on, anyway? When he hustled Miss Prudence out of the restaurant she looked like she'd been crying.''

''She had.'' Belinda sighed deeply, resolutely. ''I should be able to tell you all about what happened in a few days. I just can't say anything yet. It's really a miracle.''

''A miracle? What happened?'' Sheila giggled. ''I know, I know. You can't tell me.''

''Right.''

''What about Sam? Can you tell him? I sure hope so, because he was livid after you left. I kind of liked him, though, in spite of that. If you're not interested in him anymore, I just might be.''

"Go for it," Belinda urged. "You're a lot more worldly and well-traveled than I am, so maybe it will work out between you and Sam. I'm way too small-town for him. He doesn't understand the way I think. Or the things that are important to me.''

Sheila's voice quivered as she asked, ''You're sure you don't mind?''

"Not one bit." Their conversation had driven home the correctness of her earlier decision. ''The next time I see Sam I'm going to tell him, as gently as possible, that he and I are totally wrong for each other.''

"What if he gets mad again?''

Belinda chuckled. "I'd rather he got mad now than married me and found out the hard way that we could never be happy together.''

"I guess you're right," Sheila said with a sigh. "Well, good luck. You'll need it. Talk to you later. I've gotta go blow my nose.''

Hanging up, Belinda closed her eyes, folded her hands and turned her thoughts to God. *It's not luck I need, Father. It's divine guidance. I'm lost. I don't know what to ask You or how to ask it. How can I possibly keep Prudence's secret when it's already done so much damage? And how can I explain my feelings to Sam without hurting him or alienating him forever? And then there's Paul. What in the world am I going to do about him?*

There was no audible answer, no rushing of a mighty wind, no lightning bolt from heaven. Surrendering, Belinda let her heart continue the prayer wordlessly.

When she finally said amen, she had received a portion of the peace she so desperately sought.

Paul had tried all the way home to get his aunt to tell him what was bothering her. Several times she'd started to say something, then stopped.

Finally, he lost patience with her. "Whatever it is that's bugging you, I'm not going to drag it out of you," he said flatly. "If you don't want to confide in me, fine. Just stop crying every time you look at me, okay?"

"I can't," she wailed.

"Then either tell me or I'm leaving this house. Now."

"You'll hate me. Belinda already does. I know it."

Paul's heart began to beat faster. "What does this have to do with Belinda? Why should we both hate you?" He held his breath, waiting. "Well?"

When the elderly woman began to talk, there was no stopping her. She related the whole sordid story, going all the way back to her girlhood and the rivalry with her sister over the man they'd both loved. Paul managed to hold his tongue until she got to the part about accidentally starting the fire with a candle. Then he exploded with rage.

"All this time you kept quiet and let everybody think I did it? How could you do that? *How?*"

Weeping, Prudence managed to say, "I didn't mean any harm."

"Harm? You don't know half the harm you've done."

"I'll…I'll make it up to you, Paul. Somehow, I'll make it up to you. I promise I will."

His fists were clenched. The muscles in his jaw were twitching. "You bet you will, madam. Starting today."

"What are you going to do?" Prudence was wringing her hands and trembling visibly.

"I'm going to take your station wagon and go collect certain people so you can tell them the story you just told me," he informed her. "And the details had better be the same the second time around because I'm not going to let you hide behind your lies again. Got that?"

"Yes, Paul."

"Good. I'm glad we understand each other. Stay here and wait for me. I'll be back as soon as I can."

Eloise was in the back seat of the station wagon when Paul pulled up in front of Belinda's house and honked the horn instead of getting out.

The instant Belinda opened the door to see what was going on, Snuffy dashed out, barking wildly, to challenge their unexpected visitors.

Paul had the driver's window rolled down, and his

bent arm was resting in the opening. He didn't smile when he spoke to Belinda. "Put the dog back in the house and get in the car."

"I beg your pardon?" Belinda looked at his other passenger. "Gram? What's going on?"

"Beats me, honey. All I know is we're going to the Whitakers'. Paul says Prudence needs me. Don't dawdle. I want to get over there as fast as I can."

"I'll grab my sandals."

"You don't need shoes," Paul said gruffly. "Just an open mind, which should be a brand-new concept for you."

Belinda's heart was racing, her pulse pounding a painful cadence in her temples as she shut Snuffy in the house, slid her feet into her sandals and hurried to the car. Was this the news she'd been waiting for? Could Miss Prudence have told him the truth already? Judging by his mood, the chances were good that she had. In which case, there was really nothing to worry about.

She chose to climb in next to her grandmother instead of sitting up front with Paul. "It'll be okay, Gram," Belinda said quietly, trying to reassure her. "I'm positive everything will be all right."

Reving the engine, Paul snorted derisively. "Things will *never* be all right around here. That shouldn't surprise me. They never have been good in this narrow-minded little burg anyway, so why should I expect an improvement?"

By the time Paul finished his quest, he had collected Belinda, Eloise and Patience, whom he found having a long, intimate picnic lunch with Milton Boggs. Rather than relinquish his date, Milton had insisted on coming along. Paul had seen no reason to deny his request. Although Boggs was anything but impartial, it wouldn't hurt to include a spectator who had not been involved in the original fiasco.

Paul whipped his carload of witnesses into the Whitaker driveway, slid the station wagon to a stop and got out. "Okay. Everybody into the parlor. This won't take long."

Lagging, Belinda tried to catch his eye, intending to smile and let him know she sympathized. Rather than look at her as she'd hoped, however, Paul took the front steps two at a time and flung open the door as if he expected everyone else to follow without question, which they did.

By the time they reached the parlor, Paul had placed Prudence in a side chair in the center of the room and was hovering over her as if she were a hardened criminal.

"Sit down. All of you," he said to the others, waving his arm in the direction of the settee and sofa. "You're the jury."

"Then we're about eight people short," Belinda ventured bravely. It was obvious that Paul was so enraged he was overreacting, and she hoped to distract him enough to give him time to calm down. "Want me to run out and round up a few more folks?"

The angry glower he sent her way was enough to deter her completely. "Okay, okay. I'll sit," she said glumly, plunking down next to her grandmother.

Eloise leaned closer to whisper, "What's going on here?"

"You'll find out. Just be patient."

"But... Poor Pru looks awful."

"That doesn't surprise me much," Belinda conceded. Folding her arms across her chest, she settled back and waited for the mock trial to begin. It didn't take long.

Paul dispensed with the swearing in of the defendant and went straight to interrogating his aunt. "I want you to tell us, in your own words, who started the fire in the church ten years ago."

"I did."

Belinda heard Patience gasp and felt Eloise tense on the sofa beside her. *So far, so good.*

"And why did you do that?" Paul asked.

"It was an accident." Prudence dabbed at her misty eyes with a wadded-up hanky. "I didn't mean to do it."

"What were you doing in that church in the middle of the night in the first place?"

Prudence looked at him, her eyes pleading for mercy. "Do I have to say?"

"Yes. You do. We all deserve to hear it."

She lowered her gaze to her lap where she was nervously twisting the hanky. "I was meeting Eldon Lafferty."

Patience's resulting squeal sounded like a mouse with the croup. When Belinda looked around, Milton Boggs was patting the old woman's hands and whispering words of comfort.

Paul pressed on. "How did you know Mr. Lafferty would be there that night?"

"Because I'd arranged to meet him. Only he didn't know it was me. He thought he was meeting Sister."

"That's a lie!" Patience shrieked, shoving Milton aside so she could glare at her sister. "I haven't heard from that man for over fifty years."

"Yes, you have," Paul said, turning to face her. "Aunt Pru has a bunch of love letters that she stole before you ever saw them. Most of them were written right after Lafferty left town. A few are more recent."

"Letters to *me?*" Patience's tone was shrill, incredulous. "You mean Eldon wrote to me, just like he promised? How do you know?"

"Because I saw the letters myself," Paul said. "She had them hidden in a box she kept under her bed." He pointed toward a side table where an old tin strongbox sat at the edge of a white crocheted doily. "They're right there, if you want to see them. Right now, though, I suggest we all pay close attention to the rest of this story."

Patience fell silent, leaning on Milton's shoulder and gripping his arm for moral and physical support, as Paul continued to question the other twin. "What did you do when you got to the church that night?"

"I—I lit a candle and put it in the window of the church kitchen as a signal to Eldon, just like I'd promised. I was going to blow out the flame as soon as he got there, so he wouldn't see who it was, but my plan didn't work. Even after all those years he knew the difference between me and Sister." She sniffled, then continued. "He was furious. He started yelling and throwing things. I ran out of there as fast as I could."

Paul's voice deepened. "What happened to your candle?"

"I don't know. I swear I don't! I suppose it might have gotten knocked over or something. I forgot all about it until much later when I heard that the church was on fire."

"Or maybe Lafferty was so mad he started the fire on purpose," Paul ventured, glowering at her.

Prudence buried her face in her hands and began to weep. "I honestly don't know."

"Is that why you kept quiet and let me take the blame? Were you protecting your so-called lover?" Paul asked, hovering at the edge of self-control.

"No! I couldn't tell anybody what I'd done." She sobbed, trembling, her eyes pleading for forgiveness. "I didn't dare. What would people think of me? What would Sister think?"

Empathetic, Belinda interrupted before he could go on. "Okay, Paul, you don't have to be so hard on her. We've heard enough. What she did was horrible, but it's over."

"Horrible?" he repeated, whirling to confront her. "It wasn't nearly as horrible as what you did to me. At least Aunt Pru was acting out of love."

"And I *wasn't?*" Belinda jumped to her feet. "How dare you say that. I befriended you when nobody else would. I even lied to my father so I could sneak away to spend more time with you."

"Ah, but in the long run, you never really trusted me, did you?"

"What chance did you give me? You never stood up and defended yourself. You just ran like a scared rabbit when things got difficult. What was I supposed to think? What was *anybody* supposed to think?"

"Anybody who had loved me would have stood by me, no matter what," Paul said soberly.

"And if you had loved me, you'd have written, or called, or something. But no, you took off and left me behind to believe the worst."

"That was *your* choice, Belinda," he said with a knowing nod. "You could have come with me. I certainly asked you to often enough."

"And you could have stayed in Serenity."

"No. That's one thing you were right about when we discussed it the other day. There was nothing for me here."

I was here, she thought, fighting tears of loss and frustration. *I was here.*

Acting quickly, before she lost control completely,

broke down and gave away her true emotions, Belinda squared her shoulders and walked boldly out of the room, chin held high.

Paul let her go. In the background, both his aunts were crying. Milton was comforting Patience, and Eloise had her arms around Prudence.

The only person in the room without a visible comforter was Paul. Thankfully, he knew he wasn't alone. As always, the Lord was with him.

Thinking over what had just happened, Paul shook his head and sighed deeply. Finding out the truth had been the answer to his most fervent prayers, yet the resulting revelations had not healed the old wounds the way he'd imagined they would. If anything, he felt worse.

Belinda walked the four blocks from the Whitaker estate to her house as fast as she could, looking over her shoulder every time she heard an approaching car. If Paul chased after her she was going to flatly refuse to accept a ride home. No way was she going to get into any car with that man ever again. No, sir.

To her chagrin, the problem never came up. No one followed her. By the time she reached her house she was wringing wet with perspiration.

She'd always found that physical exertion was the best antidote for stress, so she slipped out of the damp yellow dress, donned lightweight work clothes, fastened her hair up with a big plastic spring-hinged clip and headed for the yard to take the rest of her aggressions out on garden weeds.

Fresh from a mad dash around the perimeter of the yard, Snuffy found a cool patch of shade and flopped down in it, panting heavily. Belinda was happy to have such uncritical companionship. "What's the matter, girl? Is it too hot out here for you?" She gave a stubborn weed a hard yank, shook the dirt off its roots and tossed it aside.

The little beagle's tail thumped in response to her indulgent tone. "You're smart to relax, baby. Smarter than I am." Belinda swiped the back of her hand across her brow to push aside her damp bangs without getting her face dirty. "At least you have short hair. Good thing you're not a collie, huh?" Rapid panting made the dog look like she was grinning in response to Belinda's silly comment.

On her hands and knees, Belinda leaned forward and reached for a clump of chickweed, accidentally connecting with a hidden sprig of puncture vine at the same time. That set her back on her heels in a big hurry. "Ow, ow, ow!"

Snuffy jumped into action, plunging into the flower bed in search of whatever had hurt her favorite human. Examining her hand through the layer of dirt, Belinda stopped worrying about her throbbing finger long enough to shout, "No! It's okay, girl. Come here. I'm fine."

Only she wasn't fine, was she? A painful sticker was only the most recent thorn in her flesh. Everybody else's life seemed to be getting better, while Belinda's fell apart. It looked like Paul was going to be able to negotiate a fair price for the Whitaker property, especially once she presented her brilliant tax scheme to Sam. Prudence was going to be able to afford a new place for herself and her gazillions of cats, plus, Lord willing, she was going to live long enough to see the family home restored to its former grandeur. Sam was going to be able to build his hospital just where he wanted it while looking like a philanthropist. And Sheila was happily exploring the possibilities of someday becoming a rich doctor's wife. Patience was a winner, too. She was going to be able to travel the way she'd always wanted, and it looked like she wasn't going to have to do it alone, either, thanks to her blossoming friendship with widower Milton Boggs.

The beagle chose that moment to crowd into Belinda's lap and lunge up to lick her face. "And I have you, don't I," she said, lovingly hugging her little dog. "You might not be a very good conversationalist, but you stick with me, which is more than I can say for some people I know."

Sensitive to her melancholy mood, Snuffy quieted and went back to her favorite shady spot to lie down. Belinda knew the dog had more sense than she did, at least with regard to the afternoon heat, but if she quit weeding and went inside to rest she'd have way too much time to think. To feel sorry for herself.

Which was a ridiculous, unacceptable response to the blessings the good Lord had bestowed upon others.

Determined to banish her negative thoughts before she quit gardening, Belinda got on her hands and knees again and leaned under the spent peony bushes to get at the farthest weeds. She was so preoccupied with her emotional involvement in other people's lives and the continuing throbbing of her injured finger, she failed to hear a car come to a stop in the driveway.

The first inkling she had that something was amiss was when she felt Snuffy scampering back and forth across her bare calves and whining for attention. "Ouch. Stop that. Your nails are sharp!"

"Funny," a masculine voice mocked. "I had a manicure last week."

"Paul! What are you doing here?" Belinda rose too quickly. Her springy hair clip snagged on the stems of the peony bush. Instinctively, she pulled away. Instead of providing freedom, that only poked more branches into her hair, leaving her snared in a hopeless tangle of dead leaves and twigs. Worse, she suddenly imagined she felt the tickling of insects on the back of her neck.

"I was taking your grandmother home. She insisted we stop by on the way to check on you. Besides, I needed to apologize for losing my temper earlier."

At that moment, Belinda was more interested in the presence of her most loyal supporter than in

Paul's penitence. "Gram? Are you there?" she shouted. "Help! Get me out of here!"

Paul answered instead. "Eloise is waiting in the car. Her sore ankle has started to bother her again. What are you doing under there in the first place?"

"Weeding." *As if he couldn't tell.*

"You never heard of doing it with a hoe?"

"You don't have to be sarcastic," she grumbled. "Are you going to just stand there or are you going to help me?"

"I'll see what I can do."

"Hurry. I'm getting itchy!" She felt the side of his leg brush against her waist, then saw his shoe on the ground beside her. It was one of those fancy leather loafers. Probably Italian. And no doubt expensive, she thought with disdain. There she was, wearing old, tattered clothing, her hands caked with dirt and her hair doing a good imitation of an abandoned bird's nest, while Paul remained utterly refined, as usual. When he'd changed his image from wild teen on a motorcycle to professional man, he'd certainly done a thorough job.

"Stop wiggling," he ordered. "I'm almost done."

Belinda didn't think she'd moved a muscle. "You try holding still with bugs crawling down your neck and see how well *you* do."

"No, thanks." Paul stepped away, holding part of the bush out of her way. "There. See if you can back up."

Relieved, she crawled out of the trap and staggered

to her feet, immediately edging away from him. Clearly, he thought her plight was comical. His lips were twitching in a suppressed grin, and his eyes were sparkling with wit.

"What's so funny?"

"You are." He eyed her critically.

"I wasn't expecting company," Belinda offered in her own defense, dusting her hands off on her already grubby shorts.

"Let's hope not. So, have you talked to Sam lately?"

"Not since the restaurant. Why?"

"I phoned him a few minutes ago. He bought your idea about turning the Whitaker house into a historical site."

"What about his hospital? Is he going to put it somewhere else?"

"No. He won't have to. He'll split off the one lot with the old house on it, just like you suggested to Aunt Pru, and save even more money than you figured because he won't have to pay to have it demolished, either."

"Oh, good. Then everybody will be a winner, just like I'd hoped. I was afraid Sam would be really hardheaded, especially if he knew I'd come up with the idea."

Paul made a nonverbal noise that sounded like, "Humpf," then smiled. "He probably would have been, if he'd guessed. Which is why I let him think it was *my* idea."

"You what?"

"I said, I let him think it was my idea. Is that a problem for you?"

"Yes. No." She grimaced. "I guess not."

"Good. We should have the whole deal put together in a few days."

She knew what that meant. "So, you'll be leaving?"

"As fast as I can," Paul said soberly. "I can't wait to get away from this town."

"Do you hate it that much?"

"More."

Shading her eyes with one hand, Belinda squinted at Paul. "I'm sorry. About everything."

He shrugged as he turned to leave. "Yeah. Me, too."

Chapter Twelve

Belinda kept to herself, brooding, for the rest of the day. By evening she was no closer to deciding why she felt so out of sorts. Prudence's confession had provided a direct answer to her prayers about Paul's innocence, so why was she feeling so miserable? So bereft?

"Because finding out the truth didn't make any difference," she finally admitted. "Paul still hates Serenity and he's still leaving." She knew she was going to miss him more than ever now that she'd met the man he'd become. And been kissed by that man. Boy, had she been kissed! The memory of being in his arms was so vivid it made her tremble.

She plopped on the couch, picked up the newspaper and turned to the television schedule. The little beagle rolled over at her feet, begging for more tummy rubs. Belinda obliged. "Well, here we are," she said cynically. "Just you and me, Snuffy. Another exciting evening in paradise, parked in front of the TV set till we nod off. Whoop-de-do."

Snuffy's tail thumped. "Yeah, I know," Belinda said. "I don't feel like just sitting here, either, but I'm not going to let you go outside and chase wild bunnies. You might actually catch one someday, and then I'd feel terrible. Besides, it's almost dark."

Sighing, Belinda got to her feet and paced across the room to the bank of windows above the alcove in her dining room. Outside, fireflies had begun their evening courting ritual. That reminded her of Paul. Of course, so did everything else. To be awake, to breathe, was to think of him. If she had to remain in the house with nothing to do but rehash the things she should have said, the things she should have done, she'd be climbing the walls or swinging from the rafters in another hour.

She decided to leave Snuffy inside for safekeeping and go outside to water her drooping Shasta daisies and refill the dog's water bucket. The tasks weren't a necessity as much as they were a diversion, one she desperately needed.

Belinda was concentrating on keeping the trigger sprayer on the hose nozzle depressed just enough to provide a fine mist for the flowers when she noticed a black Lexus parked across the street.

Speaking of thinking of Paul all the time! Unfortunately, the car couldn't be his. Judging by his morose mood the last time she'd bid him goodbye, she didn't expect him to ever return.

She frowned. Then whose black car was it? In a county where the pickup truck was practically the official vehicle, there weren't a lot of luxury cars of any kind, let alone another one that looked like that. And besides, why would a strange car be parked in her neighborhood?

The hair on the back of her neck prickled. Uneasy, she stopped watering and held her breath to listen to the sounds of the night. A whippoorwill called. Somewhere far off, hounds were baying at the moon. Belinda felt a sudden jolt of apprehension. Either she had another bug crawling down her shirt or something in the surrounding atmosphere was making her strangely nervous.

Even small towns had their share of crime, she reminded herself, although it had been months since anything serious had happened anywhere near Serenity. Still, it was getting pretty dark, and she was out here all by herself. The one time she might need them to watch out for her welfare, there was no sign of her nosy neighbors.

A dry stick cracked behind her. Her grip on the spray nozzle tightened. Wheeling, she aimed and fired!

Paul howled like he'd been shot, which frightened Belinda even more and prolonged her counterattack. In the long seconds before she realized she hadn't been in danger in the first place, he was drenched.

Finally, she released the trigger. "Oops."

"*Oops?* Is that all you have to say for yourself?"

"Well, you don't have to get huffy. You shouldn't have been sneaking up on me in the dark like that. You scared me silly."

"I wasn't sneaking up on you," he insisted. "I was walking around the yard looking for you. I knocked on the front door, but Snuffy was the only one who answered."

"I never heard her barking."

"Are you saying you don't believe me? I thought we'd settled all that nonsense this afternoon." He brushed at his soggy shirtfront and shook the drops of water off his hands, mumbling to himself. "This shirt was silk. If I'd known you were going to attack me again I'd have worn the one with the spaghetti sauce stains."

"What did you come back for?" Belinda asked.

"Hey, I'm glad to see you, too."

She blushed, embarrassed at the unfriendly tone of her question. "Let me rephrase that. Hello, Paul. Nice to see you. What brings you here tonight?"

"I forgot something."

"Like what?"

"To ask you a favor. I meant to do it when I stopped by to apologize this afternoon. I want us all to keep Aunt Prudence's secret. Her reputation means a lot to her, and I figure mine is already trashed, so why stir up old sins?"

Belinda was both relieved and happy. "You mean you aren't mad at her anymore? You forgive her?"

"I'm working on it," Paul said with a frown. Looking at his shirt, he added, "If I'd dreamed you'd be this unhappy to see me, I'd have phoned instead."

"I didn't squirt you on purpose," she insisted.

"Oh, yeah? Then why didn't you stop when you realized it was me? It's not *that* dark out here."

Belinda's righteous indignation rose. "I did stop."

"Right. You just have really slow reflexes for your age. That's how I got this wet." Keeping an eye on her, Paul bent, turned the valve and shut off the water supply to her makeshift weapon.

"*Now* who's not being trusting?" she demanded.

"Me." Gaze steady, movements purposeful, he straightened with the dog's water bucket in hand, holding it by its wire handle. "Fortunately, I found something to defend myself with."

"Now, Paul…" Still clutching the hose, Belinda began to back away as he walked toward her with the sloshing bucket. She heard another car approaching. It stopped in her driveway. Judging by the familiar sound of the engine, it was Sam's Camaro.

"Sam! Over here," Belinda called. "I need your help."

"What the…" The doctor's choice of a colorful exclamation was *not* one she approved of.

"Go turn the hose on for me. Hurry!" she shouted. Bracing for the surge of water, she fully expected him to comply. Instead, he came up behind her and peered at her as if she were demented. Shocked, she spun halfway around. "Sam! The water!"

That was all the diversion Paul needed. He drew back and let fly, launching the entire contents of the bucket in one mighty throw.

Belinda saw a flash of movement and a glimmer of reflected moonlight out of the corner of her eye. Acting purely on instinct, she ducked. Most of the water sailed right over her head.

She let out a high-pitched shriek, then gasped and started to howl with laughter. Paul's drenching assault had caught Sam full in the face! He was sputtering like an inept diver coming up for air after a hard belly flop.

Belinda couldn't decide which man looked the most astonished, the aggressor or his accidental victim. She always got giddy when she was overtired or stressed out, but her ensuing attack of the giggles was worse than usual. The expression on Sam's face was the most hilarious thing she'd ever seen!

Laughing so hard she was doubled over, she fought to catch her breath. Tears rolled down her cheeks. If she lived to be older than Paul's maiden aunts, she doubted she'd ever see anything this funny again.

Paul was the first to recover from the mishap. He put down the empty bucket and approached Sam with his hand extended in implied friendship. "Sorry about that, Doc. My target ducked," he said affably.

Though she was still laughing too hard to speak, Belinda did manage to punch him lightly in the ribs. Sadly, Sam was not taking their mock altercation nearly as well as Paul. Of course, Paul wasn't the one who'd been drowned in warm, greenish dog water, either. She'd scrubbed all the algae out of Snuffy's bucket a few days ago, but it had apparently grown brackish quickly, thanks to the hot weather.

Sam took a handkerchief from his pocket and wiped his face as he glowered at her. "Do you have any idea how inappropriately you're behaving?"

She'd just about regained the power of speech when his overbearing attitude started her giggles all over again. The most she could manage was, "Uh-huh."

"This won't do, Belinda. I have a professional image to maintain in this town."

"Uh…"

"I can't have you playing kid games with some delinquent from your past. Is that understood?"

"Uh…" She gasped for breath. "I… I…don't think you and I are…right for each other, Sam." He looked so flabbergasted she added, "I've been trying to tell you that for *ages*."

"You're overwrought. You don't mean it."

Belinda had laughed so hard her cheeks hurt. Taking a deep, settling breath, she cast the doctor a sympathetic look. "I do mean it. It's over between us, Sam. You'll make a great husband for some lucky woman someday, it's just not going to be me."

Brow furrowed, Sam looked from her to Paul and back again. "I see."

"No, you *don't* see," Belinda insisted. "This isn't about Paul. It's about us. You and I fell into our relationship because it was convenient. We never were right for each other."

Paul was just getting a handle on his emotional reaction to her vow that her personal problems had nothing to do with him when she decided to elaborate.

"You and Paul have the same problem, Sam. You both want me to be something I'm not. You're looking for a woman who can be a polished, refined doctor's wife, and he needs someone who loves living in the city and can fit into the new image he's created for himself. I don't belong in *either* role."

"You could if you'd try," Sam argued.

"I'm not a chameleon. I'm a person. This is the way God made me."

Chin jutting out proudly, Belinda looked both masterful and ready to cry. Paul stiffened, ready to intercede if necessary, when Sam grasped her by the shoulders, held her fast and said, "That's utter nonsense. People change all the time."

"Only if they *want* to!" Jerking free, she backed out of reach, bumped into Paul's chest and whirled around, gesturing wildly. "Ask him. He's done it. He's *nothing* like the guy I used to love."

Totally frustrated and suddenly bone weary, Belinda threw her hands in the air, gawked at the two men and shouted, "Aaaah! I give up. You're both hopeless." Pushing past Paul, she grabbed the business end of the hose and stalked toward the faucet. "Anybody who's not out of here by the time I turn this water on is going to get soaked. Got that?"

"I'm certainly not going to stick around," Sam declared, heading for his car. "She's crazy."

Belinda watched him go, then shifted her focus to Paul. "Well? Are you going to stand there and get wet or be smart and join him?"

"Neither." Slowly he began to advance.

"Don't do it," she warned. "I meant what I said."

"I don't doubt it." He'd almost reached her.

Belinda gritted her teeth and took aim. "Don't make me do this."

"I'm not going to *make* you do anything." Moving so fast his hands were a blur, Paul deflected the hose and grasped both her wrists at the same time, pushing them behind her back and holding them there. That eliminated the danger of his being squirted. It also brought Belinda's body too close for comfort.

Caught tightly against him, she froze, barely breathing. Paul was coping pretty successfully with the emotional impact of her nearness until she tilted her head back and looked directly into his eyes.

That was enough to obliterate what was left of his self-control. No matter what she said about him, what she thought of him, there was no doubt she wanted him to kiss her. He *knew* it. From his heart all the way to his befuddled mind, he knew it.

Positive he was right, he quit fighting the urge, lowered his head and kissed her. Soundly.

The moment Belinda realized what Paul was going to do she closed her eyes and surrendered. They may as well have been the only two people in the world for all the attention she paid to what any passerby would think. If her hands had been free she'd have wrapped 'her arms around his neck and pulled him even closer.

I'm making beautiful memories, she told herself. *That's all.* She desperately wanted to be sure she'd remember Paul, above everyone else, when he was long gone.

A few more moments like this and I may remember him so well I'm ruined for any other man's kisses, she thought absently, remembering how miserable both Whitaker sisters had been over the loss of their mutual lover.

Paul deepened the kiss. The spray nozzle fell from Belinda's fingers. *I love you,* she mused. *I should tell you that. No matter how embarrassing it is for me, or how you take the news, I should tell you while I still can.*

Frightened by the insistence of her thoughts, she opened her eyes, meaning to look deeply into Paul's, to try to decide if he shared her love before she spoke out of turn and made a worse fool of herself than she already had.

The corner of her eye caught a glimpse of movement. *Gram!* Her grandmother had a shovel raised over her head like a baseball bat and was aiming for Paul's head!

Belinda tried to twist away. Staring, eyes wide with alarm, she heard Eloise warn, "Let her go, mister, or I'll scramble your brains. That is, if you've got any."

Paul straightened so fast he nearly dropped Belinda onto the grass. Staggering, he regained his balance and righted her, too. "Whoa!" he declared loudly. "This isn't what it looks like."

Eloise didn't relax her stance. "It better not be, or I'll fetch the sheriff."

Belinda hurried to relieve her of the shovel and quickly placed it out of reach. "It's okay, Gram. We were just clowning around and…"

"Didn't look to me like either one of you was foolin'. I could hardly believe my ears when Liz Finnegan phoned."

"Well, that explains a lot," Belinda said, making a face at the house across the street. "I didn't think she was even home tonight. What in the world did she tell you?"

"That there was an awful row goin' on, right in front of your place. Said it looked like there was going to be a fight and I should get on over here as fast as I could. She didn't say anything about hanky-panky, though."

"No, but I'm sure she will." Belinda sounded as

disgusted as she felt. She looked at Paul. "I think you'd better go. If I know Liz, she's probably called the police. There's no sense in you getting involved if you don't have to be."

He snorted. "I'm not going to leave you to deal with this alone."

"I'm not alone. Gram is here. Go on. Go away before you get me in any more trouble."

If she hadn't been smiling he would have been worried that she might actually be blaming him for everything that had happened. He supposed he did have to take some of the responsibility for their kiss, though it had occurred on the spur of the moment. The rest of Belinda's problems, however, had been around a lot longer than he had. And they'd still be there when he was long gone.

The idea that Belinda might change her mind and eventually reconcile with Sam—even marry him— gave Paul's gut a sharp twist. It was none of his business what she did or didn't do. Feeling out of sorts, he tried to convince himself he didn't care. He'd left Serenity once without looking back, and he intended to do it again. Soon. End of discussion.

Mustering his best look of indifference, he nodded a polite goodbye in Belinda's direction, stuck his hands into his pockets, turned and walked away.

Belinda pulled aside the ruffled curtain and peeked out her kitchen window, watching Paul's car drive off. "Well, he's gone, Gram."

"For good, I hope."

"I don't." Belinda sighed and sat at the kitchen table across from Eloise, leaned forward and propped her chin in her hands. "I'm really going to miss him."

"Miss him? You two fight all the time."

"We don't fight. Not the way you mean, anyway. Paul and I just enjoy teasing each other."

"Is that how he got so wet tonight?" Eloise asked, one eyebrow arching.

"Ha! If you think Paul was wet, you should have seen Sam! He took a whole gallon of Snuffy's water right in the face. What a sight!"

"You didn't laugh at him in front of Paul, did you?"

"Nope. I roared," Belinda bragged, chuckling at the memory. "Don't worry. Everything worked out for the best. Sam started lecturing me about my undignified conduct and that gave me the perfect opportunity to explain how wrong he and I were for each other."

The stiffness went out of the older woman's posture, and she sagged back in her chair. "You really are serious about this, aren't you?"

"Deadly serious. I don't care if I wind up like Miss Patience or Miss Prudence. I'd rather stay single than settle for less than the man I love."

Sighing and shaking her head sadly, Eloise looked at her lovely granddaughter with tears in her eyes. "Don't."

"Don't what?"

"Don't settle. If you're sure Paul Randall is the only man for you, then you need to go after him and tell him so. If he really loves you, he'll come around."

Belinda couldn't believe the pep talk she was hearing. "Do you think it's possible? He said he hated Serenity."

"Did he say he loved you?"

"Well, no. Not in words. But I sensed it."

"Then go to him. Talk to him. Tell him how you feel. It's a calculated risk, of course, but I can see one of two things happening. Either he'll brush you off, or he'll ask you to marry him. If you love him as much as you say you do, you should be brave enough to force the issue and accept the consequences, whatever they are."

Paul didn't go straight to the Whitakers'. No place seemed like home to him anymore. Not without Belinda. It was as if she'd become such an intrinsic part of him, of his life, there was no peace or satisfaction to be found anywhere when they were apart.

He raked the fingers of one hand through his hair, pushing it back as he drove aimlessly. No matter how many times he told himself he was better off without her, he still couldn't make the idea sound plausible. Life without Belinda was life without zest, without harmony, without fulfillment.

And yet, life *with* her promised to be an impossible

challenge unless she was willing to relocate to Harrison with him. He considered the probability that she might. Stranger things had happened lately. Like Aunt Pru's confession, for instance. If he'd made a thousand wild guesses he'd never have suspected that she was the culprit who set fire to the church. Or that the destruction had been accidental.

Poor Prudence. No wonder she'd always brooded so much, been so unhappy. Losing the love of your life could ruin the ensuing years and leave a person bitter. That bitterness stole whatever daily joy you did manage to find.

Like losing Belinda, Paul told himself. Did she love him? Probably. But did she love him *enough?* That was the most important question. If he didn't ask it, he'd never know, would he? Maybe in the morning he'd…

No. Now, his heart and soul insisted. *Don't wait. Go to her now.*

"I can't go like this," Paul argued, looking down at his damp, wrinkled shirt. "And if I go home and change it'll be awfully late."

It's already ten years late, you dolt, his subconscious countered. *A few more minutes won't matter.*

Belinda's hair was still damp from her shower. She'd wrapped a towel around her head like a turban and was sitting on the couch in her robe when there was a knock at the door. Snuffy, who'd been napping at her feet, came off the floor running, howling and barking.

Cautious, Belinda quieted the dog, then called through the locked door, "Who is it?"

"Me. Let me in."

"Paul?" Her heart threatened to gallop out of her chest. "I can't. I'm not dressed."

"Well, *get* dressed," he ordered. "We have to talk."

"Maybe in the morning." She heard him start to pace and talk to himself. From the tone of his mutterings, she decided it was just as well that she couldn't make out most of what he was saying. Worried, she eased open the door a crack and peeked at him. He'd changed to dry clothes but he still looked pretty frazzled.

The moment he spied her eye peeking through the slit he bent to her level and stared, his gaze narrowing. "Not in the morning. Now. Unless you want me to camp on your porch all night and give your nosy neighbors something else to gossip about."

"Okay. Stay right there," Belinda told him. "Don't go away. I'll be out in a jiffy." She slammed the door and ran for her bedroom, almost tripping over Snuffy as the little beagle joined in the exciting game her mistress was evidently playing.

Giddy beyond belief, Belinda talked aloud. "What in the world am I going to wear? It's not fair! This is all happening too soon. My hair isn't dry and I haven't had enough time to rehearse my speech! And, and…''

Frantic, she began to toss outfits onto her bed, rejecting each tentative choice. *Something not too fancy and not too casual. Appealing but not too sexy.*

She finally settled on a simple white sheath, dislodging the towel when she pulled the dress over her head. Her hair was a damp, tangled mess. She'd prayed for the chance to see Paul again, but not when she looked like *this.* How did the Lord expect her to make a good enough impression to convince the poor man she'd be the perfect choice for his wife when she looked like a drowned rat?

Stopping in the middle of her bedroom, Belinda spread her hands wide, closed her eyes, took a deep breath and consciously gave her will over to God. ''Okay. I prayed about it and You sent him, Father. This is Your party. You run it, and I'll try to stay out of Your way.'' A slight smile lifted the corners of her mouth as she added, ''I might need a little help with that part, but then You already know that, don't You?''

The sense of peace she got from her prayer stayed with her until she reached the front door, opened it and saw the look of anguish and longing on Paul's face. Then he reached for her, cupped her cheek with his palm, and she forgot all about her promise to God.

Dreamy-eyed, Belinda moved her head against his

hand to encourage his caress as she slipped her arms around his waist. "I'm so glad you came back."

"Are you?"

She nodded. "Uh-huh. I was going to come looking for you in the morning, anyway."

"You were?"

Paul's lips were so near to hers when he spoke, she could feel the warmth of his breath, imagine the sweetness of his kiss once more. Everything was going to be all right. She could feel it all the way to her toes. "Yes. I didn't want you to get away from me again." Raising her gaze to his, she gathered her courage and whispered, "I love you too much to let you go without putting up a fight."

Relieved beyond belief, Paul took her face in both hands, his thumbs caressing her cheeks, his eyes growing misty with suppressed emotion. There was hope, after all. This was their second chance. The answer to his fondest dreams. He was older. Wiser. And he now had the resources to make Belinda happy, if she'd only let him. He took the chance she would.

"There's one way to guarantee that we'll always be together," he murmured.

Belinda stared at him, her lips parted, her brain whirling. Could he mean what she thought he meant, what she wanted him to mean? Or was her vivid imagination playing tricks on her again? She had to ask. "How?"

"Simple. You marry me."

Time stopped while Belinda struggled to believe what she was hearing. Could it be that her prayers had been answered so fast, so miraculously? It was Paul's look of happy expectation that finally convinced her how serious he was.

Ecstatic, she threw herself at him and kissed him with all the fervor she'd been saving for the man she would one day wed. "Oh, Paul! Yes, yes, yes. I love you so much!"

Years of unfulfilled longing, suddenly freed, surged from his subconscious, threatening to overwhelm him. Belinda, his Belinda, had just agreed to be his wife!

Breathing hard, Paul yearned to sweep her in his arms and carry her off like a princess being liberated from a dungeon. He realized he'd have to take immediate charge of the situation before they *both* got carried away by their mutual passion. It was that or say goodbye to what remained of his tenuous self-control and be sorry later.

He pulled her arms from around him, drew her hands against his chest and forced himself to step back. The love shining in her eyes was the most beautiful sight he'd ever seen. Happily, all the plans he'd made when he'd thought he was merely entertaining a foolish daydream about their future together could be put to real use.

Smiling, he said, "You won't have to worry about a thing, honey. I've already got most of our problems figured out. I'm not very well connected in the real estate business, in spite of my work on my aunts' behalf, so we will need to find a good Realtor.''

"Sure. Fine,'' she agreed sweetly. What a joy it was to picture him as a permanent part of her everyday life! What a blessing. It was amazing how quickly Paul's attitude about living in Serenity had changed. Love could do that, she supposed. To think that he was willing to give up everything just to make her happy!

"Good.'' He placed a tender kiss on her forehead. "I'm not sure how good the market is right now. If your place doesn't sell right away we can probably rent it. My condo in Harrison is plenty big enough for both of us.''

Belinda's hopes crashed in a whirl of jumbled emotion. "*What* did you say?''

"I was talking about my condo.'' Paul started to frown. "Uh-oh. I just remembered. The rules don't allow dogs. I'll bet Eloise would keep Snuffy for you until…''

"Whoa!'' She flattened her palms on his chest and firmly pushed him away. "What are you talking about? I'm not selling my house. And I'm certainly not giving my *dog* away.'' She stared at Paul as if seeing him for the first time. "How could you even ask such a thing?''

"Because it's the most logical option,'' he said, puzzled by her strong negative reaction. "At least for now. Your house is way too small. I need room for a home office with a computer, fax, copier…you know."

"Not to mention the fact that my place also happens to be located in Serenity?"

He didn't argue. "That, too. Of course."

Other serious complications were beginning to occur to Belinda now that she'd stopped being so overwhelmed by her runaway emotions. "What about my job? Have you thought of that?"

Paul slipped an arm around her shoulders and tried to pull her to his side. To his surprise, she resisted. "Don't worry about working. I told you I'd take care of you." Amused at her standoffish attitude and the childish scowl on her face, he chuckled. "You've got to stop seeing me as the penniless kid who begged you to run away with him on the back of his motorbike."

"This isn't about *money!*" She was so incensed, so disappointed, she grabbed his wrist and whipped his arm off her shoulders so she could face him squarely. "It's about caring what the other person thinks. You never even asked me if I wanted to leave Serenity."

"You know how I feel about this town. You couldn't have thought I'd agree to live *here*." Paul had to fight to keep his voice calm. Clearly, his expectations of recapturing their lost love and building a secure future with Belinda had been overly optimistic.

"Why not?" she shouted. "You want to drag me

to Harrison where I don't know a soul. How is that any better?''

"Well, for starters, nobody there hates your guts," Paul countered, trying to get her to appreciate the dissimilarity of their situations. She was free to go anywhere, do anything, while he was tied to a law practice that had taken years to build. It was a four-hour round-trip commute to Harrison, half of it on winding, two-lane roads. Even if he were willing to consider such an idiotic daily schedule, the long, tedious drives would leave him so worn out he'd be lucky to be awake during the day, let alone intellectually keen enough to do his clients any good.

Sighing with resignation, he said, "I can see I've made a big mistake. You care more about this town than you do about me. Why don't we just forget I said anything about marriage. It would never work."

She wanted to shout. To argue. To contradict him. But she couldn't. Paul was right. There was no way to refute his disheartening conclusions. Biting her lower lip so she wouldn't start to cry and make a fool of herself, Belinda folded her arms across her chest in a posture guaranteed to protect what little was left of her pride. "Don't worry," she said with as much rancor as she could muster, "I won't sue you for breach of promise. I don't know a good lawyer."

With a snort of disgust, he wheeled and stalked off the porch. Belinda's heart was breaking. How could he just give up and walk away like that? Didn't he love her enough to at least try to work out their differences?

Suddenly, she realized what crucial ingredient had been missing from Paul's marriage proposal. He'd planned the details of their future, all right, but he hadn't said the words that might have made it all work.

He'd never told her he loved her. Not once.

Chapter Thirteen

Belinda moped around for the next week and a half. The only one she confided in was Snuffy, and that was simply because the dog could never repeat anything that might reveal how badly she ached to be with Paul in spite of everything that had gone wrong between them.

Guilt was one of her biggest problems. In the course of praying for enlightenment, she realized she'd blamed Paul for not considering her side of their impasse while doing *exactly* the same thing to him.

In contrast, Sheila was delivering daily reports on her budding romance with Sam. Belinda was genuinely happy about that. If Sam had been grieving over their breakup she'd have felt responsible for his unhappiness, too.

She was sitting on her porch steps, enjoying the

cool evening air and scratching Snuffy's droopy ears, when her grandmother strolled up with a cheery greeting. "Hi, honey."

"Hi, Gram." Belinda eyed the older woman's empty hands. "No cookies?"

"Not today." Eloise tested the dirt in the flower bed with the toe of her sneaker. "Your snapdragons are thirsty."

"Probably."

"Hmm." She plopped down on the porch beside Belinda. "So. Have you had any word from Paul Randall lately?"

"No." To fill the heavy silence Belinda asked, "Why? Have you?" When Eloise surprised her by saying yes, she whipped around so fast she nearly slid off the step. "You have? What? When? Is the Whitaker deal closed?"

"If you mean, is Paul coming back here to take care of the contract the way we all thought he would, no."

Belinda's heart lodged in her throat. "No?" The word barely squeaked out beside it.

"No. Pru says the escrow company was able to fax all the necessary papers to his office for his approval. It doesn't look like he'll have to visit Serenity at all."

Staring into the distance, focusing on nothing, Belinda sensed the intensity of Eloise's questioning gaze. It made her feel like a bug trapped under a microscope. Or a kid with a sinful secret. Telling the dog her private thoughts had helped ease her conscience to begin with but she could see it was time to confide in a real person.

"When I told Paul how I felt about him he did ask me to marry him, just like I'd hoped," she confessed.

"Why didn't you *tell* me? When did this happen?"

"The night before he left."

"Well, well." Eloise's initial grin faded as she took note of her granddaughter's solemn expression. "You don't seem very happy. You didn't turn him down, did you?"

"No. Actually, I said yes." Sniffing quietly in self-contempt, Belinda shook her head. "But that was before he told me he wanted me to sell my house and go away with him."

"Excuse me?" Eloise scowled. "What's wrong with that?"

"Nothing. Everything." Throwing herself backward, Belinda rested her upper body on the porch floor, cradled her head in her hands and stared at the pink-tinged clouds of early evening. "He never even asked me what I wanted to do, Gram. He just told me how it was going to be."

"And you contradicted him with loving understanding and Christian forbearance, like the Good Book says, right?"

"Not exactly."

"Oh?" Eloise smiled indulgently. "What *did* you say?"

"I don't have a clue. I've gone back over that scene so many times, rehearsing what I *should* have said, I can't tell fact from fiction anymore."

"Well, since Paul's left and you haven't heard a word from him, I take it the outcome was not good."

Sitting up, Belinda made a throaty sound of derision. "Humpf. No kidding. If he'd just asked my opinion instead of telling me what to do..."

"You'd have told *him* what to do."

"Well, yes." Pulling a face, she let her frustration show. "I've lived in Serenity all my life. You're here. All my friends are here. Momma and Daddy are buried here. This is my life."

"It is so far," Eloise said wisely. "The question is, are you going to play it safe and turn into a hermit like poor Prudence or are you going to trust the Lord, step out on faith and meet your future head-on?"

"I always trust God," Belinda insisted.

"As long as you're comfortable, you do. Most of us are like that. It's when we're troubled or confused that our true nature shows. You were perfectly willing to support harmony and forgiveness between Pru and her sister, but you're not ready to do the same for yourself."

"Do you think I should leave Serenity? Is that what you're saying?" Tears rimmed her eyes.

Eloise put a motherly arm around her granddaughter's shoulders. "Not necessarily. I'm not the one who has to decide what's most important to you. You are.'' She leaned closer to kiss her on the cheek. ''Have you prayed about whether or not you should leave here to be with Paul?''

The truth hit Belinda like a bolt of lightning on an otherwise sunny day. She'd asked God for help and strength and a lot of other things lately, including Paul Randall's love on a silver platter, but she'd failed to ask for the Lord's *advice*. ''Um, no. Not exactly.''

''And why is that, do you suppose?''

''Probably because I don't want to get an answer I don't like,'' Belinda admitted softly, reluctantly.

''You *are* getting smarter in your old age,'' Eloise teased. ''Just remember, whatever you decide, I'm on your side. I think Paul is, too.''

''He sure had a funny way of showing it.''

Laughing, Eloise shook her head. ''I'll bet if I asked him, he'd say the same thing about you.''

Paul was determined to forget what a fool he'd been to propose to Belinda. Forgetting was a good idea. A logical idea. Only the harder he tried to put her out of his mind, the more his heart magnified the love that made forgetting impossible.

It took him ten days to narrow his choices down to only two. Simply put, he could either do things her way or let her go. After finally hurdling the worst barriers to their happiness and proving his innocence, letting her go was unthinkable. So was resigning himself to a lifetime spent in Serenity.

Grumbling, Paul stalked out to his car and slid behind the wheel, then sat there for a moment, thinking. He could do this. He had to do this. Life with Belinda might be the most difficult challenge he'd ever accepted, but life without her was no life at all.

"I have a map to get me to Harrison and Paul's business card with his office address," Belinda told her grandmother. "Snuffy's dry dog food is in the big plastic can next to the washing machine. As long as she has plenty of water she can stay out in my back yard during the day, even in hot weather. Just don't forget to keep the gate latched."

Eloise laughed. "I won't. Don't worry about us. We always get along fine. I'll even take her home with me and let her help me bake some doggie cookies if she gets bored."

"I'm glad I won't be here to see that," Belinda said, rolling her eyes.

"Take all the time you need. No hurry coming back."

"I'm not going to throw myself at the man, if that's what you mean." Belinda glanced at the load of personal possessions filling the back seat of her car. "First I'll rent my own place so he doesn't get the wrong idea about why I'm there. After that, we'll see."

"I certainly hope so," her grandmother said. "You deserve a dose of happiness."

"I don't deserve Paul. Not after the awful way I snapped at him. I wasn't seeing things from his point of view at all."

"I'm sure he'll understand when you explain it to him." She kissed Belinda's cheek and gave her a hug. "Now, get out of here before I start to boo hoo and spoil your trip."

I'm doing the right thing, Belinda insisted. Waving goodbye to the dearest person in the world, she started for Harrison and a confrontation with her future.

Correction. Gram was the *second* dearest person in the world. The dearest one was an attractive, stubborn man who was going to listen to her apology if she had to hog-tie him to make him sit still long enough. And while he was at it, he'd better admit he loved her, too, or else.

Paul went straight to Belinda's as soon as he hit town. No familiar barking greeted his arrival. Walking all the way around the house, he peeked in the windows.

"Might as well give up." The woman's shrill voice came from across the street. "She's gone."

He shaded his eyes with his hand so he could see the informant as he started to his car. "Where did she go?"

"Don't know. At least that noisy dog of hers is gone, too. Hoo-whee. What a blessing."

That news brought him up short. Belinda had been furious when he'd suggested she leave Snuffy with Eloise until they could find a place that allowed pets. If she'd taken the dog with her when she left, that might mean she wasn't coming back!

Frowning, Paul got into his car and sped toward Eloise's. Talk about illogical. Why would Belinda suddenly decide to leave Serenity when her attachment to the town was the very reason she'd gotten so upset with him?

Belinda had planned to choose an apartment and reinforce her decision to move before she contacted Paul. By the time she reached Harrison, however, she'd had so much time to think, to imagine his reaction when she told him about it, she couldn't bear to wait any longer.

Finding his office was easy. Making herself enter was a lot harder. "Okay, Father," she whispered. "I'm here. I know this is the right thing to do. I'm trusting You to take it from here."

Straightening her spine and resolving to persevere no matter what, she pulled open the heavy glass door and walked in. The waiting room was impressive, sparsely furnished yet elegantly simple in muted tones of beige and gray.

A middle-aged receptionist looked up from her desk behind a low counter. "May I help you?"

"Yes. Paul Randall, please."

"I'm sorry," the woman said. "Mr. Randall is out."

Belinda's hopes fell. "Oh." Obviously, the Lord wanted her to see to the mundane details of her life, as she'd originally planned, before she encountered Paul again. Disappointed, she said, "I see. Then I guess I should make an appointment. How soon will he be back?"

"I'm sorry. I can't say." The receptionist picked up a pen and paper. "Would you like to leave a message?"

"Yes. Tell him Ms. Carnes has decided to move to Harrison. Permanently."

"Carnes? Belinda Carnes?"

She smiled, gratified to have her name recognized. "That's me. I don't have a place here yet. I'll phone you with my new address as soon as I'm settled."

"But…"

The smile faded. "What's the matter? Did Paul tell you not to let me in?"

"No. Oh, no," the woman said. "Nothing like that. It's just that…he's gone to see *you.*"

"Me? Where? When?"

"He left this morning."

"So did I!" Belinda was ecstatic. "We must have passed each other on the road."

"Probably. I assume you came by highway 412. Since that's the shortest route, Mr. Randall would logically have used it, too."

"No doubt. He's so sensible he drives me up the wall! Thanks!" Laughing to herself, Belinda dashed out the door. Paul had gone to *her!* Praise the Lord! It was a miracle. A happy future was waiting for her at home. Nothing mattered but getting there.

Paul banged on Eloise's door harder than he'd intended. Startled, Snuffy let out a series of whoops that echoed through the house. Hearing that, Paul began to pray that Belinda was inside, too.

Eloise jerked open the door. When she saw who her visitor was, her jaw dropped. "What are *you* doing here?"

"Looking for Belinda." Snuffy was spinning in tight circles at his feet. "When she wasn't home, I thought…"

Eloise burst into laughter. "This is hilarious. She went to see *you!*"

"Me? Where?"

"In Harrison." Shaking her head, she chuckled softly. "You two are really something, you know that? I told her to call you first and tell you she was on her way but she insisted it had to be a surprise. Sure looks like it was."

Stunned, Paul caught his breath. "Why did she leave Snuffy behind?"

"Because she wasn't sure she'd be able to find an apartment that allowed dogs. This is not a permanent arrangement, believe me. I'm more of a cat person, like your aunt." Sobering, she asked, "Did you stop in to see Pru? She's really been worried about you ever since you found out the church fire was her fault. She's afraid you'll hold it against her forever.''

''There was a time when I might have,'' Paul said. ''But not anymore. Belinda once told me it's a lot easier to look back and see how God has worked in the past than it is to figure out His plans for the present. She was sure right.''

''Or His plans for the future,'' Eloise offered. ''So, what happens now?''

''I go find Belinda.'' Paul was grinning. ''If she calls, ask her where she's staying, get a phone number where I can reach her and tell her I'm on my way!''

Paul was nearly to Mountain Home before it occurred to him to alert his office. He had to wait until he'd driven out of the steepest hills before he could get a steady connection on his cellular phone. The receptionist answered on the first ring. ''Randall and Associates.''

''Alice,'' he said, wheeling around a sharp turn, ''it's Paul. I want you to be on the lookout for Belinda Carnes.'' The phone connection faded, crackled, then strengthened slightly. If he didn't know better he'd think he'd heard Alice giggling behind the static. ''What?''

''I said, it's too late, boss. The lady's been here.''

Paul's heart did a flip and landed in his throat. ''That's terrific! Did she leave a number?''

"No. I got the impression she might have changed her mind about sticking around, though, since you were gone. It wouldn't surprise me if she was on her way home. Just stay put in Serenity. I'll bet she shows up."

Tucking the phone between his chin and shoulder, he two-handed a sharp curve. "It's a little late for that. I've already started home. I'm almost to Cotter."

This time, Paul was certain he heard his secretary chuckling quietly before she said, "That should be perfect. Ms. Carnes ran out of here about an hour ago. If she's in as big a hurry as I think she is, you two should be passing each other right about now."

"If we haven't already." Paul put down the phone, slowed and began to scan oncoming traffic, hoping to spot Belinda's car among all the others approaching.

At this point, he could either turn around and go back or continue in the direction he'd been going. If Belinda had stayed in Harrison, that was where he wanted to be. On the other hand, if Alice's guess was right, he needed to head for Serenity. Without more concrete information there was no way to make a logical decision.

Totally frustrated, Paul muttered under his breath. Driving in aimless circles wouldn't accomplish a thing except to burn gasoline.

Continuing to study the traffic, he noticed that one

car was going much faster than the others. It whizzed by him in a blur. Could it be?

His pulse sped. His breath caught. He had only the witness of his heart that it was Belinda he'd seen behind the wheel of the car. That was enough.

Cutting across the grass median without concern for what the rough terrain might do to his car, Paul floored the accelerator and raced after her.

Belinda glanced in the rearview mirror. Two cars were rapidly closing on her. One was black, like Paul's. The other was white with a light bar fastened across its roof. The lights were flashing red and blue!

"I shouldn't have promised God I wouldn't speed," she murmured, slowing and changing lanes so she'd be ready to pull to the shoulder of the road if the state trooper was after her instead of the black car. She kept her eyes on the colored lights. As soon as the black car passed, the patrol car fell in behind her and blinked its headlights.

Shaking with nervousness, Belinda obediently pulled over. There was no good excuse for her excess speed. No reason the trooper should be lenient. She gritted her teeth. This was going to be one whopper of a ticket. The worst part was, she deserved it. Resigned to her fate, she unfastened her seat belt and climbed out of the car.

The approaching officer touched the flat wide brim of his hat. "Ma'am. Do you know how fast you were going?"

Belinda shook her head. "No, sir. I'm afraid I don't have a clue. You see, I was on my way—" She broke off and turned to follow his gaze when she saw him scowl and lean his head to one side to peer past her.

The black car had also pulled over and was rapidly backing toward them along the wide shoulder of the road. It skidded to a stop in front of her car. The driver's door swung open.

Belinda shrieked, "Paul!" and took off running, leaving the startled officer standing alone. Arms held wide, she smacked into Paul's chest with such force he staggered backward before grabbing her and using her momentum to swing her around, feet off the ground.

"Oh, Paul! I went to your office and they said—"

"I know." He was alternately raining kisses over her face, nuzzling her neck and laughing. "I was at *your* house."

Forgetting everything else, Belinda clung to him and kissed him until they were both breathless, then slid her cheek next to his. "Your face is all scratchy."

"I guess I forgot to shave this morning. I had a lot on my mind."

"Oh? What would that be?"

"I was busy deciding to give up everything for the woman I love."

Love? Yippee! He'd finally admitted it! Belinda was grinning so broadly her smile muscles hurt.

"What a coincidence. I just gave up everything for some guy who lives in Harrison. I sure hope he's worth it."

Paul cupped her face in his hands and gazed deeply into her eyes. "I'll do my very best never to disappoint you."

Before Belinda could reply, she heard the gruff sound of a throat being cleared behind her. *Close* behind her. She gasped and whirled, staying as close to Paul as she could. "Uh-oh. Sorry, Officer. You slipped my mind." It was a relief to see him nod and stifle a smile.

"I can see that." Looking at Paul, he asked, "You two have a fight or something?"

"More of a misunderstanding," Paul said. He wrapped his arms around Belinda. "Everything's going to be fine now."

The officer snorted. "Not if you two keep distracting other drivers. You've almost caused at least three traffic accidents since I stopped you." His smile grew. With a nod toward their cars, he said, "Go on. Get out of here before I run you both in for kissing on the highway."

Belinda glanced at Paul. "Is that against the law?"

"It is if our friend with the badge says it is." He kept one arm around her waist and urged her toward the Lexus. "Come on. Let's go somewhere more private. We have a lot to talk about."

The officer stopped them. "Hold it. You can't

leave her car here. The off-ramp to Cotter is up ahead about a mile.'' He pointed. ''Now go on. Git. Both of you.''

Carefully driving below the speed limit, Belinda led the way with Paul right behind. To her great relief, the trooper stayed on the highway when she and Paul turned off.

Parts of Cotter looked even older than Serenity. The newer portion lay nearest the highway. The rest of the town, perched on a picturesque bluff, could be reached by way of a quaint historic bridge over the White River.

Stopping at the river access because it was the first available place to pull off the road, Belinda parked and ran back to Paul. He gave her a brief hug, took her hand and led the way to a secluded patch of shade near the quietly meandering river. ''I'll manage okay in Serenity,'' he said. ''It's worth it to be with you.''

''No, no. I'm moving to Harrison.'' She was shaking her head vigorously. ''I've already decided. I can get a job almost anywhere. You don't have that option. I wasn't thinking clearly before.''

''Uh-uh. You'd hate it there. Then you'd start to hate me. I won't let you do it.''

Belinda pulled away and stepped back, her fists planted firmly on her hips. ''*Let* me? You won't *let* me?''

''Bad choice of words,'' Paul admitted ruefully. ''What I should have said is that it's not as important to me where we live. You have friends in Serenity. Folks you've known all your life. I won't ask you to give that up.''

Impressed by his sincerity and evident love, she smiled with new awareness and spoke softly, sweetly. ''Guess what the sermon was about last Sunday, Paul? Neighbors. And do you know who the Bible says our neighbors are? *Everybody.* I'd never thought of it that way before, had you?''

''And your point is?'' One eyebrow arched quizzically.

''Hearing that lesson preached was the direct answer to my prayers. It finalized the change I needed to make in my outlook. Sure, I'll miss Serenity and Gram and all my friends, but we can make a good life wherever we go. Real neighbors are everywhere.'' She swept her arm in a wide arc. ''Even right here in Cotter.''

Suddenly struck by the significance of what she'd said, Belinda scanned the area. Most of the houses on the bluff above were painted white and nestled amid massive shade trees, making the scene look as ideal as a picture postcard.

She paused to clear her head and gather her thoughts, then took a deep, settling breath. ''Paul? Are you thinking what I'm thinking?''

''In this case, I may be,'' he said cautiously. ''This town is about halfway between both our places. You could visit your grandmother pretty easily, and it wouldn't take me as long to drive to work, either.''

"And it's gorgeous here!" Belinda was warming to the idea. "We'd both have to start over, too, so it would be a fair compromise. It's perfect!"

"Does this mean the wedding is on?" he asked, grinning.

"I don't know. You took back your last proposal."

"I could always make up a new one."

Belinda was so happy she thought she'd burst. "You'd better, or I'll... I'll get my grandmother to hunt you down and conk you with her shovel."

Paul pulled her into his arms and held her close until he stopped laughing. "In that case, will you marry me?"

"Snuffy comes, too," she informed him amiably. "I already promised her she could."

"Okay. But she gets her own room. I've waited ten years for you and I'm not about to share."

Overflowing with joy, Belinda agreed. "It's a deal. Come on. Let's tour the town and go house shopping. The Lord went to a lot of trouble to bring us here. I don't want to disappoint Him."

"In a minute. I have something I want to do first." Pulling her close, Paul lowered his head and sealed their engagement with a long, slow kiss.

Belinda surrendered the last shred of her misgivings as she kissed him back. Overflowing with joy, she wanted to sing, to shout, to tell everyone who'd listen that Paul Randall was the most awesome, the most wonderful answer to prayer she'd ever received.

It didn't matter that it had taken ten years to happen. He was one answer that was *definitely* worth waiting for.

* * * * *

Dear Reader,

Everything that happens to us changes us. It's easy to notice the catastrophic events and acknowledge their immense influence, yet often it's the accumulation of the little things that makes us who we are. What we are.

Every day we're faced with difficulties and choose how we will ultimately react to them. As life goes on and those reactions become a deep-seated part of our character, we can be fooled into believing we've lost our ability to choose joy over sorrow, gain over loss, forgiveness over anger.

When Jesus said, "Blessed are the peacemakers, for they shall be called the children of God," I think He was referring to those special people who, with love and patient understanding, can open our eyes to the blessings of forgiving…beginning with forgiving ourselves for our own mistakes.

No one can go back and undo the past. But we can put it behind us, give the remainder of our lives to Jesus, ask for God's perfect forgiveness and begin again.

Every breath, every heartbeat, every moment, is a gift from God. Whether we look for reasons to celebrate that gift or bury it in bitterness is up to us.

I'd love to hear from you! If you'd like a personal reply or notification of my upcoming books, please include a self-addressed, stamped envelope. You can write to me at: Valerie Hansen, P.O. Box 13, Glencoe, AR 72539-0013 or e-mail me at valw@centurytel.net.

Blessings!

Valerie Hansen

LOVE ONE ANOTHER

A new commandment I give unto you.
That you love one another; as I have loved you,
that ye also love one another.
—*John* 13:34

To all the wonderful people in my life who are so easy to love, especially my husband, children, grandchildren and special Christian friends. And to the one person I find it so hard to forgive, for being the way the Lord has chosen to show me that I'm not perfect...yet.

Chapter One

Tina Braddock bent over a low table, up to her elbows in green and yellow finger paint and up to her knees in preschool tots. It was fortunate the colors blended with her floral print skirt because Sissy Smith had a handful of the fabric and was tugging vigorously.

"Miss Tina! Miss Tina!"

"What is it, Sissy? Is your picture finished?"

The little blond girl ignored the question. "Miss Tina, look! A *stranger*." She used both gooey hands to gather up the loose edge of her teacher's apron and try to hide behind it.

Straightening, Tina looked toward the door. Her breath caught. Sissy was right. The man standing there *was* a stranger. The best-looking one she'd seen in longer than she could remember. His hair was brown and his eyes were so dark they were almost black. As if that weren't enough, the good Lord had blessed him with about six feet of height and a stature that insisted he could pick up a small automobile all by himself and fling it across the room without even breaking a sweat.

Tina blinked herself back to reality as she smiled a greeting. "Hello. Can I help you?"

"I didn't mean to scare the kids," he said soberly. "I just came to look the place over before I enroll my son."

She extricated herself from Sissy's grasp, tossed her long light brown hair back over her shoulders without touching it, and crossed to him while wiping her hands on her apron. "I'm Tina Braddock."

As he eyed her greenish-yellow fingers he hesitated, so she withdrew the offer to shake hands. "Oops. Sorry. I tend to forget. Not everyone gets as involved in all this as I do."

"I can believe *that*."

When he smiled down at Tina, the whole room suddenly seemed a hundred times brighter. "I'll be glad to put your son on our waiting list. How old is he, Mr....?"

"I'm Zac Frazier," the man said. "Justin's just turned four."

"Oh, good. We should have several openings in the four-year-old group in a month or so, as soon as school starts and some of my Picassos-in-training go on to kindergarten."

"That's not soon enough."

"I beg your pardon?"

"I just moved here and I need a place for my son right away. I thought you understood that."

Tina remained firm. "Our rules are for the good of all the children here. Perhaps a private baby-sitter?"

"I can't do that." Frustrated, Zac raked the fingers of both hands through his thick, wavy hair. "Justin gets panicky if I leave him alone with adults. He's better when he's with kids his age."

That's odd, Tina thought. Children usually got upset when they were thrust into a group of unfamiliar kids, not when they were privy to an adult's undivided attention.

"The more distractions, the better he seems to do," Zac said. "That's why I thought…"

The handsome daddy seemed to be having trouble deciding whether or not to explain further, so she encouraged him. "Why don't you tell me a little about your son's background, Mr. Frazier?"

"There's not much to tell. Like I said, he's only four." Zac cleared his throat. "His mother died last year, when we lived up in Illinois. Since then, he hasn't wanted to let me out of his sight."

"Ah, I see." Tina quelled the urge to reach out and comfort him with a sympathetic touch. "I'm so sorry."

"Yeah, well…" He stuffed his hands into his pockets and struck a casual pose. "So, will you take him?"

"I can ask my boss. I suppose one more—"

Across the room, Sissy yowled. Tina whirled just in time to see redheaded Tommy McArthur upend a dish of yellow poster paint over her head. The thick goo pooled in her curls, then began to ooze over her forehead and trickle down her face.

"Tommy!" Racing back to the art table, Tina held out cupped hands to try to catch the worst of the mess.

Sissy chose that moment to shake her head like a kitten whose nose had been dunked into a saucer of milk. Globs of yellow pigment flew. Several caught Tina in the face. She was sure she could feel others clinging to her long hair.

The rest of the children backed away, wide-eyed and uncertain. Except for Sissy's ongoing wails, silence reigned. The boy who had caused the ruckus dropped the empty paint dish as his lower lip began to tremble.

"Hold still, Sissy," Tina said firmly. "You're just making things worse."

"My dress!" the little girl howled, looking down at her skirt. "My mama sewed it for meeee…"

"I'll wash it out for you and it'll be good as new. I promise. Just stop shaking your head!" Tina had momentarily forgotten Zac Frazier. Then she heard him start to laugh. The sound was warm and full. It filled the room and made the hairs at her nape tickle. Goose bumps stood up on her arms.

She glanced over her shoulder at him. "There are

towels in that cabinet up there,'' she said, cocking her head to indicate. "Top left. Mind handing me one?''

"You sure one will be enough?'' Zac was still chuckling as he moved to comply.

"Let's hope so.'' Tina was trying to keep from bursting into giggles and upsetting Sissy even more. "I'd get it myself but I seem to have my hands full.''

"No kidding.'' He stopped behind her and passed the towel over her shoulder. "Here you go. Anything else I can do for you while I'm handy?''

She was concentrating on wiping Sissy's face and sopping up the worst of the paint in her hair. "Like what?''

"Oh, I don't know. Hose the place down, maybe?'' He crouched beside Tina and solemnly eyed the red-haired boy who'd started the trouble. "Or maybe you'd like me to dunk this guy in a different color for you?''

Tina gave Tommy a stern glance, then smiled at Zac. "Sorry. As tempting as it sounds, I'm afraid they don't let me paint naughty children, even if they do deserve it.''

"What a shame,'' Zac said, straight-faced. "He'd look great in purple.''

"We'll have to settle for an apology, instead,'' Tina said, playing along. "Tommy, what do you have to say to Sissy?''

"She started it!'' the boy wailed. "She splashed green on my shirt.''

"Okay. That does it. Painting time is over," Tina ordered. She straightened and wiped her hands on a relatively clean corner of the towel. "Everybody to the sink to wash. Sissy first. March."

Zac stood, too. "You sure you've got a handle on them?"

"As good as I ever do," she answered, smiling fondly as her small charges headed for the low sink in one corner of the room. "They're really good kids. They just have a lot to learn about getting along with others."

"So do the kids I work with…and they're considerably older."

"Oh? Where do you work?"

"Over at the high school, starting next week," Zac said. "I'm going to substitute teach when I'm needed but I'll mostly be a guidance counselor."

"Well," Tina said, grinning up at him, "that sure will simplify things around here."

"It will?"

"Uh-huh. Once you get established in your job at Serenity High, all we'll have to do to spot the teenage troublemakers is look for the ones you've painted purple."

Tina was glad her boss, Mavis Martin, was the kind of woman who listened to reasonable suggestions. She'd waited until all the children had gone home before approaching her and explaining about wanting to add Justin to her class.

"I suppose it's okay, if you're sure you can cope," Mavis said, nodding her graying head soberly. "If it was me, I'd probably do the same thing. The poor man obviously needs help. Might as well come from us, don't you think?"

Smiling broadly, Tina nodded. "Absolutely. Bless you. You're a dear." She reached into the pocket of her apron for the card with the phone number of the motel where Zac and Justin were staying. "I'll call Mr. Frazier and tell him his son can start tomorrow."

"Okay. I just hope you aren't biting off more than you can chew. What kind of kid is he?"

"I don't really know much about him, other than what I was told. He's supposed to be overly attached to his father but adjusts better when he has other children as a distraction."

Mavis's forehead puckered in a frown. "You mean you didn't meet him today?"

"No. His daddy came by alone."

"Hmm. What do you suppose he did with Justin when he came to look us over?"

Tina was beginning to see why her boss seemed troubled. "That's a good question. Let's use the phone in your office so I can put it on speaker and you can hear, too."

"That's not necessary. I trust your judgment."

I wish I could say the same, Tina thought. But she couldn't. Being too trusting, too gullible, had cost her plenty in the past and would have ruined her future, too, if she hadn't left everything behind and started over where no one knew her.

Mavis followed her into the cluttered office. "Push aside my stuff and make yourself a place to sit down, honey. I keep meaning to get this place straightened up. I just never seem to find enough time. One look at all this and I give up because I know it'll take too long."

"My mother used to say cleaning up a big mess was like eating an elephant. It can't all be done at once. You have to take it one bite at a time."

"Well, well, well," the thin, middle-aged woman drawled, staring at Tina in amazement. "You've worked for me for over a year and that's the first time you've mentioned your family. How is your mama?"

"She passed away a long time ago," Tina said softly. Thoughts of the past had obviously caused her to let down her guard. That mustn't happen again. Once she started telling her story she'd run too great a risk of inadvertently revealing her secret shame.

"I'm so sorry to hear that," Mavis said. "Is your daddy still living?"

"No." The answer sounded crisp and off-putting, much to Tina's distress. She didn't want to be unkind, especially not to a friend and mentor like Mavis Martin, but she didn't intend to discuss any aspect of her prior family life. Not now. Not ever.

Looking for a distraction, she quickly dialed the

motel and asked for Zac's room. He answered on the first ring.

"Hello?"

"It's me, Tina Braddock, Mr. Frazier. I've talked it over with my boss, and I'm calling to invite you to bring Justin to meet me and the other children. Is tomorrow morning too soon?"

She was sure she heard a relieved sigh.

"No. That will be fine. What time?"

"If you come around ten, he can start by having milk and cookies with us."

"Good. We'll be there."

Mavis was waving at her and making hand signals from across the desk. Tina got the idea. "One question, if you don't mind?"

"Sure. Shoot."

"You said Justin didn't like to be away from you, right?"

"Right."

"So where was he today when you came by the day care center? Why didn't you bring him with you?"

"Ah." Zac let out his breath in a whoosh. "I guess that might seem odd if you didn't know the whole story. We'd been awake most of the night. He was sound asleep when I left. I figured it would be better to be by myself when I scouted out places for him to stay, so I let him sleep."

"You didn't leave him in a motel room all

alone?'' She couldn't believe a father who had seemed so concerned would have done such a thing.

"Of course not. I paid one of the maids to baby-sit. Justin never even knew I was gone."

"Oh. Thank goodness. I thought…"

"Look, Ms. Braddock," Zac said tightly. "I'm doing the best I can under the circumstances. I'd like to spend every minute with my son, but I can't. I have to work. That's why I need a place like yours to take care of him during the day. The rest of the time he's my responsibility. One I take very seriously."

Instead of attempting to justify her position, Tina fell back on her professional demeanor. "I'm sure you do. I certainly didn't mean to imply otherwise."

"Sorry." Pausing, he muttered to himself before continuing. "It's not your fault. I know I get defensive sometimes. It just galls me that so many people don't think fathers are capable of taking good care of their kids by themselves."

"All anyone can do is try," Tina told him. "No two children are alike. Sometimes, even a person's best efforts aren't good enough without the help of divine intervention." *Like she'd gotten with Craig.*

"You sound like an expert," Zac said. "Do you have children?"

Touched by the irony of his question, she gave a soft, self-deprecating chuckle. "Dozens. All other people's. And I'm certainly no expert. At least, not once they get older than about six. I'd rather face an unruly gang of twenty preschoolers than try to figure out one teenager."

"Boy, not me," he countered. "I don't envy you your job one bit. Give me a reasonable teen any time."

"There is no such thing as a reasonable teen," Tina argued amiably. "Believe me, I know."

"That sounds like the voice of experience. We'll have to compare notes sometime. Maybe I can give you a few pointers and you can do the same for me."

"I'll be glad to help you and Justin in any way I can. See you tomorrow, then. Bye."

Curiosity filled Mavis's expression as Tina hung up the phone. "I thought your specialty was little tykes. You never mentioned that you'd worked with teenagers."

"I haven't." Tina busied herself straightening piles of paper on the desk rather than continue to meet her boss's inquisitive gaze. She'd slipped again. That was twice in one day, which was two times too many. "I was just making polite conversation."

"Oh." The older woman reached out and stilled Tina's fluttering hands. "If you don't stop rearranging my papers, I won't be able to find a thing. Go on home. I'll lock up."

"You're sure?" Tina was eager to leave, to be alone where she could sort out her thoughts and gain better control of her tongue.

"I'm positive." With a motherly smile, Mavis looked her up and down. "You deserve a break.

You've either had a particularly rough day or a truck full of raw eggs crashed into you while I was busy in the other room.''

Tina laughed lightly. ''The yellow spots are from finger paint, not egg yolk. Tommy got mad at Sissy, and the rest is history. I was kind of caught in the middle.'' Recalling the funny incident, she shook her head. ''To make matters worse, it happened exactly when Zac decided to drop in to look the place over.''

Mavis's left eyebrow arched. ''Zac?''

''I meant Mr. Frazier,'' Tina said, blushing.

All her boss said was ''Of course you did.''

Justin Frazier was a miniature version of his daddy. The minute she saw the lonely little boy, clinging tightly to his father's hand, Tina's heart belonged to him.

She made sure all the other children had their cookies and milk, then approached father and son. ''Hello, Justin. My name is Miss Tina. I have an extra cookie that really wants to be eaten. Do you suppose you could help me with that?''

He buried his face against his father's pant leg.

''Okay,'' Tina said casually. ''I guess I can give it to one of the other boys if you don't want it. That wouldn't be really fair, though. They've already had theirs. I saved this cookie specially for you.''

Justin rolled his head just far enough to reveal one dark eye, and peeked out at her.

"It's chocolate chip. Of course, if you don't like that kind…"

One pudgy hand reached out. Tina quickly handed him the cookie and turned to rejoin the class, subtly motioning Zac to follow. "How about a carton of milk to go with that?"

Without looking back, she proceeded to get the milk, insert a straw and set the carton at an empty place at the low table as if she fully expected Justin to agree to sit there. "Here you go. Nice and cold."

For a moment it looked as if he was going to continue to hang on to Zac in spite of Tina's assured manner. At the last second he let go and slid into the scaled-down plastic chair. None of the other children said a word. They were all too busy studying the new arrival and his daddy.

Across the table, little blond Emily began to giggle, when Justin bit into his cookie and half of it crumbled and fell on the floor. Tina was about to offer him another, when she saw Tommy McArthur carefully break his own cookie in half and lean closer to hand the piece to Justin. She was too far away to hear what the boy said, but she figured it had to be funny because Zac had his lips pressed tightly together and was struggling not to laugh.

To her relief, Justin accepted the gift and whispered something back to Tommy before stuffing the whole half of the cookie into his mouth at once.

Zac stepped back quietly. As soon as he was far

enough away, Tina joined him. "What did Tommy say?" she asked.

Shaking his head for a moment to compose himself, he said, "I think my son just took his first bribe. He promised Tommy he'd see that I didn't dunk him in any paint."

"No wonder you looked like you were about to burst!"

"I was surprised he even remembered me. I told you I didn't understand little kids."

"Hey, don't worry about it. Nobody really does. They don't even understand themselves."

"You sure seem to know how to handle them, though. I was worried Justin would pitch a fit when I tried to let go of him. It was amazing he didn't."

"I think sometimes we underestimate the adaptability of children. All I did was act like sitting at the table with the others was the most natural choice for him to make, and he made it. It's that simple."

"For you, maybe. When I told him he was going to day care this morning, he threw a terrible tantrum. It's a wonder the folks at the motel didn't hear him and call the police."

"Have you found a house, yet?" Tina asked, keeping watch on the children as she talked.

"No. And I'm getting pretty frustrated."

"Well, as long as you don't throw a tantrum…"

"Very funny. Although I did feel like it yesterday when we drove seven miles out of town to look at a place and found out it was already rented."

"In a close-knit area like Serenity, most of the best places never get advertised. People just hear they're going to be for rent or for sale, and tell their friends."

"Terrific."

"It has its advantages. For instance, I happen to know that the house two doors north of me is going to be vacant soon. It's in a nice neighborhood and only about a quarter-mile from the high school. Would you be interested?"

"Interested? At this point I'd practically kill for a decent place to live."

Tina laughed. "I don't think you'll have to do anything quite that drastic. I'll talk to the folks who are moving as soon as I get home tonight and find out all the details for you. Hopefully, there won't be too long a wait."

"You'd go to all that trouble for me? Why?"

Looking up into his eyes, she saw how much her kindness had affected him. This was a man who apparently wasn't used to experiencing the honestly offered concern of strangers. Or accepting their help. He was never going to fit in around here if somebody didn't set him straight. Tina immediately decided it was her duty to be that person.

"In small communities like this one, Mr. Frazier, folks help each other all the time. It's how we are. We don't need specific reasons to look out for one another. We just do it. A lot of us behave that way because Christians are supposed to, but we aren't the only ones who show kindness. Pretty much every-body does. It's one of the blessings of living here.''

"I see.''

Tina decided to press ahead. ''Do you have a church home? If not, you can't beat the one I go to,'' she said enthusiastically. ''We'd love to have you visit this Sunday. At nine-thirty I teach a Sunday School class of children Justin's age. He should be comfortable enough with me by then to enjoy it. Regular church starts at eleven.''

"We'll see.'' He glanced at Justin. ''I guess I might as well try to get out of here. I do have a lot to do.''

Tina scanned the table where her charges sat. ''I think you're wise to leave him with us right away, instead of getting him used to having you stick around. He'll be fine. Just go over and tell him good-bye as if you've done it that way a thousand times. I'll take care of the rest.''

"What if he cries?''

"Then, I'll give him a hug and comfort him until he stops, the same as you'd do,'' she said. To her dismay she noticed that the man seemed a bit put off by her comment. Surely he didn't expect a mother-less child to do without a lot of cuddling, even if his father didn't view it as a natural masculine response.

"You do whatever you think is right,'' Zac said. ''You can reach me at the high school all afternoon if you need me. What time should I come back for Justin?''

"We like to lock up and be out of here by six-thirty. Will that work for you?"

"I'll make it work," he said.

Tina watched him walk stiffly across the room and bend over his son. The boy didn't seem at all upset when he bid Zac goodbye. Funny. She'd dealt with lots of little ones in the past and she'd expected at least a mild protest, especially since Justin hadn't had time to make friends yet.

Hanging back, she waited for the boy's reaction rather than anticipating difficulties and telegraphing her own concern. If he accepted his father's departure, there would be no reason to treat it as anything but routine.

Zac straightened and headed for the door. He never hesitated, never looked back. If Tina hadn't spotted the moisture glistening in his eyes as he passed, she might have believed he wasn't concerned about leaving Justin at all.

Chapter Two

Tina wasn't surprised that Zac was the first parent to claim his child that day. It was barely four-thirty when he arrived. Justin looked up from the rug where he was pushing a toy race car, broke into a wide grin when he spotted his daddy and ran to him.

Zac tousled the boy's thick brown hair. "Hi, buddy. Did you have fun?"

Nodding, Justin suddenly turned shy again and hid his face against his father's leg, just as he had that morning when he'd first arrived.

Troubled by the abrupt change in the child's attitude, Tina approached. "You'll need to sign him out on that clipboard hanging on the wall by the door. Just find his name, fill in the time and sign in the space provided."

She followed, as Zac took the boy's hand and led him toward the door. Justin was dragging his feet and not looking at anyone, so she crouched down beside him as Zac paused to check the pupil list.

"It was very nice having you in my class, today, Justin," she said amiably. "Tomorrow we're going to paint, and play with the outside toys and have lots more fun."

When the boy looked into her eyes, Tina was positive she saw a glimmer of fear. She gently stroked his bare arm to soothe him. "And then tomorrow, after school, your daddy will come for you again. Just like he did today." Still not sure she was getting through to the little boy she added, "And I'll be your special friend. If you want to keep me company while I walk around and do my job, you can be my helper, okay?"

"O-okay." His voice was barely above a whisper. As soon as he spoke he looked up at his father for reassurance.

Tina, too, looked up. "I think you should tell Justin that it's okay for me to be his friend," she said. "He seems worried that you might not approve."

"He doesn't need a friend Ms...."

"It's Braddock, remember? But call me Miss Tina. Everybody does. It simplifies things for the children."

"All right. My son needs a teacher and a caretaker, Miss Tina. That's why I brought him here. However, I don't see how becoming emotionally involved will help you do a better job. Or help Justin adjust to the new routine."

She blessed the little boy with a smile of encouragement before she straightened to face his father. The smile faded and her chin jutted out. "Everybody needs friends, Mr. Frazier. Even stubborn, hardheaded men like you, whether you choose to admit it or not."

"Ah, I see. Are you volunteering?"

Tina didn't like the self-satisfied expression on his face. Her eyes narrowed. "Why do I get the idea that's a trick question?"

"Because it is. You aren't the first single woman who's figured she could get to me by befriending my son," Zac said flatly. "And I'm sure you won't be the last. I learned a long time ago that it was best for Justin if I put a stop to that kind of nonsense before it got started."

"You think I'm pursuing you?"

"It's pretty obvious."

"Oh, really?" Righteous indignation rose. "Well, let me tell you something, mister. If I was interested in getting to know you on a personal level, which I am *not*, I'd have the backbone to come right out and say so, not hide my intentions at the expense of an innocent child."

Zac was starting to smile for real. "Are you through?"

"No." She pulled a pout. "But I think I'd better stop talking before I say too much."

"Undoubtedly. I suspect I may have to rethink my conclusions about you."

"I certainly hope so."

"In that case, I apologize, Miss Tina." He politely offered his hand. "If you want to be buddies with my son and can keep me out of the equation, then I certainly have no objection."

That's big of you, she thought cynically. For the boy's sake she took Zac's hand, intending to shake it merely to demonstrate harmony. It should have been a simple act. It wasn't. The moment he grasped her fingers some serious complications arose. Tina felt a jolt of awareness zing up her arm and spread telltale warmth across her cheeks.

A barely coherent "Thanks" squeaked out of her suddenly tight, dry throat as she quickly withdrew from his touch. No wonder he'd had so much trouble with other women! The poor guy was unconsciously sending out the wrong kind of signals. At least, the ones she was picking up were wrong. *Very* wrong. Especially for her.

Zac cleared his throat. "So, what time can I bring Justin in the morning?"

"We open at eight. I'm usually here by a little after seven, if you want to drop him off early. You'll need to knock. I keep the door locked when I'm here alone." The cautious look returning to his eyes reminded her of the conversation they'd concluded a few moments before, so she clarified her statement. "I will *not* be waiting with baited breath for you to come in with him."

Chuckling, he nodded and relaxed. "Okay, okay. I'm convinced. You're not shopping for a husband."

"You've got that right."

"Mind telling me why not?"

Tina's stomach tied in a hard knot. She *did* mind. A lot. But it wouldn't do to say so and start an unnecessary discourse. She hadn't even told her brother Craig, back home in California, what had convinced her to stay away from romance no matter what else happened. There was no way she was going to explain that kind of personal trauma to a stranger. Especially since her past history had been the obvious reason for at least one failed relationship.

"It's not relevant," Tina said, choking back any sign of emotion. "Let's just say I'm perfectly happy with my life as it is. I live in a great town, and having these wonderful kids around me all the time blesses my socks off."

"Ah, so you're happy with the status quo. Me, too. Too bad the rest of the world doesn't understand that, isn't it?"

"Do eligible women *really* chase you around all the time?" she asked, baiting him on purpose to take his focus off her life and put it back on his.

"Yes." Zac laughed softly. "Actually, that was one of the reasons I decided I needed to move to this tiny corner of Arkansas. My friends meant well, but they were fixing me up with dates so often they were driving me crazy."

"My boss, Mavis Martin, is like that." Tina

pointed to an adjoining room. "She takes care of the littlest babies over there in our nursery. She means well, too, but sometimes…"

"Don't be too hard on her. She probably wants to make sure you're not lonely." Zac paused, thoughtful. "In my case, Justin and I are doing fine as we are. We're a team." He glanced down at the boy and tousled his hair again. "Aren't we, buddy? Well, tell Miss Tina goodbye for now. You'll see her again in the morning."

Crouching to be on the boy's level, she touched his free hand and smiled with fondness. "Bye, Justin. I'll see you soon."

For an instant the boy leaned her way, and she thought he was going to break down and hug her. Instead, he whispered, "Bye," and hurried to keep up with his daddy as Zac started for the door.

Tina's heart went out to the child. Zac Frazier might be a whiz at understanding the older kids he worked with, but he had a long way to go before he met all the emotional needs of his four-year-old son. Somebody was going to have to show him the error of his ways soon, or the boy was likely to carry the scars of the lack of physical closeness all his life.

It was painfully clear to Tina that she'd been placed in a perfect position to enlighten him. The trouble was, she didn't feel even remotely qualified for such a daunting task.

"Oh, Father, why me?" she prayed softly. *"I couldn't even straighten out my own brother. How*

*am I ever going to show that man how to love his
son the way he should?''*

No easy answer came. She didn't expect it to.

It was over a week before Tina had any news for
Zac about available housing. The trouble was, the
only house she'd found was the one close to hers.
Too close. She wrestled with her conscience all day,
knowing she should give him an update about it and
hating to because she didn't want to have to deal with
him as a neighbor. Nevertheless, she gave in and
presented the address when he came to call for Justin.

"This is the rental I told you about," Tina said.
"If you haven't found a place yet, this one is going
to be vacant soon. The landlord wants to have a
chance to clean it up and paint it before he rents it
again, so I'm afraid you'll have to wait a while."
Shrugging, she said, "Sorry. It was the best I could
do."

"How about if I volunteer to do the painting to
save time? I really don't want to keep Justin in that
motel any longer than I have to. It's not enough like
a home."

"I agree. He told me a lot of his toys are in storage
and he wants to be able to get the boxes out and play
with everything. He rattled off a list of treasures that
had the other kids drooling."

"*My* son told you all that?"

"In great detail. He has a very good vocabulary

for a child his age. I suppose that comes from spending so much time with adults.''

''The only adult he has much to do with is me,'' Zac said. ''And you, of course. He talks about *Miss Tina* all the time. I think he has a crush on you.''

She laughed lightly. ''That's pretty normal, too. I can't help but get attached to these kids and they respond to me the same way. I love 'em all. Even Tommy.''

''The kid I was going to paint purple?'' Zac chuckled. ''I remember. Is he still acting up?''

''From time to time. He's a healthy boy. He can't help some of the things he does, like not sitting still or not remembering to keep his hands to himself. But he's improving. They all are.''

''Even my son?''

The man looked so concerned, she decided to go into more detail. ''Justin has never caused me any trouble. Actually, that much virtue had me worried to begin with, but I've been watching him, and he's beginning to act more normal. I've actually seen him getting into a little mischief lately.''

Zac stiffened. ''I'll have a talk with him.''

''No!'' Tina was so adamant she forgot herself and grabbed Zac's forearm, holding tight. ''Don't you dare. That would spoil everything. He's just starting to loosen up and have fun here.''

Casting a wary glance at her hand where it gripped his bare arm, Zac said, ''Looks like he's not the only one who's loosening up. Your fingernails are leaving dents. If I promise to behave myself, will you let go of me?''

"Oops. Sorry.'' Embarrassed, Tina jumped back. It would be a hot day at the North Pole before she touched that man again! She didn't have to look in a mirror to know her cheeks were bright pink. So was her neck.

"You're forgiven. It's nice to know you care so much. About Justin's welfare, I mean.'' He cleared his throat. "By the way, that's a great color on you.''

Brushing her hands over her skirt, she said, "This? Thanks. I chose it because the paint spots blend right in.''

Zac was clearly amused. "Actually, I meant the color on your face. Have you always blushed so easily?''

"Only when I forget myself and grab hold of strange men,'' Tina responded with a nervous laugh. "Believe me, it doesn't happen all that often.''

"Let's hope not.'' Looking across the room, he beckoned to his son. "Come on, Justin. We're going to go look at a house before dinner.''

The little boy raced to his dad. "A *real* house?''

"Yes. A real house. See?'' Zac showed him the paper with the address on it, then looked over at Tina. "I forgot to ask. How do we get there?''

"It's not hard. You take the main highway west, past the market and up the hill, then veer right at the first road after the vacant lot where Ed Beasley used to keep all those rusty antique cars.'' She was waving her hands for emphasis.

''Who?''

Frustrated, Tina realized they had a basic information problem. ''Never mind. I forgot. Ed sold out and moved before you came to town. I usually navigate by familiar landmarks, which is a good thing since the dirt roads around here don't have street signs posted.''

''Could you draw me a map?''

''I have a better idea.'' She glanced at the wall clock. ''If you can wait another twenty minutes, I can lead you there myself. That way you won't get lost. When I first moved here I took a wrong turn on one of those unmarked roads and I thought I'd *never* find my way back to civilization.''

''So, the house is stuck way out in the country? I'm not sure that's what I'm looking for.''

''Unpaved streets do not mean it's rustic,'' Tina countered. ''You'll see. It's a lovely house. And the yard is fenced so you won't have to worry about Justin wandering off when he's playing outside.''

Zac was shaking his head. ''That's not a problem. My son always stays where he can see me and I can see him, when we're at home.''

It was his matter-of-fact attitude that gave Tina pause. No normal child of four kept an eye on his or her parent every minute. It wasn't natural. Or healthy. Zac Frazier was a smart man, an educated man. Why couldn't he see that?

Or was it just that he didn't want to?

* * *

Zac hung around until the last of the children had been picked up, then he and Justin followed Tina out to the parking lot. He'd pictured her as the convertible or the sports car type. Instead, she floored him by climbing into an old, dusty, blue pickup truck.

He secured Justin in his seat in the rear of their minivan and got behind the wheel. Hopefully, he hadn't looked too surprised at Tina's mode of transportation. He didn't want to hurt her feelings when she was trying so hard to do him a favor.

She pulled alongside, windows rolled down. "Ready?"

"Lead the way," Zac called.

As soon as she drove off, he turned up the van's air-conditioning. Ahead, he could see Tina's long, light brown hair blowing in the wind. She might not be driving a fancy new convertible, but he hadn't been far wrong about her overall attitude. She looked exactly like the free spirit he'd been picturing ever since they'd met.

No wonder she wasn't interested in settling down and getting married. She wasn't the sweet, contented homemaker type Kim had been. Thinking of his late wife gave Zac a familiar jolt of guilt. He'd been over and over the boating accident in his mind and had never come up with a clear cause, yet his subconscious kept insisting it was his fault. It had to be. After all, he was the husband and father. Keeping his family safe was his responsibility. And he'd failed.

By the time he'd pulled Justin to safety and gone back for Kim, she'd sunk below the surface of the murky water and he hadn't been able to locate her.

Ahead, Tina signaled for a turn. That snapped Zac out of his contemplative mood. He was glad she wasn't speeding, because he wouldn't have compromised Justin's safety just to keep up with her. His days of risk-taking were over.

The road narrowed beneath a canopy of trees. Scraggly, dead tree branches stuck out here and there on both sides of the road like long, crooked fingers. If it had been dark, the scene might have seemed eerie. As it was, however, the lovely summer day lingered to bathe the countryside with rays from the setting sun. Lush growth on the healthier oaks and cedars softened the angles of their bare counterparts.

Checking Justin in the mirror, Zac saw that the boy had already fallen asleep. Good. The poor kid needed the rest. He sighed. Truth to tell, so did his daddy. Between the two of them, they'd spent many restless, nightmare-filled nights this past year. Maybe a new house, a new town, a new job were what they needed. Zac certainly hoped so. He was running out of fresh ideas.

Tina pulled into a driveway and parked. Zac followed, and couldn't believe his eyes. He stared. There were flowers everywhere. Hundreds of them. In pots, in planters, coming up in bunches in the lawn. He'd never seen anything so naturally beautiful in his life.

Climbing out of the van, all he said was "Wow."

Tina joined him in time to hear the comment. "I'm glad you like it. Gardening is a hobby of mine."

"This is your place? I thought…"

"Sorry," she said, pointing. "The one you came to see is three doors down. I turned in here by force of habit. Guess I was daydreaming. Come on. We can walk over."

Zac cast a weary glance at his sleeping son. "I hate to wake him. He has a lot of trouble getting to sleep."

"Then, leave him alone and move your car over in front of the other house where we can watch him. I'll meet you there."

She started off without waiting for him to agree. Watching her go, Zac was struck by her effortless grace and lively step. Always before she'd been inside the classroom when he'd seen her move. Now, she'd shed her shoes and was cutting across the lawn barefoot, like a child who'd just been let out of school.

What a fascinating woman. There was an easy goodness about her that spoke to his soul, made him miss the spiritual aspects of his former life. Maybe it was time to take her up on her invitation and make plans to visit her church. If even half the members were as amiable as Tina Braddock, it was a place he wanted to see for himself.

* * *

"The Nortons left their key under the mat so you could get inside," Tina said, handing it to him. "Here. Go take a peek. I'll stay out here and watch Justin for you."

"You're sure they won't mind?"

"Nope. They've moved most of their furniture already. Doris told me to give you the key and turn you loose."

"She's not worried about letting a stranger poke through her home?"

"You're not a stranger," Tina told him. "I vouched for you. Besides, the Norton's oldest boy is in high school, so they've already heard plenty about you."

Zac arched an eyebrow. "Small-town gossip?"

"You'll get used to it. Everybody means well. They like to keep an eye on newcomers, that's all."

"How long does it take to become one of the good ole boys?"

Tina laughed. "A couple of generations, as near as I can tell. A genuine southern accent helps, too. I'm working on mine."

"I thought I'd noticed a drawl in some of the quaint expressions you use."

"I'm not adding colloquialisms on purpose," she explained. "They slip into my conversation because I hear them so much. When I first moved here, I used to always catch the unusual ways people talked. Now, it's hard to pick up differences even if I'm listening for them."

"Not for me," he said, laughing quietly and shaking his head. "The other day one of the teachers I work with said he was 'fixin' to take a cold,' and I had to stop myself from asking him where he was planning on taking it."

He fitted the key into the lock and turned it till he heard it click. "Keep a close eye on Justin. I had to leave the motor running so the air conditioner would work. If he wakes up and sees I'm gone, he'll be scared. This shouldn't take long. I'm not fussy."

"Don't you worry one bit. I'm not fixin' to leave till you're as happy as a possum in a henhouse," Tina quipped, grinning widely.

Zac rolled his eyes and turned away, laughing to himself. The woman was naturally humorous, whether she knew it or not. No wonder Justin had taken to her so quickly and blossomed in her class. Tina Braddock was more than a good teacher. She was a very special person, too.

Chapter Three

Concerned about safety, Tina strolled toward the van while she waited for Zac to return. She understood why he'd chosen to leave the motor running. Justin needed the cool air. The weather was typical of summer in the Ozarks: steamy and hot, good for flowers and veggies but not as pleasant as it would be in a month or so when fall arrived.

She shaded her eyes and peeked in the van window. Justin was asleep on the bench seat in the center, close enough to the driver to be watched, yet protected from the front air bag. It didn't surprise her that Zac had chosen the best location for his son. The man didn't miss a trick where safety was concerned.

The boy stirred. Holding very still, Tina willed him back to a deeper sleep. For a few minutes she thought she'd gotten her wish. Then the boy's eyes fluttered open, and he realized almost immediately that he'd been left alone.

"Daddy!" Panicky, Justin began to struggle to undo his seat belt.

Tina rapped on the window and called to him. If he got loose, there was no telling what he might do. She made a grab for the door handle and gave it a wrench. It didn't open!

"I'm here, Justin," she shouted. "I'm right here. It's okay. You're fine. Daddy will be right back."

The child began to sob. Tina pounded on the window with the flat of her hand, then ran around to try the doors on the opposite side. They were all locked. She knew she didn't dare leave the van long enough to fetch Zac. If Justin managed to undo his seat belt while she was gone, he might inadvertently slip the van into gear and cause an accident. If only his idiotic, overprotective father hadn't locked the blasted doors!

Close to panic herself, Tina shouted at the house. "Zac! Zac!" She needn't have worried that he might not hear her. In seconds he was charging across the lawn.

"What happened?"

"He woke up and…"

Zac reached for the door. "Why did you let him get so upset? I warned you…" He jerked the handle. Nothing happened! He whirled. "Why did you lock the door?"

"I didn't lock it. You did."

"No, I didn't."

"Well, *somebody* did," Tina countered. "Maybe you pushed the wrong button when you got out."

"No way." Zac's eyes widened. "Oh, no. He's loose." Fighting to appear calm, he called, "Hey, buddy. Here I am. Come open the door for Daddy."

The child was too overwrought to respond. He threw one foot up on the back of the front seat and was struggling to scramble over.

"We have to do something. We can't let him get to the driver's seat," Tina shouted.

"I know." Zac ran around to the other side of the van and dropped to his knees by the driver's door. He'd stashed an extra key under there for emergencies. What he hadn't counted on was the mud he found caked in hard ridges where the metal key holder should have been.

Scraping frantically with his fingernails, he called to Tina, "Get me something to break this off with!"

In the bedlam, Tina heard only part of his request. She quickly hefted a rock the size of a cantaloupe and whacked the front passenger window. Safety glass fragmented into a million tiny, harmless pieces the size of peas.

Zac came up off his knees with the box in his hand and a wild look on his face. "What the—?"

"You said to break it, so I did," she explained.

"Break the mud off my spare key—" he waved the muddy box "—not break the *window!*"

"Well, why didn't you say so?"

"I *did*." He swiftly unlocked the door on his side of the van and held out his arms. Justin was just landing in the front seat. Relieved, Zac grasped his small hand and helped him step down. "It's okay, son. I've got you."

The frightened boy wrapped his arms around his father's leg and held on as if it were a lifeline. His breath came in halting, shuddering sobs.

Waiting, Tina stood back and watched father and son try to regain their composure. Zac rested his hand on the boy's hair. When he tilted his head back and closed his eyes for a few seconds, Tina imagined him sending up a silent prayer of thanks. She'd already done the same. Breaking the window might be considered foolhardy by some people—but how was she to know Zac had a spare key? Given her assessment of the situation, she'd done the right thing. Anyway, Justin was safe. That was all that really mattered.

Acting on impulse, she approached the child, dropped to one knee beside him and began to gently stroke his back, while he continued to cling to Zac. "You're fine now, honey. Your daddy's right here. You know he'd never leave you."

To her surprise, Justin released his usual hold on his father's leg, threw himself at her, wrapped his little arms tightly around her neck and began to weep anew. Tina got down on both knees to hug him close.

"Oh, baby. Don't cry. Don't cry."

Tears of empathy filled her eyes and slid silently down her cheeks. This emotionally needy child had touched her as no other had. She kissed his hair, his wet cheeks, then cupped his face in her hands so he'd have to look at her when she reassured him.

"We love you, Justin. We'd never let anything bad happen to you."

As soon as she'd spoken she realized she'd made an inappropriate inference by combining her own compassion with that of Zac Frazier. Well, too bad. Knowing there was more than one person in the world who cared about him was critical to Justin's peace of mind. If his father didn't like it, tough.

She dried the child's tears with the hem of her skirt and made sure he'd stopped crying, before she gathered her courage and stood to confront Zac. "We need to discuss a few things, Mr. Frazier. In private."

To her surprise, he still seemed aggravated.

"Insurance will probably pay for the damage," Zac grumbled, scowling at his van. "What a mess. I wish you'd asked me instead of getting so carried away."

"You're worried about the mess from a broken window?" Exasperation filled Tina's voice. "Fine. I'll help you clean it up. But I don't give a hoot about your stupid window, okay? It's your son I'm worried about."

"You weren't so worried when you dropped broken *glass* all over him."

"All the new cars have safety glass. It's not sharp when it breaks. I knew it wouldn't hurt him."

"How about scare him to death," Zac countered. "He was already having a fit over waking up alone."

She wanted to scream, *So hug him. Show him some real affection,* but she held her tongue. Yelling at the man wasn't going change him, especially since he didn't seem to have a clue he was doing anything wrong. If he agreed to rent the property she'd shown him, however, she'd have lots of opportunities to observe his interaction with his son and offer a few subtle pointers on parenting. Unfortunately, with the Fraziers so close by, she wouldn't be able to escape from that duty, either. Even if she wanted to.

"So, are you going to take this house?" Tina asked, deliberately changing the subject. "You should commit yourself as soon as possible, you know. It won't stay empty for long." In her heart, she half hoped he'd say no, and relieve her of the God-given responsibility she was feeling.

"I suppose I will," Zac said flatly. "I haven't found any other place close to my job, and the rent is reasonable."

Well, that was that, Tina thought. She was stuck. "Okay. I'll let the landlord know. He can drop the rental agreement by your office, if you like."

"That'll be fine."

Tina held out her hand as if to shake on the deal, then quickly withdrew it when she recalled the way she'd reacted when they'd touched before. "Good night, then. I've done my good deed for the day, so

I guess I'll be going. Do you think you can find your way back to your motel by yourself?''

"Probably. Can I borrow a whisk broom and dustpan before I go? I need to sweep up the broken glass.''

"And I said I'd help you, didn't I? I really am sorry. I was sure you said you wanted me to break the window.'' She flashed a wry smile.

"What I said was, give me something to break loose the dirt that was keeping me from getting to my spare key. I don't understand where all that hard mud came from. It hasn't rained since I've been here.''

"Probably from wasps. Mud daubers,'' Tina told him. "They make nests in everything, even motors. Thankfully, they're not as aggressive as the big, red, paper-wasps. Those can be nasty. If you see a nest with a bunch of exposed cells, kind of like honeycomb, *don't* put your hand into it.''

"I'll remember that. Thanks, neighbor.''

Neighbor? He soon would be, wouldn't he. Phooey. Well, like it or not, that was apparently what the Lord wanted, because the only available house in town was the one they were standing in front of.

How could she argue with providence? Clearly, God agreed that it would be much easier for her to help Justin if he lived close by. All she had to do was continue to keep his good-looking daddy at arm's length so she wouldn't be tempted to repeat past mistakes.

As Tina turned away to fetch the broom, her empty stomach growled. Combined with her guilt over not really wanting the Fraziers to become her neighbors, her hunger reminded her of Sunday's sermon about feeding a needy brother or sister. She didn't know how *needy* Zac and Justin might be, but it was long past her suppertime and she was starving to death. So why not invite them to eat with her?

Because it was a stupid idea, she argued. It was also a perfect opportunity to make them feel welcome and begin to educate Zac about children.

Hurrying back with the cleaning tools, she made her decision. "Why don't you two stay for supper? We can have a picnic in the backyard. I keep lots of hamburgers and hot dogs in the freezer, so I'm ready for any emergency."

Raising one eyebrow, Zac regarded her quizzically. "Is that local cuisine?"

"Not unless we wrap the whole sandwich in dough, dump it in a pan and deep fry it, too," Tina said with a light laugh. "Even some of the *pies* are fried around here."

"So I've heard. The thing that surprises me is how these people can live to be so old when they eat so much food that's supposed to be bad for you."

"Clean living— Was that a yes?"

"I think we could both use a break from restaurant food," Zac said, looking to his son for confirmation. "How about it, buddy? Want to eat at Miss Tina's tonight?"

"Yeah!"

Pleased, Zac nodded. "That makes it unanimous. We'll be over as soon as I get this mess..." His jaw dropped. Instead of clinging to him the way he usually did, Justin had raced back to Tina's side and immediately grabbed her hand.

"We'll wait for you," Tina said, careful to consider his feelings. He had been the boy's only refuge for a long time, and she didn't want him to think she was trying to take his place. "I'd rather cook outside in this kind of weather, and I'm probably going to need your help lighting the barbecue." Her grin widened. "I've heard that men are especially talented at getting cooking fires to burn properly."

"You heard right," Zac quipped. "We pass the secret down from generation to generation."

"I'd always suspected it was something like that. I hope you paid attention to your lessons. I don't want to use my stove unless I absolutely have to. Summer or winter."

"Spoken like a truly modern woman. Personally, I've found I like to cook. It's kind of a challenge."

"You're joking."

"No. Not at all." Bending over, he stuck his head and shoulders inside the van and continued to brush crystalline shards into the dustpan. "For instance, Justin and I love Mexican food. Around here, if you want a decent meal like that, you have to make it yourself."

"Boy, no kidding. I haven't had a good *chili relleno* since I left—" The color drained from her face.

Zac glanced up from his task. "Since you left where? Sorry. I didn't catch everything you just said."

Another close call! What was the matter with her? "Never mind. I was just rambling." All Tina wanted at that moment was to get away from him and restore her waning composure. "If you don't mind, I think Justin and I will go dig around in my freezer for something good to eat." She pushed aside her anxiety to smile down at the child.

"I'll come with you," Zac told her, straightening. "I've done about all I can with this broom. After dinner, maybe I can borrow your vacuum to finish the job."

"Sure. Always willing to be neighborly. Especially since the mess is my fault."

Feigning nonchalance, she led the way across the adjoining lawns to her house. On the outside she was calm. Inside, her thoughts whirled madly. What had lowered her defenses and loosened her tongue? It had been over a year since she'd moved to Serenity and gone to work for Mavis, yet until recently she'd never mentioned anything that might accidentally lead someone to discover her secret shame. Now, all of a sudden, she was turning into a regular fountain of information. Why in the world was that happening?

Tina felt her pulse pound in her temples. When

she'd first come to Serenity, she'd purposely adopted a new last name, a simple, traditional persona; kept to herself and had never so much as jaywalked, for fear of exposure. Her current life was an open book: Tina Braddock, volume two.

It was volume *one* she didn't want anyone to know about.

Justin lost interest in the adults as soon as he met Zorro, Tina's eccentric black-and-white cat. Its body was too long in proportion to its legs, it had the distinctive yowl of a Siamese and its favorite game was hide-and-seek. The game was in full swing on and around the back porch by the time Zac had the barbecue fire going.

"That animal is crazy." Scowling, he watched the outlandish cat hide behind the crossed legs of a picnic table and pounce on Justin's shoes as soon as the boy got close enough. "You're sure he's not dangerous?"

"Positive. I've even taken him to the preschool with me to show the children. He's never laid a paw on any of them."

"How about his claws?"

"He doesn't have any front ones." Tina took note of Zac's look of disapproval. "I didn't have his claws removed, if that's what you're thinking. It had already been done when I adopted him."

"You didn't get him as a kitten?" Listening, he leaned down to blow more air on the fire.

"No. He used to belong to one of the Whitaker sisters. When they sold their property they were desperate to find homes for Miss Prudence's cats, so I said I'd take one."

Zac arched an eyebrow as he watched the cat-versus-boy game progressing. "You picked *him?*"

"Not exactly," Tina said. "Zorro was the only one they had left by the time I got there. I took him because I felt sorry for him. If I'd known what a character he was, I'd have chosen him, anyway. They told me he got his name because he always zig-zagged when he ran." She placed a finger in front of her lips. "Look. He's hiding under the wicker chair. See his tail twitching out the back? Watch what he does when I sit down there."

Justin raced by. Zac reached out to slow his progress. "Miss Tina wants us to watch something. Over there—" He crouched down beside the boy and pointed.

Still barefoot, Tina sauntered up to the chair, carefully sat down and began to swing her feet. In seconds the mischievous feline launched his attack. Wrapping his forelegs around her ankle, he pretended to bite it while his hind feet raked at her defenseless foot. If Zac hadn't seen her giggling, he'd have been certain she was being hurt.

She bent over and began to tickle the cat's tummy. It leaped to its feet and sprinted off in a blur of black and white, followed by the little boy.

"Zorro can dish it out but he can't take it," Tina

remarked, grinning. "He loves to play that game. Especially when I act like I don't know he's there. I think he's a frustrated predator. I suppose all indoor cats are."

"Indoor? Uh-oh. You should have said something when Justin let him out. I never thought about it being a problem, or I'd have stopped him."

"It's fine as long as I'm here," Tina assured him. "Without his front claws, Zorro would be helpless if he had to defend himself, though. He acts ferocious but he's really a marshmallow." Her smile broadened. "Hey! That reminds me. I think I have a bag of marshmallows in the pantry. Want to roast them for dessert?"

Justin's loud "Yeah!" startled the cat and sent him on another wild lap over and under the raised wooden porch. On the final pass he disappeared into the shadowy recesses beneath the steps.

"Speaking as a guidance counselor," Zac gibed, "it's my professional opinion that your cat is severely disturbed."

"Oh? What treatment would you recommend? Do you want to sit down with him and ask him about his early years?"

"If he were a person, that's exactly what I'd do. You'd be amazed at the stories I've heard since I got my degree and started working with teens. It's appalling."

Turning away, Tina busied herself smoothing a fresh plastic cloth over the picnic table. *Appalling* was only the beginning. Given her experience with her younger brother, Craig, she could have added *unbelievable,* and *terrifying,* and *life-shattering.* Especially life-shattering.

The only good thing to come out of the situation with Craig was his eventual rehabilitation. Seeing him settled down with a wife, son and new baby almost made it all worthwhile. Almost.

If she had it to do over again, however, Tina knew she'd find some other way to help him. And she'd never tell a lie. Not one. Not even if her honesty meant her unmanageable sibling might have to suffer.

Justin ran out of steam right after they ate. Five minutes of whining were followed by blissful silence, when he curled up in the big wicker chair and dozed off.

"I've always preferred dogs, myself," Zac said, "but I think I may need to borrow your crazy cat from time to time. My son hasn't gone to sleep that easily for longer than I can remember."

"You could always get him a puppy, you know. Your new yard is already fenced to keep it home." Tina scanned the yard and porch. "Poor Zorro. I'll bet he's crawled off for a catnap. Chances are, he's exhausted, too."

"It wore me out just watching them play."

"I know what you mean. Me, too." She stood and began to gather up the dishes, surprised when Zac picked up his plate and rose to help her. She waved him off. "I can do this. Sit down. You're my guest."

"I'd rather help."

He sounded so sincere, she gave in. "Okay. Make a stack on the end of the kitchen counter, just inside the door. That way you'll be in sight if Justin stirs."

Complying, Zac watched her carry the uneaten food past him and put it in the refrigerator. He sighed and spoke softly. "I'm at my wits' end with that kid. I'd hoped that a change of scenery would stop his panic attacks."

"Instead of a dog, maybe he needs more family in his life so he doesn't concentrate solely on you. Aren't there any female relatives you could ask for help?"

"Oh, sure," he said cynically. "Kim—my wife—came from a big family. All three of her sisters dote on Justin."

"Well, then…?"

"No way." Zac was shaking his head. "They hate me. If I give them the chance to fill Justin's head with their unfair opinions, he might wind up hating me, too. At the very least, he'd be more confused than he already is."

Tina couldn't imagine anyone disliking a man like Zac. Even though he was clumsy at expressing affection, he clearly loved his son. Pensive, she led the way back outside and started to fold up the plastic tablecloth. "You really believe they'd do that?"

"In a heartbeat." His voice deepened. "They blame me for Kim's death."

Hoping he'd explain further, Tina hugged the folded cloth to her chest and waited quietly. She knew better than to question him on such a touchy subject, even though her curiosity was aroused. Once they officially became neighbors, perhaps he'd volunteer more information. If not, she'd just have to respect his privacy.

Finally, she broke down and asked, "What about your side of the family? Brothers? Sisters?"

Zac snorted with derision. "I was an only child. My parents live in a retirement community down in Florida. Justin and I detoured to visit them on our way here. Talk about a disaster. All my mother did when he got upset was wring her hands and cry right along with him." A wry smile lifted one corner of Zac's mouth. "It was quite a chorus. You should have seen the look on my dad's face."

"I'll bet."

Stuffing his hands into his pockets he began, "I've been thinking. Maybe…"

Tina intuitively finished his sentence. "You thought maybe I'd volunteer?"

"I suppose that's too much to ask."

"No. Not at all."

Tina had to struggle to keep from laughing at the smooth way the Lord had handled a potentially awkward situation. While she'd been needlessly fretting about how she was going to worm her way into the little boy's life without having her innocent motives misunderstood, God was setting the whole thing up. What a kick. Everything was turning out *exactly* as she'd planned, yet Zac Frazier thought the whole idea was his!

Chapter Four

Zac had offered to paint the interior of the house as soon as it was vacant because he wanted to expedite his tenancy. However, he'd had no idea how hard the job would be, especially with Justin underfoot every second.

By the time he'd finished putting one coat of paint on the master bedroom, there were already tiny sneaker prints of the same pale beige color up and down the hall.

Tina found the little boy sitting on the steps of his new front porch, barefoot. She joined him. "Hi, honey."

Justin cast her a forlorn look.

"Uh-oh," she said, smiling tenderly. "What's wrong?"

"Daddy's mad at me."

Tina drew up her knees and hugged them. "Are you sure?"

"Uh-huh. He hollered at me."

"My, that sounds serious. Why do you suppose he got so upset?"

"'Cause of that dumb old paint."

"What did the paint do?"

"It stuck to my shoes and got itself all over the rug."

"That *was* bad," she said, working hard to sound serious when what she wanted to do was laugh out loud at his childish logic. "Is that why you're sitting on the porch?"

The boy nodded. "Daddy took my shoes off and told me to stay right here." His voice quieted. "Dumb old paint."

"I'm pretty good with a brush. Do you suppose your daddy would like me to help him?" she asked, getting to her feet and smoothing her shorts as she spoke. "Maybe I should go see."

"Okay," Justin said with a sage expression, "'cept he might yell at you, too."

Tina slipped off her sandals by the front door. "I hope not, but just in case, I'll leave my shoes out here. That way I'll feel it if I accidentally step in any spilled paint, and I won't track it all over the place."

Leaving the unhappy child to mull over her common sense approach, she let herself in and called, "Yoo-hoo. Anybody home?"

"In here. Down the hall," he answered gruffly. "Watch your step. The carpet's wet."

She edged past the obviously damp portions and paused at the bedroom door. Zac had carefully covered the carpeting in that room with plastic sheeting, taped down at the edges. It was easy to see that Justin had tracked through every drop of paint he could find on the plastic, then headed for the hallway. His footprints stopped where the wet carpeting began.

Tina giggled. "I see your son was helping you paint this morning."

"Helping me lose my mind, you mean." He made a sour face. "It's not funny."

"Oh, I don't know. It proves what I've always heard. You catch insanity from your children." Taking in the room and its occupant, she shook her head and grinned. Zac had paint smeared on his shorts and tank top, plus splatters on nearly every inch of exposed skin. "Are you trying to paint the walls or decorate yourself?"

He was obviously in no mood for her sarcasm. One eyebrow arched as he stared back at her. "What does it look like?"

"Truthfully? It looks like you aren't sure. You've got paint in your hair and beige freckles all over your face and arms, among other things."

"That's probably gray you see in my hair, thanks to Justin," Zac countered. "So far, I've spent more time cleaning up after that kid than I have slinging paint at these four walls."

"So *that's* your problem," Tina gibed. "Well, no wonder. You're supposed to *roll* it on, not sling it."

"I'm glad *somebody* is amused."

"I certainly am." Laughing lightly, she waited for his expression to soften. It finally did. "That's better. Now, tell me. Would you rather I took Justin home with me to get him out of your rapidly graying hair, or pitched in and helped you paint this place?"

"I don't suppose there's any way you can do both, is there?"

"I'm good, but I'm not *that* good. Tell you what. I'll go change into some old clothes and bring Zorro back with me when I come. That way you'll have a painting partner and Justin will have something to occupy him while we finish up in here. How's that sound?"

"Like heaven," Zac said with a sigh. "I'm not real good at painting houses."

"Noooo," she mocked. "Do tell."

One corner of his mouth twitched in a wry smile, and he hefted the paint roller by its handle, as if testing it for weight and balance. "You're lucky you already volunteered to help me, Miss Tina. If you hadn't, I might be tempted to do something rash."

She quickly ducked around the doorjamb and peeked out from behind it, eyes sparkling with mischief. "You do, and I'll turn *you* purple the way you threatened to do to poor, innocent little Tommy."

"I'd like to see you try," Zac shot back.

Tina laughed and shook her head. "Oh, no, you wouldn't. Trust me. You'd lose."

"Oh, yeah?"

"Yeah. But right now, I think we'd better concentrate on getting your house painted. Are you planning on doing the other bedrooms, too?"

"That's what the landlord said he wants, and he bought the paint, so I guess the answer is yes. Since I was stupid enough to offer in the first place, I'm stuck doing things his way."

"Okay. Go tape the plastic down in the other rooms and get them ready. I'll be back in a jiffy."

Zac snorted derisively. "Do you always jump in with both feet and start giving orders?"

"Only when it's obvious I'm dealing with somebody whose expertise is sorely lacking in an area where I shine. You have a choice. You can either listen to my good advice or struggle through this project the hard way. Alone."

"Is that a threat or a promise?" he asked.

"Both." Wheeling, she flounced off down the hall.

Zac watched his charming neighbor go, then stood motionless for a few moments more after she was out of sight. He didn't realize how much her presence had distracted him until he looked down at the roller in his hand. Paint had pooled in the lowest point of the cylinder and was falling in a thin stream, making squiggle lines all over the tops of his running shoes.

* * *

Tina wasted no time returning, as promised. She found Zac crawling around on his hands and knees, securing the protective plastic sheet in the smaller bedroom.

"You don't need to mask those baseboards," she told him, pausing in the doorway. "I have a very steady hand."

"I'm glad one of us does." He looked up. "Did you check on Justin when you went outside?"

Tina nodded. "He's fine. He and Zorro are playing cat-and-mouse. Justin's the mouse."

"That's typecasting, for sure. The kid loves cheese."

"And Zorro's already a cat, so he's a natural, too," Tina added, playing along. "Did you finish the master bedroom, or do I need to go back and touch it up for you?"

"It's done. At least, I think it is. I had to stop to scrub footprints off the carpeting in the hall, and by the time I got back the fresh paint was so dry it was hard to tell where I'd left off. You might want to see if I missed any spots."

"Okay. Back in a flash."

Zac straightened and rubbed the back of his neck with one hand. That woman was a wonder. Nothing seemed to faze her. Didn't she ever get grumpy? One thing was for sure, she always managed to look good, no matter how she was dressed. When she'd first come over she'd been wearing a turquoise shirt and shorts that had set off the greenish tint of her eyes.

This time, although she'd donned tattered denim shorts and tied the tails of an old blouse at her waist, she still looked appealing.

Face it, Frazier, he told himself. *Like it or not, you have a pretty neighbor.*

Which makes no difference to me at all, he added quickly, defensively. *The only thing I care about is raising my son the way Kim would have wanted.*

Guilt instantly filled his heart. If he intended to instill the right values and set the right kind of example, he'd better start taking Justin to Sunday School again. That kind of thing had mattered to Kim. It mattered to him, too. Once, he and his late wife had led a youth ministry that had been a miraculous success, due in part to his contacts with teens through his counseling job. He could do that again. He *should* do it again.

Tina appeared in the doorway with the roller, pan and one of the partially used gallons of paint, bringing an end to his solitary contemplation.

"I found a couple of streaks in the other room and painted over them," she said. "Otherwise, you did a fine job."

"Thanks." Zac got to his feet. "Okay. You're the boss. Tell me what to do now. I'm all yours." The rosy blush rising to her cheeks made him add, "Figuratively speaking, of course."

"Of course." Embarrassed, she averted her gaze and busied herself with the painting supplies as she spoke. "I noticed that all the paint was the same color. That's good. It means we won't have to wash the brushes and roller between rooms. And I brought some plastic wrap from my kitchen, in case you don't have any, so we can cover the tray whenever we take a break. That way, the extra paint won't dry in the pan or on the roller and be wasted.''

"Sounds like you have it all figured out.''

She chanced a peek up at him. "All but the ladder part. As you may have noticed, I'm a little short on one end. And I get dizzy on ladders, so I'd prefer you take charge of the ceilings and the tops of the walls.''

"Oh, I don't know,'' Zac drawled. "Your legs must be the right length, they…''

"They reach all the way to the ground. Yeah, yeah. I've heard that my whole life.''

"Sorry. Just trying to be friendly.''

"I know. Guess I'm overly sensitive about my height.''

"Lack of height, you mean,'' Zac offered with a lopsided smile. "I suppose that's one reason you relate to little kids so well. You're practically on their level.''

"Mister,'' Tina retorted, "I'm on their level in more ways than just my size. I even think their lame jokes are funny.'' She stirred the paint remaining in the can, then poured more into the roller pan. "Yesterday, Tommy asked me why the chicken crossed the road.''

"To get to the other side?''

"Humph. That's what I guessed, too. Tommy said, nope, it crossed the road because the Colonel was after it! Broke me up."

"Sounds like that kid eats out a lot. Which reminds me," Zac said without considering the possible ramifications, "I owe you a dinner."

"Thought you'd never ask."

"Whoa." He shook his head, incredulous. "I wasn't exactly asking. I was merely making an observation. There's nothing to eat in my kitchen. Not even a table to sit at. And by the time we finish this job, I don't think either of us will be in any shape to go out to eat, so..."

"So, order a pizza delivered, and we'll eat it on the porch. I'm not fussy." The consternation on his face struck her as funny. "Don't look so scared. I'm not making a pass at you. It's local custom. We Southerners are always feeding each other. Take my church, for instance. If we didn't have a dinner on the ground once in a while after the morning service, we wouldn't think we were in the right place."

"Dinner on the *what?*"

Tina watched him stand the stepladder near the corner and wiggle it to make sure it was safe to climb. "On the ground. It's one of those old sayings we were talking about, before. Back in horse-and-buggy days, lots of folks traveled a long way to worship. After the morning service, they used to spread out blankets on the ground and share food, then fellowship together all afternoon before starting for home."

She chuckled at his cautious expression. "Hey, don't worry. We eat at tables, now. And we don't do it every Sunday. Just occasionally. Matter of fact, there's one planned for this weekend."

"Too bad it's not Sunday till tomorrow, then," Zac said. "I could use some good home cooking."

Tina handed him the roller and pan, steadying the ladder while he climbed it and started painting the ceiling. "I thought you said you liked to cook."

"I used to. I haven't felt much like doing it lately."

Pausing to decide if she should keep still and let him reveal more details at his own speed, or question him about his past, Tina suddenly realized he'd hinted he might like to come to her church. She took that as a very good sign. "You know, if you bring a covered dish to the church dinner, you'll be the hit of the afternoon. What were some of your favorite recipes?"

"I liked to experiment with ethnic food. Mexican, Chinese, stuff like that." He heard her melodic laugh below him and leaned over to peer down at her. "What?"

"Nothing. Just that I tried to get a few of my local friends to taste my homemade salsa, and they looked at me like I was crazy. Finally, I settled on a couple of recipes everybody liked, and now I take the same dishes to church suppers virtually every time."

"Maybe I should try—"

There was a howl from the direction of the front porch. Zac froze, listening. "What the…?"

Tina was already headed for the door at a trot. "Sounds like Zorro's in trouble. I'll go see what's wrong."

"Not without me, you won't," he said. Jumping down and dashing after her, he shouted, "Justin! You okay?"

Tina reached the front door a heartbeat ahead of Zac and straight-armed the screen. It swung all the way open and smacked against the house with a loud, metallic *bang*.

It didn't take a half-second for her to assess the problem. Justin was perched astride the wooden porch railing, trying to hold on to her struggling cat, while a rambunctious, half-grown, yellowish dog barked beneath them.

"How did *that* get in the yard?" Zac shouted.

"Probably jumped the fence. It's big enough."

Zac pushed past her and reached for his son, ordering the boy, "Let go of the cat."

Justin clung to the frightened Zorro for all he was worth. "No! No!"

"Here. I'll take him," Tina said.

Before she could act, however, Zac had grabbed Justin around the waist and pulled him close, leaving her poor pet pinned between them. Thank goodness the cat had been declawed or he'd have torn up father and son like a miniature buzz saw.

Zorro continued to yowl unmercifully. The stray dog apparently thought everybody had come outside to play, because he got even more excited and began leaping awkwardly into the air next to Zac, thoroughly discombobulating the trapped cat.

"Give me my kitty!" Tina shouted over the din.

Zac had his hands full. "Get that dog out of here, first."

She had to admit, the man had a point. Without the added agitation, Zorro would be a lot easier to handle. The trouble was, the adolescent canine wasn't cooperating. Every time she reached for him, he ducked away. Finally, she lunged with her whole body and managed to drape her torso over his back long enough to get both arms around his neck and bring him to a halt. Sort of.

"*Now* what do I do?" she asked, panting.

"Hang on!" Zac ordered. "I'm putting these two in the house where they'll be safe."

Tina didn't have the time or the inclination to question his decision. She was having enough trouble keeping hold of the dog. Its ears and feet were enormous. The rest of it didn't look fully developed but clearly promised to be gargantuan once it matured. Fortunately, it had an amiable temperament. Instead of trying to bite Tina, it was licking her face and wiggling all over with delight.

She wasn't nearly that happy about their close association. The reappearance of Zac looming over her would have been a more welcome sight if he hadn't been just standing there. Dodging the dog's wet tongue, she peered up at him.

"It's about time. Get this moose away from me!"

"You all right?"

"I will be when you *help* me." She suspected he was delaying because he was so amused by her predicament.

"Right. Got him," Zac finally said. "You can let go now."

Breathless, she fell back into a spraddle-legged position on the porch floor. Zac had grabbed the dog around its rib cage, the way she'd first tried to do, and lifted it off the ground, its back against his chest. Held in that position, the animal stiffened, its lanky legs pointed straight out as if they had each miraculously acquired splints. Only the dog's tail continued to move. It was hanging down between Zac's legs and wagging slightly.

"He's almost as tall as you are," Tina marveled. "Must be part Great Dane."

"No kidding. Where does he belong?"

"Beats me. Maybe he'll go home if you put him outside the fence."

"I sure hope so." Zac cautiously started down the porch steps. "I'd hate to have to go through all this again."

Exhausted from her wrestling match with the friendly pup, Tina took a deep, settling breath. "Boy, you and me, both."

She saw Zac stop at the gate, but he couldn't reach

the latch to open it because of the dog's stiff-legged posture.

"Want some help?" she called, her voice overly sweet.

"Oh, no," he replied, puffing and straining. "I'll just…hoist him up…over my head…and lower him gently on the other side of this five-foot-high fence." His voice rose. "Of *course*, I want some help!"

"Well, you don't have to get huffy." Stifling her giggles, Tina scrambled to her feet and hurried to join him. "That really is a sweet dog," she said, pausing to ruffle its satiny ears with one hand while she unlatched the gate with the other. "He could have had us all for lunch, yet he never once growled, not even when I fell all over him and grabbed him."

"Before you get too softhearted, I suggest you keep in mind that it was your *cat* he wanted to eat for lunch, not people."

"That's certainly what poor Zorro thought. What a funny picture we must have made, with Justin trying to keep him safe from this dog and you and me wrestling both animals."

"No kidding. I'm glad nobody was videotaping us." Zac lowered the dog gently to the ground, hind feet first, intending to steady him before letting him go.

Instead of standing up or running away, however, the big dog collapsed in a heap at his feet and rolled on its back in submission, its wide, pink tongue lolling out the side of its mouth.

"I think you win, Zac. Looks like he's accepted you as his boss."

Tina bent down to gently scratch the dog's stomach, and it moved one of its hind legs in unison with her ministrations, as if it were doing the scratching, instead. "Look. He's giving us the chance to conquer him and hoping for kindness, just like a weaker animal would do in the wild."

Zac wiped perspiration off his brow with the back of his hand and leaned against the gatepost. "Goody. Now I get to be his idol. Lucky me."

"Well, that's better than being his enemy, considering his size. When I first saw him, I thought he might be a yellow Lab, but he's way too big for that. If he grows into those feet, he'll be a monster. He'd better like us. We have to live in this neighborhood, too, you know."

Straightening and backing through the gate so she could close it while leaving their canine nemesis shut out, she noticed that Zac was frowning down at her. "What's wrong?"

He folded his arms across his broad chest. "Oh, nothing much. It just occurred to me that since you live around here you should know who he belongs to, unless he's a stray. He is kind of hard to overlook."

"He wasn't wearing any collar," Tina added soberly. "That's why I had to grab him like I was trying to throw a steer at a rodeo."

"He's not quite *that* big."

"Give him a month or two. He'll grow."

"Yeah. I hate to just leave him out here and hope he'll go home, but I don't know what else to do with him." Zac glanced toward the house. "Well, I suppose we'd better get back to our painting or we'll still be at it tonight."

"Painting!" Tina gasped. "Oh, no." Eyes wide, she stared up at her companion. "We left a kid and a scared cat loose inside your house with all that paint!"

Chapter Five

It wasn't hard to trace Zorro's path. Once he'd visited the room where Zac had left the open roller pan, his tracks were easy to follow. The more steps he took, however, the more his paw prints faded. Justin's bare footprints were beside the cat's for the last part of its journey. Both sets of tracks disappeared in the kitchen.

Zac raked his fingers through his hair and shook his head. "I don't believe this."

"I wonder where they went," Tina said with a chuckle.

"Out the back door, I hope," Zac mumbled, rapidly crossing to a window that looked out on the fenced backyard, to satisfy himself that his son was safe. "They're there."

"That's one thing to be thankful for. Got a mop?"

Leaning to one side, she was sighting along the shiny floor, looking for dull spots of smeared paint.

"No. But I'll buy one. I'm going to have to give up painting for the day and go rent a rug shampoo machine at the closest supermarket, anyway. I'll get a mop, too, if they have one. Can you look after Justin while I'm gone?"

"Sure. I'll take him home with me."

"*And* the cat."

Tina tried to smother a burst of giggles and failed. "And the cat," she agreed. "I wouldn't have brought him over here to keep Justin company if I'd had any idea he'd start so much trouble."

Zac was washing paint spots off his hands and forearms at the kitchen sink. "Glad to hear it was spontaneous. I'd hate to think you got up this morning already determined to ruin my day."

"Naw," Tina said with a teasing grin. "I only do that to my enemies."

"You have enemies? Here in Serenity? I'm amazed."

It was the fading of her bright smile, rather than anything she said in return, that showed him he'd touched a nerve.

Lowering her gaze, she said flatly, "No. I have no enemies. Not anymore."

All the way to the supermarket and all the way home, Zac thought about how forlorn Tina had looked when their innocent banter had gotten too close to whatever painful truth she felt the need to hide.

What she did, said or felt was none of his business, he told himself firmly. The woman had already proved she was a walking disaster waiting to happen. If he let himself get too close to her, he was liable to find out his "Miss Tina" problems had only just begun.

Kim would have liked her, he decided. Would have befriended her. And eventually probably would have become her confidant the way she had with some of the troubled teenage girls in their former youth group. How old was Tina Braddock, anyway? It was hard to tell when she acted so unrestrained. Not that her company manners weren't first-rate. She just struck him as more of a kid at heart than most other adults did—which wasn't a bad trait to have in view of her job at the day care center.

He pulled his van into his driveway and got out to unload the carpet-cleaning machine. All seemed quiet in the rural neighborhood. That was probably due, in part at least, to the uncomfortably high afternoon temperature.

Toting his rental and the special soap to fill it, Zac let himself in the back door. An unbelievable sight stopped him in his tracks. His four-year-old son was down on his hands and knees, scrubbing the floor with a stiff brush, while Tina stood over him and pointed out spots he'd missed!

It was all Zac could do to keep from cursing.

"What do you think you're doing?" he bellowed, staring at Tina.

"Cleaning up after ourselves," she replied calmly. "We make the mess, we clean it up." Her steady gaze dared him to contradict her.

"Four-year-olds are *not* responsible for scrubbing floors."

"They are if they dirty them through carelessness when they know better." Hands on her hips, she faced Zac squarely. "Or would you like to wait until he's oh, say, fifteen or sixteen, and *then* try to convince him that there are consequences to everything he does, good or bad?"

"That's not the point."

"That is *exactly* the point," Tina insisted.

Zac glanced at his son's upturned face and saw tears glistening in his eyes. His stance softened. "I'm sorry I got upset, buddy. I'm not mad at you. I was just surprised, that's all."

"We…we got it all clean in here," the boy said with a quaver in his voice. "Miss Tina helped. She did Zorro's footprints, 'cause he's her cat—and I did mine."

"I see." Zac felt like a heel. "Then, I guess I owe Miss Tina an apology."

"Apology accepted," she said with a wry grimace. "I apologize, too, for not asking you if it was all right for me to discipline your child in your absence. I get so used to doing it at work, I tend to forget I'm not responsible for every kid I meet."

"Aren't you? In a way, I think we're all responsible," Zac told her. "Or, at least, we should be."

Tina was in awe. "You mean that?"

"Every word. Which is one of the reasons I've decided to start going to church, again. Justin needs it. And maybe I do, too. Who knows? I might even be led to help with another youth group, the way I used to. I certainly have enough practical experience and the right credentials to qualify for the job." He'd been unwinding the power cord to the shampooer as he spoke, and handed the plug to Tina when she approached.

"Is that what you eventually want to do?" she asked softly. "Be a church youth director?"

"Something like that, Lord willing. It was an old dream I'd pretty much given up on. I'm beginning to believe I had to come to Serenity to rediscover what's really important."

Rather than dash his hopes, at least regarding the rules of the church she belonged to, Tina kept silent. The deacons had already rejected several unmarried applicants for the part-time job of youth pastor. They'd insisted that a man had to be settled, with a well-rounded family of his own, before he was suited to handling other people's children.

Still, though he was single, Zac *was* a father and a widower rather than a divorced man, so perhaps he would qualify. If not, there were plenty of local women who would be eager to volunteer to complete his family portrait by becoming his wife.

Tina pictured the female assault that would ensue as soon as the eligible women in town found out about his marital status. He'd be up to his eyebrows in casseroles and homemade cakes before he knew what hit him. Living practically next door, she'd be lucky if she wasn't trampled in the stampede.

"Well, at least I don't have to worry about competing," Tina muttered to herself.

"Worry?" Zac asked. "I didn't hear all that. Were you worried about the carpeting?"

"Right." Tina took it as a gift from the Lord that her companion had thought she'd said "carpeting" instead of "competing." "I scrubbed the hallway to get up the worst of Zorro's tracks. I left the rug really wet on purpose, so I think everything else will come out okay." She put on a happy face. "So, shall I stay and help you, or do you want me to take the kids home with me?"

"Kids? Plural?"

"Justin and Zorro. Our mischievous children," she explained, smiling. The smile he gave her in return had to be warm enough to melt a glacier.

"Why don't you run on home. I should have this job done in about an hour, especially if I don't have to keep one eye on my son."

"Or the other eye on my cat. When you came in just now, did you happen to see the big dog lurking outside?"

"Come to think if it, no, I didn't. Maybe he's gone back where he came from."

"Then, things are looking up," Tina said, starting for the door. "If you want, you can have the pizza delivered to my house, since I'm the one with a table and chairs. Unless you have your heart set on eating out on the porch, now that the dog's gone."

Zac had forgotten all about his half-baked dinner invitation. He was tired, in desperate need of a shower and feeling a lot less cordial than normal. However, he supposed it was best to get it over with. Cancelling his social obligations to Tina by sharing a casual meal like pizza seemed to offer a painless solution.

"You order it and I'll pay for it," Zac said. "My treat. Order plenty. And get some soda pop, too. I'm going to let Justin live it up tonight and drink that instead of having milk with his meal."

"Wow. Wild, aren't you?" she quipped.

"I've had my moments, especially when I was younger. Admitting my own mistakes helps me relate to the kids I work with. Now, go on. I have to get busy before the swamp you left in the hall dries."

Tina was thankful he'd turned away and started fiddling with the shampooer. *Mistakes?* she thought. *Oh, mister, you have no idea how bad some people's mistakes can be. Like mine, for instance.* If anyone in Serenity ever found out, they'd probably run her out of town on a rail.

She'd decided long ago not to let herself get too close to other people or make friends who might ask questions about her past. Remaining aloof wasn't easy, but it was necessary. And as long as she had other people's children to love and care for, the self-enforced solitude was bearable.

Above all, she must *never* allow herself to fall in love, she added, gritting her teeth. It would be the most unfair thing she could do to anyone, including herself. She'd found out the hard way that no decent man would want her, least of all a man in the public eye.

Least of all, a man with plans like Zac Frazier's.

Zac was worn out by the time he finished the carpet. He cut across the neighbors' lawns and headed for Tina's back door rather than take the chance of tracking dirt into her living room.

He didn't see anyone in the kitchen when he peered through the screen, so he called out, "Hi. Anybody home?"

Whooping, Justin came on the run to let him in. "Daddy!"

"Hi, buddy. Have you been good?"

Tina answered for him as she walked into the kitchen carrying two red-and-white pizza boxes. "He's been wonderful. And your timing is perfect. The food just arrived. I had plenty of sodas in the fridge so I didn't bother to order more."

"Smells great. How much do I owe you?" Zac pulled out his wallet.

She waved him off. "Nothing. I took care of it."

"Oh, no, you don't," he insisted. "Either you let me pay, or Justin and I are out of here."

"Aw, Da-a-a-ad," the boy whined.

"Okay, okay." The printed bill was taped to the top box. Tina pulled it loose and passed it to him. "Sorry. It looks like we could have had a fancy dinner at Linden's for less money."

"Linden's?"

"It's a big buffet over in East Serenity. Practically everybody goes there after church. It's an all-you-can-eat place."

Laying the money on the kitchen counter, then taking a seat at her table, Zac helped Justin into the chair beside him and checked the boy's hands to make sure they were reasonably clean. "I thought you said there was a potluck coming up at your church?"

"This Sunday there is. We don't do it all the time, though." As soon as she'd provided their drinks, Tina sat down across from her guests and began to dish up the pizza. She smiled as she handed a plate to Zac. "So, what were you planning to bring?"

One dark eyebrow arched. "A bag of potato chips?"

"Well…"

"A *big* bag?"

"That'll do if you want to pretend you're a helpless bachelor with a poor, starving child to feed."

Justin laughed. So did his father.

"It will also mean that every single lady for fifty

miles in any direction will be showing up at your door, trying to win you over with her cooking.''

''Are you serious?''

''Count on it,'' Tina said. ''That's why we don't have many bachelors left around here. At least, not ones with teeth.''

Zac sounded as if he was going to strangle. He covered his mouth with his napkin till he got better control of himself. ''I'm so glad you told me that.''

''Just trying to warn you.''

''Maybe I should build a brick wall around my house and dig myself a moat.''

''Wouldn't help,'' she countered. ''The ladies I know would get past a little obstacle like a moat, even if it was full of alligators.''

Zac froze, a wedge of pizza halfway to his mouth. ''You don't really have alligators in this part of Arkansas, do you?'' He cast a sidelong glance at his young son. ''If I thought…''

''Nope. Just enough ticks, chiggers and mosquitoes to make life miserable in the summer and enough ice on the roads to make it interesting for a few days each winter. Other than that, this is a pretty nice place to live.''

''I'll buy some bug repellent the next time I go to the store. Anything else you think I need?''

''Not unless they've started selling a product you can spray on to keep the women away,'' she teased.

The man was staring at her in disbelief, acting as if he didn't know how attractive he really was.

Maybe he didn't. But he was sure going to find out. He really was the best-looking, most appealing guy in Serenity—or in all of Fulton County, for that matter—and his son was a charmer, too.

Truth to tell, if she hadn't considered herself unacceptable wife material for anyone, let alone Zac Frazier, she might have jumped in line with a casserole of her own and given the other single women a run for their money.

Justin had asked to be excused from the table and had promptly fallen asleep in an overstuffed chair in Tina's living room. She was combining the leftover pizza into one box, when Zac returned to the kitchen to report why the boy was suddenly so quiet.

"I noticed he could barely keep his eyes open." Tina gestured with the open box. "Here. Sure I can't talk you into one more slice?"

"Uh-uh. I ate too much already." Rejoining her at the table, Zac leaned back in his chair and lazily studied the kitchen. "You know, this is a cute little house. I like the way you've fixed it up."

"Thanks. It's exactly the same as the one you're renting, except the floor plan is reversed."

"You're kidding! This place feels a lot more homey."

"Must be because of the frilly curtains on the window over the sink," she alibied, hoping he'd drop the subject before she began to blush.

"I don't know." He laced his fingers behind his

head in a classic pose of relaxation. "I suppose I could try that at my place and see if it helps. You've got little statues and things sitting all over, too. And houseplants. I never was any good at keeping those alive. I got so I felt guilty for dooming the poor things by buying them in the first place."

"Then, why did you?"

Zac sighed. "Because Kim had always liked them so much. Keeping the house full of greenery made it seem more like she was still around."

"I'm sorry. I shouldn't have asked."

"It's okay. As long as Justin's not here to listen to us, I don't mind talking about her."

Tina began to frown. "You don't talk to him about his mother? Why not?"

"It brings back the trauma."

"How do you know?"

"Because I've seen how he acts when I mention Kim. He gets all tense and red-faced, then he starts to cry."

"Every time?"

"Every time. I took him to several doctors, but they couldn't even get him to talk to them, let alone to explain what was bothering him."

"His mother died. That's what was bothering him."

"I mean, specifically," Zac said soberly.

"Isn't he more likely to tell *you* something like that than he is to confide in a stranger?"

"Not necessarily. I told you, I don't relate well to small children. Not even Justin."

"Maybe that's because you think of the little ones as being more different than they really are. If he were a sad teenager, what would you do? How would you approach him?"

Tina saw his relaxed posture stiffen, his jaw muscles tense.

"I'd do the same thing I already did," Zac said flatly. "Find my son a capable, professional counselor."

"Which is exactly what *you* are. Plus, you love him. I know you do. Is there some good reason why you don't step into that role yourself?"

Zac got to his feet and stood facing her, pausing only long enough to say "Yes. I'm the one who's responsible for his mother's death, and he knows it. He saw it happen with his own eyes."

Tina was so overburdened by her turbulent emotional reaction to Zac's surprising revelation about his late wife, she didn't sleep much that night.

The following morning she pondered Zac's parting words for the thousandth time as she dressed for church. He'd bared his soul. And she'd just sat there like a ninny, with her mouth hanging open, and stared at him. The anguish in his expression had made her stomach hurt then—and it was doing the same thing, again and again, every time she relived the poignant scene.

She didn't recall saying anything relevant to Zac as he'd picked up his sleeping son and walked out the door. Now that she'd had more time to think about it, she realized that she should have at least expressed sympathy. If she hadn't been so busy trying to figure out exactly what he'd meant by his shocking confession, she might have. Unfortunately, she'd been so dumbfounded over the whole thing, her mind had gone blank.

"Of all the times to keep my mouth shut," she muttered to herself. "Now they probably won't show up for church this morning and it'll be my fault." Full of self-disgust and regret, she closed her eyes momentarily and prayed, *"I'm sorry, Father. I really blew it this time. I wanted to comfort him but I just didn't know what to say."*

Of course, saying nothing was probably better than blurting out the wrong thing, she reasoned sensibly. Well-meaning people were notorious for making someone's grief worse when all they meant to do was offer solace.

Tina picked up her Bible and scanned the room blankly, wondering why she felt as if she were forgetting something. Nothing came to her, so she gave up and headed for her truck, continuing to ponder the puzzle that was Zac Frazier.

Actually, it was just as well she hadn't openly expressed too much concern. She didn't want the man to get into the habit of confiding in her, because then he might expect her to reciprocate with details from her own past. That, she would never do.

Starting her truck, Tina headed toward the opposite side of Serenity, more than ready for the worship service to come. *"Okay, Lord,"* she said softly and with relief. *"I know if the Fraziers are meant to be in church with me, they'll get there in spite of my mistakes. I just pray they go* somewhere *to worship."*

Almost positive she wasn't going to see Zac and Justin in church, Tina grimaced. They were going to miss the dinner-on-the-ground if they didn't show up. That would be a real shame. The picnic atmosphere would be a wonderful way to get Justin more involved with some of the other children his age, and...

Suddenly, she realized what had been nagging at the fringes of her spinning consciousness all morning. "Oh, no! Dinner-on-the-ground!" The bewilderment surrounding Zac's statement of responsibility for his wife's death had made her forget to fix or bring any food. Well, it was too late now. There was only one thing left to do. She'd have to stop on her way to church and pick up something. Anything.

Wheeling into the market parking lot, she skidded to a stop, jumped out of her truck and rushed into the store. The instant she spotted the rack with all the bags of potato chips, she knew *exactly* what to take.

Chapter Six

Growing more and more disappointed, Tina kept an eye out for Zac all morning, even though Justin had failed to show up to enroll in her Sunday School class.

Mavis took her aside when they ran into each other after the eleven o'clock worship service. "What's wrong, kiddo? You look distracted."

"Nothing," Tina said quickly, scanning the crowd.

"I see you wore your prettiest dress today. Could that be because Zac Frazier is here?"

"He is? Oh, that's great!" Unable to quell her natural excitement, she stood on tiptoe to try to peer past the older woman's shoulder. "Where? I don't see him."

"That's probably because he's out in the kitchen," Mavis said. "At least, he was a few minutes ago when I got my cake out of my car and brought it inside.''

Tina studied her boss's smug expression and began to frown. "What's he doing in the kitchen?"

Laughing softly, Mavis said, "Beating 'em off with a stick, from the looks of it. Except for Miss Verleen, I don't think there's one volunteer worker out there who's over the age of thirty. And to think...we usually have to beg the younger ladies to help out with kitchen chores unless their age group is the one sponsoring the meal."

"Oh, dear." Tina grimaced wryly. "I warned him that would happen. *Now* he's in for it."

"We could go offer to rescue the poor guy," Mavis suggested. "A few minutes ago, the Gogerty sisters had him practically backed into a corner and Lela Pierce was moving in for the kill. He's probably still trapped right where I last saw him."

"Great idea. I don't want him to get scared off. Come on." Grabbing Mavis's hand, Tina began to drag her through the crowd that was gathering in the narrow hallway leading from the sanctuary to the fellowship hall. It wasn't easy to make headway with so many bodies crammed into such a small space.

"Pardon me! Excuse us! Coming through! Sorry," Tina mumbled. Her short stature made it impossible to see most of what was ahead, so she just kept pressing in the right direction. She'd almost made it to the closed double doors leading into the fellowship hall, when the pastor asked for quiet and began to say the blessing. Tina skidded to a halt. The moment he said "Amen," she let go of Mavis, forged ahead, and burst through the swinging doors before any of the others even got moving.

The sight that greeted her was almost too funny for words. Six—no, seven—women had Zac surrounded in the kitchen doorway, barring his escape. They were all babbling at once. Justin was clinging to his daddy's leg in the same frightened way he had been when she'd first met him. Zac might be flattered by all the attention he was getting, but the poor kid was obviously overwhelmed by it.

Tina called to him. "Hey, Justin! Over here."

Letting out a joyful squeal, the little boy abandoned his father and ran straight into her open arms. She crouched down to give him a big hug. "Hi, honey! I'm so glad you're here."

Directly above her, a deep, masculine voice said, "Good morning."

Tina managed to keep from looking at Zac right away. Listening was bad enough. The sound of his voice had made the hairs on the back of her neck tickle and sent goose bumps galloping up and down her bare arms.

Finally, she got command of her errant emotions and straightened, holding the child's hand. "Good morning." She glanced past Zac at the retinue he'd left behind. "I see you've met some other members of our congregation, already. How nice."

"Yes. It was." He paused to cast a winning smile

at the kitchen crew. Three of them waved back. "I whipped up a gelatin-and-fruit salad at dawn this morning. These ladies were kind enough to put it on a serving plate for me."

"How special."

Zac laughed softly. "You don't sound like you really mean that. What did you bring? Cold pizza?"

"Why do you want to know?"

"So I can taste your cooking."

"Why would you want to do that?" Tina was scowling.

"Just trying to be sociable. If you don't want to tell me what you brought, you don't have to. I'm sure somebody else will be glad to fill me in."

"Undoubtedly." She decided to redirect their conversation. "You missed Sunday School."

"I know. We got here late," Zac explained. "I needed to use the refrigerator at the new house to cool the gelatin and—"

"And my *doggie* came back!" Justin shouted gleefully, tugging on her hand. "He got us all dirty."

Zac nodded. "We had to go back to the motel to change into clean clothes. By then, it was almost too late to come at all."

"Oh, my." Tina was struggling not to laugh. "I can just picture that happening."

"No doubt. If that mutt doesn't quit being such a nuisance, I may have to call the dog pound."

"You can't. Serenity doesn't have one."

"Then, what do the folks around here do with strays?"

"Keep them. Find homes for them. Or..." She glanced at Justin and decided not to put the rest of the thought into words. Instead, she sobered and said, "This is the country, Zac. Not everybody around here values animals as pets instead of livestock, the way you and I do. What we see as an unacceptable solution to the problem was a necessary element of survival for years. Old habits die hard."

His expression hardened, his eyes narrowing as he searched Tina's face. "You mean to tell me they'd just...?"

"Some would, yes, if they saw no other choice. It's a way of life that's been around since pioneer days, and it's certainly no worse than the city folks who drive out to the so-called country to dump their unwanted dogs and cats, expecting us to take care of them."

"Hmm. I'd never thought of it quite that way." Pensive, he took Tina's arm and said, "Come on. Let's eat," and ushered the three of them into the chow line, together.

The touch of his warm, steady hand made her shiver. Everybody was staring. The Gogerty sisters looked like they were about to cry, Lela was wide-eyed and incredulous, and Cheryl Smith, the only blonde in the bunch, had whipped out a lipstick and was smearing it on thick.

That wasn't the only thing *thick* around there, either, Tina mused. You could have fried bacon using the heated atmosphere of female rivalry in that room!

The spirit of neighborliness at their long dining table was alive and well. Zac met the infamous Ed Beasley, whose old car collection had cost the city a lawsuit after he'd moved to a house in town and left the rusty relics behind. Then there was Miss Verleen, one of the older workers from the kitchen, who had brought him a special helping of her homemade meatballs.

Tina spent most of the mealtime either helping Justin cut his food or laughing at Zac's reaction to having so much bounty heaped upon him, whether he wanted it or not. He'd been sitting there eating for as long as she had, yet his plate remained piled high.

During a rare lull in the conversation, he leaned toward her to whisper "I'm stuffed. What do I do now?"

"Why, you've hardly touched your meal," Tina cooed. "What will all your girlfriends think?"

"What girlfriends?"

"Maybe I should have said your *fan club*. It's a good thing your fridge is working, because I'll bet you leave here with enough leftovers to feed you and Justin for a week."

Zac grimaced. "I don't *want* leftovers. Well, maybe another piece of this peach pie, but otherwise, no."

"I knew you'd love it. That's why I told you to take a slice. Eloise made it. She's famous for her pies."

"I hope she's married," Zac said. "I'd hate to give her an innocent compliment and have her think I was making a pass at her."

"Around here, that could happen," Tina told him, her eyes twinkling merrily. "A fella from Harrison bought a peach pie at a charity auction last year and wound up marrying the one who baked it."

"It must have been some pie."

"Guess so. I didn't know many people in Serenity at the time, so I didn't go to the auction. I heard all about it later, though." She noticed that Zac was staring at her. "What? Do I have food stuck to my teeth or something?"

"No, no." He shook his head slowly, thoughtfully. "I'm just surprised, that's all. I remember you told me you hadn't lived in Serenity your whole life, but somehow I got the impression you'd been around here for a long time."

"Nope." Tina was starting to regret being so chatty. He already knew as much about her as people who'd been a part of her life since her arrival. Being that open with anyone was not good.

"So, where are you originally from?" Zac asked.

"Why? What difference does it make?"

He looked surprised, then troubled. One eyebrow arched. "If you and I were just having a casual conversation, I'd say it didn't make any difference at all.''

''It doesn't,'' Tina said quickly. Her smile was forced. If only she'd named a hometown! Any hometown. Any except the real one.

When Zac leaned closer to talk quietly, there was an unspoken warning in his tone. ''As long as you are entrusted with the care of my son, it makes a tremendous difference…to me. The way I see it, if you had nothing to hide, you wouldn't hesitate to tell me everything.''

''Oh, really?'' So angry she was trembling, she crumpled her paper napkin, pushed back her folding chair and got to her feet. ''Well, think again, mister. My private life is just that. Private. So get used to it. If you choose to take your son out of our day care because of that, fine.''

The noise level in the room fell dramatically, and Tina realized her outburst was the reason. Her cheeks flamed. Once again, being around Zac Frazier had resulted in calling undue attention to herself, to her reluctance to share details from her past.

Tears of frustration pooled in her eyes. She knew she didn't dare look at Mavis or any of her other Christian friends, or she'd see their sympathy and start to cry for sure. The only way to salvage her pride and continue to protect her privacy was to leave the room. Immediately.

The outer exit seemed miles away as she circled the long table and started for it, her sight blurred by her tears. Twenty feet to go. Now ten. Five. She put out her hand to open the door. *Almost there.*

Just as she pushed aside the heavy glass door and passed through, a shrill little voice filled with pathos called out, "Miss Tina!" and she thought her heart would break.

A short time later, Zac and his son found her sitting in her truck in the church parking lot, sniffling. The windows were rolled down. He handed her Bible and purse to her through the opening on the driver's side. "Here—you left these at the table and I figured you'd need them. Especially your keys."

"Thanks."

"Don't mention it." He reached down and lifted Justin in his arms, then said, "See, buddy? Miss Tina is fine now. She just didn't feel very good so she came outside to get some fresh air."

Tina smiled wanly, hoping to reassure the worried child, then searched his father's expression. "Is that what you told everybody inside?"

"I didn't have to. Your boss took care of it for me. Do you really have an ulcer, like she said?"

"Not that I know of," Tina admitted, making a disgusted face. "Although it's becoming a distinct possibility."

"I'm sorry if my questions upset you," Zac said. "You obviously have a lot of friends here. They all went out of their way to assure me you were wonderful with children. They vouched for your character one-hundred percent.''

"I'm glad.'' Tina fished a tissue out of her purse, blotted her tears and blew her nose. "I feel like a fool. I'm not normally so touchy.''

"And I don't usually act so defensive.''

"Only where Justin is concerned.'' Tina reached out to gently caress the child's arm. "That's understandable. I know you love him very much. I just wish…''

"What? That we could spend a little more of our free time together? The three of us? Hey, what a coincidence. I've been thinking the same thing.''

Tina stared at Zac, incredulous. Why would he make a pass at her when they'd both insisted they weren't interested in pairing up? Then she noted the deep concern in his eyes as he chanced a sidelong peek at his son, and she suddenly understood his motives. Perfectly. As a professional counselor he was in his element, in control of things, but as a single father he still felt lost. All he was doing was asking her for more help. How could she refuse when his plea was a direct answer to her ongoing prayers for Justin?

"I suppose we could get together once in a while,'' Tina finally said. "Since we'll be neighbors, it'll be easy.'' The relief in Zac's expression was so transparent that it threatened to bring back her tears, so she switched her attention to the boy. "Only, you have to promise to keep your doggie on a leash when

Zorro's outside with me, at least until they get to be friends. Okay?''

"Okay!" Justin shouted eagerly.

Zac began to scowl at her, his dark eyes narrowing. "Now, wait a minute. I never said anything about keeping that dog."

"You did feel sorry for him, though. I could tell. And he has to stay somewhere while we advertise to try to find his owner. Might as well be at your place."

"Oh, sure. No problem," he countered. "All I have to do is get used to dodging his muddy paws every time I walk out the door."

The cynical look on the man's face made Tina chuckle, in spite of her personal problems. "He's just one of God's poor, lost creatures. I have a way with animals. I can teach him to stop jumping on you, if you want."

A smile brightened Zac's countenance, lit his eyes. "It's a deal. That'll be something you and Justin can do together when you visit us." He gave his son a quick hug as he put him down. "Right, buddy?"

The child nodded enthusiastically, holding tight to his daddy's hand. "Uh-huh. Can we do it now? Today?"

"That's up to Miss Tina."

She leaned out of the truck window to smile down at the little boy. "If the dog is still hanging around when we all get home, I'll come over and we can start training him. I promise."

Zac mouthed a silent *thanks,* and backed away with his son, watching as Tina started her truck and drove away. He began to frown. There was something about her that still bothered him. Maybe it was the contrast between her normally loving attitude and the defensiveness he'd glimpsed when she'd gotten upset and fled the fellowship hall.

He took a deep breath and released it as a quiet, pensive sigh. Tina Braddock's past, whatever course it had taken, really was none of his business. Her good reputation in Serenity was unquestioned, unmarred. On the surface she appeared to be just about perfect, from her skill with small children to her beautiful flower garden to her membership in the local church and participation in all the charitable activities he'd been told about that morning.

So, what was her problem? And why did he care? Zac asked himself. *Why, indeed.* Because his pretty neighbor was getting to him, that's why. Beneath the calm surface of the image she presented to the world, he'd sensed uneasiness, foreboding, even fear. But what was she afraid of? What could possibly affect her so deeply that she refused to even tell him a simple thing like where she was from?

He was going to find out what was causing her reticence and unhappiness, he vowed silently. Somehow, he was going to find out everything. And when he did, he was going to use his professional skills to help her face her fears and put them behind her. That was the least he could do in return for her willingness to help his son.

Verleen spotted Zac before he and Justin reached their van. Waving, she called, "Hey, there. Wait up! You forgot your meatballs."

"Sorry about that," he said, pausing politely as she approached. "But I'm sure there are plenty of other folks who can use some extra food."

"Nonsense. Any man with a hungry boy to feed and no wife to cook for him needs all the help he kin get." She motioned toward the group coming out the back door of the fellowship hall. "Over here! I caught 'em in time."

Zac's eyes widened. A parade of women was marching across the parking lot, obviously bearing leftovers intended for him. "Really, ma'am, I—"

"Now, son, there's no need to be shy," Verleen said, giving his arm a motherly pat. "We want you to have plenty to eat." She stepped back as the others approached to present him with their specialties, one by one.

The last in line placed a package of homemade cookies atop the stack of foil-and-plastic-wrapped goodies already in Zac's arms, smiling at him with confidence. "I'm Inez Gogerty, remember? I'm afraid they ate all my chicken salad. Always do. I saved you a few sugar cookies, though." Her smile widened, her expression eager. "I'll drop by your place with a fresh chicken salad in a few days, when you've had time to eat up all this other stuff.''

"You don't know where…"

"Where you live? Of course I do," she said, giggling nervously. "Everybody gets curious when we see a new face in town. We probably knew which house you were renting before the ink dried on the lease." She glanced at the others who were still crowded around Zac's van. "Didn't we, girls."

There was a twittery chorus of happy agreement and broad smiles from all the women.

Zac was beginning to feel like the star attraction at the zoo. Tucking the tall stack of odd-shaped packages under his chin to steady it, he managed to open the sliding side door of the van without dropping anything. Justin clambered in and climbed into his safety seat, while Zac carefully piled the food on the floor.

"Watch that plate o' beans," Verleen warned. "They could leak a might if they was to get tipped."

Zac had already found that out, thanks to the sauce he'd noticed on his fingers when he'd put everything down. "They'll be fine," he said, wiping his hand on one of the paper towels he kept in the van to clean up after Justin. This was turning out to be the most unusual visit to church he'd ever experienced. He'd thought Tina had been exaggerating when she warned him about the reception he'd receive, but she hadn't even begun to cover the present situation.

He slid behind the wheel and shut the door. "Well,

I'd better be getting on home so I can put all this food in the refrigerator. Wouldn't want any of it to spoil in the heat.''

Everyone was still standing there, waving a hearty goodbye, when he glanced into his mirror as he drove away. It looked as if he was going to be eating a lot of chicken salad, and who knows what else, in the weeks and months to come. Like it or not, he was definitely on more than one woman's list of needy single men.

Zac laughed to himself. So, this was what it was going to be like to live in a small town! How bizarre. He supposed it wouldn't do any good to announce that he was permanently unavailable. Knowing human nature, a declaration like that would only intensify the interest in changing his mind, especially if he explained fully.

Sobering, he shook his head. The last thing he intended to do was tell everyone what had happened to his wife and wind up being pitied for his loss. In that respect he could identify with Tina's wish for privacy.

He'd gone over and over the details of the boating accident, looking for some logic, some peace of mind about Kim's death. The water had been unusually swift that day, but she knew how to swim. Their son didn't. So Zac had towed the boy to shore first, then gone back to rescue her. What else could he have done? How could he have known she had hit her head and slipped out of her unfastened life vest?

And now it was just the two of them left. Father and son. Alone. Did Justin remember much about the accident? Or blame Zac the way he blamed himself? Considering the nightmares the boy kept having, both were possible, at least subconsciously.

Zac gritted his teeth in senseless anger. He'd made the wrong choice and there was no going back. Nothing he did was ever going to cure what ailed his family, or make things right again. God help him, there were times when he looked at his son and almost wished...

No! No! his conscience screamed. Sickened by the gravity of his wild thoughts, Zac pulled the van to the side of the road, set the brake and quickly climbed into the back seat next to Justin. His voice broke before he could finish saying "I love you, buddy."

The child, reacting to the intensity of his father's feelings, reached out his little arms.

Without a word, Zac embraced him, held tight, and began to pray wordlessly, letting his tears and his returning faith start to wash away the guilt that had been tainting his life, and his soul, for far too long.

Chapter Seven

Tina had stopped after church to pick up a leash and collar for Justin's dog, when suddenly she began to feel uneasy. Pivoting, she scanned the other shoppers. Most of them, like her, were dressed as if they'd just come from church. Only one person didn't fit. A gaunt, blond woman wearing a stretched-out tank top over shorts was squinting at her from across the store.

Curious, Tina stared back. The woman did look sort of familiar, although she couldn't place where she'd seen her before. Could she be the mother of one of the preschool students? Tina tried to picture her in different clothes, with her stringy hair styled better, hoping that would help. It didn't. Moreover, there was something about the woman's steady gaze that was unnerving.

The moment the strange woman started to approach, Tina looked away and slipped into the nearest checkout line. She knew she should be pleasant to everyone, even if their appearance was a bit off-putting, but this time was different. There was unspoken menace in that woman's eyes. Only a fool would stay to face it without first knowing what she was up against.

Hurrying out of the store with her purchases, Tina kept her gaze lowered, her head bowed, her shoulders slightly slumped. It was when she reached her truck that she relaxed enough to realize where she'd been when she'd learned to assume that kind of submissive posture.

Tina was surprised to see that she'd arrived home before her new neighbors. By the time she'd changed from her good dress into shorts and a T-shirt and walked over to the Frazier house to deliver the dog supplies she'd bought, she was starting to get a little worried. Zac had indicated they were coming here, not going back to the motel, so what could have delayed them?

The stray dog was lounging on Zac's front porch, half asleep. The moment she entered the yard, it leaped to its feet and barreled toward her.

Ready, Tina braced herself. Timing was everything in a situation like this. She didn't weigh nearly enough to overcome its forward momentum and muscle that big a dog into obedience, and she wasn't going to get a chance to win it over through friendship first, either. Unless she reacted properly in the next few seconds and caught it off guard, it was going to knock her flatter than a flitter.

The dog jumped at her, its front feet hitting her nearly as high as her shoulders. Tina raised one knee to meet its broad chest and jostle it without hurting it. At the same instant she shouted, "No! Down!"

Both of them staggered to regain their balance. The overgrown pup cocked its head and looked up at her as if she'd suddenly become a confusing giant. Tongue lolling, tail wagging, it headed for her again.

This time, all Tina had to do was raise her voice and deliver a firm "Down," and it stopped in its tracks. "Oh, good boy," she crooned. "What a smart boy you are."

Circling in front of her, begging for approval, it got so dizzy it almost swooned under her light, calming touch. Tina laughed. "You sure had Zac fooled, didn't you, you big baby? He thought you were incorrigible."

The wide, pink tongue laved her hand. "I know, I know. I'm the boss now." Laughing softly, she slipped the supple, link collar over the dog's broad head and fastened the ring at the end of it to the snap on the leash. "I sure hope my authority is transferable. One of your new masters is even shorter than I am, and four-year-olds don't have good enough reflexes to stop you the way I just did."

She cupped the dog's face in her hands and looked into its warm brown eyes, willing it to understand her words. "If you want to live here, you're going to have to learn to take it easy around the little guy, or you'll wind up back on the streets. We certainly don't want that to happen, do we?"

As if on cue, Zac and Justin pulled into the driveway. Tina straightened and waved a greeting with her free hand, taking care to watch the dog's behavior at the same time. Excited and trembling all over, it waited until the boy was inside the fence, then charged, forgetting that there was a restraint around its neck.

Just as it reached the end of the long leash, Tina yelled, "No!" as loud as she could, did an about-face, and headed in the opposite direction to counteract the dog's forward momentum. Her end of the leash might as well have been tied to a freight train.

"Wow," Zac said, astounded to see the result. "I'm impressed. What do you call that move?"

"Effective," she said, smiling and warmly welcoming the bewildered canine as it returned to her side. "And painless. The last thing you want to do is allow a stubborn moose like this to turn a nice walk into a contest of strength. One or two firm lessons should be enough to keep him from dragging you around behind him. He seems to learn really quickly."

"I thought for sure he was going to jerk you off your feet just now. Where did you learn to do that?"

"In 4-H," she said, immediately sorry to have spoken without censoring her answer.

"Can you teach me to handle him like that?"

"Probably. Do you learn as fast as the dog does?"

Zac gave a wry chuckle. "I doubt it." He gestured toward the van. "I wasn't clever enough to avoid accepting enough food to keep us in meatballs and desserts for weeks."

"Verleen's rubber meatballs?" Tina asked, knowing the answer but wanting to tease him.

"Those are the ones. Must be at least three or four dozen in here. I hate to waste food. Do you suppose I could freeze some of them?"

"Not if you value your life." Tina was shaking her head and grinning. "Anybody in town will tell you she makes up a big batch every couple of years, bags them, and stores them in her freezer. By the time she serves the last of them, they're pretty freezer-burned and dried out."

"Is that why she had so many left today?"

"Yup."

"Why didn't you warn me?"

"Oh, they won't kill you. Not yet. But if you refroze them after they'd been sitting at room temperature for so long, they might be pretty deadly by the time you finally decided to eat them."

"Terrific." Zac gathered up as much of the food as he could carry without dropping it, and headed for the front door. "Justin, you and Miss Tina come with me. And leave that flea-bitten nuisance outside."

"But, Da-a-a-ad…"

"One training lesson is not enough to teach him

the manners he needs to get along in the house," Zac explained to his unhappy son. "Besides, he needs a bath."

"He also needs a name," Tina interjected. "The only thing I've heard you call him so far is a nuisance."

"That'll do fine," Zac said, flashing a self-satisfied grin. "We'll call him Nuisance."

She made a sour face. "Ugh. What an awful name."

"Then, you pick one," Zac challenged.

"Maybe Justin would like to choose his name." Tina looked expectantly to the boy. "What do you think we should call him?"

"Tina!" Justin shouted. "Just like you."

Wide-eyed, she struggled to control her urge to burst into laughter. "Um…that's flattering, honey, but I'm afraid it would be awfully confusing, having two of us with the same name. Living so close together, I mean."

"Oh." Justin sulked for a moment, then said, "How about Mean Max?"

"I like the 'Max' part," she said. "Let's not scare people by saying he's mean, okay?" As soon as the child nodded, she added, "Hello, Max." Patting the newly christened dog, she carefully slipped the training collar off its neck, then turned to Zac to ask, "Want me to carry the rest of the stuff in for you?"

He'd paused at the screen door, propping it open with his shoulder so Justin could pass through ahead of him. "Sure. Thanks. About all that's left is a soggy plate of baked beans." When she bent to reach into the van he added, "Be careful. It leaks."

"Yuck. Too late." Tina balanced the plate on the flat of one hand and shook the wet fingers of the other like a kitten with a milky paw. Max took that as a clear invitation to play with his new friend. Free of his leash and collar, he lunged, catching Tina by surprise.

She staggered backward. Tripped. Screeched. Sat down on the lawn with a plop, instinctively hugging the plate of cold beans to her chest, vertically. The thin, foil cover stuck to her shirt while the gooey contents pooled at the bottom, then squeezed out all over her stomach.

In less than a heartbeat, Max went for the food. His bulk and enthusiasm pushed Tina onto her back. Helpless to rise, she rolled from side to side and tried to fend him off with her hands and feet. "No! Stop! Aghhhh…" Her screeching grew so high-pitched it was unintelligible.

Zac set aside the packages he'd been carrying and ran to Tina's aid. He pulled the dog off her and stood there, stupefied. Instead of screaming in pain, as he'd assumed, it looked like she was…*laughing!*

"What's wrong?" Zac demanded. "Are you hurt?"

Tears were streaming down Tina's cheeks, and she could hardly catch her breath. She rolled over and clambered to her feet, wiping her eyes with the backs of her hands. "Tick…" she gasped between bouts of wheezing and rasping giggles. "Tick…"

"Where? I don't see any tick."

She waved her hands in front of her and shook her head for emphasis. "No. Tick…tickle. Tickle me…"

"Oh, for crying out loud. You scared me to death. I thought you were being killed!" Disgusted, Zac let go of the dog. It headed straight for Tina.

Though her breath was still coming in great, deep gulps, she managed to holler "No," and raise her knee enough to remind Max he wasn't supposed to jump on her. This time, she didn't even need to touch him or pull on the leash to get him to settle down. To her chagrin, Zac didn't look impressed with her prowess as a dog trainer. Actually, he looked pretty upset.

"Sorry," she said. "I'm…"

"You're a mess, that's what you are," he interrupted in a gruff tone. "Why didn't you do that in the first place and stop him from knocking you down?"

"Because I *like* wearing baked-bean-flavored clothes," Tina wisecracked. She rolled her eyes for emphasis. "It's my favorite flavor." Looking down, she lifted the hem of her sticky shirt away from her body and saw what a mess the mishap had made of her midriff. A heartfelt "Oh, yuck" slipped out before she could censor it.

When she looked back at Zac, however, she was glad she'd made the candid comment, because the corners of his mouth were starting to twitch up. Tina made a face at him. "I suppose this means you're not going to invite me into your house."

"Can't. I've already returned the carpet cleaner." His smile grew. "You're still dripping beans."

"I know. I guess I should be thankful your stupid dog ate most of them off me. He's probably starving. When did you feed him last?"

"I didn't. I'm not used to having pets. I didn't think of stopping on the way home from church to pick up dog food."

"Well, no wonder!"

Tina could tell that his spreading grin was mostly because of the comical condition she was in. Good thing she wasn't trying to impress him the way all the other women had been that morning, she thought cynically, because right now she looked more like a ruined picnic than a delectable pick.

"If you'll excuse me, I think I'll go home and change," Tina said in an overly sweet voice.

"Good idea."

"I knew you'd like it." She glanced down at Max. "The leash and training collar are over by your van. Would you mind restraining him so he doesn't follow me home?"

Zac chuckled softly. "Why? Maybe he'd rather be your dog. He does seem overly fond of you."

"No way." Tina cast Zac a look of mock disgust. "Feed the poor thing some of your extra meatballs to hold him for a while. I'll borrow a couple of cups of dry food from the Petersons till you can get to the store and buy him a big bag of his own.''

Starting for the gate, she paused. ''And get him a decent food dish, will you? I'm sick of him using me as his dinner plate.''

The sound of Zac's rich laughter was still echoing when Tina got to her own back door and let it slam behind her.

As soon as Tina had showered and changed into clean clothes, she dashed up the street to borrow the dog food and returned to Zac's.

Justin and Max were both on the front porch. To her delight and relief, the gangly, energetic pup had laid down next to the boy, rested his chin on his front paws, and was behaving beautifully. He raised his head when she approached, but otherwise remained quiet.

Holding the paper sack of dry dog food behind her to hide it, she smiled at the pair and spoke softly, maintaining the atmosphere of calm. ''Hi, fellas. What's up?''

''Daddy's painting again,'' Justin said.

''Oh.'' She started up the steps past the boy and dog, certain Max would smell the sack of food and cause trouble. Amazingly, he stayed put, so she asked, ''Did your dad give the dog some of those meatballs like I told him to?''

''Uh-huh.'' The boy laid his hand on the dog's

broad head and stroked his fur gently. "He even let me feed him in the kitchen."

Wow. They were making great progress. "How nice. Was Max a good boy?"

"Uh-huh. Real good. He ate lots. We didn't have to come outside till he threw up on the floor."

It was all Tina could do to keep from chuckling out loud as she made her way into the house. Poor Zac. He couldn't win. Detouring through the kitchen, she left the sack of dry kibbles on the back of the counter, carefully out of Justin's reach so he wouldn't overfeed his new pet. Again.

She located Zac in the second bedroom. It looked like he'd already finished painting the hall. "I'm impressed," she said with a smile. "You've gotten a lot done since the last time I was here."

"I'm getting the hang of it." His gaze traveled over her from head to toe, then he grinned. "You cleaned up pretty well, considering. I don't think I'll ever be able to eat another baked bean without cracking up."

"Good. You didn't seem to think it was all that funny at the time. I was afraid you'd hold it against the dog. He was only doing what came naturally, you know." When she noted Zac's souring expression, she added, "He really is a wonderful pet for Justin. You should have seen them just now, sitting out on the porch together like old pals."

"Did my son tell you I got the chance to use my new floor mop, thanks to that mutt?"

"He might have mentioned it, yes." Tina cleared her throat to stifle her giggles. "I thought you weren't going to permit the dog in the house because he was dirty? You didn't let *me* in."

"That's because you were in worse shape than the mutt."

"Be nice or I won't help you finish painting," she warned.

Zac arched one eyebrow. "Is that a *promise?*"

"Fine. If you don't want my help, I'll go home."

"Okay, okay. You can stay. How about helping Justin wash the mutt instead of painting with me? He's been begging me to let him do it, and I know he couldn't manage a job like that alone."

"What makes you think he and I can handle Max's bath by ourselves?"

"I look at it this way," Zac said, busying himself with his painting supplies rather than continuing to face Tina. "It's a hot day so it won't hurt Justin to get wet, and even if you two make another big mess, watching you struggle with that stubborn dog should be worth a good laugh."

"I ought to wash him in your bathtub," Tina taunted. "You'd probably *never* get the ring out."

"How about using your tub, instead?"

"Not a chance. I'll get a hose and do it outside. We'll need some shampoo, too, unless you happen to have a bottle of flea soap handy."

"Never use it, myself," Zac responded. His smile faded. "I sure hope bringing Max in the house once in a while doesn't mean I'll have to start."

It took some careful planning to bring both their dog-bathing supplies and their unwilling victim into close proximity. Max acted as if the hose were a toy, until Tina tried to wet him down with it. If she hadn't put his collar on him and snubbed the leash to the fence, he'd probably have jumped out of the yard the same way he'd first gotten in.

Justin threw his thin arms around the dog's neck to hold him still. That technique did work, but it also brought the little boy into position to get nearly as good a washing as the dog.

"Let go," Tina ordered. "He's wet enough, now. I don't want to get soap in your eyes."

"I'm not scared," Justin declared.

"I know you're not, sweetie, but the shampoo might sting your eyes and make you cry. We don't want that, do we?"

Backing away, he shook his head. "Uh-uh."

"Good. Hand me that green bottle, please."

Max had stopped struggling and was watching her warily, head lowered and floppy ears folded back against his head. As soon as she poured shampoo along his spine and began to lather it by vigorously scratching his back, he started to relax and actually leaned toward her.

"See, Justin? He likes it." Tina edged aside. "He

just needed to know we weren't going to hurt him. Come closer so you can rub his back, too.'' The child was quick to obey. ''That's it. Wiggle your fingers as hard as you can.''

While the dog was being distracted, Tina went to work on his neck and the sensitive areas of his face.

''Won't he cry, like me?'' Justin asked, concerned.

''I'm being very careful around his eyes so I don't get soap in them. He'll be fine.''

The child was quiet for a few moments, then said soberly, ''Daddy cried.''

Although she was embarrassed to be told about such a private incident, Tina didn't want the boy to think he'd done anything wrong, so she treated his comment as casually as she could. ''Everybody cries sometimes.''

''My daddy doesn't. He never cries—'cept today.''

Tina's gaze darted toward the house. ''Today?''

''Uh-huh. I made it all better.''

''I'm sure you did,'' she said tenderly.

''I did. I gave him a hug, just like Mommy used to do.''

Tears of gratitude and empathy filled Tina's eyes. Many young children had the ability to accept a loss simply, with a pure faith that most adults found so astounding they couldn't relate to it. This was the opportunity she'd been praying for. Her heart focused on her heavenly Father once again. *Please, Lord, tell me what to say, how to help.*

When she opened her mouth to speak, the words were there. "You miss your mommy, don't you."

"Uh-huh. She was pretty." Before Tina could comment, he added, "She died and went to see Jesus."

"I know. Your daddy told me. It made him very sad."

"Yeah. But it's okay."

"Why is that?" Tina was fighting to keep the emotional quaver out of her voice. Clearly, Justin had accepted the inevitability of his mother's death without question.

"'Cause Jesus loves her. She said so. He loves me, too. And Daddy." Looking at Tina he began to smile. "Jesus loves you, too. He really does!"

Turning to him without thought for anything around them, she pulled the little boy into her arms and held him tight. "I know He does, honey. Lots of people have told me that, but I've never heard it said as well as you just said it."

Zac had been listening to barking, screeching and giggling in the yard for the past fifteen minutes. As soon as he was done painting, he gave in to his curiosity and went to see what was going on.

An outrageous sight greeted him. Tina was holding Max on the leash. Justin, soggy from his hair to his bare feet, was apparently trying to hose him down with a spray nozzle, and the agile dog was dodging so well that Tina was getting hit with most of the water.

Incredulous, Zac stood on the porch and shook his head. What a trio. Not a rational one in the bunch. At least he had sense enough to stay out of the melee.

Tina spotted him and waved her whole arm. "Come on in. The water's fine."

"I can see that."

"Your dog's clean."

Zac chuckled derisively. "How can you tell?"

"Because he smells so good. Like lilacs." She had to pause to duck another squirt from the hose. "Take a sniff of him and see for yourself."

"No, thanks. I think I'll pass."

Tina was in such high spirits, she refused to let Zac's stodgy attitude get to her. "What's the matter, Frazier? Afraid of a little water?"

"No. I just have more common sense than the three of you put together, that's all."

"Oh?" She noticed that he had carelessly wandered awfully far from his front door. Trying to look innocent, she edged closer to the porch, crooking her finger at Justin to join her.

"Don't even *think* of turning that hose on me," Zac warned, wary.

"I wouldn't dream of it." Relieving the boy of his dog-rinsing duties, Tina started to carefully run water over Max's back, scratching him into a state of bliss as she worked her way from his head to his tail. "There. See?" she finally said to Zac. "He's a lighter golden color than we thought. By the time he's dry, you won't recognize him.''

"Oh, I'll still know him," Zac replied with exaggerated disdain. "Considering all the *fun* we've had so far, I imagine he's going to be pretty hard to forget."

"In that case…" Before she could change her mind, Tina stopped scratching the dog's back to deter his shaking, stepped in front of Justin as a shield, squinted her eyes, pressed her lips tightly together… and let go.

Max started to tremble, then he shook. Cascades of water flew off him in all directions. The deluge began at his head, soggy ears flapping, then quickly worked its way down his body to the end of his long tail, before starting over at the front.

Zac howled and ducked to try to stay dry, but he was too slow. Spitting and muttering, he wiped his face with his hands and looked down at his water-speckled clothing. Then, he focused on Tina.

The moment his gaze fastened on her, she read an unspoken threat of retaliation. With a shriek she grabbed Justin by the hand and darted around the side of the house. Max was running in wide circles, stopping occasionally to shake himself and obviously enjoying this new game. Which meant there was no way Tina could effectively hide and wait until Zac cooled off. The friendly dog would undoubtedly give away her hiding place. Nevertheless, she ducked behind a bush at the rear of the house and crouched, pulling the boy with her.

What had possessed her to purposely get Zac wet like that? Was it his smug, self-righteous attitude? His direct order practically *daring* her to turn the hose on him? Or did the impulse to raise his spirits go deeper?

When Justin had told her that his father had wept, the simple story had touched a place in her heart she'd thought she'd walled off for good.

Tina chewed on her lower lip. Somehow, someday, she knew she must find a way to gently tell Zac that he'd been wrong about Justin's lack of adjustment after Kim's accident.

Difficulty accepting the loss wasn't his son's problem. If it was anyone's, it was Zac's.

Chapter Eight

Zac's exaggerated growling and grumbling as he searched for them made Justin giggle. Tina bent down beneath the overgrown, purple-flowered, rose of Sharon bush and hushed him with a finger to her lips.

"Shh. Quiet. We can't hide from your daddy if you keep making noise!" She could tell the boy was trying to be still but was having so much fun that it was impossible.

As Max galloped past, dragging his leash, Tina reached out to grab it. She missed. The effort caused her to turn slightly, and she thought she spotted a flash of movement out of the corner of her eye. *Oh, no!* Zac must be trying to sneak up on them!

Tina bolted from behind the bush and took off in the opposite direction. Behind her, Justin squealed. In the split second it took her to glance back to make sure the boy was all right, she ran full tilt into a solid, soggy chest. A solid, soggy, *masculine* chest. If the collision hadn't knocked the wind out of her, she'd have screamed.

Zac's arms instantly locked around her waist. "Well, well, what have we here?" he drawled. "Could it be my troublesome neighbor?"

She pushed her hands hard against his chest and leaned her upper body back to look up at him. "Let go of me!"

"I will. As soon as I've decided how I'm going to get even." He was smiling with smug self-confidence. "I suppose I could turn the hose on you but you're already soaked, so there's not much point in doing that, is there?"

"Just let me go. I promise I won't do it again."

Zac chuckled. "No way. I know you too well. Even if you don't sic a wet dog on me the next time, you'll think of something else to do to drive me crazy. You're…"

As he stared into her eyes, Tina saw his smile fade, his gaze darken, as if he'd just realized how close he was holding her. How intimate they had suddenly become. Any observer who didn't know better would easily assume their innocent pose was that of two sweethearts.

The significance of that concept replaced Tina's rational thoughts. Her eyes widened. Her lips parted slightly. Staring up at Zac, she wondered absently if he, too, was awestruck by their accidental embrace.

The answer came without words. Moving as if in a fog, he lowered his head and gently kissed her.

Zac spent the ten minutes following their kiss arguing with himself about what had transpired. The last thing he'd meant to do was kiss his pretty neighbor after he caught her. He certainly hoped he hadn't given her the wrong impression. Nothing had changed. He still intended to raise his son alone. The Lord had taken his first wife from him, and he wasn't ever going to choose a second one.

Muttering to himself about personal stupidity, he realized he'd just taken a big step in that very direction by thinking about being married while considering his blossoming relationship with Tina Braddock at the same time. If only he hadn't given in to his subconscious urge to kiss her!

Disgusted, Zac shook his head, remembering the taste of her lips, the tenderness of their embrace. He wasn't the only one who had gotten lost in the spirit of the moment. Tina had reacted with a lot more enthusiasm than he'd expected, especially in view of her earlier insistence that she wasn't interested in romance.

When he'd released her and stepped back after their spur-of-the-moment kiss, the befuddled look on her face had been impossible to interpret. Only one thing was certain. She hadn't wanted to hang around his place after he'd let her go. Though her abrupt departure had brought tears to Justin's eyes, she'd gathered up her dog-washing paraphernalia and insisted she had to leave.

"So, *now* what do I do?" Zac asked himself cynically. "I've got a sulking kid who's hiding in his room and won't even talk to me, a wet dog the size of a pony that I didn't want in the first place, a house without a stick of furniture in it, and I've alienated the woman who takes care of my son every single day. How much more can go wrong?"

That thought brought him up short. Given the daily possibilities of tragedy and loss, his current problems were insignificant. And fixable. All he had to do was swallow his pride and apologize to Tina.

He was halfway to her house when it occurred to him that he didn't have the foggiest idea what he was going to say.

Zorro was the first to realize that they had company. Arching his back and hissing once, he ran into Tina's bedroom and hid under the bed.

She bent down, lifted the dust ruffle and peered at him. "What's the matter, baby? What scared you?" Zorro stared at her, his yellow eyes wide.

Straightening, she smoothed the hem of her clean T-shirt over the outside of her shorts and began to towel-dry her clean, damp hair. "Never mind. I suppose it has to be at least one of the Fraziers. Poor kitty. I know exactly how you feel. The boy and the dog aren't so bad, but that man scares the stuffing out of me."

Zorro peeked out from under the ruffle, responding to Tina's calming tone of voice. A sharp knock at the front screen door sent him scrambling back into his sanctuary.

"If you're selling something, go away," she called, starting for the door.

"How about if I'm giving away apologies? Free. Would you like one of those?"

The truly contrite look on his face did more to convince her than his words. She kept the screen between them and continued to dry her hair, as she said, "I might be interested. How sorry are you?"

"I'm the sorriest guy in Serenity."

Tina chuckled softly at his choice of the local vernacular for some object or human that was miserably useless. "*Now,* you're talking."

How irresistible he looked, standing there with his hands stuffed into his pockets and his hair all tousled. Every time she saw him, he was more endearing. So was his little boy. As a matter of fact, their resemblance was strongest when Zac was acting contrite. Like right now.

"I really do apologize," he said seriously. "I shouldn't have kissed you. It was way out of line."

"It was terrible," Tina teased, working hard to keep a straight face.

"Terrible?"

"The worst."

"Oh. Well. If you say so." Half of Zac's mouth canted up in the beginnings of a smile. "On a scale of one to ten, I'd probably give it at least a seven, myself. I didn't think it was all that bad.''

"You didn't?'' Her lips twitched like his, and she gave in to the smile that wouldn't go away.

"Nope. It certainly was a surprise, though. I had no idea you were going to kiss me back.''

"Me? Kiss you? No way!''

"You did so.''

"Did not,'' Tina insisted. She wrapped the towel around her head, assumed a standoffish posture and folded her arms across her chest. "Well? Go ahead. I'm waiting.''

"For what? I already said I was sorry I kissed you.''

"So you did. I guess I was hoping for something a little more eloquent in the way of an apology. After all, your dog did knock me down and spill food all over me, and your son did douse me with my own hose when all I was trying to do was help him wash the dog. A yucky job like that should have been *yours,* I might add.''

"Oh, really?'' Zac mirrored her stubborn stance. "And whose fault is it that I have a dog in the first place?''

"Well, don't look at me,'' Tina retorted. "I didn't tell Max to jump your fence. He thought up that cute little trick all by himself.''

"Lucky me.''

"Actually,'' Tina said, mellowing, "I think you

are pretty fortunate. I'm not sure you realize *how* fortunate."

"If I don't, I'm sure you'll enlighten me any minute now."

"I might. Do you think it would do any good to try?"

Her question was designed to generate Zac's retrospection without requiring an answer, so she was surprised when he sobered and said, "I doubt it. I haven't been very good at counting my blessings lately."

Tina knew she was taking the chance of getting in over her head with her handsome neighbor, but she couldn't just send the poor man away when he was so obviously in spiritual need. She opened the screen door and joined him on the porch, seating herself in an oak swing that hung on chains from the exposed rafters. "You can sit here and tell me about it, if you like."

Zac hesitated, warily eyeing both Tina and the swing. "You sure?"

"No," she said, shaking her head and smiling up at him, "but do it, anyway."

He eased onto the empty end of the swing, putting himself as far from her as possible. Together, they set the swing in motion by pushing their feet against the porch floor. The slow, smooth, back-and-forth movement added to the feeling of peace and helped Tina wait patiently for whatever was to come. As before, she sensed the Lord's hand in this encounter.

That was all the encouragement she needed to cope with the long silence.

When Zac spoke again, there was a marked poignancy in his voice. "I don't know how to explain it. Every now and then I'm overwhelmed by the miracle that Justin is still with me." He hesitated, staring blankly into the distance as he went on. "Then, when I should be counting my blessings, I get so mad I can hardly see straight."

"Because your wife didn't make it, too."

Zac's head snapped around, his dark eyes flashing. "How did you know?"

"It made sense. I don't think there's anyone who can't look back and wish his or her life had been different. That awful things hadn't happened. Don't waste the happiness you have right now by reliving events you can never change, no matter how often you try to figure out what you should or shouldn't have done."

"I should have been able to save them both when the boat capsized," Zac said flatly. "Kim was wearing a life vest. So was Justin. I knew she could fight the current better than he could, so I helped him to shore first."

Tina sensed he was playing out the accident in his mind, so she gently prodded, "That's logical. Then what?"

"I went back for her. The boat was still upside down with its prow jammed against a tree that had fallen into the river. I could see her empty vest floating off downstream. I dived and dived but I couldn't find her—'' His voice broke. ''She shouldn't have died.''

Putting aside her own concerns, Tina reached out and laid her hand over his. ''You're not God.''

''What's that supposed to mean?''

''Just that I know you did the best you could. Did what you believed was right. No man has any power beyond that.''

''So, the alternative is to blame God, right?''

''If that's what you need to do to get through a crisis, I'm sure the Lord will understand,'' Tina said tenderly. ''I've done it, and He's forgiven me.''

She noted the glimmer of unshed tears in Zac's eyes as he looked away.

''I didn't consciously realize what I'd been doing until today,'' he said. ''The whole thing became clear to me when I was driving home from church. It scared me to death.''

''I understand.''

''No, you don't,'' Zac insisted. ''It's not God I've been blaming. It's not Him I need to ask for forgiveness. It's my innocent son.''

Tina's fingers closed around Zac's as she fought back her own tears. So *that* was why his fathering hadn't seemed quite normal. Chances were he'd been so caught up in his grief, he didn't even know why he'd kept Justin at arm's length. Well, he knew now. And he was sincerely contrite. That was an excellent sign. It meant he was healing.

A lone tear slipped out to slide down her cheek. Zac turned to face her and brushed the drop away with his finger.

"Don't cry for me, Tina. I don't deserve anybody's tears."

"Let me be the judge of that. Okay?" Clearly, he'd solved his problem of placing unearned blame on someone else and replaced it with a big dose of self-pity. Should she tell him so, or had he had enough soul-searching to deal with for one day?

That decision was God's, not hers, Tina decided, more than happy to pass the accountability on to Him. So far, The Lord had done just fine arranging chances for her to minister to Zac. Unless that job was done—and she didn't believe it was—there would be plenty of future opportunities to speak her mind and set him straight.

Besides, she loathed confrontation. That was one of the quirks of character that had made taking charge of her headstrong, teenage brother, Craig, so difficult. So ruinous.

Tina sighed. Boy, talk about wallowing in self-pity! She sniffled and managed a wan smile. "Frazier, you and I are a mess. If we got any more down in the dumps, we'd have to borrow a ladder to climb out."

"You do have a way with words," he said. Cupping her face in his hands, he used his thumbs to gently wipe the remaining tears from her cheeks.

Tina wasn't sure whether it was the compassionate

look in his eyes or the touch of his hands that made her tremble. Something serious was going on here. She and Zac had connected, spiritually as well as physically, and the result was so awe-inspiring, so perfect, it made her question its reality.

Blinking to clear her head and focus her whirling thoughts, Tina forced herself to take a deep, settling breath. If she was dreaming, this was the most true-to-life fantasy she'd ever concocted. Even when she'd told herself far-fetched stories all night long because she'd been too overwrought to sleep, she'd never managed to make her tales this believable. This wonderful. Then again, her dreams had never included a man like Zac Frazier.

She saw his gaze darken and narrow to concentrate on her lips. His head began to tilt slightly to one side, the way it would if he were planning to kiss her again. Her eyes widened. That was exactly what he intended to do!

Tina flattened her palms against his chest so she could push him away. *Do it!* her conscience ordered. *Give him a shove and tell him to go home.*

I will, Tina assured herself. *Any second now. Yes, sir. I'll call a halt to this whole ridiculous game we're playing.*

Only, she didn't. There seemed to be a short-circuit in the communications between her will and her body. There she sat, practically stupefied, while a man she cared about prepared to make his second terrible mistake. The first had been their first kiss.

The second would be more of the same. Unless she stopped it.

The weak protest she finally managed to make wouldn't have been enough to deter anyone who didn't respect her. Fortunately, Zac did.

He got to his feet and backed away from the swing, staring at her as if he'd just realized she was sitting there. "Oh, boy," he said, a bit breathless. "We have to stop meeting like this."

Tina managed a faint "Yeah," surprised to note a strong urge to follow Zac, to slip her arms around his waist and step into his embrace. When he'd left her just now she'd felt empty, as if she'd wither like a thirsty, summer flower and blow away without him there to sustain her.

"I guess I should be going," Zac said. "I left Justin pouting in his room. He's bound to miss me pretty soon."

Thoughts of the lonely child helped Tina concentrate on something aside from her own needs. "When will you be getting your furniture out of storage and moving in?"

"Soon. I brought our camping equipment, so we can sleep in the house tonight," he said. "Justin will think it's a big adventure. Tomorrow, I'll stock up on food—and dog food. I've already checked out of the motel."

"That's good."

Which was the truth, as far as it went. It would be good for Justin to have a stable, permanent place to live. It would be good for Zac to establish a new home and get on with his life. The only one it would *not* be good for was her. Having Zac living so close was going to pose innumerable problems, the most disastrous being the growing attraction between them.

He's just lonely, she told herself. Lonely and finally making peace with his past. Soon, he'd probably realize he was ready to fall in love again, too. Given the choices of available women in Serenity and their eagerness to please, he shouldn't have any trouble finding the perfect mate.

Tina exhaled loudly. All she had to do was make sure she stayed away from him long enough to keep him from deciding he should pick *her.*

Walking home slowly, Zac gave himself permission to broaden his outlook. There were worse things than spending more quality time with Tina Braddock. He snickered. Yeah. Like spending time *without* her, for instance.

What was wrong with him? Was he crazy? The last thing he wanted to do was give Tina the idea he was getting serious about her. He wasn't. Well, he *wasn't,* he insisted. She was just fun to be around. And Justin liked her. There was something oddly appealing about her offbeat character and crazy sense of humor.

Her hesitancy to reveal much about her past intrigued him, too. Maybe she was holding back because she felt she didn't know him well enough yet. Zac's imagination kicked in. Or maybe she was keeping secrets because there was something in her background that she was ashamed of.

"No. No way," he muttered to himself. Tina Braddock was the most honest, loving, sincere, sweet woman he'd ever met. There was no way she could be hiding a checkered past.

"Listen to yourself," he said, shaking his head in disgust as he opened the front gate and entered his yard. "You sound like a one-man fan club. So, she made you laugh and gave you a shoulder to cry on. So, she gets along with Justin. So, she's nice. So what? Lots of people are like that. Why should you go nuts over *that* one?"

A weary Max yawned and got up as his master climbed the front steps to the porch.

Already out of sorts, Zac glowered at him. "Oh, lie down and go back to sleep, you good-for-nothing, useless dog. It won't do you any good to kiss up to me. I'm all out of meatballs."

Max began to wag his tail. When Zac sighed in passing, the dog put his cold nose against his hand and gave him a loving lick.

Zac paused long enough to ruffle the dog's droopy ears and smile down at him. "Okay, okay. I'm sorry. But you're still totally useless, you know." Panting in response, Max looked as though he might be smiling, too. The wagging of his tail increased until his whole rear half was dancing the hula.

"Sit," Zac ordered, testing. When the dog obeyed, he swung back the screen door and held it open. "Okay. You can come in. But one false move and—"

Max disappeared through the door in a blur and left Zac standing there alone. Seconds later, he heard Justin's whoop of happy surprise. "Maybe we'd better make that two false moves," he added to himself. "I have a feeling you're going to need at least one second chance."

Hovering in the back of Zac's mind was the impression that the same principle could easily apply to him.

Chapter Nine

The bulk of Zac's belongings arrived early Tuesday morning. A crew was unloading the moving van, when Tina backed out of her driveway on her way to work. Zac was standing on his porch. The minute he spotted her pickup truck, he jogged to the street and flagged her down.

Reluctantly, she pulled over in front of the van and let the truck's engine idle. She'd made a grave error when she'd helped that man find a house so close to hers. At the time, all she'd considered was what would be best for Justin. Now, she had her own well-being to think about, too. Running into Zac all the time and having to pretend he didn't already have a special place in her heart was exhausting. It was going to have to stop. Her nerves couldn't take the constant pressure. Neither could her conscience.

"Morning!" Zac said cheerfully.

"Good morning."

"Got my furniture."

"I can see that." Tina pointedly glanced at her watch. She didn't want to seem unkind, but she had to make sure he understood that she hadn't been making a play for him the way other single women had. "Well, I don't want to be late."

"Just one thing before you go," he said. "My phone's not connected yet, and I need to call the school to see if an in-service meeting has been scheduled for this afternoon. Can I borrow yours?"

Tina almost laughed out loud. When Zac had hailed her just now, she'd been convinced he was doing it for purely personal reasons, when all he'd actually wanted was access to her *telephone!* Oh, well. It wasn't the first time she'd felt like a fool and it surely wouldn't be the last.

"I leave my back door unlocked," she said. "Help yourself. Just be careful you don't let Zorro out."

"Right. Thanks." Zac nodded toward the house. "Justin's still sleeping like a log in spite of all the noise. I'll keep him with me today if I don't have to go to work." Stepping back, he gave her a quick wave and a smile. "Have a nice day."

"Thanks. Bye." Tina glanced in her rearview mirror as she drove away. Zac hadn't moved, but he wasn't looking in her direction anymore. The approach of a bright red, four-wheel-drive pickup had captured his attention.

Tina's stomach knotted. Her mouth went suddenly

dry. The only person she knew who drove a fancy truck like that was Lela Pierce.

Tina slowed, hoping to delay long enough to see for sure. She gritted her teeth. It was Lela, all right. Zac was helping her down from the high cab of the truck. And it looked like she was handing him a casserole dish.

Refusing to believe she could actually be jealous, Tina insisted, "Well, so what? What do I care?" It didn't matter to her if Zac Frazier was up to his neck in fawning women and homemade food. All she cared about was his relationship with his son, which was definitely improving.

Not satisfied, she began to theorize. Okay. If all that was true, then why did it feel like her stomach was twisted into a knot the size of a Cave City watermelon? And why had she suddenly pictured herself slamming on the brakes, making a U-turn, driving back to Zac's and letting all the air out of Lela's tires?

Zac opened the back door of Tina's house and called to her cat, not terribly surprised when Zorro didn't appear. Cats were reserved like that. Give him a dog any day. He might trip over Max every time he turned around, but at least a man knew where he stood with dogs. They were too goofy, too amiable, to hide their feelings the way a cat did.

He paused. Tina's kitchen was just the way he remembered it. The sink was immaculate, the curtains were frilly lace, and there were pots of blooming violets and various other small plants lined up along the windowsills. What he didn't see was a telephone.

Wandering farther into the house, Zac continued to search, sorry he hadn't thought to ask Tina where her phone was located. It seemed improper to go prowling through her house when she was gone—but what else could he do? He had to stay available while the movers were still unloading. And besides, he couldn't go looking for a pay phone unless he woke Justin and took him along. That wouldn't be fair. The poor kid needed all the sleep he could get.

Pausing, Zac looked around the living room. Tina's decor was a combination of styles. All the elements fit together beautifully. Again, there were houseplants, some by the front windows, some sitting in the dimmer corners of the room on stands of their own. The whole effect was homey. Welcoming. And yet...

He frowned, studying the room further. There was something missing. ''You came here to borrow the phone, not to analyze the furniture,'' he reminded himself aloud.

Quickly scanning the entire room and deciding he'd have to move on, he headed down the hallway. Tina had told him her house had the same floor plan as his, only in reverse, so it was easy to find his way. He peeked through the doorway to the master bedroom. Zorro lay curled up in the middle of Tina's neatly made bed, sleeping. A beige telephone was on the nightstand.

Hesitant to invade her private space, Zac reminded himself that she'd known where the phone was when she'd given him permission to use it. Therefore, as long as her cat didn't get spooked and attack him, he'd go ahead, make his call and be done with it.

Reaching into his pants pocket for the card with the phone number of the school office, he kept one eye on Zorro and reached for the receiver. Suddenly, his subconscious locked on to the elusive missing element he'd been searching for. It was pictures. More precisely, family photographs.

Scowling, Zac systematically scanned the four walls of the room he was in and every flat surface where a framed picture of a loved one might be placed. There were no photos. None.

Forgetting his original reason for being there, he checked the other bedroom, then retraced his steps. A professional decorator might eliminate the personal touch that family photos provided, but that couldn't be the case here. Tina's house was already artistically cluttered. Framed photographs would have added to its charm.

So, where were the faces of all the special people she loved and wanted to remember? Surely there must have been someone, somewhere.

The idea that she might have no one to love—or to love her in return—disturbed him greatly.

* * *

Tina's phone was ringing when she walked in the door at six-thirty that evening. She ran down the hall to answer. "Hello?"

"Hi. It's me," Zac said. "I'm checking my new telephone to see if it's working and give you the number."

"It's working." Tina grimaced, mad at herself for being so delighted to hear his voice. The phone wasn't the *only* thing that was working. Her keen memory was fired up, too, displaying vivid images of Zac and making her recall all the special moments they'd spent together. The watermelon-size knot in her stomach had predictably recurred, too.

"Good." He recited his new number, then asked, "You hungry? I've got plenty of supper for three."

Tina's racing pulse began to pound in her temples. In spite of all her misgivings about seeing Zac again, the urge to accept his invitation was overpowering. She was so exasperated by her apparent lack of self-control that a touch of irritability crept into her reply. "If you're offering to feed me Lela's casserole, never mind."

"It smells pretty good. Is there some reason we shouldn't eat it? Or are you just in a bad mood tonight?"

"I'm never in a bad mood. I'm always sweet and kind, like the Bible says we're supposed to be." She could tell he'd grasped her intended sarcasm because she could hear him laughing in the background.

"Ah," Zac finally said, "the old 'Christians are

perfect' defense. I'm disappointed. I thought you had more imagination than that.''

Imagination? Boy, did he have that right! She sighed. ''Don't pick on me, Frazier. I've had a rough day.''

''Okay. Back to the original reason I called. Why not tell me about your day over dinner?''

''I might tell you about it, but not while anybody's trying to eat,'' Tina explained. ''A lot of what pre-schoolers do is *not* acceptable mealtime conversation.''

''Granted. So, does this mean you're coming over?''

''Do you have any chairs yet?''

''Four of them. And a table. Very civilized.''

''Good. I'm too beat to sit on the porch steps and wrestle your dog. You did buy him some food, didn't you?''

''I did. And more. He now has a doghouse that looks like a plastic igloo, a bed stuffed with cedar shavings, a food dish the size of a turkey roaster and a watering system with a jug that holds five gallons so he won't run out of drinking water while I'm at work.''

''Boy. When you go to the dogs, you really do it up right, don't you.''

''I try. You still haven't given me a direct answer. Do I put three plates on the table or the usual two?''

''Three,'' Tina said with a sigh. ''Just give me ten

minutes to change and feed Zorro. What can I bring?''

''Not a thing,'' Zac said. ''We have enough food over here to last till Christmas. Whoever said the way to a man's heart is through his stomach must have lived in Serenity.''

Think ugly, Tina told herself again and again. *Major ugly.* She was rummaging through the bottom drawer of her dresser, looking for the perfect outfit to wear to Zac's and rejecting each article of clothing on the grounds that it was too attractive. Finally, she settled on an old, faded sweatshirt that was missing its arms, a pair of jeans with holes torn in both knees and worn sneakers.

To complete the transformation, she pulled all her hair straight back and fastened it with a clip. The image she presented when she glanced in a mirror was even less appealing than she'd hoped it would be. ''Good. That should do it,'' she told herself, starting for Zac's with newfound energy in her step. ''At least the man won't get the idea I'm trying to impress him.''

Justin was waiting for her on his porch. ''Miss Tina!''

She swept him up in her arms. ''Hi, sweetie. I missed you, today. Did you have fun with your daddy?''

''Uh-huh. We got my toys!''

The little boy started wiggling to be put down. The

minute his feet hit the floor, he grabbed Tina's hand and tugged. "Come look at my room!"

In the background she heard Zac calling them. "We'll be there in a minute," she shouted back.

Tina knew that having a place he could call his own was crucial to Justin. And it was also important that he be able to share his feelings of joy and belonging with someone other than his father. When he made little friends in Serenity he could invite them over to admire his treasures, but right now, she was the closest thing the boy had to a buddy.

Racing through the bedroom door, Justin hit the floor on his knees and quickly held up a model of a bright red truck. "Look! This one's new. Lela gave it to me," he jabbered. "It's just like her real one."

Tina's jaw dropped open. She snapped it closed and forced a smile for the child's sake. "How nice of her."

"Yeah. She helped me carry all the boxes to my room. I got to ride in her truck, too!"

"Wow. You must have had a very busy day," Tina managed to say.

When a deep voice behind her said "We did," she was so startled that she almost lurched into a pile of plastic building blocks. Staggering to regain her balance and catch her breath, she whirled, eyes wide, to face Zac. "Don't sneak up on me like that!"

"I thought you knew I was here." Looking her up and down, he smiled and raised an eyebrow. "I like the new look. It's kind of cute."

Cute? That was hardly the effect she'd been aiming for. Making a face at him she said, "It's for self-preservation. Every time I visit you I wind up a mess. This time, I'm ready for anything."

"Even Lela's casserole?"

"Well, *almost* everything," Tina answered cynically. "It probably won't kill me."

"Not unless you choke on it," Zac teased.

Tina mumbled, "That could happen."

"I know. I can tell." Turning, he was chuckling softly as he started off down the hall. "Come on, you two. Playtime's over. Time to eat. If you don't come now, you won't get any dessert."

"Dessert!" Justin barreled past Tina and ducked around his father to lead the way.

"Looks like he's finally getting caught up on all the sleep he's missed," Tina said. "How long did he stay in bed this morning?"

"I think it was about ten when he finally wandered out to the kitchen and asked for breakfast. I didn't see any reason to wake him earlier if I didn't have to."

"No in-service meeting today?"

"No," Zac said. "By the way, thanks for the use of your phone. I hated to get all dressed, show up at the school, and *then* find out there was no meeting. Besides, this way I had time to get more stuff unpacked. I hate living out of boxes."

"I know what you mean." She couldn't help noticing the inquisitive look he was giving her as she followed him into the kitchen. Averting her gaze, she concentrated on taking a seat at the table. "It's always difficult getting settled."

"Have you moved often?"

The hairs on the back of her neck prickled, sending a silent warning. Was Zac trying to trip her up? Or was she imagining his undue interest? It could be either. Or both. The man was certainly clever enough to take advantage of any momentary slip of the tongue she might make if she carelessly relaxed her guard.

Tina thought it best to redirect his attention to the feast he'd assembled. There was so much food, it left barely enough room at the table for their plates. "This looks and smells delicious. Even the casserole."

"Thanks. Is milk okay? Or would you rather have coffee?" Zac glanced at a stack of unopened cardboard boxes in the far corner of the room. "I think I know where the pot is. I just didn't have time to dig it out yet."

"Milk is fine, thanks." Tina smiled at the boy. "It's very good for you. I drink it at day care, too."

"Daddy says I can ask Tommy over to play," Justin piped up. "But I can't. I don't know where he lives."

"Well, now that you have a telephone, I can give your number to Tommy's mom, if you want, and she can call you."

"Super!"

Zac delivered three glasses of milk to the table, sat down and began to put dabs of food onto his son's plate. The green beans were the only choice that elicited a childish protest.

"They're good for you," Zac said. "And it looks like they have cheese sauce on them, so I expect you to at least taste them."

"But, Da-a-a-ad…"

Tina couldn't help smiling at the father-son exchange. Zac was getting the hang of solo parenting, all right. When he'd first brought Justin to meet her, she'd sensed that all the boy had to do was pout or cry to get his own way. This firmer approach was a big improvement.

"I'd like some beans, too, please," Tina said, accepting the bowl from Zac. "I know they're good because I can tell Miss Mercy made them. She used to cook for the whole school district, back when it was much smaller."

"I suppose you do recognize most of these dishes," Zac conceded. "I'm beginning to wonder if that church of yours is actually a catering company in disguise."

Tina laughed lightly. "Nope. We just love to eat." Waiting for Zac to pass another entrée, she helped herself to a roll and butter. "I'll bet Miss Tessie made these biscuits."

"Beats me," Zac said. "This stuff was delivered so often today, I lost track. Well, almost." Grinning over at her, he held out a deep, steaming dish with a serving spoon sticking out the top. "I do remember who brought this one."

"Lela!" Justin informed them. "It's got dinosaurs in it. She said."

Tina's hand hovered over the handle of the spoon while she leaned closer to peer at the contents of the casserole. Her eyes narrowed in a frown. "Dinosaurs?"

"The pasta kind," Zac explained. "She figured Justin would get a kick out of it."

"How thoughtful." Smiling with exaggerated sweetness, Tina held out her plate to him and asked, "May I have a tyrannosaurus rex, please. They're my favorite."

"Yeah!" the boy shouted. "Me, too. I want that kind."

"Since Miss Tina knows all about them, I'm sure she'll be happy to help you find some." Zac handed the spoon to her and leaned closer to whisper, "Troublemaker."

Determined he wouldn't best her, she stirred around in the deep ceramic dish for a few seconds before filling the spoon and plopping its contents onto the boy's plate. "I just saw a tyrannosaurus hide in that scoop," she said. "If he didn't fool me, he should still be there. They're sneaky, you know."

Zac muttered, "They're not the only ones," as he picked up his fork. "Well, let's eat." When Tina didn't rush to begin right away, he wondered why, until he saw her close her eyes for a moment and fold her hands in her lap. "Oops. We forgot to say the blessing."

"We *never* do that anymore," Justin told him. "Not since…" His shrill voice quieted.

"Well, it's about time we started again." Zac bowed his head. A few seconds later he merely said, "Amen."

"That's not how Mama did it," the boy complained, pouting.

Tina spoke up. "Next time, we'll take turns praying. How's that?" To her relief, the suggestion was enough to stop the child's protest and preserve what was left of Zac's upbeat mood.

His gaze met hers. "Thanks."

"You're welcome."

"You're very good with kids."

"I'd better be. I spend half my life with them."

"What about the other half? What's that been like?"

She pretended to misinterpret his reference to the past. "It's blessedly peaceful. Serenity is a wonderful place to live, as long as you aren't the kind of person who has to have all the amenities a big city can offer."

"How about before you came here?" Zac pressed. "Don't you miss it? Miss your family?"

"My parents are dead," Tina said flatly.

"I'm so sorry. I know how tough that kind of thing can be. But at least you have your mementos, photographs, that kind of thing."

''No. We...I...lost everything.'' She could have added more but instead simply sighed quietly. There was nothing to be gained by airing sad tales of personal loss. She'd found that out the hard way. Her brother Craig didn't have any idea where she was because of the new last name she'd adopted when she'd first settled in Arkansas. Nobody from her past did. And that was just the way she liked it.

Tina sensed that Zac was studying her. ''I appreciate your concern,'' she said formally, ''but if you don't mind, I'd rather not discuss my past.''

''No problem.'' He shrugged and turned to his son. ''Hey. Find any dinosaurs yet, buddy?''

''Not good ones,'' Justin mumbled with his mouth full.

''Well, you let me know when you do.'' Zac smiled over at Tina. ''Speaking of that casserole, Lela tells me she's originally from Chicago, like me. She moved down here with her folks when she was fifteen. Her dad was transferred.''

''Peachy.'' Tina busied herself pushing the food around on her plate so he wouldn't notice her flushed cheeks.

''I think I'm going to like the milder winters here,'' he went on. ''I suppose this southern climate takes a lot of getting used to the rest of the year, though.''

''You'll adjust pretty quickly. The different seasons can be kind of a bother to begin with. You're already used to those kinds of changes, so I wouldn't worry.''

''You mean like trees turning color in the fall?''

''That, and the cultural changes. The first few months I was here I went nuts trying to predict what would be for sale in the stores. I'd go to town to buy something I needed, and nobody would have it in stock. The worst part was, I couldn't find live plants anywhere. I finally figured out that was because it was the middle of winter.''

''Well, you've sure made up for it since then. Your yard is beautiful.''

''Thanks.'' She carefully speared some green beans and put them in her mouth, then went back for more.

''I suppose you were used to working outside year-round back in California.''

Tina's head snapped up, her eyes widening. ''How did…?'' The pleased look on his face answered her question. ''You're guessing.''

''Assuming. There's a difference.''

''Oh, yeah? Well, how do you know I'm not from Florida.''

''Because you didn't act like it when I mentioned stopping there to visit my parents.''

''Arizona, then. Or New Mexico.''

Zac put down his fork and watched her closely. ''I wouldn't expect you to lie, especially not in front of a child. Are you telling me that's where you're from?''

Blinking, Tina glanced at Justin. He was watching her reaction as intensely as his father was. ''I'm not telling you anything,'' she finally said. ''You don't play fair.''

Zac's eyes seemed to darken, and the deep vibration of his voice made her shiver when he said, ''Maybe I'm not playing anymore.''

Chapter Ten

Nervous and frustrated, Tina spent the rest of the night and all the next day trying to recall the exact words in her telling exchange with Zac. It was a useless effort. All she could remember was the look on his face and the sound of his voice when he'd said he wasn't playing games anymore.

She hugged herself and paced the floor of the day care facility, thankful that none of the children had arrived yet. What was she going to do? Zac seemed determined to dig into her past, no matter how often she told him not to. She didn't dare confess. Or did she? Would that be best? Maybe he really *was* different from all the others. Suppose she explained exactly what had happened?

"Oh, sure," Tina grumbled. "That would fix things *really* well."

If Zac cared for her, he'd probably insist on trying

to help, which could only make things worse. She couldn't chance hurting Craig. Not when he was finally leading a normal life and had a loving wife and family.

Tina sighed as she considered the other conceivable outcome of telling Zac everything. If he chose not to keep her secret, she'd probably have to move again. Even if she was able to find another job in Serenity, she was sure the rumors about her would make staying here unbearable.

Mavis breezed through the door, spotted Tina and greeted her with a cheery "Good morning!"

"Oh, hi. I didn't hear you drive up."

"I'm not surprised," the older woman said. "You looked like you were a million miles away just now."

"Only about two thousand." Tina took a deep breath and sighed. "Life is complicated."

"It beats the alternative."

That brought a smile. "You're right. I won't mind going to heaven someday, though."

"Well, don't rush things," Mavis countered. "The good Lord gave each of us a special amount of time on earth, and He expects us to use it wisely. I wouldn't want to have to face God sooner than He'd planned and explain why I was there early. Would you?"

"No way. I have enough other mistakes to account for."

"We all do, sweetie. That's what's wrong with

churches, you know. They're full of sinners." She laughed. "'Course, that figures. If we were all perfect, nobody would need to go to church in the first place!"

"I love your logic," Tina said. "I just wish there was some way I could go back and live my past ten years over again, knowing what I know now."

"If you figure out how to do that," Mavis quipped, "sign me up for thirty years or so."

Tina looked away and busied herself straightening the children's plastic chairs. Her mind was spinning. Oh, how she yearned to share her concerns with Mavis and ask for advice!

Pensive, she sighed. Maybe there was a way, providing she was very careful. "Suppose you wanted desperately to do the right thing. Even prayed about it. Only, later you discovered you'd made the wrong choice because you didn't have all the facts to begin with. What would you do, then?"

"Hypothetically?" Frowning, Mavis studied her young employee. "Well, I suppose that would depend upon whether anyone else would be hurt if I went back on my word. Then again, you have to remember that the good Lord didn't give us the ten *suggestions*. He called them commandments for a reason. There's no excuse good enough to swap right for wrong. It either is, or it isn't. Right or wrong, I mean."

"What if it's already too late to change anything?"

"Ah, that's where asking for forgiveness and being truly sorry comes in. If Jesus expected us to go back and fix everything we'd done wrong so far, we'd probably mess it up worse and never live long enough to get it all straight!"

Tina nodded in agreement. "*That* I can relate to."

Zac hadn't casually run into his neighbor since the night he'd invited her over for dinner. The only time he saw Tina was when he delivered Justin to day care, and even then she was usually so busy she barely said hello.

Had he scared her off by speaking his mind? Maybe. At the time, telling her he was no longer playing games had seemed like the most sensible thing to do. Now, he could see the folly of his bluntness. Thank goodness he hadn't told her he thought he was falling for her, too!

Sighing in disgust, Zac entered his office and shut the door behind him, glad for the files piled high in the middle of his desk. Thinking about other people's problems would help take his mind off his own. He had less than a week left to prepare for the students' return. Given the severity of the offenses he'd found in the first few files he'd looked at, he was in for a tough year.

Zac snorted. Good thing the school board didn't know how much trouble he was having deciding how to live his *own* life, or they'd never trust him to sort out the problems of confused students!

His intercom buzzed. He answered, assuming correctly that it was the office receptionist. "Yes, Rosemary?"

"I have a package out here for you, Mr. Frazier."

"Put it in my in-box."

"Sorry." She tittered. "No can do."

Frustrated by the interruption, Zac quickly got to his feet. This was one of the things about small-town life he was having trouble adjusting to. Nobody seemed to think a thing about stopping whatever they were doing to visit, even if they were swamped with work. The last time he'd ventured out of his office he'd been cornered by a Mrs. Fitch, the militant mother of one of the boys he was assigned to counsel. If this was her again, he was going to have to have a serious talk with Rosemary.

Rounding the corner so he could see what awaited him, he began to grin. *Oh, no! More food.* Inez Gogerty was standing at the counter with an eager look on her face. She cradled a covered glass bowl in both hands.

"Here's the chicken salad I promised you," she said with obvious delight. "There's enough for your supper, too."

"Thank you." Zac took the chilled bowl from her. "But you really shouldn't have."

"Oh, fish. What're friends for? Besides, I know how hard it must be for you, working all day and taking care of that dear little boy, too. Jason is such a darling."

Zac corrected her. "His name is Justin."

Color crept up her neck to bloom on her cheeks. "Oops. Well, I was close. They both start with a *J*." Pointing to the chicken salad, she added, "My name and number's on a sticker on the bottom of the bowl. Give me a call when you're finished, and I'll drop by your place to pick it up."

"You've gone to enough trouble already," Zac said politely. "I'm sure we'll see each other in church. I'll just put your bowl in the car and return it some Sunday."

"Well...I suppose that would be simpler." She waved as she turned and headed for the door. "Bye, now. Bye, Rosemary."

"Uh...goodbye."

Looking out through the office window, Zac watched Inez walk away. He was successfully holding his amusement in check, until he noticed the comical expression on the receptionist's face. Poor Rosemary had her fingers pressed to her lips, and her face was so red she looked like she was about to explode. In seconds, she was laughing so hard there were tears streaming down her cheeks.

Zac didn't think the situation was quite *that* funny. He held up the bowl. "Want to join me for lunch? This stuff is really pretty good."

Gasping for breath, the receptionist blotted her tears and managed to say "No kidding?" before she had to stop to blow her nose. "I'd heard you were popular but that's just plain ridiculous. Did you see what I saw? Inez was wearing false eyelashes! It looked like a couple of caterpillars had crawled up her face and died on her eyelids!''

''Really?'' Zac shrugged. ''I didn't notice.''

''Probably just as well.'' Rosemary glanced out the window as she wiped her nose again. ''Uh-oh. Look out. Here comes that Mrs. Fitch again.''

Zac didn't move quickly enough to escape. The wiry woman burst into the office and confronted him, not bothering with a greeting. ''Have you got it straightened out yet?''

''I did look over your son's file,'' he said calmly.

''Well? You can read, can't you? Those teachers last year had it in for my Bennie. He don't deserve to be held back again.''

''According to his transcripts, he does,'' Zac told her. ''There was a period of nearly a year when he was truant more than he was in school. When he did go to class, he refused to turn in any homework. Surely you're aware of that.''

She waved a thin hand at him, rolled her eyes and cursed fluently. ''It wasn't Bennie's fault. My sister was keepin' him for me, back then. She didn't give a rat's… Hey, wait a minute. I'll bet those idiots in the other school sent you the wrong records.'' Glaring at Zac, she leaned on the counter to get closer to him, and her strident tone softened noticeably. ''Sure. That's gotta be it. You look into it for me, okay?''

''I assure you, Bennie will be treated as fairly as

any other student at Serenity High," Zac said. He gestured with the bowl. "Now, if you'll excuse me, I have to go put this in the refrigerator."

"Sure, sure. I need a smoke, anyway, and it's against the rules to light up in here. Gotta keep all the stupid rules. Oh, yeah. I'm a great one for keepin' the rules."

Rosemary waited until the woman had left, before saying "Whew. That woman's going to be trouble."

"*Going* to be?" Zac shook his head sadly. "I haven't met her son but I can guess who he takes after just by reading the teachers' comments in his file."

"Well, at least he hasn't been bragging about the awful things he's done or how tough he can be, the way she does. I'd say that's a point in his favor."

Interested in knowing more, Zac put down the bowl and perched on the edge of Rosemary's desk. "His mother actually brags about having a bad reputation?"

"You bet she does. Goes around telling everybody what a rough customer she used to be, like she's proud of it."

"Could that be why Bennie was staying with her sister?"

"Probably. According to what I heard, that woman's been in and out of trouble since the poor kid was little. No wonder he turned out like he did."

"I'll make a note to have a talk with him as soon as school starts," Zac said soberly. He got to his feet and picked up his bowl of chicken salad. "Come on, Rosemary. I hear voices in the staff lounge. Let's go share this. I want to catch all the teachers at once and find out what else they may have heard about Bennie Fitch."

"It's hopeless," she offered.

Zac silently disagreed. There was always hope. Sometimes it was impossible to see from a human standpoint, but with faith, it was always there.

His thoughts immediately turned to Tina—to his hopes that they might develop a deeper personal relationship. Making her a permanent part of his future wasn't a new idea, it had simply grown from an inkling to a definite goal. The Lord had brought them both to Serenity and arranged their lives so they couldn't avoid each other. The more Zac was around her, the more he was beginning to feel that they were meant to be together.

Now, all he had to do was convince Tina Braddock.

Zac called for Justin a little before five. Tina sensed his presence before she actually saw him. The subconscious warning gave her enough time to find something to do on the opposite side of the room. Her intent was to appear far too busy to stop and chat.

The ploy failed. Peeking out of the corner of her eye, she noted Zac's approach. The only thing to do was face him.

"Justin was very well-behaved, today," she said with an amiable nod of greeting.

"I'm happy to hear that."

When he just stood there looking at her instead of going on with their conversation, she asked, "Was there something else you needed?"

"Actually, yes," Zac said, nodding. "First, I want to apologize for the other night. I didn't mean to upset you."

"You didn't upset me." Tina folded her arms across her chest. "I just think we need to remember that two people can be friends without getting too involved."

"I agree completely. You forgive me, then?"

"There's nothing to forgive." She managed a tiny smile.

"Good. Then, we can have dinner together, tonight."

How had he managed to deduce *that* from their otherwise noncommittal discussion? "I don't think so."

"Why not? You said you weren't mad at me."

"That doesn't mean I think it's a good idea for us to spend a lot of time together. Justin is already getting far too attached to me because he sees me here all the time."

"Is that so bad?"

Tina pulled a face. Either the man was dense, which she doubted, or he was trying to trap her. "Not bad. Unwise," she said flatly. "You were right when you said Justin didn't need a friend like me. If you want your son to be happy, you need to find him a mother, not just a neighborhood pal."

"Ah, I see." Zac was beginning to smile. "You talk about brotherly love but you don't want to live it. Too bad. I was hoping I could count on you to help me with a youth group I'm thinking of starting."

"A youth group?" Had she dreamed up his romantic interest simply because she *wanted* it to be so? Tina clenched her teeth. What a ridiculous idea! Of course she hadn't. She'd merely misunderstood his motives because she'd misread his mood.

She gazed up at him. "What kind of youth group?"

"I'd like to see it made up of some of the kids I've been assigned to help," Zac explained. "You know. The ones who don't come from homes that teach the same ethical standards you and I grew up with. Kids who're already on the wrong path. If I don't try to turn them around, who will?"

"There's a great group for teens at my church," Tina said. "You could always tell them to go there."

"Once they get to know me, maybe. If I tried it now, they'd think I was railroading them. It'll be hard enough to convince them I can work at the high school and still be on their side."

"I don't know what to say."

"How about telling me it's a great idea and agreeing to have dinner with me so we can talk it over?"

Watching her expression and waiting for an answer, Zac kept smiling. He didn't know who was more surprised about the idea of starting up a new youth group—Tina or himself. Until he'd started telling her about it, he hadn't even considered organizing anything that complicated in his spare time. Not that it was a bad idea. It was a wonderful one. It just wasn't a project he'd consciously planned out.

Then again, maybe the Lord had wanted him to take on that very job. For all Zac knew, God might have planted the concept in his head in the first place. It was not only a perfect task for him, it was an answer to his prayers for a way to draw Tina deeper into his life.

When she said "Oh, all right," Zac breathed a silent sigh. "Good. We can stop at the market on the way home and get some steaks to barbecue. How does that sound?"

"I don't get off work for another hour."

Zac took her arm and started to lead her toward the door. "Yes, you do. It's all taken care of. Mavis volunteered to close tonight. We can leave anytime."

"Whoa. Wait a minute." Tina jerked free and faced him. "I just now agreed to go with you. When did you make those convenient arrangements with my boss?"

"Well..."

"That's what I figured. You think you can talk me into anything, don't you? Well, you *can't.*"

Doing his best to look chagrined, Zac shrugged.

"Okay. My mistake. I suppose I can get someone else to volunteer to work with the kids." He brightened. "Tell you what. How about a temporary commitment? Just until I can get the program set up and find another assistant?"

"What? I wasn't talking about the youth group," Tina said, frowning. "I was talking about being manipulated into having dinner with you."

"Oh. I didn't think keeping company with Justin and me was that disagreeable. If you'd rather come on over after you eat, we can make our plans then. Either way is fine with me." Long minutes passed. Zac had to force himself to breathe slowly, evenly.

"Porterhouse. Medium rare," Tina finally said. "And this is a business meeting, not a date, so it'll be my treat. I'll get my purse and follow you to the store."

Zac decided to let her have her way rather than argue and take the chance she'd balk. There would be plenty of time to repay her for whatever she spent, this time or any other.

He loved a tough challenge—even one as perplexing as Tina promised to be. Now that he'd decided to allow himself to get to know her better, he was starting to view her as more than just a friendly neighbor. That outlook gave him such an enhanced perspective, he felt he was seeing her for the first time. There was a double dose of spunk and wit packed into her small self, and that was only the beginning.

Her beautiful eyes were more green than blue, Zac noted, and her hair looked so silky and touchable, he had to fight the urge to reach out and run his hand along its full length. And her lips? Remembering their taste, he felt his pulse quicken. Even when she was scolding him she looked physically ready to be kissed. Holding himself in check until she was *emotionally* ready was going to be exhausting.

But worth it, he added. Definitely worth it.

Chapter Eleven

~~

The market parking lot was crowded by the time Tina pulled up beside Zac's van. He got out carrying Justin. The boy was asleep, his head resting on his daddy's shoulder.

Tina grabbed her purse and joined them. "Poor baby. Looks like we wore him out today," she said, gently stroking the child's back.

"He always goes to sleep the minute I start the car," Zac told her. "Has ever since he was a baby." They headed toward the store together. "For the past year or so, I think he's done more sleeping in his car seat than he has in bed. Hopefully, that'll change now that we're back in a real home."

"He's getting older, too. It won't be long before he refuses to take naps. That usually helps kids sleep better at night." Tina laughed softly. "I think it's because they're so exhausted."

"Good." Zac turned so she could see his expression and rolled his eyes dramatically. "*I* could use the rest."

She chose an empty shopping cart and steered it toward the meat department. "You said he used to have a lot of nightmares. Does he still?"

"Not nearly as often."

Maybe this was the opportunity she'd prayed for. It certainly had the potential to be. Shooting a silent prayer toward heaven, she decided to speak her mind. "I'm not surprised he's doing so well. I've had a couple of opportunities to talk to him about his mother, and he seems very well adjusted."

"You did *what?*" Zac's voice rumbled low, raising tiny goose bumps on Tina's forearms and zinging up her spine to infuse her nape with an unexpected tingle.

"I talked to him," she said boldly. "Or, rather, I listened to what he had to say. Children don't usually fear death the way adults do. They find it a lot easier to trust God than we do, too. If we tell them their loved one has gone to be with Jesus, they accept it as a good thing."

Following, Zac stepped closer and spoke so quietly that Tina had to strain to hear. "You told him that?"

"No. He told me. Your wife apparently taught it to him. At least, that's the impression I got. She must have been a very special lady. Even after she was gone, her faith was powerful enough to comfort Justin and eventually bring him through."

The melancholy expression on Zac's face made her want to caress his cheek to console him, the same way she would if he were a heartbroken child. When moisture began to glisten in his eyes, she had to look away or she'd have wept.

All he said was "Thank you," but those two words encompassed their entire discussion and assured Tina she'd done the right thing. That was all that mattered.

Zac hadn't offered much advice about anything while they shopped, so Tina had chosen their steaks, then picked out some chicken strips for Justin. "All the kids go crazy over these when we serve them for lunch," she said, holding up the package. "Anything else you can think of that we need?"

Zac didn't answer. He didn't even bother to shrug. She waved her hand in front of his eyes. "Yoo-hoo. This whole thing was your idea, remember? If you've changed your mind, we don't have to do it."

Blinking, he marshaled his lagging awareness. "No, no. I'm still a little dumbfounded, that's all. I can't believe how perfectly God has taken care of Justin, including bringing us all the way to Arkansas to meet you."

Her resulting laugh sounded nervous. "I don't know if I'd go quite *that* far."

"I would."

The intensity of his gaze captured hers and held it. Tina leaned on the handle of the shopping cart to steady herself. She was certainly glad they were in a public place. And that Zac's arms were fully occupied holding his son. If they'd been alone, she wasn't sure she could have resisted the alluring combination of Zac's rich voice and intense, hungry stare.

Time seemed to stop. All they were doing was standing there, looking at each other, yet she felt embarrassed, as if everyone could read her innermost thoughts. She certainly hoped that wasn't so. It was bad enough that *she* knew what she was thinking!

Tina was trying to decide what to do or say next, when Zac broke eye contact and glanced over her shoulder. His expression immediately hardened.

"What? What is it?" She pivoted. All she saw was the normal crowd at the checkout counter.

"At the end of the far line," Zac whispered.

Tina caught her breath. Her heart fluttered. It looked like the woman who had stared at her so fiercely the last time she'd shopped here! Could it be the same one? The stringy blond hair and bony shoulders sticking out of a sleeveless knit top made it likely.

"Who is she?" she asked.

"The mother of one of my cases. I'd just as soon not tangle with her here, especially with you and Justin around. When she comes to my office, every other word is a curse."

"She kind of gives me the willies."

"I know what you mean." Zac stiffened. "Uh-oh. Duck. I think I've been spotted."

The blowsy blonde stormed past Tina and went straight for Zac. "Well, well. You have a boy, too? Good. Then, you should understand why I'm tryin' to help mine."

"I do understand, Mrs. Fitch." Turning to hand Justin off to Tina, he quickly refocused on the irate parent. "Why don't we go outside to discuss this?"

"Why? You afraid to talk in front of your girlfriend?" The woman's hard eyes fastened on Tina. "Don't I know you?"

Seeing the woman up close settled Tina's questions. They *did* know each other, if only in passing. How in the world had they both wound up in the same little Arkansas town? The odds against that happening were tremendous!

"No," Tina blurted out. Lord help her! Near panic, she hugged Justin to her chest and prayed the other woman wouldn't remember where they'd first met.

Zac stepped forward, placed himself between the two as a buffer and spoke to Tina over his shoulder. "Think you can handle Justin and the groceries, too?"

She nodded numbly and clung to Justin as she watched his father shepherd Mrs. Fitch out of the store. The icy look in the woman's eyes gave away no secrets.

Shaking inside and sick to her stomach, Tina pulled herself together enough to place a kiss in the little boy's dark hair and urge, "Wake up, sweetheart. I have to sit you in the basket for a minute while I pay.''

The child roused slowly, yawning and mumbling in protest. When he saw who was holding him, he brightened. Tina kissed his cheek and fought back tears as she leaned over to slip his feet through the openings in the shopping cart's child seat.

Justin started to look puzzled. "Where's Daddy?"

"He went out to the car for a minute. I told him you and I could handle the groceries by ourselves. Do you think we can do that?"

The boy nodded. Tina could tell he was still concerned. No wonder. He'd gone to sleep in the van with his father, and awakened in a grocery store with only her for company. Anyone would find a switch like that confusing. He might also be intuitively sensing her inner turmoil.

Watching for Zac, she kept an eye on the outer door as she placed her purchases on the conveyor belt, interrupting her vigil only when she had to write a check to pay the bill. When she looked up again, there he was! Alone. *Thank God!* She pointed.

"Look, Justin! Here comes Daddy. See?"

Zac joined them quickly and leaned closer to speak privately with Tina. "A whole year of that woman, and I'll have gray hair for sure. It's no wonder her boy is so hard to handle. You should have heard her cut loose when I got her outside."

He took over and started to push the cart toward the door, slowing when he noticed that Tina seemed to be hanging back. "Don't worry. It's safe. I waited till she drove away before I came back for you."

"Okay." Relieved, Tina hurried to keep up. If her feet had been racing as fast as her imagination was, she'd have beat him to the car.

As it was, she didn't even remember driving home.

They decided to gather at Tina's house because her barbecue was already set up. It was a good thing Zac had volunteered to do most of the cooking. Tina had so much trouble concentrating, she had to let Justin tell her how to warm the precooked chicken strips.

Max lived up to his reputation of being a nuisance. He parked on her back porch and acted as if he owned it. "I shut Zorro in my bedroom," Tina told Zac as she cautiously stepped over the dog. If it chose to leap up while she was passing, she knew she'd be knocked down, no matter how careful she was. Adding a scared cat to the mix practically ensured an accident.

"Smart lady," Zac said. He poked at the steaks on the barbecue with a long-handled fork. "How did you say you wanted this? Rare?"

Distracted, she was fussing over setting the picnic table, so her concentration wasn't on what he was saying. *Or* on her reply. "Whatever. I'm easy. Just don't get carried away."

If Tina hadn't heard him chuckle, she might not have noticed the double meaning of her innocent statement. She chanced a peek at him. His smile was smug. No doubt he was enjoying her slip of the tongue immensely.

Placing his right hand over his heart, Zac assumed a humble expression. "You have my word, Miss Tina. I will *never* get carried away with you."

"That's a load off my mind."

"I figured it would be. So, where did Justin go? Is he sleeping again?"

"No. We put his chicken in the microwave, and he's minding it for me. I imagine that's why your dog is guarding my back door. Between smelling the chicken strips and knowing his favorite kid is inside with a *cat*, Max is probably on the verge of a nervous breakdown." Tina glanced over at the dog. "Either that or he's already had one. I wish *I* were that relaxed."

"Me, too. I hope he turns out to be a good watchdog, especially where Justin is concerned."

"I don't think you have anything to worry about in Serenity," Tina offered. "This is a peaceful town. Folks here look out for each other. Country people are some of the nicest you'll ever meet."

"You mean like Mrs. Fitch?" Zac asked pointedly.

Tina swallowed the knot that threatened to close her throat. Had he referred to that particular woman simply because she was so difficult to deal with? There was only one way to find out.

"Lots of people blow off steam by talking tough, and nothing more ever comes of it."

Zac concentrated on the barbecue instead of facing Tina, and gave a resolute sigh. "I know. I don't have all the facts yet, but I'm planning to look into her past. In the meantime, I don't want you to let that woman anywhere near my son. She may even be dangerous."

"Dangerous?" Tina's pulse sped faster and faster.

She looked so distressed that he put his arm around her shoulders for moral support. "Don't worry. Just keep your eyes open and watch out for the kids the way you always do."

"*Why?*"

"Because, even if I wasn't worried about what Esther Fitch might try to do, I *still* wouldn't want Justin to be anywhere around her. She's a rotten role model. That kind of negative influence can stick with a kid his whole life." Zac paused, studying Tina's pained expression. "It's not just her foul language that bothers me," he said slowly. "It's everything about her. Rosemary tells me she's even been heard bragging about how rotten her reputation is."

Suddenly, Tina felt as if she were being smothered. No coherent thought surfaced to rescue her. No viable prayer arose from her soul to call out to God on her behalf.

She stared at Zac, acknowledging a facet of his character that didn't fit the image of perfection she'd created for him. By telling her how he felt about a woman like Esther, he'd joined all the hypocrites who always judged others without bothering to search for good qualities. They didn't care what their prejudicial attitude cost. All they wanted to do was stick a label on other folks so they'd have an excuse to exclude them from their lives.

Anger filled her, taking the place of all rational emotion. "And you call yourself a counselor!" Tina was nearly shouting but she didn't care. "You've passed judgment on that poor woman without even looking at what kind of person she really is. No wonder you can't talk to her without getting into a fight."

"Whoa." Zac held up his hands in mock surrender. "What's the matter with you?"

"*Nothing's* the matter with me," Tina insisted. "You're the one with the closed mind. I thought you were different. I thought you were intelligent enough to show compassion and tolerance. I see I was wrong."

"Maybe you're mistaking compassion for stupidity," Zac countered. "If I see a thunderstorm coming, I'm going to take cover whether the hills need the water or not. Only an idiot stands outside in a storm and makes himself a human lightning rod when he knows what can happen."

Tina was facing him, hands on her hips, feet in a wide, confrontational stance. "Meaning?"

He purposely lowered his voice and slowed his speech, a tactic designed to calm. "Meaning, there are some things no one can change, no matter how much we wish we could. Our past is one of them. Bennie Fitch's mother is what she is. And it's my duty as a father to protect my son.'' Zac's forehead creased in a frown. "Can you give me one good reason why I shouldn't do that?''

"What about forgiveness? Isn't everyone entitled to that?''

"From God, maybe. Not necessarily from me. It's a matter of priorities. Justin has to come first. He's all I have left.''

The sadness in his eyes touched Tina enough to temper her animosity and give her the added wisdom to grasp a deeper truth. "I get it. You don't think you're capable of granting unconditional forgiveness to anyone, do you. And you refuse to try, because you know the Lord would want you to start by forgiving yourself.''

"That's ridiculous,'' Zac said flatly. He turned away to concentrate on the barbecue, jabbing at the meat on the grill with his cooking fork. He didn't look at Tina when he said, "Call Justin and grab your plate. The steaks are done.''

Chapter Twelve

They never had talked about Zac's plans for a youth group after Tina had blown up at him, which suited her just fine. All she wanted to do was hide, thanks to running into her past, head-on. She'd prayed all night that Esther wouldn't remember when or where they'd met.

This mess can still turn out all right, Tina told herself. All she had to do was stay calm and remember that God was in charge. That was a comforting thought, until she took it one step further. Suppose the Lord had been responsible for both her and Esther coming to Serenity? What then? And how was she supposed to avoid the woman in such a small town? The more often Esther's memory was jogged by seeing her, the greater the chance she'd remember.

Believing she was still temporarily in the clear,

Tina went to work as usual. At one o'clock she received a telephone call from Esther Fitch.

"How did you know where to find me?" Trembling, Tina clutched the receiver.

"I've been watchin' you."

"Why? What do you want?"

"Just to talk. Nothing fancy. Come on over. I'll be home all afternoon. If you don't want to run into my Bennie, you'd best hurry."

"No way."

"If you don't come, I'll drop in on you while you have all those cute little kids hanging around. Want them to listen to what I have to say?"

"I can't just leave work."

"You'd better find a way," Esther threatened. "Grab a pencil. I'll give you directions to my place."

The house Bennie and his mother lived in was at the end of a narrow, unpaved county road. Tina was glad she was driving a pickup instead of a low-slung passenger car because the dirt lane was mostly potholes and gullies, the result of rain runoff and ongoing neglect.

Esther Fitch was waiting on the rickety-looking porch, a cigarette in one hand, a tea-colored beverage in the other. Tina hoped the drink was iced tea. She parked and started for the house.

"You're late," Esther said, as Tina climbed the front steps.

"I came as soon as I could."

The atmosphere surrounding them was charged, making the hair on the back of Tina's neck prickle. Nervously, she added, "Okay. I'm here. Now, what do you want?"

"Shut up and sit down," Esther ordered.

The threatening tone made Tina shiver. She perched on the edge of the seat of a metal lawn chair. Obviously, it had been foolish to agree to come way out here without telling anyone where she was going. If she jumped up and made a dash for her truck, would the gaunt woman be quick enough or strong enough to stop her from leaving? She wasn't sure, so she prayed for God's guidance and waited to see what would happen next.

Esther was staring at her, shaking her head and cursing under her breath. "You might as well stop pretending you don't know me."

So, the game was over. "All right," Tina said, managing to keep her voice from quavering. "But it won't do you any good to try to blackmail me. I don't have much money."

"I don't want your money. Not that I wouldn't take a little if you twisted my arm." Esther stepped closer. "All I want is for you to have a talk with your boyfriend—get him to let my boy go on to the twelfth grade so he can graduate with his friends."

"*That's* why you made me come out here?" Tina was flabbergasted. "That's all?"

"It's plenty to a teenager," Esther said. She blew smoke in Tina's face. "Bennie would of done fine if

I hadn't been away his whole junior year. It ain't his fault he got behind in school. You talk to Frazier. He can fix it.''

Wide-eyed, Tina gaped at her. "I can't do that. I *won't* do it.''

"If you don't, I'll tell the world just who and what you are and where we met, missy.'' Grinning broadly she stepped back to look Tina up and down. "I'll bet your holier-than-thou friends will sing a different tune when they hear you're a jailbird!''

Oh, how she hated that expression! Tina was desperate to find some way of escape from the inevitable. "It won't do me any good to try to influence Zac,'' she insisted. "We aren't close friends. We're just neighbors. Why should he listen to anything I say?''

"Not close? Hah! I saw you two in the store together, saw how he looked at you. You might be able to fool some folks, but you can't fool me. That man's in love with you. I'll bet you've got it bad for him, too.''

"You're wrong,'' Tina said firmly, loudly. "There's nothing between us. Absolutely nothing.''

"Okay.'' She shrugged her bony shoulders. "In that case, you won't care if I start out by tellin' *him* I know you from when we were both in prison. It should be a real interesting conversation, don't you think?''

"Don't... Please don't do that.''

"Okay. Then, this is how it's going to be. You

want a favor from me, you need to get busy and earn it.''

''You'll only be hurting your son in the long run if you try to interfere,'' Tina argued. ''He needs to be held responsible for his grades.''

Esther wasn't impressed. ''I'll give you a week to see that Bennie gets put back with his old class. After that…''

After that, Tina thought, *I'll need to leave Serenity and find some other place to start over. Someplace where no one knows me. Just like twice before.*

Heartbroken, she gave up and headed for her truck. Was she never going to finish paying for the lie she'd told to protect her brother? It had seemed like such an inconsequential act at the time. One little lie.

Just one little lie.

Exhausted, Zac was glad to see the first week of school come to an end. He'd been too engrossed in his new job to do anything aside from eat, sleep and work. After the first couple of days, Tina had offered to take Justin to day care with her every morning, so Zac wouldn't have to. Since he finished his workday earlier than she did, he always drove the boy home.

He hadn't had an in-depth conversation with Tina since the night she'd gotten so mad at him over his comments about Esther Fitch. In retrospect, he had to admit his pretty neighbor was right. He had been judging the Fitch woman on past offenses, which was a pretty easy thing to do, considering her current erratic temperament and colorful way of expressing herself.

Tina's personal observations about him, however, were a lot harder to deal with. Even if there was a touch of truth in her theory, he didn't intend to bother God about it. After all, Zac reasoned, it was perfectly natural for him to continue to lament the decision he'd made after the boat had capsized. Anyone would. Life was full of missed chances and false starts. A man who claimed he was never sorry about anything he'd said or done was either a liar or a fool.

One of the reasons Zac looked forward to picking up his son every afternoon was that it meant he'd get to see Tina. It wasn't enough that they were neighbors and friends. He wanted more. Needed more. She'd made a permanent place for herself in his heart before he'd even realized he was beginning to care. That was why her criticism of him, personally, had been so hard to take.

Opening the door to the day care building, he began to smile at the happy noises that welcomed him. The place always sounded like a bunch of munchkins were holding a party. It smelled like paint, plastic and whatever the lunch entrée had been. Today, it had *definitely* been spaghetti.

Zac paused and scanned the room, looking for the two most important people in his life. Justin was close by. Tina wasn't. The boy was engrossed in the structure of wooden blocks he was building with

Tommy. He didn't even look up until Zac called, "Hey, buddy. You about ready to go home?"

Reluctantly, Justin went to his father. When he was close enough, Zac reached out and tousled the boy's hair. "So, did you have a nice day?"

"I guess."

Immediately concerned, Zac crouched down and touched his son's forehead. "No fever. Are you feeling all right?"

"Uh-huh."

"Then, what's wrong? Why are you acting so sad?"

"Miss Tina left."

"She did?" Straightening, Zac looked around the large, open room once more. No wonder he hadn't spotted Tina when he'd arrived. What could be wrong? She'd looked fine when she'd stopped to pick up his son that morning. Maybe she'd come down with a bug since then. "Was she sick?" he asked.

"I dunno. She just left." Justin pointed to a tall, blond woman who was busy straightening some toys on shelves. "That's Miss Vicki. She's mean."

Zac took him by the hand and led him toward the nursery area, looking for Mavis. "Come on. We'll go find out what happened to Miss Tina."

The nursery door was ajar, saving him from having to decide whether to knock and chance waking the babies. He peeked inside. "Excuse me?"

Mavis instinctively assessed Justin's mood, then asked, "Is there a problem, Mr. Frazier?"

"No. Everything's fine...I think. I was just wondering— Where's Tina? I mean, Ms. Braddock."

"Hang on. We'll talk out there." The older woman quickly joined him and pulled the nursery door shut behind her. "Okay. What do *you* know?"

"About Tina?"

Nodding, Mavis pressed her lips into a thin line and folded her arms across her chest. "Yes. She's been acting strange lately. Distracted. Like she had something important on her mind. I thought you two might have had a fight or something."

"She did get pretty mad at me the other night," Zac admitted, "but I've seen her since then and she's seemed fine. I don't think she's still upset." He paused to review their past meetings. "We haven't really had an opportunity to discuss much of anything since school started."

"She didn't go to see you today?"

"No. Why would you think that?"

"Because she was acting evasive. She got a phone call, then asked me for time off. You're all she's talked about, lately, so I figured it had to have something to do with you." Mavis smiled down at Justin. "You and the little guy here. If you two ever need a cheering section, call Tina. She's had lots of practice."

To Zac's chagrin, he felt a blush warm his face. "We like her, too."

"Is that *all* you feel for her?"

"No." His sense of embarrassment refused to go

away, so he dealt with it and kept talking. "It's much, much more. Only, please don't tell Tina, okay? The minute I tried to get her to consider a serious relationship, she started to avoid me. I really think we're right for each other. I just don't want to move too fast. I want to marry her, not chase her away. She's a very special lady."

"I agree." Mavis's wide grin crinkled the corners of her eyes, and her enthusiasm made them sparkle. "You can count me as being on your side. I've given Tina the whole afternoon off, so I doubt she'll come back here. Why don't you go on home. I'm sure she'll show up at her place before too long."

"Thanks." Zac vigorously shook the older woman's hand.

She leaned closer to whisper, "Remember, I get invited to the wedding."

Zac chuckled nervously. "I sure hope I do, too."

Tina saw both Fraziers sitting on their front porch steps when she drove into her own driveway. Max was chasing a ball one of them had thrown. The picture of a happy family nearly broke her heart. She hadn't been forced to admit how deeply she loved Zac and his son until today.

The idea of leaving Serenity—of leaving Zac—was unthinkable. Yet what choice did she have? Now that Esther knew who she was, it was only a matter of time before the woman told someone, who told someone, who told someone else. The result was inevitable. At best, all Tina could hope for was the week's time Esther had promised to allow her.

One week. Was it fair to dream of spending every spare minute with Zac? Was it right to pretend everything was going to be fine and lead him on? Tina shook her head sadly. No. She couldn't do that. No matter how much she yearned to be with him, to make fond memories that would comfort her someday, she couldn't take the chance of hurting Zac. Or Justin. She loved them too dearly.

The only sensible thing to do was continue to keep her distance and pray that Zac was not already in love with her. Tina's aching heart refused to allow such a prayer. She *did* want him to love her. She wanted to love him in return. And most of all, she wanted to find a way to banish the old mistakes that kept coming back to haunt her. That was the most unattainable part of her dream.

She'd changed clothes and was pouring herself a glass of iced tea when there was a tentative knock on her back door. Zorro bristled and hissed.

Tina immediately saw why. Both Justin and Max were peering at her through the screen door, while Zac waited at the foot of the porch steps. Justin was licking an orange Popsicle and holding up something small that was wrapped in white paper.

She couldn't bring herself to ignore the boy or send him away, so she smiled wistfully. "Hi, honey. What'cha got?"

"One for you," he said eagerly. "I think it's

cherry. Daddy wouldn't let me look 'cause this dumb ol' dog keeps tryin' to lick it, and he said you wouldn't like that.''

"They do taste better without dog lips on them," Tina said, feigning seriousness. She started to open the screen door to accept the treat. "Thank you."

Before Justin could hand her the Popsicle, Max barged through the door—headed straight for the cat!

"No!" Tina shrieked.

Zorro didn't need a warning. He zoomed around the corner into the hallway so fast that his black-and-white image blurred. The big dog chasing him was far less agile. Its nails clattered and scraped against the tile floor as it scrambled to overcome forward momentum and negotiate the same quick turn the cat had made. Instead, it began to slide sideways, feet still paddling, and crashed into the side of the refrigerator with a *thunk*.

That caused enough delay for Tina to throw her arms around the dog's neck and gain temporary control. At least poor Zorro had plenty of favorite places to hide. The only thing that worried her was keeping the excited dog from tearing through her house in a frenzy and knocking over all her plants and knick-knacks while he pursued his quarry.

Zac quickly came to her rescue. He burst through the back door, slid to a dead stop in the center of her kitchen, stared for a second, then exploded into laughter.

Tina was not amused. She'd had to drape herself

across the dog's back to keep him from getting to his feet, and her arms were aching from holding on so tightly.

"I thought…" Zac gasped for breath. "I thought something *terrible* had happened."

"It nearly did," she snapped. "Your dog tried to have Zorro for lunch."

"Dinner," Zac said. "It's too late for lunch."

"I stand corrected." Tina didn't dare let go. She glowered up at Zac. "Are you going to help me, or are you just going to hang around and make jokes?"

That started him chuckling again. "Okay, okay. I'll help. I take it you aren't trying to ride the dog, so you must be restraining him. Right?"

"No kidding. If I let him get up, he'll wreck my house, not to mention my poor cat. Why isn't he wearing his collar?"

"The one you bought for training?"

"No. The red one that buckles on."

"Ah." Zac had crossed to stand beside her. "We think he ate that one. Justin found a little piece of it in the yard. We still don't know what happened to the buckle, but I can guess."

"Me, too," Tina said. "As big as he is, I don't think it'll hurt him, though." She nodded toward a nearby cabinet. "We need a rope or something. I think there's some old clothesline in there."

"I'll see." Zac quickly located the bundle and displayed it proudly. "Got it." He made a slipknot, formed a loop and put it over Max's head before saying, "Okay. I've got him under control. You can let go."

Moving slowly, Tina eased back into a crouch. Sensing impending freedom, the dog lurched to his feet and sent her sprawling.

She couldn't squelch the loud "Ouch!" that escaped, but she did manage to keep from rubbing the spot that hurt the most. Fuming, she sat flat on the floor and glared up at Zac. "If you laugh, so help me, I'll…I'll…"

He held up his free hand as if swearing an official oath. "I promise I'm not going to laugh at you."

Tina could see the corners of his mouth twitching as he fought to keep his promise. Justin was standing right behind him, holding high his melting Popsicle, while the dog licked at the sticky, sweet drops running all the way from his fist to his armpit.

Zac was in passable command of his emotions, until he heard his son begin a high-pitched giggle. That was all it took to push him over the edge of his tenuous self-control. By the time Tina got to her feet, the man was roaring.

The hilarity was contagious. Unable to keep a straight face, she laughed along till tears rolled down her cheeks and she was doubled over.

Finally, she pointed at Max. "Will you please… take *that* out of my kitchen?"

"Sure." Zac wiped his eyes as he started to lead his dog to the door. "I don't know why you invited him inside in the first place."

"*Invited* him?" Waving her hands, Tina loosed another spate of laughter, then grabbed her ribs. "Oooh. Ouch."

"You okay?"

"I'm fine…just…a stitch in my side."

"Maybe you hurt yourself when you wrestled the dog," he speculated. "Hold on a sec. I'll be right back."

"No!" Disgruntled, she watched him shepherd both dog and boy out the door and latch the screen so they couldn't reopen it on their own. "You're not listening to me, Zac. I said, I'm fine."

He marched back to her like a man on a mission. "I heard you. You're fine. Now, lift your arms so I can take a look at those ribs."

"No way, mister. Hands off. You're no doctor."

"I have studied first aid," Zac countered. "And I wasn't asking you to take your clothes off. Just stop hugging yourself, put your arms up and hold still. This won't take a minute. Turn around."

Tina gladly turned her back on him. Anything was better than having to meet his gaze and wonder if she was giving away the secret of her love for him. Did he already know? If he was as sensitive to her moods as she was to his, he probably suspected. After all, he was trained to be perceptive.

At the touch of Zac's hands on her shoulders, she shivered. He froze. "Did I hurt you?"

"No."

"Then, relax. I'll be gentle," he said as he began

to press his thumbs against her spine and splay his fingers along both sides, working his way down. "Tell me if you feel anything."

Feel anything? Oh, yes! But those feelings had no relation to her fall.

It was all Tina could do to keep from moaning with pleasure at Zac's deft, tender strokes. In the loving caress of his hands lay the ultimate answer to her question about his emotional involvement. With a heartfelt sigh, she closed her eyes, accepted the full truth of what she was sensing and leaned back against his chest.

Zac didn't hesitate. His arms encircled her. Held her. She felt his warm, sweet breath tickle her ear, her cheek. Felt the press of his lips against her temple. *This is all wrong,* she told herself, over and over. Knowing her conclusion was the right one wasn't enough to make her pull away from him.

"Oh, Tina," he murmured against her hair. "Tina."

Laying her arms on top of his, she swayed within their mutual embrace. Zac hadn't touched her anywhere he shouldn't have, yet she was completely his. How could this have happened? How could she have let it? She'd vowed to stay away from him for his sake, to give him up without revealing how much she loved him *because* she loved him.

Well, it was too late for all that now. There was no way to go back and undo what had just happened. Even if she broke her solemn promise to God and purposely told another lie, she'd never be able to convince Zac she didn't share his affection. Which meant she had only the pure truth to work with. Truth could hurt. It could also heal. She just wasn't sure how she was going to tell one from the other until it was too late.

Steeling herself for the inevitable, Tina turned around, determined to tell Zac everything about her past. But at the last instant she lost her nerve. Flattening her palms against his chest, she bowed her head and prayed silently, *Oh, Father, You know what a mess I've made of my life. Help me. Please. I don't want to lose him but I don't want to hurt him, either. I don't know what to do. I'm really scared.*

Zac pulled her close. He began to caress her hair with his hand—and her soul with his voice. "It'll be okay. We'll make it work. Don't be afraid, honey."

Struggling for self-control, Tina blinked back tears and drew a shuddering breath. Zac deserved to know all about her before he said any more. As soon as she got her emotions under better control, she was going to sit him down and make him listen to her whole story, even if he resisted.

A yowl from the backyard made them jump apart in unison. Zac recovered first. "What the—?"

"Sounds like Justin!" Tina headed for the door.

Zac beat her outside and leaped off the porch. He reached his son in two long strides and bent over him. "What's wrong?"

"My Popsicle stick," the boy wailed. "I was gonna save it to make a boat."

"Hey, no problem." Zac whistled in relief. "You can save the stick."

The child stamped his foot and began to pout. "No, I can't. It's all gone. Max ate it!"

Chapter Thirteen

"It was after closing time but I spoke to the vet's assistant," Tina told Zac. "She said we should watch him and not panic. Dogs eat weird stuff all the time. We're supposed to call their emergency number if he starts to act funny over the weekend."

"Humph. How will we know the difference? That dog always acts funny."

"True."

Zac was holding on to the makeshift leash that was still around Max's neck. "So, want to walk us home?"

"No."

"Oh, come on. It's either that or replant your entire garden after a boy and his dog get through remodeling it for you. My yard was already pretty trashed when I moved in, so they can't hurt anything over there. We can sit outside and watch the monsters play. It's probably more interesting than whatever's on TV.''

"Probably." She sighed. "Well, okay. For a little while. I don't know if I'll be very good company, though. I'm really tired tonight."

"You were wonderful company a minute or so ago," Zac offered. "At least *I* thought so."

She took a mock swipe at him and pulled a face. "Could we forget about that?"

"Not a chance, lady."

"That's what I was afraid of." Following Zac and Max down the street, Tina felt Justin take her hand, and she turned her most loving smile on him in spite of his gummy fingers. "Hi, sweetie. Do you know you're all sticky?"

"Uh-huh. My Popsicle melted."

"I know. I saw. They're really messy." Another thought struck her. "Whatever happened to the one you brought over for me?"

The boy reached into his pocket and withdrew a packet of white plastic. Two hard bumps showed where the sticks were. The rest jiggled and pooled in the lowest point. Tina stifled a grin.

"I'm afraid it melted."

"That's okay." Justin held his gift up to her with solemn dignity. "You can put it back in the freezer and eat it later."

Zac took the drippy mess for her, grasping its edge between his thumb and forefinger and holding it at arm's length. "I'll refreeze it for you, Miss Tina."

His mischievous wink was carefully aimed at her alone. "I have lots of them in my freezer, so it won't be lonesome."

The little boy rolled his eyes. "Da-a-a-ad, food doesn't get lonesome."

"Oh, sorry," Zac said. "My mistake."

He opened the gate to his yard and led the way with Max, not releasing the excited canine until they were all safely inside. As soon as he was loose, the dog galloped off with Justin in hot pursuit.

Tina couldn't help being amused at the father-son exchange. "Imagine that. A grown man not knowing that food doesn't get lonesome."

"Yeah. I can't win. That kid learns something new every day. He's growing up a lot faster than I thought he would."

"They all do. Children learn at a more rapid rate when they're little than at any other time in their lives. Think about it. They have to figure out how to move their bodies where they want them to go *and* master language in their first few years—all with no base of prior knowledge to build on. It's a phenomenal challenge."

"I'd never thought of it quite like that." Zac dropped the melted Popsicle into the trash, then led the way to his backyard and unfolded two mesh lawn chairs, placing them in the shade of a native oak.

Tina sat down and settled back to watch Justin and Max playing keep-away. "You know, that's really a great dog,'' she observed, not trying to hide her admiration.

Zac coughed and cleared his throat noisily. *''That?''*

''Yes. See how careful he is? He never bumps into Justin and he never leaves him too far behind, either. If that were you or me out there, instead of a child, Max would probably flatten us.''

''I still may never forgive him for interrupting us a few minutes ago,'' Zac drawled, arching his eyebrows and looking at her sideways, teasing. ''Want to go into the house with me? I didn't finish checking your sore ribs.''

''Oh, yes, you did. I suspect the Lord may have used that dog to rescue us from each other.''

''Hah! I didn't need rescuing,'' he insisted. Breaking into a wry smile, he added, ''Of course, maybe *you* did.''

''I considered that possibility.'' Blushing, Tina knew she should take advantage of his good mood to bring up her past. When she searched her heart for the abundant determination she'd had earlier, however, she found little of it left.

Relieved, she rationalized, *It wasn't the right time to confess, and God stopped me. Okay. I'll just wait till He gives me another chance and then I'll speak up.*

The concept of actually explaining everything to Zac sounded easy until she began to think seriously about doing it. Reality hit her hard and fisted in the pit of her stomach. Where could she start? Where *should* she start? If she didn't choose every word carefully, Zac might get so upset he'd stop listening before she got around to the most important details. That was exactly what had happened with her other so-called friends in the past.

Moreover, what in the world should she do—or not do—till the Lord cleared the way for her to confess? Now that she and Zac had quit pretending there were no romantic feelings between them, all she wanted was to be near him. *Very* near him. The pink color in her cheeks deepened.

Zac had been watching her. "Hey. You're blushing. Want to tell me what you're thinking about?"

"Not a chance, mister."

With a smug grin he leaned back in his chair and laced his fingers behind his head. "That good, huh? Thanks. I'm flattered."

"Well, don't get a swelled head," Tina countered. "You weren't the only thing on my mind."

"Oh? Is there something or somebody else you want to tell me about?" Zac brought himself forward, leaning his elbows on his knees and giving her his full attention.

"I…not yet." Tina refused to meet his gaze. "I will soon. I promise."

He reached for her hand and clasped it in both of his, his thumbs skimming across her skin in a simple caress. "You don't have to worry about leveling with me, honey. Don't you know that?"

Not worry? *Hah!* Tina immediately thought of lots of good reasons to worry. Zac might hate her. Or be afraid she'd be a bad influence on his son. Worst of all, getting serious about her could ruin his whole life! That last conclusion was a doozy—one she'd managed to put out of her mind when she'd been fool enough to imagine a happy future with Zac. Well, it was back with a vengeance. Whether she liked it or not, he'd never realize his dream of becoming a Youth Pastor if he chose a jailbird for a wife. No one would hire him under those circumstances. And she didn't blame them.

Tina sighed and forced herself to look at him so she could spot the slightest reaction. "You once told me you wanted to be part of a ministry. Is that still your goal?"

The enthusiasm brightening his eyes seemed to shine all the way to his soul, telegraphing his answer. When Zac began to explain, she felt worse than before.

"I'd love it," he said. "So will you, honey. We'll make a great team. You'll see." He sobered and gazed at her with undisguised longing. "And while we're on the subject of love—I love you, Tina. I was going to put off asking you this until I was sure how you felt, but I can't stand the suspense. We belong together. Will you marry me?"

Watching her eyes widen and her lips part, Zac waited for her to throw herself into his arms and promise to love him forever, the way Kim had when he'd proposed to her. Long seconds passed. He saw Tina's eyes begin to glisten as tears tipped over her lower lashes and trickled down her cheeks. Her lower lip trembled.

Zac held tight to her hand so she couldn't run away, and tried desperately to undo his mistake. "Don't say no, honey. Please, don't say no. Don't say anything right now. Just think about it. Take your time. Take all the time you want. I won't push you to decide. I promise I won't."

Tina nodded and sniffled, trying to smile. Her course had suddenly become clear; the answer she must give, obvious. "I know exactly how much time I'll need," she said, almost whispering. "Give me eight days."

The odd length of time puzzled him. *Eight days? Why not a week?* Zac was intrigued, yet wary. Tina must have a good reason for specifying exactly eight days. But what could it be?

Zac subdued a reckless urge to question her further. "Okay. No problem. Eight days is fine."

"Good. Then, I'd better be getting home."

"Already? You just got here." It was hard to convince himself to release her hand when she stood up and pulled away. Feeling instantly bereft without her touch, he shoved his hands into his pockets to quell the temptation to reach for her again. "Would you like a cold drink before you go? I can make some lemonade. Iced tea? I know, I'll get you a fresh Popsicle! What flavor would you like? I think we have cherry, orange, and maybe grape.''

''No. Nothing, thanks.'' Head down, heart heavy, she started for home.

Zac dogged her footsteps. ''Hey! How about supper? We can order another pizza.''

''No.'' The more Tina thought about what she was planning, the more difficult it was to stay convinced she was doing the right thing. Steeling herself against Zac's predictable negative reaction, she paused and faced him. ''I want my eight days. All of them.''

''Sure. No problem. I won't press you.''

''Starting now.'' Not totally conscious of her actions, Tina swayed toward him slightly. Before she could right herself and make him understand exactly what she was trying to say, Zac reacted by taking her in his arms once more.

She closed her eyes and rested her hands flat on his chest. The rapid pounding of his heartbeat was echoed by an intense, throbbing pulse in her temples. No matter how much she wanted to be with him, she knew she couldn't stand a whole week of this kind of hopeless yearning. Neither could Zac. If they were together, he'd begin to ask questions—questions she wasn't ready to answer. The only sensible thing to do was insist he leave her alone.

Was there any chance Esther Fitch might take pity on her and back off? Tina wondered. Probably not, unless the Lord intervened to soften the woman's heart. Tina knew that in answer to prayer, God could do anything He wanted. However, she also knew that believers who'd been forgiven still had to accept the consequences of their mistakes. Chastisement, even when it was well deserved, was one of the hardest lessons to accept.

Tina exerted a light pressure on Zac's chest, and he loosened his hold. She eased away so he wouldn't think she was asking for another kiss when she tilted her head back to look up at him.

"I think we should give ourselves time apart to cool off and think this through," she said softly. "I have something important to tell you. Then, if you still want to marry me…"

"What do you mean, 'if' I still want to marry you?" A deep scowl creased his forehead. "Why should I change my mind?"

She saw the skeptical look on Zac's face begin to include a trace of annoyance. Well, too bad. It was probably foolish of her to dream that their love was ever going to have a chance to bloom and grow, anyway, given all the obstacles she'd brought along. Yet she couldn't help hoping they'd find some way to make the relationship work.

There were certainly a lot of "ifs" standing in the way. If Esther chose to keep silent, Tina would have to decide how much to reveal to Zac—and if it was fair to accept his marriage proposal. However, if she put off telling him anything until after Esther started spreading rumors, as she'd threatened, he'd be deeply hurt.

On the other hand, Tina knew that if she told him more than she needed to, he might leap to her defense, take her side against Craig, reveal the whole story and ruin more innocent lives back in California. Zac had a strong sense of right and wrong. She admired that fine quality in him.

It also scared her silly.

Sunday dawned bright and beautiful. Tina wasn't impressed. Scrunching down in bed she pulled the coverlet over her face to hide from the rays of sunshine streaming through her bedroom window.

Zorro batted at a partially exposed wisp of hair that trailed over her pillow. Getting no response, he gave up, jumped silently to the floor and began to chase the dust motes swirling in the sunbeams.

Tina felt his weight leave the bed. She peeked out, saw what he was doing and groaned. Must be nice to be a house cat, she mused. No responsibilities. No cares. Just eat, sleep and play. What a life. And what a contrast to her present disconcerting existence.

Lucky for them, cats had no conscience. She, on the other hand, could hardly wait to go back to work on Monday so she'd have something to do aside from fret about Zac. No matter how many times she rehearsed the story she planned to tell him, it never sounded plausible.

She would come across as a complete fool unless she mentioned having been her brother's legal guardian and then explained why she'd felt such a strong responsibility for his foolish actions. But if she went into detail about Craig's guilt, there was no way she could continue to shield him. He now had a family, a good job, and was leading a productive life. That was important. It meant her sacrifice had paid off, even if the cost had been far higher than she'd imagined. No way was she going to place him in jeopardy if she could help it.

Poor Craig. This time, he deserved her loyalty. And this time she wasn't sure how she was going to deliver it.

Hoping a hot shower would stimulate her weary brain, Tina got up and padded to the bathroom. This was Sunday. If she skipped Sunday School and church, she'd regret it all week. On the other hand, if she stayed for the main service and happened to run into Zac, it would be more than merely tough to ignore him. It would be impossible. She was already getting a familiar knot in her stomach every time she pictured his handsome face. Reality was bound to be worse. Much worse.

"I don't *want* to be in love!" Tina shouted. Her protest bounced off the bathroom walls and dissipated down the narrow hallway.

Turning on the shower full force, she stepped into the stinging spray. To her chagrin, she realized she didn't want to go to church, either.

Duty won out. Tina was arranging the crayons and pages to color when her first Sunday School students arrived. Little Connie Cain was holding the hand of a red-haired girl Tina didn't recognize. She was so busy making the new child feel at home, she didn't notice Justin at first. When she looked up, he was standing by the open door, staring at his shoes and kicking an invisible object on the rug.

It took her a few seconds to catch her breath and convince her hammering heart that Zac was nowhere to be seen. Relieved, she said, "Hi, Justin. Come on in and have a seat. We do things a lot like your other school does, so you already know my rules."

He didn't move. He also didn't look at her.

"Justin?" Tina approached and cautiously touched his shoulder. "Are you okay, honey?"

He shook his head. She crouched down to be on the same level. "What's the matter?"

Sniffling, he wiped away a tear with his pudgy fist. "I'm sorry, Miss Tina."

"For what? You didn't do anything wrong, did you?"

"Uh-huh." Starting to cry in earnest, he threw his arms around her neck, nearly toppling her.

Tina hugged and soothed him until she sensed he was calm enough to explain. Then she held him away so she could see his face, and dried his tears with a tissue, ending at his nose. "Here— Blow. That's better. Now, can you tell me what upset you so much?"

"It's all my fault," the boy said with a shuddering breath. "I...I didn't mean to make you mad."

"Oh, honey," Tina said lovingly. "I'm not mad at you. Why would I be?"

"Your Popsicle. I messed it up."

"It just melted, that's all," she assured him. "They're made out of ice. They're supposed to do that." Judging by his pained expression, the boy was not fully convinced, so she added, "If they didn't melt, we couldn't eat them."

"But…but you left. And you didn't come back."

Tina drew him to her in a motherly embrace, kissed his damp cheek and smoothed back his hair. "Oh, baby. I'm the one who's sorry. I should have told you goodbye before I went home. Of course I'm not mad at you." Unshed tears misted her vision. "You're very special to me."

"My daddy says you're crazy," he told her solemnly. "But I don't care. I love you, anyway."

Before she straightened, she paused long enough to smile at him and quietly whisper, "I love you, too."

The little boy beamed with delight. "Will you come over and play with me?"

"I'm pretty busy today," Tina hedged. "But you'll see me in regular preschool tomorrow."

Justin began to pout. "Daddy says he has to drive me. I want to go with you, like always."

"I don't see any problem with that," she agreed, finishing her classroom preparation while they talked. "As soon as Sunday School is over, I'll go find your father and tell him I'll be glad to keep taking you. How's that?''

From the doorway came a familiar, deep voice. ''Why not tell me now?''

Every fine hair on Tina's arms prickled and stood on end at the sound of Zac's voice. Her heart flipped, then seemed to lodge in her suddenly constricted throat. She spun around to face him, barely managing to control her instinctive urge to flee. If he hadn't been blocking her escape, she might have given the concept more serious consideration.

Instead, she stood tall, her chin jutting out, and faced him. ''Fine. I'll be happy to take Justin to preschool with me in the morning, as always. There. How was that?''

''Well done. Quite explicit,'' Zac said.

''Good.'' There was one more question she felt compelled to ask. ''Why would you assume I'd stop taking him?''

Zac shrugged. ''I don't know. I don't seem to be able to tell *what* you're going to do or say, so I thought it would be best to prepare him, just in case. I didn't want him to be disappointed if you didn't show up tomorrow.''

''Did you really think I'd purposely disappoint an innocent, little boy? I would *never* do that. *Never.*'' It had gotten so quiet behind her, she knew she had the complete attention of every four-year-old in the small room.

Nodding slowly, Zac flashed a wry, lopsided grin.

"In that case, I have only two more things to say to you, Miss Tina."

"What two things?" She eyed him with suspicion.

"I wish I were a lot shorter…and about thirty years younger."

The endearing smile on his handsome face tied Tina's stomach in a knot the size of a beach ball. Nevertheless, she managed to reply, "If you were thirty years younger, Mr. Frazier, we wouldn't be having this conversation in the first place."

"That's probably true. Tell you what, Justin and I will save you a place so you can sit by us during church." Zac looked hopeful.

"Thanks, but I won't be staying today. I just came to teach my class. I'm going home right afterward."

That said, she boldly closed the classroom door to shut him out, and turned her attention back to the children.

Chapter Fourteen

The first hint of trouble came the following day. At first, Tina assumed her preschool classes were smaller because some of the children were sick. It wasn't unusual for germs to make the rounds, especially among the youngest students. Chickenpox was noted for its yearly attacks on any kids who hadn't already been exposed.

Monday, two were absent. Tuesday, it was five. By Thursday, Justin and Tommy were the only ones who showed up, and Tina's reasoning powers began to work overtime. Common childhood diseases all had specific incubation times, which tended to stagger the absences. When the first batch of kids was getting well, the second was just coming down with it, and so on. Even colds and flu didn't spread instantly.

So far, she hadn't heard any rumors pertaining to

herself. Then again, she wouldn't, would she. That was the insidious nature of gossip. It skipped the very people who *should* be told what was being said behind their backs so that they could refute it.

Pensive, Tina sighed. Justin and Tommy were playing peacefully on the rug by the toy shelves, and since her class had dwindled, she had no pressing duties. She eyed the nursery door. It was time to go and have a talk with Mavis.

The older woman was sitting in a rocking chair with the Carter twins, cradling one in each arm and slowly rocking. When Tina entered, she looked up, smiled, and nodded toward a matching chair beside her.

Leaning close so she could speak without waking the babies, Tina said, "I need to talk to you about my class." Her heart began to race. "Do you know why so many kids are absent?"

"I've heard some silly gossip, but don't worry about it, dear. This, too, shall pass, as the Bible says. As soon as everybody realizes how foolish it is to believe vicious rumors, the children will be back. I can't imagine how it's gone this far. I mean, *you* with a prison record? That's absolutely unthinkable!"

Steeling herself for what she knew she must do, Tina mustered her courage. She laced her fingers together, squeezed tight and said simply, "It's true," and watched her boss's reaction. Doubt was followed by astonishment.

"What? How? When?" Grimacing, Mavis shook

her head. "I don't believe it. How could you do this to me? I trusted you!"

"I'm so sorry." Remorse weighed heavily on Tina's conscience. "It happened a long time ago." She paused. "You don't have to fire me. I'll go."

"I think that's best."

The twins were stirring, so Mavis got up to return them to their cribs. Tina heard her mumbling words that had probably never been heard in that establishment in all the years she'd owned it.

Tina followed to help her place the first twin in bed without waking the second one. When both babies were comfortably settled, Tina took Mavis aside and told her, "You've been wonderful to me. I never meant to hurt you or your business. I just wish there was some way I could make it up to you, fix things."

Mavis scowled. "I'm afraid it's too late for that. The damage is done."

"I know. I've been through this kind of thing before, in other towns. Look at all the kids who are being kept home because of me. The situation won't get any better, either. It never does."

"I can't afford to wait and see."

"I know that, too." Tina started for the nursery door. "Can you get Vicki to come in to take my place this afternoon?"

"I'll get someone." Mavis accompanied Tina out of the nursery and closed the door behind them. "I wish there was another way to handle this."

"There isn't. Serenity is close-knit. People won't forget. That's why I need to leave."

"Leave this job, you mean?"

Standing tall, Tina accepted the inevitability of her choices. Slowly, sadly, she shook her head. "No. Not just the job. I need to leave town, too. Start over. Otherwise, I'll never be able to lead a normal life."

"Why didn't you tell me the whole truth in the first place?"

"Oh, sure. I apply for a job taking care of little kids, and before you even have a chance to get to know me or see how well I work, I tell you I have a prison record? I don't think so. In a big city they'd have done a background check on me first thing."

"So you came to a place like Serenity where we go on trust and our gut-feelings?"

"Yes." Tina sighed. "I hope you can forgive me."

"Was it very bad in prison?" Mavis asked.

"I got through it. That's all that matters." Tina smiled wistfully. "And just between you and me, I wasn't guilty in the first place."

"Then why…"

"It's a long story."

"Shorten it," Mavis ordered.

Pensive, Tina slowly shook her head. "The whole thing sounds so silly when I tell it. After my parents were killed in a car accident, I applied for custody of my younger brother, Craig. He was a real handful. I guess he was mad at the world, me included."

"That's understandable, losing his folks and all."

"I know. That's why I cut him so much slack, I suppose. Anyway, I'd loaned him my car so he could take some friends out for pizza, and he got in a wreck. When he came running into the house, he was scared silly and babbling something about wanting me to say I'd been driving because he'd had a few beers with his friends."

"You didn't!"

"Unfortunately, I did," Tina replied. "Before I'd had a chance to ask Craig anything about the accident, the police burst in and started shouting at us. I didn't know what to do so I took the blame to protect my brother. At the time, I didn't know he'd driven away from the scene and made the crash a hit-and-run."

"But surely, when you found out..."

Tina sighed. "There's more. When they searched my car they found drugs." Noting Mavis's concern she quickly added, "No! They weren't mine. Craig's so-called buddies had stashed them in my car after the accident so they wouldn't get in trouble if they were caught by the police. I hired a lawyer, of course, but by that time, even he didn't believe I was innocent. If I had it all to do over again, I sure wouldn't sell my house to pay his exorbitant fee."

With a concerned smile Mavis relented and patted Tina's arm. "Oh, honey. I do believe you. You don't have to say any more."

"Thanks." Tina's thoughts turned to Zac Frazier.

It would be a minor miracle if he hadn't already heard the juicy gossip about her. She'd foolishly let nearly a week pass, hoping and praying Esther would have a change of heart and decide to keep quiet.

Had Zac seemed out of sorts when she'd stopped by to pick up Justin that morning? She didn't think so. That probably meant he hadn't yet heard. Tina shivered. He might have by now, though, meaning it could already be too late to salvage the touchy situation by confessing.

Oh, Father, she pled silently, *I love him. What am I going to do now?* No booming voice from heaven answered. Instead, she felt a strong compulsion to race to Zac's office—a compulsion she knew better than to deny.

It took Miss Vicki half an hour to respond to Mavis's harried call. The minute Tina saw her replacement walk in, she grabbed her purse and headed for her truck.

The only traffic light in Serenity was red when Tina hit the main crossroads. It seemed to take *hours* for the signal to change. With no special left-turn lane or green arrow to indicate right-of-way, she was stuck waiting until Inez's grandmother, Lillian, managed to pilot her old green Buick through the intersection. By that time, the light had switched to yellow.

Tina was too frantic to endure another whole cycle. She floored the gas and whipped left, making it through at the last minute. Getting to Zac had become an obsession, although she didn't know what she was going to do or say when she reached him. Her befuddled brain refused to concentrate enough to form even one coherent thought. Given the erratic way she was driving, she figured that was just as well. One crisis at a time was her limit.

Wheeling into the high school faculty parking lot, Tina found it crammed full. She simply gave up and abandoned her truck in the aisle nearest the main building. Zac's office had to be close to the reception area. If not, she knew Rosemary could tell her where to find him.

The office receptionist looked more surprised than happy, when Tina burst through the door. *She's heard,* Tina reasoned. *And if she knows...*

Forcing herself to slow down and take deep, calming breaths, Tina smiled and approached the counter that separated the public from the faculty and support staff. "Hi, Rosemary. I'm here to see Zac Frazier. Is he available?"

"No. He's with a parent."

"That's okay." She sat down on the padded bench beneath the window. "I don't mind waiting."

"His appointment may take a long time. Could be hours."

Tina set her jaw and folded her arms across her chest in a pose of defiance. Her eyes narrowed. "I'll wait."

The other woman shrugged. "Have it your way."

Have it *my* way? Tina mused. It would certainly be nice to feel that normal for a change, wouldn't it? She shook her head slowly, thoughtfully. Given the defensive way she'd been forced to conduct herself lately, would she even recognize a normal life if she saw it?

Yes, if she remembered her family the way they were before she'd been left alone to raise Craig. At nineteen, she'd had no idea how to cope with a precocious sixteen-year-old. Poor Craig had been mad at the world. The last thing he'd wanted to do was allow his sister to discipline him, even though the courts had given her custody.

Tina closed her eyes and breathed a sigh. Thank God, Craig hadn't killed anyone when he'd wrecked her car! If he hadn't panicked and fled, he wouldn't have called undue attention to himself and nothing more would have come of it. But he ran. Like the kid he was. *And I took the blame because I was supposed to be in charge.*

The hands on the large, black-rimmed clock on the wall ticked off the minutes while Tina waited. She watched the red second hand jerk its way around the full three-hundred-and-sixty degrees, then do it again and again. If she hadn't been so worried about facing Zac, she might have been lulled into boredom. Instead, she remained so alert that she bolted off the bench every time anyone entered the reception area.

Finally, in the distance, she heard Zac's warm, familiar voice. He'd apparently opened the door to his private office while bidding someone goodbye. Tina smoothed her skirt and nervously tucked the sides of her long hair neatly behind her ears. Soon, she'd know if she was too late. One look at his face and she'd be able to tell.

A couple she recognized from church came around the corner ahead of Zac. When the husband nodded to her, his wife jabbed him in the ribs with her elbow. They hurried past without speaking. Tina hardly noticed. She had eyes for only one person, and he was gazing at her the way a thirsty, desert traveler stares at an oasis.

Tina quickly approached. "Don't worry. Justin's fine. I thought maybe you and I could talk, if you have a few minutes free."

"I'll make time," Zac said. He ushered Tina straight to his office, placed a chair for her, and perched on the edge of his desk next to it, grinning expectantly. "Well? Are you ready to give me an answer? I know the eight days aren't quite up yet, but..."

Tina didn't sit down. Instead, she eased close enough to lay a finger across his lips. "Shh. Let me do the talking. Please?"

Zac kissed her fingertips as he took her hand and held it. "No problem."

So much unrestrained emotion was coursing through her that she could hardly bear it. Oh, how she loved this dear man! He was strong and commanding, yet there was a gentle side to him, too. Her fondest hope was that his heart was also overflowing with compassion, because she was going to need all the forgiving he could muster.

Start with the most important thing, Tina told herself. Smiling through unshed tears she said, "I do love you, Zac."

"I love you, too." He was still holding her hand, and tried to pull her closer.

Tina resisted. "Wait. There's more."

"Nothing else matters," Zac said. "We love each other. We're both single and available. And Justin thinks you're almost as much fun as Max is."

She could tell by the pleased, confident look on his face that he expected her to laugh at that final observation. Instead, she sobered. "You don't know as much about me as you do about that stray dog."

Zac wouldn't give up. "I know you're a lot cuter than he is. Your long hair is prettier, too."

"This is serious. I'm trying to tell you something very important. Will you please stop kidding around?"

"I can't. I'm too happy." He raised one eyebrow as he continued to grin at her. "Guess you'll just have to muddle through as is."

Growing more and more frustrated, Tina threw her hands in the air and strode away from him, hoping distance might help her concentrate. It didn't. She was so flustered, she was ready to scream instead of making a sensible effort to salvage their floundering relationship.

Tears pooled behind her lashes. *Terrific.* Crying wasn't going to help one bit, and now she had *that* urge to deal with, too.

Fighting the impulse to give in to her turbulent emotions, Tina took a deep breath and faced Zac. "Okay. It started a long time ago, when I was nineteen. My—"

Zac interrupted. "Hey, I don't have to hear every detail. Make it easy on yourself. Just spit it out and get it over with."

"No. I have to make you understand, first."

"No, you don't." He was shaking his head and smiling benevolently. "There's nothing you can tell me that I haven't heard a thousand times in my job as a counselor."

He looked so open, so ready to accept whatever she said, that Tina's prior misgivings seemed suddenly foolish. She and Zac loved each other. She was about to ask him to take her just as she was. How could she not do the same for him?

"Okay," she began tentatively, "I have a record."

"I prefer CDs, myself. They sound better."

"No, Zac. A *record.* As in prison. I was charged with hit-and-run and drug possession and sentenced to three years."

He came off the edge of the desk with a lurch. "What?"

"I'd hoped nobody would find out. I wouldn't be telling you now if Esther Fitch hadn't threatened to expose me."

Zac was shaking his head, talking to himself and pacing in random circles. "That's impossible. You and that woman have nothing in common. Nothing!"

"Nothing but incarceration. That's where she and I met. We were in the same jail," Tina said. It was killing her to see him looking so disappointed. "I'm not proud of my past. It's just there. I can't change it. Or make it go away so it won't impact your career. That's one of the reasons I kept telling you I didn't want to get serious."

Still in shock, he stared at her. "My career?"

"Yes. That was why I asked if you were sure you wanted to be a youth minister."

"Ah, my career," Zac muttered.

Tina saw his eyes narrow, his jaw clench. Befuddlement was gone. Anger had taken its place.

"What about my *son?* Did you bother to think of him?"

"Of course I did!"

Shaking his head in evident disgust, Zac asked, "And what about everybody else's kids? How did you manage to get a job taking care of children?"

"Mavis didn't know. Not till this morning. I told her the truth just before I quit."

"So, I'm the last to hear?"

"Only because you aren't part of the town grapevine," Tina insisted. "Esther tried to blackmail me into doing her a favor. When I refused, she said she'd give me a week to change my mind. That was why

I asked you to wait eight days. Only, she lied. She must have started blabbing right after I left her.''

"I heard there was no honor among thieves.''

"I'm not a thief!'' Tina cried.

"Then, what are you?'' Zac's harsh tone sounded almost menacing.

Tina had had enough. "I'm a fool!'' she shouted. "A stupid, idiotic fool. I thought love would be enough.''

"Love without honesty is worthless. A counterfeit. It's not even close to the real thing,'' he declared. "If you'd been as sincere as you claim, you'd have told me the truth up front, when it might have made a difference.''

"Oh, it would have made a difference, all right. I learned *that* when I heard your expert opinion of Esther Fitch. The only mistake I made was not remembering how you felt.'' Whirling, Tina headed for the door.

"Where are you going? I'm not through.''

"Oh, yes, you are.'' She jerked open the door and made a dash for her truck.

The outburst of hysterical weeping didn't seize her until she was halfway home.

If her emotions hadn't been so raw, Tina would have stopped at the preschool to speak to Justin that same afternoon. Because she didn't want to upset him, she decided to wait until her plans were firm before bidding him a final goodbye.

One of her first steps the following day was to visit the church and drop off the Sunday School teacher's guide and other materials for her class. She'd intended to slip in and out without having to speak to anyone. Unfortunately, one of the deacons was cutting the lawn when she got there. He waved, shut off the mower and started up the grassy slope to where she'd parked.

"Mornin' Tina."

"Good morning, Sam." Judging by the warm greeting, she suspected he hadn't heard. She climbed back into her truck. "Sorry I can't stop to talk. I've got a million things to do today."

He removed his cap and mopped his brow with a bandanna. "I heard you was movin'. That's a shame, you ask me. You've been real good for this church, no matter what they say."

Tina was flabbergasted. "You *know?*"

"About your trouble? Shoot, everybody does. I just don't understand why you don't hang around and let all the hoo-haw die down. This ain't a bad place to live. Them that talk the worst about others are usually the ones with the most secrets of their own to hide." He chuckled. "I could tell you a few wild tales, that's a fact."

"Well, don't," Tina said, finally breaking into a smile. "I've had enough stories told about me to know what kind of trouble gossip can cause. I suppose that's why the scriptures list it right up there with murder."

"Prob'ly so." Sam touched the brim of his cap and backed away. "You take care, Miss Tina. You'll be sorely missed around here."

"Thanks. It's sweet of you to say that. I'll miss this place, too."

"You can always come on back."

Her smile waned. "No. I'm afraid that's one thing I've learned the hard way, Sam. What's done is done. We can never go back and undo anything."

"Well..." His grin spread to crinkle his sun-weathered skin and light the eyes below his bushy gray brows. "Just remember, nobody's perfect. If it wasn't for Jesus takin' care of our sins, we'd *all* be in deep...manure."

Tina couldn't help smiling at his candid observation. "Maybe you should get up and preach next Sunday's sermon, Sam. I've never heard forgiveness explained so clearly."

Chapter Fifteen

Tina made arrangements with her landlord to leave most of her furniture behind in exchange for a month's rent. Considering where she was planning to go first, she didn't know how long it would be until she decided to set up housekeeping again.

She hadn't seen Zac for days. That was just as well. It was Justin she needed to talk to, not his father. Keeping careful watch on the Frazier house, she finally saw the little boy come outside to play with his dog.

Max saw her first and greeted her through the chain-link fence as if she were a long-lost buddy. Justin, however, was not as sure of himself. Silent and still, he stared up at Tina.

"I came to talk to you," she whispered. "Can you leave the dog in there and come out here for a second?"

He cast a wary look toward the house. "I guess so."

"Good." As soon as he joined her, she crouched down to be on his level and took his hands. "I didn't want to leave without saying goodbye."

"Leave?" His high voice trembled.

"I'm moving away," Tina explained.

"No!" It was more a wail than a word. He launched his little body at her, wrapped both arms around her neck, buried his face against her neck and began to cry.

Tina's eyes were filled with tears, too. She held him close and rocked gently, patting his back and making soothing noises. As soon as he'd calmed down some, she said, "Shush, baby. It's okay. I'll miss you bunches, too. I'd like to stay here but I just can't. Someday, when you're older, you'll understand."

He sniffled and lifted his face to look at her as he asked solemnly, "Are…are you gonna die like my mommy?"

The poignant question fractured her heart into a million pieces. "Oh, Justin, no. I'll be living someplace else, that's all. Why would you think I was going to die?"

"When I ask about my mommy, Daddy always says I'll understand when I'm older."

Of course. His mother had left him suddenly, unexplainably, and now Tina was about to do the same thing. To a child, the comparison of the two events made perfect sense.

"Tell you what," Tina said, trying to sound joyful. "I have your telephone number. I promise I'll call you from wherever I am, just so you'll know I'm all right. Would you like that?"

"Uh-huh." The sound of a banging door came from the direction of his house, making Justin jump.

Tina quickly straightened. With Max standing guard on the opposite side of the fence and directing his undivided attention toward his young master, there was no way Zac could keep from noticing. Therefore, unless she wanted to undergo another inquisition—or worse—she'd better head for home.

"Okay," Tina whispered hoarsely. "It's a deal, but it'll have to be our special secret." She laid her index finger across her lips. "No fair telling. Promise?"

In the distance, Zac began calling to Justin. Eyes wide, the boy whirled. Tina backed away as she said, "Go on, honey, before you get in trouble."

"But…"

She darted back to place a quick kiss on the child's forehead and give him a parting hug. "I'll call you. I promise. Cross my heart."

"Lots of times?" he asked, sounding lost and insecure.

"If that's what you want." She ducked around the nearest shrubbery to hide. "Now go on. Scoot."

Waiting behind the overgrown hedge, Tina

watched the little boy slip through the gate and heard him answer his father. In seconds, Zac had scooped the boy up in his arms and was carrying him back toward the house.

Peeking over his father's shoulder, Justin smiled and waved a private goodbye, then mimicked her sign of secrecy by placing a finger against his lips.

Tina bit her lower lip. When she'd decided to give up Zac she'd consoled herself with the assurance that she was acting for his ultimate good. Until this moment, she'd believed that nothing else she ever did would hurt as much as that had. She'd been mistaken. The sight of him carrying that dear little boy away from her for the last time caused such agony of spirit that she had to clench her fists and clamp her jaw shut to keep from crying out.

The monumental effort stole her breath and overwhelmed her mind. She wanted to weep, to wail, to frantically beat her fists against the ground and scream at God for letting her fall in love with Zac and his son in the first place, yet she was too numbed by grief to do any of those things.

Instead, she slowly made her way home and continued to pack without caring what she took or what she left behind. Material possessions no longer mattered. Nothing did.

Zac was at work when Tina threw the last of her belongings into her truck and left Serenity for good. His first clue that she'd actually moved was a call from her landlord asking him if he wanted to rent her house because it had a much nicer yard. That's when reality set in.

He pushed back from his desk and stared, unseeing, at the office wall. Tina was gone. Really gone. It seemed unbelievable. All his favorite memories of Serenity included her. Like it or not, that woman had become an integral part of his life. And of Justin's.

Thinking about her, remembering their time together, made him happy, and exasperated, and melancholy, all at the same time—a confusing condition that didn't help foster an amiable disposition.

His unexpected encounter with Esther Fitch in the school parking lot later that afternoon capped the dismal day. If she hadn't accosted him, Zac gladly would have passed her by without speaking.

"Did she tell you all about it?" Esther jockeyed to block his way and stood firm.

"If you want to see me, Mrs. Fitch, you need to make an appointment. I should have a little time later in the week."

"It's not my fault, what happened," Esther insisted, ignoring his formal manner. "I told her I'd keep my mouth shut, but oh, no, she had to get on her high horse about it. I just want to make sure you're not blaming my poor Bennie."

Zac took a deep, settling breath before chancing to speak. "Blaming him for what?"

"For runnin' your girlfriend out of town. All she'd

of had to do was one little favor for me and nobody'd have been the wiser about her past."

Had Tina mentioned something about Esther wanting a favor? He wasn't sure. At the time, he'd been so shocked that he hadn't been able to focus on her confession enough to ask for details. Now, he wished he had.

Clenched fists were the only outward sign of Zac's roiling emotions as he asked, "What kind of a favor?"

"For Bennie, of course."

The woman was giving him a look that plainly said she thought he was dumber than dirt. Zac didn't care. Rather than guess what she'd done to Tina, he wanted her to spell it out. "What does Ms. Braddock have to do with Bennie?"

"Not her. *You!* All she'd of had to do was talk to you. Get you to bend a little. Give my son a break. It's not like I was wanting a lot." She snorted derisively.

Zac's voice was gruff. "Tina refused?"

"Right off. Wouldn't listen to reason. Gave me some stupid line about honesty and Bennie needing to take the blame himself when he failed."

"You should have listened to her. She was right. The more you keep trying to bail your son out of trouble, the harder it will be for him to learn how to function as a responsible adult."

"I love my boy!" Esther insisted. "I may not be

much, in your eyes, but I'm his mother and I love him.''

''I can see that, Mrs. Fitch. The question is, do you want him to stand on his own someday, or wind up following in your footsteps because you taught him how easy it can be to cheat the system?''

Her response was pretty much as he'd expected. Muttering curses, she turned and stalked away.

Zac shook his head slowly, sighed, and started for his car while he mulled over the importance of what he'd just learned. Tina could have prevented her own exposure by simply lying and trying to manipulate him, yet she'd risked everything and refused because she'd felt it was the right thing to do. That kind of pure integrity was rare. To find it in a person who had served time in prison...

And he'd been so hardheaded that he'd driven her away. Instead of accepting Tina, faults and all, he'd judged her without giving her a chance to explain. The fact that she'd kept him in the dark, at first, had bruised his male pride, and he'd retaliated without even realizing what he was doing until it was too late. Maybe Esther Fitch's unspoken opinion was right. Maybe he *was* dumber than dirt.

But maybe it wasn't too late! ''I'll crawl if I have to,'' Zac told himself as he drove toward the day care center to pick up Justin. ''I don't care what Tina did in the past. I'll find her and keep apologizing until she gives me—gives us—another chance.''

That decision lifted his spirits enough that he actually smiled for the first time in longer than he cared to admit.

By that evening, Zac was down in the dumps again. He'd figured Mavis would know where Tina had gone, but she was as much in the dark as everyone else he talked to. He was rapidly running out of people to ask.

Well, at least Justin isn't depressed, Zac thought, watching his son push a toy car across the floor while making noises like a motor. The kid was as energetic and cheerful as ever—maybe more so. He hadn't wanted to go outside to play that evening the way he usually did, but that was understandable since the late summer heat lingered until sundown. Other than that, Justin's behavior seemed perfectly normal. He'd obviously adjusted to Tina's absence a lot better than his daddy had.

Zac was in the kitchen fixing supper, when the telephone rang. Before he could reach it, Justin had answered and was already saying, ''Hello?''

''I'll take that.'' Zac held out his hand.

The boy refused to relinquish the receiver. ''Hello? Hello?'' he repeated.

Zac pried the phone from his fingers and listened. A recorded, computerized sales spiel was just beginning. Disgusted, Zac slammed down the receiver and headed back to the kitchen. Behind him, Justin started to wail.

That unexpected reaction tempered Zac's grumpy

disposition. "You know I've told you not to answer the phone. I'm not mad at you for doing it this time, if that's what you're upset about. I'm mad at the people who call us and try to sell us something right at supper time."

Surprisingly, the explanation didn't begin to halt Justin's emotional outburst, so Zac crouched down to reassure him. "Hey. I'm not mad at you, okay? Honest, I'm not. I know I've been kind of short-tempered, lately. I'm sorry if I scared you." He patted the boy's back as he spoke. "Just don't forget the rules and answer the phone again. Okay?"

All he got out of Justin was more shuddering sobs, so he took him by the hand and led him to the bathroom where he helped him blow his nose and washed his face with cool water. "There. Isn't that better? Now—"

In the other room, the telephone started to ring. Justin bolted from his father's grasp and dashed down the hall. Zac went after him. When he reached the living room, he found Justin hiding behind the sofa. He had dragged the telephone back there with him!

Zac peered over the couch. "Hey, buddy, what are you doing down there?"

Justin's shoulders slumped as he hung up the receiver, got to his feet and returned the phone to the side table. "Nothin'."

"Who was that?"

"Just some man."

"Who did you *think* it might be?" Zac asked. He was beginning to suspect why his son hadn't wanted to go out and play before supper lately. And why he hadn't once lamented the fact that Miss Tina was gone. The child's subsequent refusal to answer was further proof. "Justin..." he said coaxingly, "tell Daddy what's going on."

The boy shook his head energetically and stared down at his shoes.

Zac took his hand, led him around to an easy chair, sat down and lifted him into his lap. "Okay. You can keep your secret if you want to."

"I can?" Justin whispered.

"Yes, you can. And I'll do the talking for you if you're out playing or something when Miss Tina calls."

"No!" He tried to wiggle free and jump down, but he was being held too securely.

"Don't you want me to talk to her?" Zac asked with careful nonchalance.

"No. She promised she'd call *me*."

Nodding, Zac said, "Uh-huh. I thought so." Justin continued to squirm, so he turned him loose. "Do you know where Tina went, son?"

"She moved away."

"I know that. I mean, did she happen to say where she was going?"

"No." Pouting, the child stared up at his father, then glanced over at the silent telephone.

"Well, don't worry," Zac reassured him. "I won't

spoil your talk with Miss Tina. You can answer the phone anytime it rings. But if the call is for me, you have to promise to come get me right away. How does that sound?''

"Fine!''

"Then, it's settled.'' He crossed to the window and began to shift furniture around. "Look. I have an idea. If we open the front window and set the phone right here on the sill, you can go out and play with Max and you'll still hear it if it rings. I won't answer it, I promise.''

"All right!'' Justin galloped out the door with a whoop.

"One more thing,'' Zac muttered to himself. Reaching for the telephone directory and flipping it open to the front pages, he dialed, then waited impatiently until a young voice answered, "Customer service. How may I help you?''

"I want to order Caller ID,'' Zac said. "I don't care what it costs. And I need it *yesterday.*''

Tina called Justin three days later, on a Sunday afternoon. Zac didn't have to hear her name to know who it was. The delight in his son's expression and the way he held the receiver so tightly told Zac everything.

"I did go to Sunday School,'' the boy said. "Yeah. It was okay. I miss you.''

Imagining the other side of the conversation and picturing Tina, Zac sighed.

"I'm fine. He's okay, too." Justin looked up at his father, then said, "Yeah. He's right here." There was a long pause. "No. He's not mad at me. I think he misses you, too."

It was hard for Zac to keep from shouting confirmation. Afraid that any such outburst might cause Tina to hang up, he held his tongue. He'd encouraged his son to pose some leading questions when he finally talked to her. He just hoped the boy remembered.

"Do you have a nice house?" Justin asked, listening carefully. Then he said, "Maybe I could come visit you. Is it far?"

The way his expression sobered when he said "Oh," told Zac she hadn't provided an invitation.

"My dad could drive me," the boy offered, sounding hopeful. Then he asked, "Why not? Oh. I thought you kind of liked him. He likes you."

Zac was pacing, praying Tina would listen to the child's simple wisdom. Even if she never forgave him and they didn't wind up becoming a family, he needed to see her face-to-face. To tell her how wrong he'd been, how truly sorry he was. To convince her he didn't care what she'd done in the past—he loved her, anyway. Just as she was.

"Okay. Bye," the boy said sadly. He hung up and turned to his father. "Did I do okay?"

"You did fine," Zac told him with a pat on the head. "It's not your fault Tina left us. I'm the one who made all the mistakes. I'm really sorry, buddy."

Justin hugged his leg the way he had when they'd first come to Serenity and he'd felt so insecure. "It's okay."

"What did she say about me?" Zac asked, almost afraid to hear the answer.

The boy straightened and shrugged. "Nothin'."

"How about when you told her I liked her? What did she say then?" Zac leaned over the small, black Caller ID box he'd had installed and started to write down the number. No wonder it had taken so long for her to call. Judging by the area code, she'd traveled all the way to Southern California.

"I don't know," Justin said.

"Why not? You just talked to her a second ago." Though he was at his wits' end, Zac managed to maintain a calm, even tone for the boy's sake. Heaven help any parents who tried to carry on a logical, meaningful conversation with their four-year-old!

"'Cause."

Zac tried once more. "Because *why?*"

"'Cause Miss Tina was cryin' too hard. I couldn't hardly understand her." Justin gave his father a curious look that indicated he was surprised it had taken a grown-up so long to figure things out.

"Crying? She was?" Awed by the possible implications, Zac couldn't keep the joy out of his voice. "All right!"

Justin blinked and stared at him. "Is that good?"

"It's wonderful," Zac shouted, scooping him up

in his arms and whirling around and around till they were both so dizzy they collapsed on the sofa together.

Zac caught his breath, his heart pounding with anticipation, and reached over to pat Justin on the leg. "How would you like to fly in an airplane?"

"A jet?"

"Well, not a fighter plane like you see in the movies, but the trip will still be fun."

"Where are we going?"

Zac thought about the phone number he'd jotted down. If he couldn't get the address information he needed from the Internet, he might have to call a friend in law enforcement for help, and that would take longer. One thing was certain. If he didn't find out where Tina was and go after her soon, she might move again and disappear for good. He couldn't let that happen. Even if taking unscheduled time off cost him his current job.

"I'm not quite sure yet." Zac purposely hedged, not wanting Justin to accidentally give away their plans if Tina called again before they left. "I have a few arrangements to make first."

"Can we go camping in the van, too?"

"No. We'll have to leave that parked at the airport for when we come back." A comical scenario popped into Zac's head, and he laughed as he ruffled the boy's dark hair. "Tell you what. We'll take along our sleeping bags. How's that?" He could picture

Tina opening her front door some morning and finding them camped on her lawn!

"Yeah!" Justin hollered.

It was all Zac could do to contain the same feeling of elation. This whole idea kept getting better and better.

The name Braddock was not associated with the west coast address Zac finally acquired. Confused, he still had to follow the only lead he had. If it turned out to be a dead end, he'd come home and try again until he located Tina—or ran out of money trying.

Justin slept during the flight and most of the ride through the San Gabriel Valley to their destination, a modest tract house in Arcadia, California.

Slowing the rental car, Zac cruised past the address, trying to decide if he should call first or go knock on the door. He opted for the element of surprise. That way, if Tina *was* there, she wouldn't have a chance to run.

Nervous as a teenager on his first date, Zac pulled into the driveway of the strange house. He'd been rehearsing what he intended to say to Tina ever since he'd decided to find her, but all of a sudden the pat phrases seemed trite. Any words of wisdom he'd managed to come up with on his own were gone, too, floating off into oblivion like the fragile soap bubbles Justin liked to blow.

Zac found a shady place to park right next to the small porch, so he temporarily left his sleeping son

in the car, its windows rolled down, when he went
to the door. The screen was closed, but the door itself
was open. He decided to call out rather than ring the
bell.

"Hello. Anybody home?"

A small, red-haired child of about three peeked
around a corner, then ducked out of sight. In seconds,
a young woman carrying a baby against her chest in
a blue canvas sling came to the door. "Yes? Can I
help you?"

"I hope so," Zac said. "I'm looking for Tina
Braddock."

"I'm sorry, there's... Wait a minute. Stay right
there," she said. "I'll be right back."

Zac fidgeted. *It was the wrong house.* Dejected
beyond belief, he started back to the car.

He was reaching for the door handle when a familiar voice said, "I'm not Tina Braddock. My real
name is Christina Ferguson."

Zac whirled. It was her! It was really her!

"Around here they call me Chris," she explained.
"My brother's name is Craig. When we were kids
we were always called Chris and Craig, probably because those names sounded so good together."

Speechless, Zac stared. She'd cut her long hair.
The new style made her look thinner, younger somehow. There was also sadness in her eyes. "I...I
thought I had the wrong house," he stuttered.

"You do. You shouldn't have come."

"You shouldn't have left us," he countered.

"You know very well why I had to." Tina began to scowl at him. "What *are* you doing here?"

Zac approached cautiously, hoping she wouldn't slam the door in his face before he had a chance to tell her how he felt. "I came to apologize to you," he said. "I shouldn't have lost my temper. I was wrong."

She agreed with him. "Yes, you were."

Beginning to smile with relief, he noted that she, too, was having trouble remaining emotionally distant. "Okay. That's a start. How long do you think it may take you to forgive me for being such a jerk?"

"You're already forgiven," Tina told him softly. Instead of resisting when Zac opened the screen door, she stepped out and joined him on the porch. "But that doesn't change anything. I'm still not going back to Serenity."

He laid his hands gently on her shoulders and felt her tremble at the touch. "Fine. We'll start over someplace else. Get new jobs. I'll probably be fired, anyway."

"Fired? Why?" Looking into his eyes, she was so overcome by deep, passionate emotion that she barely heard him reply.

"Because I took an unscheduled leave to chase after the woman I love."

It took a moment for his statement to sink in. Tina gasped, her mouth agape. She finally managed to squeak, "Me? You still love me? Even now?"

Zac was so overjoyed to have found her that he felt light-headed. "I always said you were smart."

"Stop teasing. I'm not smart. If I were, I'd never have gotten sent to jail in the first place."

"True. But whatever you did, I can tell you're totally honest now, and that's what counts. Whatever mistakes you made years ago shouldn't change how I feel about you. Not as long as you've totally reformed."

Tina stiffened. "Yes, they should."

"Why? There's no question that you've turned your whole life around. And you certainly don't brag about being in prison or carry on the way Mrs. Fitch does."

"But...you saw what happened when the people in Serenity found out about me."

"No," Zac said, shaking his head. "All I saw was the beginning of a good lesson in loving one another, no matter what. When you ran away, you ended it before most folks had learned what I think the Lord was trying to teach them." He bent and kissed her parted lips to silence her before she could argue.

Tina slid her arms around his neck and kissed him back. Confusion reigned in her heart and mind. Could Zac be right? Was it conceivable that the Lord could actually use her terrible past to His advantage? Of *course* He could! She'd just never opened her mind enough to consider that possibility before.

She stared up at the man who had accepted her without condemnation, even though she hadn't loved him enough to trust him to do so. When he whispered, "Marry me, Tina?" she felt as if she were floating a hundred feet off the ground.

Could this be happening? Was she finally free to follow her desires and accept the blessings God offered—without hesitation, without guilt and without reservation?

"You're sure?" she asked, her voice barely audible.

"I'm sure." Zac cupped her face in his hands and gazed down at her with pure, unquestioned love. "Was that a *yes?*"

"Yes!" was all she managed to say, before Zac grabbed her and kissed her breathless. When they came up for air, she planted her palms flat on his chest and gave a halfhearted push. "Wait. You have to listen to me."

"Not if you plan to change your mind," he said, leaning down to reclaim her lips. "I don't think I could stand it if you did that."

Tina caressed his cheek and smiled. "I'm not going to change my mind. Ever. I just want you to know the truth about why I went to prison. Let me tell you? Please?"

His slight nod gave her the go-ahead, and she explained how she'd been made her brother's guardian, how she'd felt responsible for his mistakes, and how she'd taken the punishment meant for him.

When she saw anger start to color Zac's expression, she added, "Don't blame Craig. The accident was his fault, but my involvement, afterward, was strictly my own stupid decision. By the time I realized I'd done the wrong thing and tried to take back my confession, it was too late. No one believed me. Not even my lawyer.''

''Your brother walked off scot-free?''

''Not exactly.'' Tina flashed a satisfied grin. ''Craig's whole life changed because of that accident. He turned back to the Christian faith he'd had as a child, cleaned up his act, finished school and built a good life. He has a wonderful wife and two great kids. That's why I've never tried to clear my name. I can't take the chance he'd be sent to prison and lose everything he's worked so hard for.''

She took Zac's hand and squeezed affectionately. ''This is Craig's house. Come on. I want you to meet everybody. And remember what you told me about forgiveness. Craig needs it as much as I did. He's even offered to go back to Serenity with me, stand up in a town meeting and admit his guilt.''

''Well, that's better. When?''

''Never. I told him to forget it. He's already made full restitution to the man he hurt in the car accident. That's enough for me.''

Zac raised an eyebrow but refrained from telling her that it wasn't nearly enough for *him*. As he mulled over the situation, a plan started to take shape in his mind. If Tina's brother had meant it when he'd volunteered to speak out and clear her name, *somebody* should encourage him to go ahead and do it.

Since Tina wasn't willing to be that somebody, Zac knew it was up to him.

He turned toward the rental car. "Okay. I'll get Justin."

"Justin's *here?* Why didn't you tell me?" Thrilled, Tina dashed by him and jerked open the rear door.

The instant the little boy awoke, he recognized who was bending over him. Giving a happy shriek, he held out his arms to her. "Miss Tina!"

"Hi, sweetheart," she said, fighting tears of joy while she unfastened his seat belt. "I missed you."

"Me, too!" The child leaped into her arms and hugged her neck as if he never intended to let go.

Zac helped her straighten, still holding Justin, and enfolded both his son and his bride-to-be in a wide embrace.

Tina heard his voice break with emotion as he whispered, *"Thank you, God."*

Blessed beyond belief she added a heartfelt, "Amen."

Epilogue

❞

Zac's private talk with Craig had gone well. So had the wedding plans. Although Zac would have preferred that he and Tina be married in their home church in Serenity, she was adamantly against it, so they'd settled on the small church where Craig and his family worshiped.

The ceremony was intimate. To Tina's delight and relief, Zac had asked Craig to be his best man even before she'd decided to make her sister-in-law matron of honor. Seeing the two men she loved most standing at the front of the sanctuary together, waiting for her to walk down the aisle, was wonderful. Almost as wonderful as becoming Zac's wife and Justin's mother.

Their honeymoon was necessarily short, which was just as well since they'd decided they should include Justin. Tina would never have agreed to go home to Serenity with Zac afterward if he hadn't convinced her he'd lose his job if he didn't return to work as soon as possible.

Filled with misgivings, she was unusually quiet during the drive north from the airport in Little Rock. Justin napped in the back seat of the van.

When they'd almost reached Serenity, Zac noticed that Tina was getting fidgety. He reached over and took her hand. "It'll be okay, honey. I'm right. You'll see."

"I wish I could believe you," she said softly. "It's never been okay before."

"Just remember, you can't expect to please everybody. No matter what we do or say, there's always someone who takes offense. That's part of living. We're not accountable to them. Our job is to stay true to the Lord and try to behave the way He'd want us to." Zac squeezed her fingers. "You're only responsible for what *you* do, honey. How other people respond is up to them."

"You mean 'Love one another...,' like it says in the thirteenth chapter of John?" Tina chewed her lower lip. "I don't know if I can do that, Zac. Some really awful things were said about me behind my back."

"And to your face, especially if you count me." He brought her hand to his lips and kissed her fingertips. "I'll never forgive myself for putting you through that."

"It's over." Tina's voice echoed the love and forgiveness in her heart.

"That's exactly what I've been trying to tell you for the past two weeks. It's all over. Now we start again. Together."

Turning north on highway sixty-two at Ash Flat, he began to grin.

Tina noticed immediately. "What are you smiling about?"

"Oh, nothing."

"Za-a-a-ac. I know you better than that. What have you got up your sleeve?"

"My arm?" He made a silly face as she gave him a playful whack on the shoulder. "Okay. We're almost there so I guess I should tell you. I bought us a house."

"A *what?*"

"We don't have to keep it if you don't like it. I got such a great deal on the place, I couldn't turn it down. You'll love the yard. It's got more flowers than I've ever seen in one place before. Used to be rented by a gardening nut who took off for California and left it vacant."

"My house?" Tina gasped. "You bought *my* house?"

"Sure did. I've had the Peterson kids looking after Max at my old place. And I hired them to water your yard while we were gone, too, so your plants should be in pretty good shape. I knew how much they meant to you."

"Oh, Zac…" She leaned as close as the separate front seats in his van would allow and laid her cheek on his shoulder. "You're so sweet."

"See that you remember that in the future," he cautioned. "Now, close your eyes. We're almost there."

"Why should I close my eyes?"

"Because your husband asked you to?"

Tina made a pouting face. "Okay. Since you put it that way. Don't make me keep them closed too long, though. I get dizzy on curves if I don't watch the road."

"Hang tough. Just a little farther." Pulling to a stop in front of their house, he saw the result of Craig's visit to Serenity while they'd been honeymooning. It was better than Zac had dared hope. Big yellow bows were tied on the porch posts and hung from every branch and stem strong enough to support them. Ladies from Tina's church had tables laden with food set up in the driveway.

"Can I look now?" Tina asked.

"Not yet. Stay right there. And don't peek." Zac circled the van, opened her door and helped her out. As soon as he'd turned her to face the unofficial welcoming committee, he said, "Okay. You can look."

Tina couldn't believe it. Dumbfounded, she pressed her fingertips to her lips and stared. So many folks had shown up to greet her that she couldn't count them all! Everybody was standing very still, apparently waiting for her to make the next move.

And grouped in the very front, holding hands, was her brother and his whole happy little family.

Blinking back tears of joy, Tina gazed up at Zac and slipped her arms around his waist. "You did this for me?"

"I can't take all the credit," he said. "Craig played a big part, too."

"Oh, Zac! You didn't let him—"

"Hush. No harm was done. I looked into it and found out the statute of limitations on his crime had run out. He's not in any danger of being arrested."

Tina was incredulous. "He's not?"

"No, he's not. And even if he were, he'd have come here and told the truth for your sake. He really is a straight-up guy. You should be proud of the way you raised him."

"Thanks. I did everything the hard way, though. I wish I had it all to do over again."

Zac laughed. "You will. Wait till Justin gets old enough to drive a car."

"Oh, dear… I hadn't thought about that. He's already a handful. I'll bet his teenage years will be awful."

"Maybe not. I'm hoping he'll want to set a good example for his younger brothers and sisters."

"What younger…?" Tina blushed. "Oh, *those* younger brothers and sisters. Well, before we can start to do anything about *that*…" She smiled and waved at the folks who'd been waiting for a sign that she'd forgiven them. "You'd better bring Justin and come on. We have company."

"A welcome home party seemed like a good idea when I thought of it," Zac said, lifting his son out of the van and falling into step beside her. "Only, I didn't dream half the town would show up!"

Laughing gaily and feeling as if the sun was shining more brightly than ever before, Tina approached the crowd and opened her arms wide to include everyone.

Craig ran to her first, his wife and children close behind, and gave her a bear hug. "Surprised?"

"Flabbergasted." She saw him offer his hand to Zac, saw them shake like brothers, and asked, "Okay. How long have you two been in cahoots?"

"Long enough," Craig said. "Zac made most of the local arrangements. Even convinced your pastor to let me speak from the pulpit and explain what kind of person you really are—" His voice broke. "And what you did for me."

Stepping between the two men, Tina slipped one arm around each of their waists and squeezed them tightly. "I was no hero, Craig. What I did was tell a lie that came back to bite me." Blinking back tears of joy and relief, she glanced up at her brother. "It was the stupidest thing I've ever done. But thanks for coming here like this and setting the record straight."

"You're welcome." He winked at Zac and added, "Besides, somebody had to drive your old truck home and get it out of my yard. My stuffy, citified neighbors were beginning to complain that it was a terrible eyesore.''

"Well, it fits in just fine around here," Tina said, gazing fondly up at her husband. "And so do I...now."

Zac kissed her forehead. "You mean, you don't want to sell the house?"

Laughing lightly and standing on tiptoe to whisper in his ear, she told him, "Nope. At least, not until we fill it up with children and run out of room."

*   *   *   *   *

Dear Reader,

I've really struggled and prayed over what to say in this letter. If I were a perfect Christian, it would be easy.

Then again, if I were perfectly loving, the way Jesus commanded His disciples to be to each other in John 13:34, I might not have been able to create the characters and situations in this book.

When I was younger, I thought the Bible was like a textbook, full of rules to follow using my own willpower. Anyone who has tried to do that, without the help of the Holy Spirit, knows it's impossible. When I made the conscious decision to turn my life over to God, through Jesus Christ, and began to study with new insight, I realized that my rebirth as a true believer was just the beginning. I still had a *long* way to go!

My point is not that Christians are fallible, which we are, it's that once we've turned to Jesus, we're enrolled in God's school. Sometimes we do well. Sometimes we don't. But the Lord knows what's in our hearts, and with His help we will learn to love one another as He has loved us.

I'd love to hear from you! If you'd like a reply, please enclose a self-addressed, stamped envelope. Or look me up at www.valeriehansen.com and read all about my upcoming books.

Blessings,

Valerie Hansen

Valerie Hansen, P.O. Box 13, Glencoe, AR 72539-0013.

Love Inspired

PRECIOUS BLESSINGS

BY

JILLIAN HART

From bestselling Love Inspired
author Jillian Hart comes
a new McKaslin Clan tale!

THE McKASLIN CLAN

Being a single father was
hard on Jack Munroe's faith
and patience, and he didn't
need the all-perfect
Katherine McKaslin telling
him how to impose
discipline. Yet he began to
see the positive effects she
had on his daughter...and
on him. Jack hadn't been
looking for a relationship,
but this strong and beautiful
woman made him wonder
if God wanted him to risk a
second chance at love.

*Available February 2007
wherever you buy books.*

Steeple
Hill®

www.SteepleHill.com

LIPBJH

REQUEST YOUR FREE BOOKS!

2 FREE INSPIRATIONAL NOVELS
PLUS 2
FREE
MYSTERY GIFTS

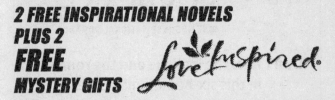

Love Inspired®

YES! Please send me 2 FREE Love Inspired® novels and my 2 FREE mystery gifts. After receiving them, if I don't wish to receive any more books, I can return the shipping statement marked "cancel." If I don't cancel, I will receive 4 brand-new novels every month and be billed just $3.99 per book in the U.S., or $4.74 per book in Canada, plus 25¢ shipping and handling per book and applicable taxes, if any*. That's a savings of 20% off the cover price! I understand that accepting the 2 free books and gifts places me under no obligation to buy anything. I can always return a shipment and cancel at any time. Even if I never buy another book from Steeple Hill, the two free books and gifts are mine to keep forever.

113 IDN EF26 313 IDN EF27

Name	(PLEASE PRINT)	
Address		Apt. #
City	State/Prov.	Zip/Postal Code

Signature (if under 18, a parent or guardian must sign)

Order online at www.LoveInspiredBooks.com

Or mail to Steeple Hill Reader Service™:

IN U.S.A.: P.O. Box 1867, Buffalo, NY 14240-1867
IN CANADA: P.O. Box 609, Fort Erie, Ontario L2A 5X3

Not valid to current Love Inspired subscribers.

Want to try two free books from another series?
Call 1-800-873-8635 or visit www.morefreebooks.com

* Terms and prices subject to change without notice. NY residents add applicable sales tax. Canadian residents will be charged applicable provincial taxes and GST. This offer is limited to one order per household. All orders subject to approval. Credit or debit balances in a customer's account(s) may be offset by any other outstanding balance owed by or to the customer. Please allow 4 to 6 weeks for delivery.

Your Privacy: Steeple Hill is committed to protecting your privacy. Our Privacy Policy is available online at www.eHarlequin.com or upon request from the Reader Service. From time to time we make our lists of customers available to reputable firms who may have a product or service of interest to you. If you would prefer we not share your name and address, please check here. ☐

LIREG07

Love Inspired®

SUSPENSE
RIVETING INSPIRATIONAL ROMANCE

Don't miss the intrigue and the romance
in this six-book family saga.

THE SECRETS OF STONELEY

Six sisters face murder, mayhem
and mystery while unraveling the past.

FATAL IMAGE
Lenora Worth
January 2007

**THE SOUND
OF SECRETS**
Irene Brand
April 2007

LITTLE GIRL LOST
Shirlee McCoy
February 2007

DEADLY PAYOFF
Valerie Hansen
May 2007

BELOVED ENEMY
Terri Reed
March 2007

**WHERE THE
TRUTH LIES**
Lynn Bulock
June 2007

Steeple
Hill®

Available wherever you buy books.

www.SteepleHill.com

LISSOSLIST

Love Inspired.

SUSPENSE

RIVETING INSPIRATIONAL ROMANCE

THE SECRETS OF STONELEY

Six sisters face murder, mayhem and mystery while unraveling the past.

Little Girl Lost
SHIRLEE McCoy

Book 2 of the multiauthor The Secrets of Stoneley miniseries.

Portia Blanchard had been planning to spend time with police detective Mick Campbell to keep tabs on the family investigation, but she soon finds herself drawn to him. Is it because he's a single dad or because his faith is strong under fire?

Available February 2007 wherever you buy books.

Steeple Hill

www.SteepleHill.com

LISLGL

Love Inspired

FROM BESTSELLING LOVE INSPIRED AUTHOR

Janet Tronstad

COMES A NEW MINISERIES
ABOUT FOUR CANCER SURVIVORS
WHO MAKE A PACT TO BETTER THEIR LIVES.

The Sisterhood
of the DROPPED Stitches

In this story, Marilee Davidson challenges herself to go on three dates! She hadn't let any man get close to her since her diagnosis. But with the help of her friends, she put herself out there… and learned that sometimes love can be found in the most unexpected places.

Steeple Hill®

Available February 2007 wherever you buy books.

www.SteepleHill.com

LITSOTDS